PASSION'S AWAKENING

Slowly, Two Arrows pulled Glory close, bent his head and kissed her lips. It was a tender kiss, almost a caress across her mouth.

For a moment, she was too surprised to move. Then, though she didn't mean to, she reacted instinctively, her arms going up around his neck as she kissed him in return. At this encouragement, he pulled her hard against him, his arms holding her so close that she felt the heat of his body and the urgency of his desire.

She didn't think, she only reacted, clinging to him, pressing against him, returning his passion with her own. No man had ever kissed her like this and she had never responded with the fire she now felt deep in her very soul.

Somewhere in the distance, she heard little Grasshopper calling, "Two Arrows, Proud One, where are you?"

They jerked apart abruptly, Glory both appalled and stunned that she had returned his kiss with such ardor.

"No wonder the lieutenant wants you back," Two Arrows whispered. "A man would move heaven and earth to keep you!"

"I—I must be losing my mind!" She pulled away from him and ran for the camp. She didn't look back.

PREVIOUS BOOKS BY GEORGINA GENTRY

Cheyenne
Song

Georgina Gentry

Zebra Books
Kensington Publishing Corp.
http://www.zebrabooks.com

ZEBRA BOOKS are published by

Kensington Publishing Corp.
850 Third Avenue
New York, NY 10022

First Printing: March, 1998
10 9 8 7 6 5 4 3

Printed in the United States of America

For my longtime editor, Carin Cohen Ritter, whose wise counsel and good editing has saved some of my books from disaster. Every writer should be lucky enough to have such an editor. Thank you, Carin.

MAP OF 1878 CHEYENNE FLIGHT

Prologue

A second chance. How many of us have hoped, or maybe even prayed for another chance to redeem our pasts, correct the mistakes we've made? Most never get that opportunity.

This is a love story about a rescued stallion, a failed cavalry sergeant, a drunken Cheyenne dog soldier who hates whites, a disgraced cavalry officer who hates Indians, and a beautiful woman with a scandalous past.

More than that, it's a saga of the northern Cheyenne tribe who made a mistake and then risked their lives to change it. In 1878, three hundred starving Cheyenne walked away from Fort Reno, Indian Territory, stubbornly determined to reach their beloved homeland, fifteen hundred miles to the north. Ten thousand soldiers were sent to block that escape.

Along with the Indians, all the players in this drama desperately need a second chance. . . .

One

Fort Reno, Indian Territory
The night of September 7, 1878

Two Arrows wanted the woman from the first moment he saw her. Whether it was simply desire as a man wants a woman or revenge because she was Lieutenant Krueger's lady, he wasn't sure and didn't care.

In fact, the Cheyenne brave didn't care much about anything tonight as he leaned against a tree and watched her riding through the moonlight with the silhouette of the fort in the background. The full moon threw distorted shadows of the horse and rider across the prairie. Two Arrows knew the leaf shadows hid him, so he could watch her as he had done before without anyone knowing. The hated Lieutenant Krueger would not like a drunken Indian watching the beautiful Glory the way Two Arrows watched the dark-haired woman now, desire in his heart and groin.

He grimaced and rubbed his hand across his mouth. He was drunk, he thought, but the white man's liquor no longer took away the painful memories the way it used to. Now it only made him sad, but he was drunk more often than he was sober these days. When he was sober, he rode as an army scout. It was sometimes hard to remember that once he had been a respected dog soldier of the Cheyenne, bravest of the brave. Now his own people laughed at him, and his family was dead or scattered like the autumn leaves.

He watched the white woman tap her gray mare with her little whip, and the fine thoroughbred broke into a gentle lope across the prairie. If she kept coming, she would be riding beneath the trees, but first she would have to pass the soldier on guard duty.

She had dark eyes and very black hair that had come loose from its ribbon like a wild filly's mane. Tonight, she wore cream linen—men's pants—and she rode astride. Lieutenant Krueger would not like that. That thought made Two Arrows smile. He did not like the lieutenant, and he knew the feeling was mutual.

The cheap liquor was pumping through his blood, and Two Arrows felt a stirring in his groin as he watched her canter up to the post guard. She was not beautiful in the way white men judged beauty, and she was no longer a young girl, but there was something about the way she carried her head high and proud that appealed to him. Two Arrows had watched her many nights and thought about her often, since he had no woman of his own. She might soon be marrying the lieutenant; everyone said so, even though the women at the fort gossiped about her past and her scandalous behavior. Two Arrows took another big drink from the bottle and moved farther back into the shadows of the bois d'arc trees.

Glory Halstead rode toward the sentry, who raised his hand. "Halt! Who goes there?"

She reined in and smiled at the red-faced Irishman. "Mercy, Corporal Muldoon, surely you recognize me? Do I look dangerous?" She laughed, and Misty danced under her, eager as she for a swift gallop.

The old soldier looked shamefaced in the moonlight. "Aye, of course, Mrs. Halstead, but it's regulation, you know; I'm tryin' to do everything by the book these days."

Glory nodded. "I understand. I'm sure you'll get those stripes back." Everyone on the post knew Muldoon had been broken from sergeant and was trying to regain his stripes. "Well, good night." She smiled and started to ride past him.

"Beg pardon, ma'am, but does the lieutenant know you ride out alone after dark and in men's trousers?"

"I'm not a callow girl, Muldoon," Glory snapped, "and I'm not Mrs. Krueger yet, so I do what I wish."

"My apologies, ma'am, but your riding alone causes all the old ladies' tongues to waggle—"

"I've survived a divorce, Muldoon, so I'm already a scandalous loose woman as far as the old biddies hereabouts are concerned."

His beefy face softened. "Aww, don't you pay them no mind, Missus."

"I don't." But she knew she lied. "Don't worry about me, Muldoon, I won't ride far."

Before the corporal could object again, Glory nudged Misty and cantered toward the ragged grove of trees that grew just outside the fort's perimeters. Riding alone at night, the wind blowing her hair, was the only pleasure she had at Fort Reno. She had thought when she came here to help her sick father in the post sutler's store that she might leave the scandal behind her in Virginia; but it had followed her. Now she had met David Krueger, and he hinted that he wanted to marry her, scandalous divorcée or not. She was not an innocent girl anymore. Her practical side told her that at thirty-four, she might not get a better offer.

Glory rode through the shadows of the trees, her mind wrestling with that decision. She would have security with David, if not passionate love, but then, Glory had never believed such love actually existed. Certainly with the lieutenant's society credentials, it would end the gossip about her scandalous past.

A man stepped out of the shadows, causing her horse to rear. Glory gasped and almost slid off as she reined in. "Mercy! Are you crazy! What do you—?"

He caught Misty's bridle, and the mare snorted and ceased

rearing. Glory clung to the cantle and stared back into the stranger's handsome dark face. She realized suddenly that he was Indian, one of those encamped near the fort's perimeters, no doubt. She didn't like the naked hunger she saw in those burning eyes.

"I watch you all the time," he said, but he didn't let go of the bridle.

"You're drunk." The hair rose up on the back of her neck. After dealing with a drunken, brutal husband, she was all too aware how unpredictable and dangerous a drunk could be. She must stay calm. "Let go of my horse this instant."

He swayed a little, looking up at her. "Or you'll do what?"

She recognized him now with a sense of relief. Big, rugged, wide-shouldered, dressed in buckskins; this wasn't some stray savage. Two Arrows was one of the Cheyenne scouts who rode for David. "I shall scream loudly, and you'll be in a lot of trouble."

He grinned arrogantly, but he didn't let go of the bridle. "You aren't the type to scream for help, and anyway, it would only add to the gossip."

Even the Indians had heard about her. It wasn't fair; it wasn't fair she should be branded so. "Let go of my horse, damn you!" She slashed out with her riding crop, catching him across his dark, high-cheekboned face.

He let go of her horse, one hand going to his injured face as the other reached out and caught the riding whip, his powerful hand covering hers as they struggled for it. The fury in his eyes frightened her, but she had too much pride to cry out for help and bring Corporal Muldoon running. For a split second, they fought for the little whip as the delicate mare snorted and danced nervously.

Then the virile brave yanked it from her hand and broke it in half with a sneer. "If you were a man, I would have killed you for that."

His sultry eyes left no doubt what he would like to do to her; desire mixed with anger in his dark, handsome face. Glory had never sensed such virile, dangerous power in a man before, not from her drunken, brutal husband, certainly not from the gentle, civilized Lieutenant Krueger.

Shaken, Glory did not answer. Instead, she wheeled Misty and galloped back toward the fort, past Corporal Muldoon, who started as if he'd been dozing at his post, and called after her, but Glory didn't acknowledge him.

Good, at least the big Irishman probably hadn't seen the encounter to tattle to his commanding officer. Muldoon and David had served together many years, beginning in the Civil War.

No, she shook her head as she rode through the silent post. She didn't want to be reprimanded by her cautious fiancée. David had enough reason to hate Indians without her adding any fuel to his fire.

She rode back to the stable, put her horse away, went to her small house, and flopped on her bed. Now she'd done it. Had Muldoon seen the confrontation? She considered appealing to the soldier, but she was too proud to do that, just as she had been too proud to stay in an abusive marriage. Though many women endured such silently, she had divorced her husband. Unable to find a job in her shocked small town, she had finally come to live with her father here at the post, hoping for a second chance, but the gossip had followed her. Lieutenant David Krueger needed a second chance, too, and keeping company with a divorced woman certainly wasn't going to help him get his captain's rank back. Still, he hinted he would soon ask to marry her, and she ought to accept. Most wives were boycotting her little sutler's store at Fort Reno, and she was struggling for a living.

Maybe Muldoon hadn't seen anything. At the moment, she didn't want to think about Muldoon or solid, dependable David Krueger. Her mind went to the Indian scout, Two Arrows. He must have been very drunk to throw caution to the winds the way he had done and grab her bridle. What would have happened if she hadn't slashed at him with her little whip?

Glory shivered at the possibilities. Would he have dragged

her off her horse if she hadn't broken free? And if so, then what? Had he watched her before? Yes, now that she thought of it, she remembered seeing him staring at her from a distance. The Indian scout knew her pretty well if he sensed she was too proud to scream for help.

Two Arrows. Glory had seen the emotion in his dark eyes above the whip welt and felt the virile strength of his hand as he tore the riding crop from her fingers and broke it. There was something dangerous and disturbing about him. Raw power, that was it. He could just as easily have pulled her from the dancing mare and broken her in his two strong hands, or carried her deeper into the shadows and . . . no, she wouldn't imagine those possibilities. Yet she had a sudden image of herself lying in the shadows with her pale cream riding coat torn down the front and the savage, muscled Cheyenne lying between her thighs, his brawny body dark against her white skin as his big, hard hands cupped her breasts.

She took a deep breath and put her fingertips over her eyes to block out the thought. The thought of sex revolted her. Howard Halstead had been a drunken brute and she had dreaded it each time he forced her to perform her "wifely duty."

Maybe that was why she was still not certain about David; she dreaded the marriage act. David was gentle and kind, perhaps he would be patient and not insistent on claiming his rights too soon.

Gradually, Glory drifted off to sleep and had troubled dreams wherein she seemed to feel the Cheyenne brave's callused hand covering hers again, the smoldering heat of his dark eyes. This was no gentle male, this was a stallion of a man. In her troubled dreams, he pulled her from her horse again and again, carried her into the woods to strip the cream fabric off her and cover her pale body with his dark one, his hot mouth claiming hers, his tongue deep in her mouth and his big, throbbing manhood probing her velvet places, his seed coming warm in her womb as she dug her nails into his hard-muscled back and urged him deeper still.

Glory awakened suddenly and sat up, breathing hard, startled and disturbed. She'd never had dreams like that before; was she losing her mind? Glory got out of bed and went to stare out the window at the warm night. Off in the distance, the Cheyenne tipis were stark against the moonlight, drums throbbing in a rhythm that seemed to call to something very deep and primitive within her. Was Two Arrows sleeping off his drunk somewhere, or was he lying on an Indian girl's dark breasts, satisfying the hunger Glory had seen in his smoldering eyes? Glory returned to bed, putting her hands over her ears to block out the sound of the distant drums. Sleep was a long time returning.

Glory slept heavily. The light was streaming in her window and onto her face, warm as a man's fingers trailing across her cheek. Mercy! Where had a thought like that come from? She got up, knowing she must open the store, even though she had fewer customers all the time.

Quickly, she dressed, thought about putting on the black of mourning, decided it was too hypocritical, selected a simple blue calico instead. She put her black hair up in a respectable twist of curls, remembering wistfully the feel of it blowing loose in the wind last night.

After a quick cup of coffee, she walked across the fort's grounds through the mild September warmth.

The other women seemed not to see her as she hurried through the busy post, but Glory carried her head high and ignored them. She knew when she passed, there would be a buzz of disapproving gossip, but she didn't care anymore. She and her father had been on the worst of terms, so she hadn't worn black since the day she buried him, and that had only added to the scandal.

As she expected, business was slow. Glory busied herself with restocking shelves of merchandise. Her stocks were low, but she might not be in business much longer anyhow. She would have to make a decision soon about moving where she wasn't known and starting fresh or marrying David. The gossip would probably follow her to a new town. People just weren't willing to give an independent and divorced woman another chance. Perhaps that was why David was hesitating; a captain needed a proper society wife. Marrying Glory would make it even more difficult for Lieutenant Krueger to regain the rank he had lost at Powder River.

Glory looked around at the bolts of cloth and boxes of nails and small tools. A barrel of crackers and another of pickles added their scents to the still, warm air. Her thoughts went to the dark man who had grabbed her horse last night. Next time, she should avoid that shadowy area near the Cheyenne camp.

The bell on the screen jingled, and she looked up as a small Indian girl peeked shyly at her.

"Hello, there." Glory smiled. "Come on in."

The child hesitated, then entered, barefoot and ragged. She looked hungry, Glory thought. She ought to run the Cheyenne urchins out when they ventured in to stare at the merchandise, knowing they had no money to buy anything and the ladies of the fort disapproved of them coming into the store, but Glory didn't have the heart for it. "How are you today?"

The child stared up at her with wide, dark eyes and slowly smiled. "Me *Hah'kota,* Grasshopper."

She might not speak English, Glory thought, but the girl caught the friendly tone.

"Well, Grasshopper, good morning."

The little girl only stared back at her, then moved silent as a shadow to stand before the big glass jars on the counter full of peppermint sticks and horehound drops.

Glory chewed her lip, watching the little girl. Of course the Indians had no money. They didn't even seem to have enough to eat, much less money for white man's candy. It was not good business practice, but Glory found herself reaching into the jar of peppermint sticks. Silently, she presented the candy to the little girl. "This is a gift from me to you."

For a long moment, the child looked from Glory to the candy.

Then she took off a small, beaded bracelet she wore and offered it gravely.

"Oh no." Glory shook her head. "The candy is free; you don't have to give me anything."

"Gift in return," the child said insistently, holding out the delicate bracelet.

There was a matter of pride here, Glory realized, as she recognized a spirit so much like her own. "In that case, my small gift shames me; I must give more." She took a small sack of flour, a slab of bacon and added them to the candy as she accepted the bracelet. "Your gift is better than mine."

The child brightened at the sight of the food, grabbed it up as if afraid Glory might change her mind. She turned to scurry out the door and collided with the formidable Mrs. Frost, who was just entering.

The wife of an employee of the Indian agent was certainly well named, Glory thought, but she put on her friendliest smile. "Hello, how may I help you?"

"Humph!" The dumpy lady looked after the running child with blue eyes as cold as her name. "You shouldn't encourage them. You'll have a store full of those redskin urchins."

"The Cheyenne children seem to be so hungry and ragged," Glory said.

"It's their own fault if they're hungry; my dear husband and the agent are doing their best to get the lazy savages to farm. Your sympathy is misplaced."

She must not offend a customer, Glory reminded herself, noting that Mrs. Frost didn't appear to be missing any meals. She slipped the bracelet on her wrist.

"Injun junk!" The other sniffed disdainfully.

"Quite the contrary, I think it's lovely." Glory was determined to hold her temper. "How may I help you, Mrs. Frost?"

"I'm in the middle of a cake, and I've run out of sugar," the older woman snapped, "otherwise . . ."

Otherwise, she would have driven into the settlement instead of shopping here, Glory thought. "How much do you need?"

Georgina Gentry

"One pound, and hurry, please." The woman's thin lips were tight with disapproval as she looked over Glory's dress.

"Of course. Lovely day, isn't it?" Glory put on her best smile, reached for the metal scoop and a brown paper bag. She scooped sugar from the big barrel, weighed the sack on her scale, and tied it up with a string.

The stout woman took the package, put some coins on the counter, looked Glory up and down again. "Bright calico? With your father less than six months in his grave?"

"How nice of you to notice." Glory met the other's gaze with a firm smile. She was not about to apologize or explain to the gossipy old biddy.

"Tsk! Tsk! But then, I suppose we shouldn't expect any better from a divorced—"

"Good day, Mrs. Frost. Think of those hungry Indian children while you're enjoying your cake and don't slam the screen on your way out."

"Why, I never!" the other huffed in righteous indignation. "No wonder you're the talk of the post!" Mrs. Frost sailed out of the store like a big ship under full sail, and she did slam the screen.

"Mercy, Glory, now you've gone and done it," she muttered to herself. "Why couldn't you be humble and bow and scrape a little? Then she might have considered you a poor, unfortunate wretch and urged the other ladies to do a little business with you."

She would not cower, Glory thought as she glared after the outraged woman. Glory had too much pride, her father had said; she would not lower herself and grovel or beg to save her own life, much less her business.

Glory went to the store window and stared out at the dusty parade grounds. The big regulator clock on the wall ticked loudly as time passed, but no other customers came in. She did have an order to fill for elderly Mrs. Brown, who didn't seem to care what people thought . . . or maybe it was because the old lady was infirm and had trouble shopping at a more distant store. Glory filled her basket with the order, hung the "Be Back Later" sign on the door, locked up, and left. She walked over to the small houses on the edge of the post, delivered her order, visited a moment with the old widow, and started back.

Passing the barracks, she was abruptly aware of the buzz of conversation and the crack of a whip. Curiously, Glory changed her path and went around the buildings. A line of cavalrymen were standing stiffly at attention while a man stood tied with his hands above his head against a stable wall. The man was stripped to the waist and his muscular brown body gleamed in the light as David brought the quirt down again. "I'll teach you to molest a white woman! How dare you touch Mrs. Halstead!"

Even as she opened her mouth to protest, the riding crop came down across the brown back again, leaving another red welt there. The Indian flinched, but he did not cry out.

"David, no!" She ran forward as the whip came up again.

The officer paused with the whip in the air. "Glory, stay out of this. This scout deserves to be disciplined, you know that."

"Don't, David, he's had enough."

The stoic Indian never moved or even gave a sign that he had heard her.

David hesitated, his square blond face uncertain. She had placed him in a humiliating situation before his men—she knew that—but that didn't matter to her at the moment.

"All right," he snapped curtly to a sergeant, "cut him down. I think he's learned better than get drunk and lust after a white woman again!"

As Glory held her breath, a sergeant stepped forward and cut the ropes binding the man's hands. Two Arrows sagged against the barn wall, but he did not fall. He turned his head ever so slightly and looked at her. Glory shivered at the scorn and hatred in the handsome dark face, still marked by the welt she had put across his cheek with her tiny whip. And yet there was still that passion burning deep in those intense eyes—passion so strong, it unnerved her.

Because of her, he'd been whipped like a cur, and yet, the

intensity of his gaze told her that even after all that, Two Arrows still desired her. That wasn't what scared Glory and caused her sharp intake of breath. To her horrified surprise, as she stared into his burning eyes, something primitive deep inside her stirred in response!

Two

Glory held her breath, terrified that David might realize that something electrifying had just passed between her and the scout.

However, David seemed too busy with his duties to notice her response. "Get him out of here!" Lieutenant Krueger ordered, and threw down the whip in a gesture of disgust.

Soldiers stepped forward, tried to get their arms under Two Arrows's sagging wide shoulders. He shook them off, stepped forward alone, even though he swayed on his feet.

David snapped, "Aren't you forgetting something? Salute me, Scout."

Instead, the Cheyenne's lip curled in disgust and very deliberately, as Glory watched, he strode away.

David turned to the burly sergeant. "Dismiss the squad."

"Yes, sir." The man snapped him a salute, gave his orders, turned smartly to join his men, and the soldiers marched away.

Glory gritted her teeth, watching the scout, his brown back stiff with resentment. She waited until the soldiers had marched out of hearing distance. "Oh, David, I wish you hadn't done that."

David confronted her, his earnest face red and confused. "I thought you'd be relieved that he'd been punished. Instead of behaving like a proper lady, your interference made me look like a fool."

"I'm sorry." She caught his arm. "But David, this isn't like you. I can't imagine you flogging a man, especially since it's against regulations—"

"You think I don't know that?" He kicked the whip with disgust. "I let my temper get the best of me because of what Muldoon told me—"

"I don't think I was in any danger, not really."

"More than you know, Glory." David put his big, square hand over hers and patted it gently. "I saw the way that savage looked at you just now, like he was willing to risk any punishment to possess you."

To possess you. In her mind, the strong hand reached up and caught hers as they struggled for her little whip. Shuddering at her own reactions, she took the lieutenant's arm, and they began to walk. "You're imagining that, David. You're letting your own terrible tragedy affect your judgment."

The lieutenant winced, and she was sorry she had mentioned his wife's death. "You're probably right; Two Arrows is a good scout; except when he's drinking, which is more and more often this past year. You know what drove me to fury?" He paused and looked down at her. "I couldn't bear the thought that he had put his hands on you. All I could see in my mind was Susan alone and screaming, while a pack of savages—"

"Don't think about that, dear." She kept her voice low and soothing, and they began to walk again.

He shook his head. "It's never far from my mind. The Comanches are allies of the Cheyenne, did you know that?"

She didn't answer because he seemed to be talking to himself. "The way that savage looked at you just now—"

"I'll try to be a little more careful so I won't worry you." She felt the blood rush to her face, remembering the way the big, virile savage had stared at her. Even with his back cut and bleeding, he was thinking how it would be to take her in his arms. She felt guilty because, just for an instant, she had imagined it, too.

"Glory, you make me crazy sometimes. I pride myself on

calm judgment, yet, when Muldoon told me about Two Arrows trying to drag you off that horse—"

"Did your old corporal also tell you I hit the scout across the face with my riding crop?"

David blinked. "No. I wondered where that mark came from. I hear he's killed men for less. Still, that doesn't matter; he's a savage. Two Arrows was once a top dog soldier, bravest of all the warrior clans. Now even his own people resent him for being an army scout."

"How'd he come by those two bad scars on his chest?" She stopped suddenly, not wanting to admit she'd been staring at the Cheyenne's muscular brown nakedness, but the lieutenant didn't seem to notice.

"Sun dance scars. Hard to believe that drunken redskin was once a respected warrior." David laughed without mirth. "But then, so was I, once."

"You'll regain your rank, be a captain again, and then you'll be promoted to major. Your father will be so pleased." Glory comforted him, patting his hand absently like a sister would.

He seemed to notice her beaded bracelet for the first time and frowned. "Where'd you get that?"

She smiled and turned it over with the fingers of her other hand. "Isn't it pretty? One of the children gave it to me."

"It is difficult to hate the children," David admitted. "The women and children are always the innocent victims when men fight."

She didn't say anything, aware that David was probably still thinking of his own personal tragedy. They paused to watch a troop of cavalry drilling on the parade ground, the September sunlight reflecting off the shiny brass buttons and rifles. A captain sat a bay horse, surveying the marching troops.

"I've got to regain my rank," David muttered, pain in his pale blue eyes as he stared at the other officer's back. "Glory, you don't know how important this is, almost as important as you are. When I regain my rank, perhaps we will talk of marriage."

She paused and, taking both his hands in hers, looked up at him. "Have you even mentioned this to your father?"

He looked shamefaced. "Well, no, I couldn't seem to put it in a letter, but I've got an idea I'd like to talk to you about."

"Oh, David, you know as well as I do that he will explode. From everything you've said about him, your father will be so upset if you marry a divorcée—"

"The colonel!" he snorted. "He's let me know all my life how much I've disappointed him; what a shame it is that of his three sons, I'm the only one alive. If I could ever catch him in a good mood when I'm home on leave, and tell him about you—"

"Marrying me wouldn't help your career," Glory reminded him.

"Perhaps not, but then, I wrecked my own career at the Powder River fight against these same Cheyenne I guard now," he said ruefully. He squeezed her hand and smiled. "I love you, Glory, you know that; no man could ever love you as much as I do."

She patted his arm absently. "I know that, David. It's just that, well, I don't know if I want to be married again."

"You wouldn't regret it." He kissed her fingertips.

But you might, she thought. Besides, from what she'd seen so far of marriage, she didn't want any more of it. True love and passion were only for silly storybooks.

The scent of sweating horses and the rhythmic sounds of troops marching drifted on the warm September air.

"This is no time to discuss it, David." She gave him a warm smile. "I've got to get back to the store."

His earnest face wrinkled into a frown. "I don't know why you bother to try to keep that store open; you know some of the ladies are trying to run you off this post."

"Even more reason I should try." Her head came up proudly.

"You're too brave for a woman, Glory," he said softly. "You should have been a man." He reached in his pocket for his pipe.

"Now you sound like my father," Glory snapped. "He never

let me forget that he would have preferred his only child be a son."

David paused in filling his pipe. "That's not what I meant, and you know it."

"I'm sorry"—she raised her chin—"I just don't have much patience with these spineless lady types."

He laughed out loud. "What they would say if they heard you talk about them that way!"

"That's the least of my worries." Glory shrugged. "I'm not afraid of them and what they think."

He grinned as he lit the pipe. "May I call on you this evening?"

"I suppose." Glory tried to sound more enthused than she felt. "I'd planned to go to bed early, didn't sleep very well last night."

"Well, no wonder," David grumbled, puffing and blowing sweet-scented smoke. "I suppose you couldn't stop thinking about that Indian grabbing you."

How could he possibly know? She didn't look at him as he leaned over and planted a prim, dry kiss on her lips. In her mind, she imagined how the Cheyenne scout's hot mouth would feel against hers.

"Glory, I didn't mean to embarrass you with my little show of affection," the officer apologized. "You've flushed brick red."

"It's all right, really." She was flustered and confused, glad he couldn't read her guilty thoughts. "Why don't you come to supper tonight, David? We'll talk."

"I'd like that." He smoked his pipe, his earnest features lighting up with pleasure. *Dependable, solid; maybe even a little stodgy,* she thought, and was immediately ashamed of her disloyalty.

"Fine. Six o'clock then. Good-bye now." She turned and fled toward her store, upset with herself because of the shocking images of that savage that kept coming unbidden into her mind.

* * *

Of course there were no customers waiting for her to reopen. Glory went in, scolding herself. Her rash actions last night had stampeded a slow and deliberate man into losing his temper and whipping one of his own scouts. It was all her fault for not doing what was expected of her and behaving like a prim and proper lady. Ladies did not go out riding alone at night.

And white men's docile Injuns did not try to drag white women off their horses. This Cheyenne was not docile; he was as untamed and defiant as she herself.

She thought about the scout's wounds. He'd been whipped like a dog in front of other scouts and a squad of white soldiers. She felt both guilty and angry. There was no doubt from the way he had glared at her that he thought she had tattled to David. Maybe it shouldn't, but that thought bothered her.

"Mercy! Are you crazy?" she scolded herself. "He brought it on himself, grabbing your horse and then grabbing you."

But he hadn't touched her hand until she had struck him across the face.

Glory leaned against the cabinet, staring at the supplies within and thinking about the marks on Two Arrows's back. The northern Cheyenne had been sent down here under orders from Washington to join their southern relatives. The tribe was poor and had little in the way of medicines; they didn't even get enough food and clothing, although David said requisitions had been sent repeatedly asking for more supplies. Washington wasn't interested in savages thousands of miles from politician's offices, especially Cheyenne. It had been only a little over two years since Custer had been killed at the Little Bighorn.

She wondered if Two Arrows had been there. In her mind, she saw him half-naked and smeared with war paint, galloping into battle. Something in that image appealed to the wildness in her own soul.

And because of her, he'd been beaten and humiliated. It didn't seem just. The least she could do would be to take some ointment over and give it to his woman to soothe his scarred back.

She waited until four o'clock, but no customers came in. Mrs.

Frost had probably already told everyone on the post about this morning's confrontation. What was Glory to do? She was running out of options. It did no good to keep the store open if she had no customers.

At least this day was almost over, except that now she had to deal with David for dinner. Taking the ointment, she saddled Misty, the beautiful thoroughbred David had lent her. The only finer horse on the post was the chestnut stallion, Second Chance, David rode. The Kruegers were famous for the fine horses from their northern Kentucky stable.

She managed to avoid anyone seeing her as she cantered away from the post, telling herself she was obligated to relieve the scout's suffering. It was because of her, he'd been whipped like a dog.

As she rode closer to the circles of tipis, she was acutely aware of the dark, silent people pausing to stare at her as she passed. How ragged and thin they were, she thought with dismay. The northern Cheyenne had been crowded onto the reservation of their southern relatives here in the Indian Territory last year. The soldiers said they weren't happy and wanted to return north, where the air was cold and there was still enough game to feed the children.

The Indian people stared at her with open hostility as she rode into their camp.

A prickle of alarm went up her back, but she kept her head high and proud, not wanting them to know she was uneasy. Glory wished she had not come now, but she had thought it would be perfectly safe since it was broad daylight. Her conscience had been pricked by the welts on the man's broad back. No doubt David was feeling the same, but he'd never admit it. Glory would give the salve to Two Arrows's woman and ride out.

Dozens of silent, angry Indians surrounded her as she rode in. Yes, the people were thin, and most were dressed in rags. It was so much worse than the whites at the fort realized . . . but many who had lost relatives in Indian raids or at the Little Bighorn would not care.

"I have brought some medicine," she began, but the women stared up at her blankly. The only friendly face she saw was the little girl she had given a candy stick to this morning. The child smiled shyly from behind an older woman's skirt, probably her grandmother.

They don't understand English, she thought. Glory held up the small jar of salve. "Two Arrows," she said.

The little girl started to speak, but the grandmother shushed her and stared back at Glory. "Him hurt."

She looked away so the guilt wouldn't show in her dark eyes. "I—I know. I bring medicine to give his woman."

"No woman," the wrinkled grandmother grunted. "Her dead; him child dead."

Two Arrows and David had something more in common than their hatred, she thought. "Two Arrows," she said again, and the old woman gestured toward a tipi away from the others.

Glory looked around. "Who cares for him?"

The old woman shrugged. "Nobody; white man's scout."

Glory regretted coming at all. She would put this ointment in the tipi and go home before David found out she was here; before it got dark. She dismounted and marched toward the tipi, the crowd following her silently. Glory hesitated, then stooped and went into the lodge.

Inside, a small fire burned in the center, casting a glow of light across the furs and weapons there. With a start, she realized he was here. Two Arrows lay on his belly against the back of the lodge. *He must be either asleep or unconscious,* Glory thought as she took a deep breath. The inside of the lodge smelled of smoke, cured meat, and the scent of a man.

Until she stood looking down at him, she had forgotten how big and powerful he was. She felt a sense of shame as she stared down at the muscular, bare back, crisscrossed with whip marks. If David hadn't been so jealous and so worried about her safety, he never would have struck the scout. Besides, it was against regulations to strike a soldier, had been since before the Civil War. Maybe that didn't apply to Indian scouts.

What to do? She would leave the ointment by his head, so that when he woke up, he could get someone to apply it to his back. Even if he didn't have a woman, there must be one who cared about him. Glory leaned over to place the ointment by his hand.

Abruptly, his hand snaked out and caught her wrist, yanking her down to her knees. She gave a small cry of dismay, but he only glared at her as he rolled over on his side. "Why do you sneak up on me, white woman? And where did you steal that bracelet?"

"I didn't steal it; little Grasshopper gave it to me. How dare you call me a thief!" Glory tried to pull away from him, remembering again how strong his hands were. "I—I brought some ointment for your back. I came because I was sorry—"

"You came to gloat," he whispered, "you come to see what your telling has done—"

"I didn't tell; I never would have." Glory was as angry as she was scared. "I'm trying to help you—"

"I don't need your help." He seemed to spit the words at her as he let go of her arm, and she scrambled to her feet, dropped the salve, and backed away.

"I didn't tell the lieutenant; I've been looking after myself for over a year now. I'm not a weak girl who goes crying to a man for help."

His dark, handsome face was stoic as he glared back at her. "Keep your salve, white girl; I don't need charity."

She couldn't keep her gaze from sweeping across his big frame. He was taller than David and more powerfully built. She had a sudden feeling that he could pick her up with one arm, and she was not a petite type. "Surely there's a woman who cares—"

"There was a woman." He almost whispered it, but there was pain in his dark eyes. He no longer seemed to see Glory; he was talking to himself. "We were camped on the Washita when the Yellow Hair and his soldiers came riding in at dawn. They're all dead; my woman, my children." He seemed to have forgotten Glory as he reached to pick up a bottle of cheap whiskey from the buffalo robe and took a long drink. "Sometimes at night, I hear them crying for help, and I wasn't there; I wasn't there. . . ."

Glory waited, torn by the pain in his face as he stared into the fire, which threw grotesque shadows across his tired features. Abruptly, she felt like an intruder. How could she have thought she would make everything right with a stupid little jar of salve? Silently, she turned and left the tipi, brushing past the crowd of stoic people.

"Somebody needs to see about Two Arrows," she said to the old woman as she mounted.

She shrugged. "When the ghosts come, he drink. Him no dog soldier now, him white man's Injun. No belong here."

Heads nodded in agreement.

Glory nudged Misty and rode out, thinking the scout was as bad off as she was; she didn't belong anywhere either since she'd been scandalous enough to divorce her faithless, abusive husband. Other women stayed in such marriages. Trouble was, Glory wasn't like other women; how often she'd been reminded of that by her outraged father. Like the scout, no one cared about her. No, that wasn't true. David cared about her. Yet David was haunted by his own ghosts. Three misfits, she thought, thrown together by chance and circumstances. No, four, if she counted Corporal Muldoon.

Glory rode back to the fort, put her horse away, and freshened herself up. She put on David's favorite dress, the one with the tiny blue flower pattern, and began preparing dinner. She just hoped no one had seen her riding out to the Indian camp. David would scold her for her reckless disregard for her personal safety.

He arrived promptly at six. David was always prompt. She served beef, well-done, as civilized men preferred it.

Afterward, they went into her small parlor and in the deepening twilight, David sat down at her piano and began to play and sing. He had a fine baritone voice. *"In the gloaming, oh, my darling, when the lights are dim and low,"*

She leaned on the piano and smiled politely, knowing he was singing words of love to her, but her mind kept returning to the hostile, moody brave.

"and the quiet shadows falling, softly come and softly go." David looked into her eyes as he sang, and the expression on his square, aristocratic face told her how sincere he was about his feelings for her. *"When the winds are sobbing faintly with a gentle, unknown woe, will you think of me and love me . . ."*

Her mind drifted away as she listened to the beautiful melody and played with the beaded bracelet she still wore.

"Glory, your mind must be a million miles away. What on earth are you thinking about?"

She realized then that he had finished the song. "Oh, I was just enjoying the music." She clapped politely. "You have such a fine voice."

"I was hoping you were paying attention to the words; I mean them deep from my heart."

"I know, David." She patted his hand absently.

"Glory, I know your marriage was hell, but I'll make you forget all that. With your charm, you could win over my father. Besides, no man will ever love you as much as I do."

He would never marry her as long as his father disapproved; the colonel's opinion meant too much to him. Good, dependable, dutiful David. "Yes, I know, dear. Would you like another cup of coffee?"

He shook his head. "When I finally leave the service, we could live on my father's estate; Father won't live forever, and someday I'll inherit the place."

She busied herself lighting the lamp. "I thought you own a big spread in Texas you bought just before the War started?"

"I do." David frowned. "Even though the Comanches have been corralled, the memories haunt me; until I learn to deal with them, I could never live there."

"Then I don't know what you'll do," Glory said. "As far as the Kentucky estate, I'm not sure the colonel wouldn't disinherit you over marrying a divorcée."

"I'm the only son he has left, Glory, with William dead in the War and Joseph killed . . ." His voice trailed off and she knew he felt guilt and responsibility over both his kid brother and his dead wife.

"Play something lively," Glory urged him, thinking that David and Two Arrows had more in common than they knew. Maybe that was why they disliked each other so much.

"Only if you'll play a duet." He reached out and pulled her down on the piano bench beside him. "What'll it be?"

She wanted to change the subject and the mood. "What about 'Camptown Races'?"

They both began to play and sing and finished laughing. Glory got up then because she was afraid that if she stayed there beside him, he would put his arms around her and talk of love again. Tonight, she didn't want to think about love.

"It's getting late," David said, standing up and looking toward the door regretfully. "I need to go. I don't want the ladies gossiping about you."

"They do anyway," Glory said.

He put his arms around her protectively. "If you were married to me, they'd soon forget your past. I have money, Glory, if we get far enough away, no one will remember—"

"That's what my father counted on, but you see, the scandal followed me all the way to Indian Territory."

"Think of it, Glory, we could start fresh. I own the finest thoroughbred stallion in the western U.S. Second Chance will be the foundation sire for the best stable in the country. You've got the best mare I own."

She looked up at him. "You shouldn't have, David. Gray Mist is quite valuable."

"I want you to have her, my dear. When we're married, that pair of horses will start the best herd in America."

She twisted out of his arms and went to stare out the window into the darkness.

He came over, stood behind her, put his square, capable hands on her shoulders. "What's the matter, my dear? You seem so preoccupied."

Oh, dear God, was it so apparent? She kept seeing Two Arrows's tortured face as he talked of his wife and children. "Oh, nothing. A little Cheyenne girl came into the store today; I gave her candy. I told you about the bracelet."

"You're such a soft heart, but I love you for it." He nuzzled the back of her hair.

Glory kept her body stiff. "She was ragged and hungry-looking. All the Indians here look pretty desperate."

He sighed against Glory's dark hair. "I know. Even though I've got good reason to hate Indians, I feel sorry for the poor devils. It seems old Dull Knife and Little Wolf brought their people all these miles down here at government insistence. They say the White Chief told them they could go back home if they didn't like it here."

"Did they tell the Indians that?"

She felt David shrug. "Who knows? They probably told them anything that would get them to come peacefully, but of course, they won't let them go back."

She turned, looking up at him. "Why not?"

"Well, I suppose that Washington figures if other tribes see it, they'll all start clamoring to change reservations."

"It seems like such a small thing," Glory said.

"To be honest, I suspect Washington's trying to keep them away from their old friends, the Lakota. If they linked up again like they did two years ago, we might have another big Indian war."

"David"—she took his face in her hands—"that pitiful child haunts me. Won't you talk to the colonel and the Indian agent; see if something can be done?"

"It won't do any good," David said, "believe me, we've tried. Even I'm not so cold-hearted that I can watch women and children go hungry, but Washington just sends letters telling us to control them. The northern Cheyenne have been grumbling that they've been promised they could return home, and they want to."

"How would they get there? Isn't it a long way?"

David nodded and made a gesture of dismissal. "Of course it's a silly threat. It's almost fifteen hundred miles back up to the Dakotas, and they only have a few good horses; they'd have to walk all the way."

Glory chewed her lip. "Isn't that what the Nez Perce did last year up north?"

David frowned. "Lot of good soldiers killed there."

"Indians, too," she reminded him.

"Glory, I don't know what's gotten into you." David frowned at her. "I didn't come here to talk about Indians, yet that seems to be almost all we've done."

"I'm sorry, dear, that pitiful child unnerved me." She gave him a quick kiss to mollify him.

David took her in his arms and held her close. She put her head against his shoulder, thinking if she would let him, and if his father gave permission, she could be David's wife, protected and secure. When they returned to Kentucky, with his family connections, no one would dare gossip about her, and she wouldn't have to worry about money.

He kissed her then, a prim, dry kiss. She felt nothing, but then, she didn't expect to. Everyone said that women were not expected to feel anything, just submit to a man's baser appetites.

David took a deep breath. She could feel his body grow tense against her. Abruptly, he sighed and took her by the shoulders, seemed to step away from her by sheer willpower. "I must be going, my dear; it's late."

She saw him to the door, handed him his hat. "You do look so dashing in your uniform, dear."

He smiled at her. "I'll look even better when I get my captain's bars back. All I need is some heroic action, a chance to clear my record of the mistake I made at the Powder River almost two years ago."

"It was an honest mistake; and you'll get your rank back,"

she assured him as she let him out. "I do hope it happens for Muldoon, too."

"Ah, the old rascal; if we hadn't served together all these years, I'd give up on him. If he'd stop gambling and be a little more spit-and-polish, he wouldn't have lost his stripes. Another chance; that's all we need."

"That's all most people need," she said softly, and gave him a quick peck on the cheek. " 'Night, David." She closed the door behind him.

Preoccupied, Glory lay down across her bed fully dressed in the blue-flowered calico. In the warm darkness, twisting and turning on her lonely bed, she was unable to sleep. Through the open window, the prairie wind carried the scent of wildflowers, campfire smoke. She got up and went to the window, stood staring out at the silent fort, turning the small bracelet over and over absently. The restless breeze rustled through the dry prairie grass and carried the rhythm of throbbing drums from the Cheyenne camp to her room. She felt suddenly closed in in the small, cramped box of a house. She would go for a ride. No one need ever know. Why, she'd even use a sidesaddle; that would hush everyone. Quickly, she slipped out to the stable.

"Hello, Misty," she crooned, patting the sleek dapple gray head. The mare nuzzled her hand, and Glory gave her a sugar cube. "Are you as bored and restless as I am?"

The mare snorted.

"Then we'll go for a short ride," Glory declared. "I've got too much on my mind to sleep."

She saddled up and rode out at a walk, holding her breath. What would she do if she were discovered? No doubt David had told all the soldiers on guard duty to watch out for her, so she rode out a different way to bypass the sentry. The drums seemed to be louder, even though she was not riding in that direction. She reined in, hesitant, listening and curious. What could the Cheyenne be doing this late at night? The soldiers never seemed to pay much attention to the rhythmic drums. The sound seemed to be drawing her like a magnet.

Maybe she'd just watch from a distance. Glory took a deep breath, pulled the ribbon from her hair, shook her hair loose so that it blew in the breeze. Now she felt as free as some mustang filly. Glory laughed aloud and raised her chin proudly. Then she wheeled her horse and rode toward the Indian camp.

Three

Two Arrows stood in the darkness just beyond the big campfire, watching the meeting of the Cheyenne leaders. Once, as a proud dog soldier, he would have been welcomed there, his words would have been heard with great respect. Now, as a white man's Injun, the men paid him no more heed than if he'd been a skulking cur lurking about the camp.

His head ached from cheap whiskey, and the quirt cuts on his back still throbbed, though he had put on a buckskin shirt to hide the humiliating marks.

The arrogant white woman crossed his mind, and he shook his head to chase her spirit away. She was the woman of the lieutenant and had brought him nothing but trouble. When he had grabbed her bridle to save her from falling as her mare reared, she had mistaken his intentions. He both hated and desired her; desired her as he had not wanted a woman in a long, long time. Yet he had been wrong about the white woman; she was no different and no better than the rest. Two Arrows would have thought her too proud to run and tell the lieutenant about last night. Aieee, what did it matter?

He crept closer, listening to the warriors talk. Important things were being decided on this moonlit night; even the children knew it and ran about through the tipis, chortling with excitement, although their mothers tried to shush them and urge them to sleep. Children. His were dead.

Old Dull Knife held the ceremonial pipe aloft, offering to

the four directions, to the spirit of the sky and earth, before taking a solemn puff, then passing it on around the somber circle, moving as always, right to left. It was so quiet, standing in the shadows, Two Arrows could hear the crackle of the flames, the snorting of restless horses. In a nearby tree, cicadas whirled their wings, and on a distant hill, a wolf threw back his head and sang with all his soul to the moon.

Dull Knife paused, tilting his head, and listening, the flames of the circle throwing distorted shadows across his lined face. The chief nodded with approval. "He sings the Cheyenne song," he said solemnly. "Our brother sings to *Heammawihio,* the great God Above, of freedom."

The others grunted agreement.

"It is good medicine on this night we decide this important thing," another warrior said.

Little Wolf, the honored war leader, stared into the fire. "Like us, our furry brother grows weary of this hot, foreign land. We are and will ever be strangers here. Maybe he signals us to go north, to our own wild, free country, and he will run before us to guide us."

Another man with many battle scars puffed the pipe and passed it to the next. "There are only a few hundred of us as the white man counts, and most of them are women and children. Where will we get the horses to carry them?"

An older woman, with gray streaks through her black hair, stepped into the firelight, her shadow distorted by the flames. "I helped scalp the soldiers when our people killed Yellow Hair and his soldiers up on the Greasy Grass that whites call the Little Bighorn. May I speak for the women?"

Two Arrows watched from the shadows as the men considered a long moment, respecting her age and her bravery. Once Moccasin Woman had been pretty, but hardship and heartbreak had taken their toll. Her husband had died at the Sappa Creek massacre, and she'd lost both sons at the Rosebud Creek battle against the white leader called Crook. Her daughter had died from malaria since they had come to this place, and her ancient mother was even now dying, so Moccasin Woman was rearing little *Hah'kota,* Grasshopper.

Little Wolf nodded. "Speak for the women."

"We will walk all the way if we have to," Moccasin Woman said, "even though it is a long, long distance and many will not live to see the high, cool country we love. The women say: take the chance; we may not get another. It is worth our lives to try."

There was silence, broken only by the crackle of the fire and the murmur of the women in the shadows agreeing with old Moccasin Woman as the men considered her words.

Thin Elk, who had often annoyed Little Wolf lately by paying unwanted court to the leader's young daughter, asked, "Will the soldiers let us go or will they try to stop us?"

"The soldiers will try to stop us," Two Arrows blurted loudly, and then paused in confusion. He was not one of them anymore. They did not want his opinion.

The men in the firelit circle turned to frown at his effrontery.

Behind him, he heard a young woman whisper, "Who is that who dares to speak?"

"No one," sneered another. "His soul belongs to the soldiers and their whiskey—"

"Hush, woman," Dull Knife thundered, his pockmarked face stern and solemn. "Come to the fire, soldier scout, I would see you."

Two Arrows took a deep breath. By his boldness, he had drawn their attention, and he had no right to voice an opinion among these brave men. He stepped forward, trying not to stagger with the whiskey that still ran hot through his veins, and stood silent.

He felt the stares of curious scorn, but he only looked into Dull Knife's eyes.

The chief studied him a long moment. "You say 'us.' Since when does the white man's servant include himself with the people?"

"I was not always a white man's scout," Two Arrows said respectfully. "Many of you elders knew my father, Clouds

Above, and my brother Lance Bearer and my cousin, Iron Knife."

A murmur of approval went around the camp circle and heads nodded. "Brave men all."

Two Arrows ripped open his buckskin shirt and showed his scarred, mighty chest. "Only a few among you carry the scars of the sun dance as I do. I once counted many coups and my woman wore my coup marks proudly."

"Then why did you abandon this?" Dull Knife looked puzzled, and the elderly, bent Cheyenne sitting cross-legged next to the leader leaned over to whisper in his ear. Two Arrows caught the word *Washita*.

The word and the terrible memories it brought back made Two Arrows take a deep breath and wince, wanting, no, needing a drink of whiskey. When he was very drunk, he didn't hear the screams in his mind. His life had ended that frozen dawn ten winter counts ago; he only went through the motions of living now.

Yet last year, he had been among those who helped track down the escaping Nez Perce. The guilt he'd felt over his part in catching those sad, defenseless ones, so much like his own wife and children, had pushed him over the edge. He'd hardly been sober since.

"Why do you not answer me, Scout?" Dull Knife snapped.

"I am sorry, Great One, my thoughts were gone on the wind like the running wolf."

"I said, why do you talk as if you would cast your lot with us when you have food and gold riding for the soldiers?"

He listened to the distant singing of the wolf, so wild and free, and blurted out the truth that only just now did he recognize. "I tire of being the white man's slave," he answered. "I serve him well, yet today, I was whipped like a cur before other bluecoats." He pulled off his shirt, turned, and showed his back to the circle, silently enduring the humiliation of them all seeing his marks of shame.

"This is no way to treat a man," a warrior muttered. "It shames him and our people."

"It is nothing to the white men," said another. "They even whip their children this way."

A disbelieving murmur of excitement went around the circle. The Cheyenne never raised a hand to a child—they were disciplined with love, not pain.

Two Arrows turned around to face the warriors in the firelit circle. "Once I brought honor to the people; I would like a chance to do so again."

"Don't listen to him." An acclaimed warrior called Broken Blade spit in the dust and frowned. "Two Arrows has ridden for the soldiers for many years now against both our friends and enemies."

"That is true," Two Arrows agreed. "Only last year, I was the scout who helped the army find the Nez Perce as they tried to escape across the great northwest to Canada. Perhaps because of me, Chief Joseph's people were captured. Sometimes a man sees that he has been wrong, that he still might change. I ask for a second chance."

"I lost three brothers in fights with the bluecoats; the last one at Powder River against the bluecoat chief called Mackenzie," grumbled Broken Blade to no one in particular. "I hold the Cheyenne who ride as scouts responsible. Why should we trust this traitor?"

"Because I have ridden with the soldiers long enough to know how their minds think," Two Arrows said, but he winced at the scorn and anger he saw on the stony faces staring back at him. "If you do this thing, if you try to take these people and go back to our own country, you will have to outwit the soldiers because they outnumber you."

"But why should they care?" another argued. "Did not the Great White Father in Washington say that we only had to try this Indian Territory and that if we did not like it, we could leave?"

"Washington speaks always with a forked tongue; you know

that," Two Arrows said. "They say whatever they think will get them what they want and think nothing of the truth and what they promised."

A murmur of agreement went around the circle.

Broken Blade scrambled to his feet. "I say we finish what the soldiers began," he shouted, gesturing with a closed fist at Two Arrows. "I say we whip this cur out of our camp, once and for all!"

Again more muttering and uncertainty on all faces.

"Be silent!" Dull Knife thundered. "We cannot think while mouths chatter like foolish women."

All fell silent as the old chief stared into the fire a long time. Now the others waited patiently. Time, as the white man counted it, meant little to the Indians, Two Arrows thought impatiently; they saw no reason to be slaves to the white man's clock and what was a few minutes when measured against eternity? "Little Wolf, what think you?"

The great war leader stared into the fire. In the silence, the wolf howled again and the sound echoed and reechoed across the lonely hills. "It is a good sign," Little Wolf grunted finally. "I say we can use the knowledge of the soldiers' scout."

"What if he betrays us?" grumbled Broken Blade.

Dull Knife looked at Little Wolf and then directly into Two Arrows's eyes. There was no mistaking the cold promise on that stern, pockmarked face. "If he betrays us, I will kill him myself!"

Now an excited buzz went around the fire and then spread across the camp. Murder of a fellow Cheyenne was the most serious of crimes. On the few occasions it had happened, the killer and his kin were exiled from camp and ceased to exist as far as other Cheyenne were concerned. A serious crime, Two Arrows thought, but the decision they were facing was deadly serious.

"If I betray the people, I absolve you from blame," Two Arrows said, "or may the soldiers catch me and hang me!"

A mutter of awe went through the crowd. To be hanged was

more dishonorable than being whipped. All knew a person's soul escaped through his mouth as he died, but if he were hanged, his soul was trapped in his dead body forever.

Dull Knife gestured to him. "Sit with us, then, and give us your knowledge."

Two Arrows had not felt pride in a long, long time. He had been a hollow man that walked and talked, but his heart had been empty. Even though his back burned and his mouth ached for a drink of whiskey, once again, he felt like a dog soldier, bravest of the brave among the Cheyenne. It was a good feeling.

He sat down cross-legged in the circle and someone handed him the pipe. He tried not to let his hands tremble with the power of this important thing. It had been many winter counts since he had been offered the pipe. Two Arrows took a long puff and stared into the fire for wisdom before passing it reverently to the next man.

"What the people are considering is dangerous and perhaps foolish," he said. "They have little chance of success, but freedom is worth dying for. All we want is another chance to live as we choose in our own country with our brother wolf."

"Whiskey is a powerful thing," Little Wolf said. "It becomes more important to a man than anything else. I fear you may have good intentions, yet fail when the craving gets too strong."

Even now, Two Arrows's body cried out for a drink. If he closed his eyes, he could almost taste the flavor on his tongue. He had not been completely sober for a long, long time. "All I ask is that the people give me the chance to prove myself," he said.

Broken Blade snorted in disgust. "Have we come to this, then, that we place the lives of our people in the hands of a drunken white man's Injun?"

Yes, how far he had fallen, Two Arrows thought, from an esteemed dog soldier to a drunken redskin. "I am what Broken Blade says I am, and yet, I would ask to regain the place of honor I once held."

He saw sympathy in some of the other faces now, but not Broken Blade's; never Broken Blade's. The other man would never forgive him, Two Arrows thought. Sooner or later, he and Broken Blade must come into terrible conflict.

Again, there was silence, broken only by the crying of a baby somewhere in the camp and the crackle of the big campfire.

Dull Knife sighed. "Perhaps we have little choice. Two Arrows is the only one who knows what the soldiers might do. Does another wish to speak?"

A frail elder stood up, old Sitting Man. "I was a friend of Two Arrows's father. This was a fine family of many honors that this warrior has disgraced. It is only right that we give him the chance to redeem that honor."

Two Arrows felt the moisture come to his eyes at the mention of Clouds Above. "Somehow, I have lost my way, but I now promise on my father's bones that I will change."

Again, silence as each man considered.

Little Wolf looked around the circle. "Does any man feel strongly enough against him to speak out?"

A young warrior, a friend of Broken Blade's, got to his feet. "I do not trust this drunken scout, yet like Dull Knife, I do not know who else knows what the soldiers might do." He glared at Two Arrows as he returned to his place by the fire.

Little Wolf paused, considering. "Then we are in agreement. We will take a chance on this warrior, and woe be to him if he fails us. Now, tell us, Two Arrows, what must we do?"

He had not made a decision on his own in many years. As a scout, he followed the white man's orders without thinking. Now lives might depend on his choices. "I say we leave in the middle of the night." Two Arrows looked around at the other men. "The soldiers will not expect that."

"Tonight?" asked another.

"Tonight," Two Arrows said.

"Ancient One, mother of Moccasin Woman, is sick," Broken Blade said. "We cannot take such an old, sick woman. Perhaps we should wait—"

"No." Moccasin Woman strode into the circle, in her haste committing a great wrong. Cheyenne had been trained to listen respectfully as another spoke, and it was unthinkable that a woman should interrupt a warrior's words. "Two Arrows is right; it will take several moons to cross all those miles to our country. Already the leaves turn yellow. Soon the chill breath of winter will blow across the land. If we travel in the snow, we will lose many to the cold."

Everyone thought about her words. Moccasin Woman was stating the facts, and yet Two Arrows knew how hard this must be for her. "Ancient One is your own blood," he whispered. "Perhaps we could wait."

"And others will die of disease and hunger while we wait." Her lined face betrayed no emotion, but her voice shook. "Ancient One would be the first to tell us to leave while there is still time to go north before the winter winds blow snow upon our trail."

No one spoke, knowing what a sacrifice Moccasin Woman was making. Besides Ancient One and the little granddaughter, Grasshopper, Moccasin Woman had lost all her kin. Ancient One was much loved, but people were dying every day in this hot climate without enough food. More would die unless they left soon.

After a long moment, Dull Knife stood and gestured. "It is decided then. We will leave late tonight when the soldiers at the fort are asleep. Let the men gather the horses and the women pack the travois."

Now Two Arrows's knowledge of the soldiers could help his people. "It will be best," Two Arrows said, "if we leave most of the tipis standing and campfires burning so they will think we are still here. Perhaps we can be many miles to the north before the soldiers know we're gone."

Dull Knife's dark eyes showed a hint of respect. "Two Arrows speaks true. Let us make haste."

Glory had tried to keep herself from riding toward the Indian camp. Twice she had cantered Gray Mist across the prairie, her long black hair blowing wild and free behind her, enjoying the freedom of the ride while she wrestled with her decision about David. If she married him, she would be safe and secure. He was so dependable . . . and so dull. Then she was immediately ashamed. He loved her more than any man possibly could, and not many would want a divorcée.

She realized suddenly that she had turned her mare and without any conscious effort, was riding again toward the Cheyenne camp. Even as she scolded herself for her recklessness, her heart quickened with excitement at the pale glow of the many campfires in the distance and the soft beat of the drums echoing across the rolling prairie.

Somewhere on a hill, a wolf sang, and the sound echoed and reechoed through the September night. The wolf seemed to be calling to her; it sounded so wild and free. The big savage came to her thoughts unbidden. Two Arrows was a lot like that wolf, she thought, wild and dangerous. His dark, high-cheekboned face and his brooding eyes came to her mind. She almost seemed to feel his hard, strong hand grasping hers after she had hit him with her riding crop. She shuddered, thinking what a foolish thing that had been; the virile, powerful savage could have killed her with his bare hands. He was such a contrast to blond, civilized David Krueger.

She slowed her horse to a walk and rode nearer. Strange, the camp should be settling down for the night; it was very late. Yet there seemed to be a lot of activity; people hurrying about, horses being saddled with the little Indian saddles, children awake and running about chortling with excitement. Just what was happening here?

Glory rode closer, curiosity overcoming her caution. David would be so upset with her for coming out here again, but he didn't have to know about it. She wondered if Two Arrows was still in the camp and if a dark, beautiful woman had finally stroked Glory's salve into the wounds of his powerful, naked back?

In her mind, Glory dipped her fingers in the creamy ointment as he lay half-naked on a blanket. She ran her fingertips across the welts on his muscular back, feeling the strength and the warmth of the man's flesh.

Was she losing her mind to be thinking such things? Why, he was a savage! She realized she had ridden up in the shadow of a grove of sand plum bushes overlooking the Indian encampment. Her mind had been on the image of Two Arrows lying half-naked under her fingertips for her to pay much attention to what she was watching. Now she took a good, long look.

"Mercy! Why, they're packing up to leave!" she said in a shocked whisper, "I must tell David so he can stop—"

A big hand reached up out of the darkness and caught her wrist.

"Let go of me!" She tried to fight him off, spur her horse to escape. Misty snorted and reared even as the man reached up with both hands and jerked Glory from her horse.

Misty neighed in fright and took off at a gallop. Glory's heart pounded against her ribs as she struggled with her assailant in the darkness. If she could just catch her horse and remount, she could escape and go for help. Maybe she could scream and alert the guard at the gate, even though it was a long way from here.

She barely got a whisper of sound out before a hard hand clamped over her mouth. He was big and powerful; even in the dark, she could feel the size and power of him as he turned her so that he held her against his body with one hand under her breasts and the other over her mouth. She could feel the strength of him all down her back as he pulled her hard against him. The heat of his bare chest and the mound of his manhood pressed against her through the sheer dress. She was going to be raped or killed!

Sheer terror caused Glory to fight, clawing at her captor, trying to bite his hand. If she could pull her mouth free for an instant, she could scream and maybe the sentry—

"No, you don't, Proud One." He cursed under his breath as he jerked his hand away, then put it over her mouth again.

Two Arrows. It was Two Arrows; she recognized the voice.

At that moment, she didn't know whether to be relieved or terrified, remembering the way his eyes had smoldered as he
looked at her this morning and last night. In their struggles, his
hand had gradually moved up to hang on to her until it was
under her breasts. She felt the heat of it through her sheer blue-
flowered dress.

How dare he! Even David had not dared touch her so familiarly. Now she was as indignant as she was scared. What to do?

He was too big to break away from; in fact, he could break
her like a matchstick across his knee. She would have to outwit
him to escape. Oh, she'd make him rue this day! Next time,
she'd wield the whip and laugh when the lash cut into his back.

She forced herself to relax and go limp as if she had fainted.

"White girl?" he whispered. "Are you all right?"

She didn't answer. She didn't know exactly what she was
going to do, but she'd decide as things played out. Mercy, suppose he carried her out under a bush and raped her?

By the great god *Heammawihio,* he had killed her! Two Arrows relaxed his grip a little, sick at heart. Why hadn't he realized how soft and fragile white women were? He had been
too rough with her, and maybe crushed her or broken her body.
"White girl? Proud One?"

She didn't answer, only slumped in his arms like a crushed
butterfly. In alarm, he ran one hand up over her heart. It was
still beating. She had fainted, he thought with relief. White
women at the fort were always fainting and reaching for smelling salts according to the soldier gossip.

He became suddenly aware that in putting his hand over her
heart, he was now cupping her breast. He could feel her nipple
through the cotton of her bodice and her sharp intake of breath.
In his mind, he imagined her naked. If this were a different
night, he would be tempted to lie with her under the sand plum
bushes and take her as conquering warriors of all nations availed
themselves of the enemies' women. It was a gesture of both

hatred and contempt. Two Arrows had never wanted anything as much as abruptly; he wanted to lie between her satin thighs and put his mouth on that nipple. For that, Lieutenant Krueger would have him executed. The thought crossed his mind that it might be worth it.

He had not yet removed his other hand from her mouth. She had tensed and taken a sharp breath when he put his hand on her heart. Could she be pretending? White women were no doubt as good liars as their men. How much had she seen? He must not take a chance that she would go back to the fort and bring the soldiers.

It was difficult to tear a strip from the hem of her calico dress without taking his hand from her mouth, but he managed to do it. He knelt and quickly put the strip of cloth in her mouth, gagging her. At that point, she came to life, fighting and scratching again.

"Just as I thought!" he said, relieved that she was not hurt, but angry with her for her trickery. Lieutenant Krueger's woman deserved whatever she got. Two Arrows flipped her over on her belly, put his knee on her to hold her down as she struggled to get the gag out of her mouth. She was no match for him, even though she fought like a bobcat, clawing and snarling in her throat.

"Hold still!" he commanded, but she struggled to get out from under his weight while he grabbed for her hands. Her flesh was soft under his knee. In their struggles, her dress had worked its way up so that he could see a large expanse of stockings and small riding boots.

He resisted the urge to reach down and run his fingers up the backs of those long, slim legs. Instead, he tore another strip from her dress, twisted her hands behind her back, and tied them together. How fragile her hands and wrists seemed to him. "Now," he said, "you're my prisoner."

He flipped her over and swung her up in his arms as she struggled. Her dusty dress had slipped off one shoulder showing the swell of her bosom, but in the moonlight, she looked more angry than frightened. Her dark eyes gleamed with indignation and hatred, promising revenge when she could run and tell the lieutenant as she had last night. At that moment, Two Arrows hated her with a vengeance as the marks on his back throbbed and reminded him how much pain and humiliation Lieutenant Krueger's lady had caused him.

What to do with her? He threw her over his broad shoulder like a sack of flour and strode toward the camp. She didn't weigh much, he thought, and she was full-breasted. He could feel her nipples against his scarred, bare back. He felt his manhood tighten in sudden desire. It had been a long time since the need for a woman had had more urgency and appeal than whiskey.

She was long-legged and, that night, she wore a dress that had slid upward as he threw her across his shoulder. He had his hands on the back of her bare legs. She tried to kick at him, and, without thinking, he reached up and slapped her across the rear. "Stop that!"

She froze in abrupt surprise, and he seemed to feel the fury at his unthinkable gesture in her rigid body, but she stopped fighting. Her soft breasts pressed against his back through her thin dress. He ran his hand down the backs of her silken stockings from the backs of her thighs to her calves. Two Arrows had never wanted a woman as much as he wanted this one right now. Her skin was soft and silky, and she smelled of rose petals.

If he'd had any thoughts of changing plans, not leaving tonight, that was lost now, Two Arrows thought grimly as he strode toward the camp. There was no turning back; not when he had just handled the lieutenant's lady so familiarly. If the Cheyenne didn't escape tonight, no doubt Lieutenant Krueger would mete out terrible punishment tomorrow with the approval of Major Mizner. The problem was—just what in the hell was he going to do with this woman?

Glory hung limp over the savage's massive shoulder, her black hair hanging almost to the ground, her face against his bare back as he strode through the darkness. Her breasts were pressed against his warm flesh and his hands clutched the back of her bare legs. How dare he touch her so crudely? Her fury outweighed her fear, and she tried to shake his hands from her legs. She recoiled with shock as his big hand slapped her bottom so brazenly while he ordered her to stop. Did this big, insolent savage think he was dealing with some tavern wench or Indian whore? And just what was he planning to do with her?

The way his hand stroked the backs of her legs, she knew abruptly what he must be thinking. She had a sudden image of herself sprawled under a bush with her dress shredded while this virile savage forced himself between her thighs and put his hot mouth on her nipples. With her hands tied, she would be helpless to stop his insolent touch. She could do nothing while he toyed with her until he came in a rush of hot seed in her depths.

And if he got her with child! No doubt, this savage would do that the minute he coupled with her, unlike her weak husband, who had never managed to put a son in her belly. This savage was built like a stallion. Glory remembered only too well the feel of his hard bulge of manhood against her back as they had struggled. Of course he would rape her; she could only hope he wouldn't kill her.

Mercy! Where was he carrying her? She must not think about what was about to happen, she must think about how to save herself. Maybe some soldier would spot Glory's riderless mare and awaken the lieutenant to bring a patrol out to investigate. As late as it was, the chances of them finding her horse before Glory was raped and murdered were pretty slim. No, she must think of ways to save herself.

If she could just get the gag out of her mouth. . . . Glory rubbed her face against the scout's muscular back, feeling the heat of his dark flesh against her face, smelling the scent of smoke and maleness.

She realized from the sudden confusion around her that he had carried her into the Indian encampment. He slid her easily from his shoulder to his arms and glared down at her, but she could see the hunger in his eyes.

She glared back at him over the gag, telling him with her own dark gaze how much she hated him and what the soldiers would do when she told them how Two Arrows had put his hands on her. Indians were coming from everywhere to see what the commotion was.

"I found her spying on us," Two Arrows said, evidently speaking in English for her benefit.

A mutter of dismay went through the crowd. In the glowing light of the big campfire, she saw the dark, hostile faces, and she had never been so afraid. Probably all the warriors would rape her. Why hadn't she heeded David's command to behave like a proper lady and stay safely indoors and ride only when escorted? Now the Indians were talking in their own language, and their hostile tone told her it did not bode well for her.

Two Arrows looked down at the bound woman in his arms. He hated her for the feelings she created in him, warring with each other, hatred and desire. "What say you, Dull Knife?"

The chief looked from the girl to Little Wolf. "If we turn the woman loose, she will bring the soldiers."

Broken Blade snorted. "Then I say we kill her to stop her mouth."

Two Arrows clutched her protectively against his great chest. "Do we now act like the soldiers and kill helpless women and children?"

Little Wolf frowned. "If we kill her, the lieutenant will hunt us down and slay us like rabbits."

"Perhaps we could leave her tied in a tipi," Thin Elk suggested. "By the time the soldiers find her, we will be long gone."

Two Arrows did not want to let her out of his embrace. She just fit the curve of his arms as if she belonged there. How could his enemy's woman feel so right in his arms? It was revenge he hungered for, he thought. "Perhaps we could use her to protect us if we took her along."

"What do you mean?" old Dull Knife asked.

"As long as we have Lieutenant Krueger's woman as a hostage, the soldiers will not dare to fire on us for fear of hurting her," Two Arrows said.

"We had hoped the soldiers would not care enough to chase us," Broken Blade grumbled, "yet if we have his woman, you know the lieutenant will chase us to the ends of the earth rather than lose her."

Two Arrows looked down at the helpless woman in his arms, her long black hair a tumble like a mustang filly's mane, her dark eyes blazing back at him with anger and hatred, her sheer dress falling off one white shoulder, exposing the swell of her breasts. If she were his woman, he would pursue her captors to the ends of the earth rather than lose her. "Broken Blade speaks true," he admitted, "but killing her would bring even more wrath from the army."

He would not let them kill her, he realized that suddenly, even if all the council voted in favor. She was his captive, and he would not let anyone hurt her. The thought made him angry with himself all over again that a mere woman could have such power over him. It was hatred, he thought, looking down into her blazing eyes, hatred and lust. No, he could not possess her, not ever; that would bring even more vengeance down upon the people. While the soldiers mated with Indian girls often, the thought of a warrior touching a white woman brought with it terrible retribution.

"It is decided then," Dull Knife said. "We will take this captive with us. Two Arrows, you are responsible."

Two Arrows grinned down into the woman's blazing eyes. "Don't worry, Honored One, she is now my slave. I will see to it that she does not escape!"

Four

Glory looked from one to another of the Indians as she hung in Two Arrows's arms. Obviously they were arguing over what to do with her.

All she could do was hold her breath, listening to the hostile tone of the savages' voices, wondering what was being said. The gag tasted dry and starchy, and she could feel the heat from Two Arrows's virile body burning through her dress as he held her against him.

Finally, after some talk, they must have reached a decision because Two Arrows threw her across his shoulder again and carried her to his horse, a big fine paint stallion and put her up on it before mounting behind her. "I just saved your life," he said close to her ear in a mocking tone, "but since you're white, I don't expect you'll appreciate it."

Damn him to hell! She twisted her neck and glared up at him, hoping all her hate and anger showed. And to think she had pleaded his case with David, felt sorry for this Indian. She wished now David had beaten him to death!

Two Arrows pulled her up against his body. That gesture put her hands, which were still tied behind her back, up against his body. She tried to jerk away as she heard his sudden intake of breath and felt his maleness swell at her touch. He moved even closer, so that her hands were against his manhood, and there was no way she could pull away from the contact. His arms went around her and he pulled her so close that she could feel his warm breath stirring her hair. His body seemed tense, and she thought his hands trembled as he held her so closely that she could scarcely breathe.

How dare this savage touch her like this! If she could only get this gag off, she'd scream loud enough to be heard at the fort!

Abruptly, she twisted her head before he could realize what she was up to, tried to rub the gag off against his bare chest. She felt the hardness of his nipple against her face and he grabbed her head and held her face there a long moment. "Stop it, Proud One," he demanded through clenched teeth. "Stop it before your value as a woman makes me forget your value as a hostage!"

She froze and looked up into his intense eyes. She had never seen such burning emotion in a man's face before. It both startled and frightened her, and in that moment she hated him all the more because she was helpless in his arms and couldn't claw or spit or even say anything cruel.

"Don't worry," he snarled. "I won't do it; the lieutenant wouldn't want you back then; not if I'd had you in my blankets."

Would David want her back if she'd been raped by an Indian? Glory wasn't sure. She'd heard stories about white women who'd been outraged by Indians, and how the white men didn't want them after that.

At least, she could feel relief in realizing that of course they weren't going to kill her; she had more value as a hostage. Oh, when David came riding to her rescue this arrogant savage would rue the day he had touched her. She gave him her most hateful glare.

"Behave yourself, Proud One," he snapped, and jerked her close against him again, his face against her hair. She not only could feel the heat and weight of his big manhood against her bound hands, she could hear his heart beating in her ear like war drums. Her struggles had only aroused him, and it was silly for her to fight, knowing how much bigger than she he was. She'd bide her time and outwit this savage.

Glory forced herself to relax her body and settle into the

muscular planes of his. The night had turned cool, and his warmth seemed to envelop her protectively.

"That's better," he grunted. "You're being smart now." One of his hands went to rest on her thigh, the other went around her to grasp the reins.

Except for the indignity of this arrogant male holding her as if she belonged to him, she sensed that she was in no immediate danger. Around her, Indians were gathering up a few meager possessions, children and dogs running everywhere. A small girl paused in mid-stride to look up at her. Grasshopper. The child said something in an anxious tone to Two Arrows, and he shook his head, and said a few words in a soothing tone, evidently reassuring the child that Glory would be all right.

What time was it? Sometime in the middle of the night, Glory guessed as she watched the flurry of activity. Horses were hitched to travois, small sacks of dried meat and corn were tied to the few horses the Cheyenne had saddled. The horses looked as thin and tired as the people, Glory thought with pangs of conscience; these people were in a bad way.

Mercy, was she losing her mind? Here she was feeling sorry for these savages and their animals when she was their captive. No doubt somewhere along the way, when they were certain they were out of the reach of their pursuers, they would kill Glory rather than deal with a troublesome captive. Before they killed her, would all the warriors rape her?

An older woman with a lined face and gray streaks in her braided hair came looking for Grasshopper. The grandmother caught the little girl's hand, then turned to look back at a tipi in the shadows. She wiped her eyes slowly. Why was the woman crying? Glory thought. It was only a tipi she was leaving behind.

In fact, the Indians were leaving most of the tipis in place, and they had built up big campfires. Only a little food and a few weapons and supplies were tied to the thin horses. Glory looked around. Why, there weren't near enough horses for all these people. Just where did they think they were going and how did they think they would get there with all these children and old ones? Some of them would die doing this. The thought made her tremble.

"Don't be afraid," Two Arrows whispered, and pulled her even closer against him. Again her bound hands touched his manhood. Glory determined that she would not give him the satisfaction of recoiling in horror. She would act as if she didn't know—or didn't care what rested against her hands, but if she could ever reach that knife in his belt, blamed if she wouldn't attempt to geld him with it. It might cost her her life, but it might damned well be worth it.

In the firelit circle, the people were ready now, moving out of the camp, leaving their tipis standing, their campfires burning brightly. Now Glory realized what they were doing; they were trying to fool the soldiers into believing the Cheyenne were still in camp. Why, it might be midday, noon, or even tomorrow evening before the soldiers finally noticed that there was no one walking around in that distant Indian camp.

Glory's heart sank. By tomorrow afternoon, there was no telling where these Indians would be. If they got enough distance between themselves and the fort, they might not need a hostage anymore and would cut her throat if she caused them any trouble.

At that point, she resolved not to be any trouble and to plan her escape. As they rode out of the camp, another brave rode past, turned and looked at her with lust in his eyes, said something to Two Arrows, and laughed.

Two Arrows replied defiantly, and slipped his arm around her waist possessively. For once, Glory was glad to lean back against his big chest and let him hold on to her. Obviously the other had made some lewd suggestions or threats, and Two Arrows was making it clear he didn't intend to share his prize.

Share her? How dare this arrogant savage put his hands on her, hold her so familiarly? Oh, yes, David would have him hanged or shot, all right, but before he did, she wanted the pleasure of taking a whip to this impudent brave!

She would focus on her anger and what she would do to this

scout once they were recaptured—that would keep her mind off the danger and indignities of her ordeal until she could find her opportunity to act.

Somewhere on a distant hill in the dark September night, the wolf howled again, as if singing to these people. It was a sad, lonely sound that seemed to call to her very soul, which surprised her.

They rode out toward the north, with a handful of men, including Two Arrows, bringing up the rear. He seemed nervous and tense, looking about.

It was the scout in him, she thought, ever alert for trouble or danger. The Indians were moving north; even those who walked were moving fast. Glory saw the old woman who held little Grasshopper's hand hesitate and look behind her toward the distant tipi once, then, with a sigh, she turned toward the north and began to walk with the others.

Oh, David, where are you? I'm being kidnapped within sight of the fort with a sentry asleep at his post and the whole encampment unaware of what's happening. In her mind, she pictured David leading the troop to her rescue. Oh, if she managed to survive this, she would never behave rashly or headstrong again. Or maybe not. It wasn't in her to be meek and mild, no matter what kind of scrapes she got herself into. That had cost her her marriage—and many a beating.

As they rode through the darkness, Two Arrows put his face so close to her ear, she could feel his warm breath along her neck and in her ear. "I know that gag bothers you. When we are far enough away, I'll take it out of your mouth."

She nodded, pretending to be pliant and agreeable. Maybe she could trick him into untying her hands, too. Glory was an excellent horsewoman. Given half a chance and a little surprise, she could gallop away, leaving the Indian shouting in protest behind her.

The moon had gone down, creating a night as black as the bottom of a well. A gradual chill descended on the landscape as they rode north at a quiet walk. In spite of herself, Glory shivered in her sheer dress.

Immediately, Two Arrows pulled her into the warmth of his arms and big body as they rode. "I'll warm you," he said, and then, almost with satisfaction, "I'll wager you have never allowed the lieutenant to hold you this close."

It was true, but the satisfaction in his tone annoyed her. Oh, the nerve of this savage! However, in spite of his mocking words, she found herself fitting her body against his hard-muscled frame, taking warmth from him. Even his rigid manhood against her hands seemed hot as coals. *Just wait*—she promised herself to control her fury—*just wait until David strips you to the waist, ties you up, and hands me the whip; oh, I'll make you rue the day you ever put your hands on my person!*

It seemed to Glory they had ridden for hours, but it was not yet dawn, and sheer exhaustion caused her to doze off. She awoke with a start to find herself cuddled against Two Arrows as he rode.

"It's all right," he said softly. "I've still got you."

Was that supposed to be a reassurance or a brag? It wasn't very comforting. Her arms ached from having her hands tied behind her back and her mouth was so dry, she felt as if she might choke with the gag in her mouth. Somewhere off to the east, the first gray light of dawn kissed the rolling prairie. She just had to get this gag off. She twisted to look up at Two Arrows and made a pleading sound in her throat, hating herself for it.

He looked down at her, reined in. "You're begging? I didn't think you knew how, Proud One. Well, I don't suppose anyone can hear you scream now." He reached and untied the gag, pulled it away.

Glory sighed with relief. He stared at her mouth for a long moment in the dim light, slowly reached to run one finger across her lips. She saw the desire in his dark eyes and jerked her head away. "Do you—do you have any water?"

"How like an officer's lady!" he sneered. "Not even a 'please'?"

She snorted. "I should be grateful to you for kidnapping me?"

He laughed under his breath as he reached for a canteen hanging from his saddle. "I forget what it is about you that appeals to me, Proud One. No man rules you, does he?"

"And never will!" she shot back, glaring up at him, fury in her voice.

"Breaking a spirited, fine-blooded filly is a challenge for any horseman."

"I wear no man's bridle."

He smiled ever so slightly. "We'll see." He took the cork from the canteen and put his arm around her shoulders, tipped it so she could drink. The water tasted so good and cold, she gulped and it dripped down both sides of her mouth.

"Easy," he commanded, "you'll choke."

"You stuff a rag in my mouth, half smother me for hours, and now you worry about me choking?"

"You try my patience." He held her a long moment, frowning, then, abruptly, he pulled his arm away and took a drink from the canteen himself.

She watched the way he swallowed, thinking he was like some big, lithe animal. She had better not push him too far; he might beat her as Howard had often done. If she made her captor angry, he'd never relax his guard so she could get away. She forced herself to say meekly, "Thank you."

He blinked at her unexpected politeness, then nudged the horse into a lope again. "There's a small spring up ahead," he said. "The white men call it Turkey Springs. Everyone will be stopping just a moment to refill their canteens and water their animals."

The spring might be her chance, Glory thought; besides, she needed to relieve herself. She looked around as they rode on. The Indians were strung out over a long trail, some riding, some walking. They passed the old woman she remembered from last night, the one with tears in her eyes. The woman now rode a bony old paint horse pulling a travois with little Grasshopper asleep in it. The woman's face was stony, but tragic, and she stared straight ahead.

Somehow, her expression touched Glory's heart even though she hated these people for kidnapping her. "Who is that and why does she cry?"

"Moccasin Woman?" Two Arrows sighed. "She had to leave her mother, Ancient One, behind."

Glory was horrified. "She left her back there at camp?"

"There was no help for it," Two Arrows said, and he stared straight ahead as if to look in Glory's eyes would bring some emotion from him. "She was dying, and we had to go. We must reach our country before the snows begin; to be caught on the trail in the cold would bring death to many."

" 'Our country'?" Glory stared up at him. "You don't mean these people intend to walk all the way up to the Dakotas?"

He nodded, his attention on the trail ahead of them.

"Why, that's the craziest thing I ever heard," Glory declared. "Do you know how far that is?"

"We know better than you." He kept riding. "They mostly walked it when they were sent down here."

"But then you had food and tents the army furnished," Glory argued. "Now you've got almost no supplies. Soldiers will catch you before you get out of the Indian Territory."

"Maybe not." He looked down at her now and smiled without mirth. "You see, we have something Lieutenant Krueger wants very much. He won't risk endangering my hostage."

"He'll kill you for this!" she snapped without thinking.

"He'll have to catch me first." The handsome savage grinned at her. "In the meantime, he'll be torturing himself, wondering what might be happening between us."

There was a long pause as they stared into each other's eyes, and Glory had a sudden feeling that they both had the same image of the two of them meshed naked on a blanket, writhing in the mating ritual under the September moon.

Her chin went up proudly "I'm not a giddy girl; you can't scare me with threats."

He wasn't smiling now. "I wasn't threatening, Proud One, although, I'll admit, mating with the lieutenant's woman would be the ultimate revenge."

"Only for revenge?" Somehow, she was annoyed.

"I didn't say that. Now be still; I have more important things to think about."

Oh, such arrogance! She should have let David whip him to death. No, she wanted to do it herself. She must not let her temper get the best of her brain, Glory thought, she must seem meek and agreeable while she figured out how to escape and find her way back to the soldiers, who were surely on her trail by now. "My arms are aching," she complained, "and I can't possibly get away. Can't you untie me now?"

"When we get to the spring," he said, "if you'll promise not to try to escape."

"You'd believe my promise?"

"I might."

Anything to get her arms free. Of course a promise made under these conditions wasn't binding. She wouldn't have any qualms about breaking her word to a savage who was holding her captive.

Up ahead, in the dawn light, a warrior held up his hand and shouted.

"The spring," Two Arrows said.

He nudged his horse, and they rode forward up under a small grove of scrub oak trees. He swung down, turned, and held his arms out for her.

Glory hesitated, then decided there was nothing to do but slide off into his arms. She certainly couldn't dismount alone with her hands tied behind her back. As she came off the horse, she slid down the length of Two Arrows's body, her skirt catching on the saddle and pulling up so that her long legs were bare.

He held her against him a long moment, looking down into her face, and she saw both uncertainty and desire there. His big hands seemed to burn into her back. She wasn't sure whether it flattered her or scared her. David was too civilized to look at her that way, and certainly her husband had always taken her in a bored manner as if he were only interested in the end result—the son which she never bore.

"My arms," she said.

"Oh, yes." He reached for the knife in his belt, blinking in confusion. She knew he had been envisioning throwing her down right there in the prairie grass and taking her. He reached around her with both muscular arms and cut the strip of cloth.

For an electrifying instant, she was keenly aware of his hard chest brushing against her nipples, then her arms came free and she brought them to the front, rubbing her wrists and sighing with relief. "You tore a perfectly good dress."

"How like a woman," he snorted. "With everything else that's happened, you're worried about a torn dress."

She stepped away from him. "Remember, the lieutenant may not want me back if I've been . . ." She couldn't bear to say the word.

"He doesn't love you then"—Two Arrows shrugged—"or nothing would matter to him but your return."

"He does love me!" She almost shouted it at him, and those over near the spring turned to stare. "He loves me more than any man possibly could; he's told me so."

His face was like stone. "Maybe he loves you as much as a white man is capable of loving."

The way he sneered when he mentioned David made her grit her teeth. David did love her. It wouldn't matter to him if she was raped—would it? "If—if you don't mind," she said, "I need to go over to those bushes and . . ."

He nodded as he tied his horse to a fallen log. "All right, I'll fill the canteens at the spring."

Glory watched his broad back as he gathered up the canteens and started toward the spring. He was all muscle but as lithe as a mountain lion, she thought. She stared at the faint red welts on his back and felt a moment of guilt. *Mercy, Glory, are you losing your mind? This savage has kidnapped you; if David gets his hands on him, he'll hang him*—but not before she got the pleasure of whipping the insolent savage herself.

Cautiously, Glory looked around. It was still such faint light with a bit of early-morning haze that people moved like ghosts toward the spring or checked their horses' gear. She looked toward the stolid Moccasin Woman, now filling her canteen along with the others, and felt a twinge of pity for her. What nerve it had taken to leave a dying mother behind for the good of the people. If she weren't careful, she would soon be admiring them and empathizing with them. However, if the army had let them go back to their own land, Glory wouldn't be in this spot.

She went off into the bushes and relieved herself. Then she looked around, trying to decide her next move. Two Arrows had the best of the horses and that big paint grazed where he'd been tied, some distance from the others. All the people were scattered about in the early dawn, women nursing babies, old people resting, their lined faces already weary. Many of these would never survive this long walk, but they were going anyway. These were either the craziest or the bravest people she'd ever met, but she didn't intend to make that fifteen-hundred-mile trip as their hostage. The way that warrior called Broken Blade had leered at her and the way Two Arrows kept looking at her gave her grave doubts that she'd survive the trip without getting raped.

Quietly, Glory tiptoed through the grass to the grazing paint. She patted its neck, trying to appear casual while looking around. Two Arrows was kneeling by the spring, filling his canteens. No other man was close enough to grab her. It was now or never!

Glory jerked the reins loose and swung up on the paint, her skirts hiking high as she forked the horse. "Hah!" She lashed the startled horse with the reins and dug her riding boots into its sides. She saw Two Arrows turn, startled, even as the paint took off at a gallop.

"Woman, come back here!" She heard his furious cry of protest, but she lashed the horse and kept riding.

Mercy! Suppose they shot her out of the saddle? She must not think about that; she must concentrate on getting away. Behind her, she heard another horse and glanced back over her shoulder. Two Arrows was coming after her on a big bay at a gallop, and the anger on his handsome face was terrible to see. It scared her even more than being shot.

Glory lashed the horse and kept riding. Behind her, she heard the other horse closing the distance. Then Two Arrows whistled long and loud and her horse slammed to a stop and she went over its head in a tumble. Oh damn! Why hadn't she realized that his own personal horse might be trained? She hit the ground, momentarily stunned, rolled over to see his horse coming hard, Two Arrows's face a cold mask.

She scrambled to her feet and began to run, her long black hair blowing wildly about her face. He was gaining on her. She couldn't outrun a horse, she knew that, but she was too stubborn and proud to give up. Besides, the fury on his features terrified her. Now he was alongside her, reaching to scoop her up with one strong arm, lifting her to his horse while she fought and bit. She sank her teeth into his arm and he swore and let go of her. She landed in a heap, momentarily knocked breathless, then stumbled to her feet as he dismounted, with the horse still running.

She had never seen such anger in a man's face. Patient David would never be capable of such passionate fury. "Lying white woman!"

Glory took one look at his expression and turned to run. When Howard had gotten even slightly annoyed, he would beat her, and Two Arrows looked furious. What would such a man do to a woman who had made a fool of him?

She hiked her skirts and ran hard, gasping for air, but he was running easily behind her. He caught up to her, grabbed her shoulder, and her dress tore as they fell.

"Your tongue is as forked as the soldiers'," he snarled, and flipped her onto her back, pinning her there.

She lay there, gasping for breath, afraid of the anger in his dark eyes.

"Are you hurt?"

"Why do you care?" She spit it at him and tried to get out from under him.

"You lying white—!" He pinned her down as she struggled and she winced, and closed her eyes, waiting for him to strike her.

"What is the matter with you?"

She opened her eyes and glared up at him. "Go ahead; I refuse to beg! I'm used to it; I can take it."

He seemed to read her expression. "You think I'm going to beat you?"

"Are—aren't you?"

For a split second, his hard eyes softened. "What kind of man was your husband?"

For a moment, she felt tears cloud her eyes, but she blinked them away. She had never cried when Howard beat her; she would not cry now. "That hardly concerns you."

His dark face was only inches from hers and he was lying half on top of her. She felt the sudden tension, abruptly aware of the heat of his hard, muscled body against her. He looked down at her, and his body tensed.

"Damn you for lying to me." He stood up, reached out, caught her wrist, hauled her to her feet, and dragged her toward the horse.

"Mercy! Just what did you expect?" she snapped at him, struggling to break his hold. "You don't expect me to keep my word under duress, do you?"

He glanced back over his shoulder as he dragged her along. "I'm just a simple savage, remember? I don't know the meaning of that word."

"Well, it means—"

"Be silent! I'll break that defiant spirit of yours; you won't make a fool of me twice." He grabbed her, threw her up on the horse, and took the reins as he mounted the other. "By the way, now that you've broken your word, I don't see any reason to keep mine."

"About what?" She felt a chill go down her back.

He looked her over, caressing her body with his dark, smoldering gaze.

Startled, Glory glanced down, realized her torn bodice exposed much of her bosom.

Just the slightest smile played along his sensuous lips. "You know about what."

Five

A woman screaming . . . screaming. Flames licking around the frame house, smoke rising up across the Texas plains.

Garish colors; war paint and blood. Half-naked Comanche warriors shrieking as they gallop lathered ponies around the burning ranch house.

The woman's yellow hair reflects the early-morning sun as she takes off across the yard, running clumsily, too heavy with the imminent child to escape the howling savages that chase her while she screams and screams.

Behind her, the blond young man, hardly more than a boy, tries to hold them off with his rifle, covering her escape, but he is out of ammunition and the shrieking savages surround him. He fights them now with the butt of his rifle, swinging it vainly, but at a shout from their leader, the war party lets loose a volley of arrows and the boy goes down, jerking like a bloody pin-cushion. He is not yet dead, but the savages are on him, taking his scalp with triumphant shouts.

As he writhes in agony, they turn their attention to the woman, trying so desperately to escape through the cornfield.

Yelping like hungry coyotes, the Comanches chase her down, surround her. They laugh as their leader grabs her, ripping her dress away.

"Please," she screams, "oh, please, have mercy!"

The Indians advance on her, painted faces grinning with de-light, waving the bloody scalp of the boy in her face as they throw her to the ground. There in the dirt of the cornfield, they violate her, grunting with pleasure. All the while, behind them the acrid smoke of the burning ranch drifts up into the pale Texas sky.

Sated, the leader reaches for the knife in his belt, grabbing the woman by her long yellow hair.

Their ugly faces grin down at her as she struggles to escape from their merciless circle.

"David," she screams, "oh, David, where are you? Please help me! Please! David! David! David!"

Lieutenant David Krueger came awake with a start, sweat soaking his body, blinking at the sunlight streaming through his window.

A nightmare; the same old nightmare. His younger brother dead and his pregnant wife screaming his name, but David was thousands of miles away in the war.

He put his folded arms over his face and sighed. He had failed Susan in more ways than one. He had not really loved her; she was the girl his father had chosen for him.

Savages. The vivid nightmare reminded him again of why he hated Indians. The Comanches and the Cheyenne were allies. How ironic that he was stuck here in the Territory with the same band of Cheyenne who had cost him his rank at Powder River during the winter of '76. It was adding insult to injury that he also had to work with Cheyenne scouts.

Two Arrows. David grimaced and swung his legs over the side of his bed. When Corporal Muldoon had told David about Two Arrows trying to jerk Glory from her horse, David had lost all reason, remembering what had happened to Susan.

It was a good thing he was off duty this morning; he had obviously overslept after a restless night. He lingered over getting dressed and sipping coffee in his quarters.

Glory. What was he to do? He was deeply in love with her and bedazzled by her fiery disposition and proud, defiant behavior. He paused in polishing the epaulets on his blue jacket and frowned. He might have to defy his father to marry her, and he had not yet discussed it with old Colonel Krueger. David was the middle son, always craving his father's approval and never getting it. He knew what Father would think of his marrying a divorcée, what it would do to his military advancement.

Smiling, he made a decision. He had ordered an expensive gift from a New York store for Glory's Christmas. He would arrange to have the gift sent to the horse farm. Then he would invite Glory to accompany him home for the holidays to meet the colonel. Surely her beauty and spirit would sway his father. When his father adored her as David did, David would ask her to marry him. But suppose his father still objected? David wouldn't think about that right now. However, he did drop by the office and ask the soldier at the desk to send a letter about the gift.

Now David walked across the parade grounds in the crisp morning air toward Glory's little store. Yes, he was due a leave; this Christmas visit would be a great idea. He lit his pipe as he walked, enjoying the taste and scent of fine tobacco. Glory. Sometimes he wished she were a little less independent; she made it difficult for herself around here—and for him. David usually behaved in a slow and methodical manner, but the tempestuous Glory could cause a man to lose all reason. He had lost his temper and whipped one of his Cheyenne scouts because of her. If she'd been home at night like any respectable woman, instead of out riding in the dark, that incident wouldn't have happened.

David paused at the store's entry. A *CLOSED* sign still hung on the door. *Odd;* he tapped the pipe against his teeth. It wasn't like her to sleep late. Maybe she was ill. A bit worried, he strode toward her small house and rang the bell. No answer. He rang again, longer and more insistently.

"Glory?" He shouted and banged on the door. It came open under his hand. David hesitated. It was not at all proper for a gentleman to enter a lady's quarters unless invited. He stuck his head in the tidy home. "Glory? Are you here?"

He waited a long moment, straining to hear any answer over

the sound of soldiers drilling on the parade grounds and a bird singing in a nearby oak tree.

His concern caused him to forget that it wasn't proper either to enter or to smoke his pipe inside a lady's home without permission.

"Glory?" He strode through the house, looking about. No breakfast dishes in the kitchen. Her bed appeared mussed as if she had lain down across it, but her nightdress was still thrown across the foot as if she had begun to get ready to retire, then changed her mind.

A feeling of dread began to build in him as he turned and strode out across the porch, walking toward the stable. If she wasn't at home or at the store, perhaps she was out for a morning ride. David smiled in anticipation. He would saddle up Second Chance and join her. The weather was good, and it sounded like a marvelous day.

"Lieutenant?" Corporal Muldoon hurried toward him, faster than the old Irish trooper usually walked. "One of the men found that gray filly grazing along the road near the barns."

"Oh, good." David puffed his pipe with a sense of relief. "So Misty got out of the barn and Glory's out looking—"

"Lieutenant"—Muldoon's red face mirrored concern—"the filly—she—she is saddled and bridled."

Oh, Lord. David paused, his pipe halfway to his lips. In his mind, he saw Glory riding recklessly through the darkness. The mare had stumbled and thrown the woman, then limped back to the stable. Even now, Glory was lying out there on the prairie somewhere, injured. Or maybe dead.

No, he shook his head. He had lost one woman, one he didn't really love; he wasn't going to lose this one he adored. "Get a patrol, Muldoon, we'll begin an organized search—"

"Lieutenant Krueger, sir." Skinny Private Tanner ran up, puffing with exertion and saluted. "Major Mizner wants to see you in his office right away."

David had saluted automatically, his mind on Glory. "See me? If it's about the missing Mrs. Halstead—"

"Sir?" The young man's black brows knitted together. "I don't know what it's about, but he said it was important. There were a couple of southern Cheyenne in his office when I left."

Cheyenne. What the devil was that about? David looked into Muldoon's eyes, but his old friend appeared as baffled as he.

"Dismissed," he snapped. "Come on, Muldoon, I'll need the major's help if we have to send more than one patrol looking for Glory."

The two of them strode toward the major's office.

"Laddie, I'll give you eight to five," Muldoon grumbled, "that this ain't going to be good news."

"Now, Muldoon, you promised you'd stop gambling or you'll never get your stripes back." He was making tense conversation, but his mind was on Glory. Where was she? Was she hurt?

"Aye, sir, we'll both get our rank back together. We've got many years ahead of us with honors and a good retirement."

"Of course. I've got to make at least major; it's important to my father." They were almost running as they crossed the parade ground and went into the office.

"Good morning, sir." David and Muldoon saluted the stern officer behind the desk, studied the ragged savages standing there. "I'd like to request a search party—"

"At ease, men. We've got trouble." The major motioned for silence as if he hadn't heard the other. "These southern Cheyenne tell me their northern cousins took off last night."

"Took off?" David blinked. "You mean, they're gone?"

"Bag and baggage, damn their sneaking hides!" Mizner's stern face turned an angry red, and he slammed his fist on the desk. "These two told because they're afraid it's going to bring trouble to their people."

The two cowardly ones did not look at the men, they looked at the floor.

"I don't understand," David began. "The sentries—"

"Didn't see a damn thing." The senior officer stood up and began to pace the floor. "They left tipis, fires burning to fool us; the sort of thing you'd expect from a smart general, not ignorant savages."

"Well, sir, I'm sure they won't get far." David tried to soothe his commander, his concern only for Glory. "Now there's another problem—"

"You don't think this is a problem?" The major whirled on him. "I'm responsible for keeping the northern Cheyenne on this reservation. With a mess like this on my record, I'll never get that promotion, get a transfer out of this hellhole back to Washington. Of course, with your record, you don't have to worry about that."

David swallowed hard. "Both Corporal Muldoon and I intend to erase that, sir."

"I know your father." The other man looked at him, shaming David with his unrelenting stare. "Damned good officer before he was wounded in the Mexican War."

"Yes, sir." Was there anyone who didn't know the colonel?

"Your older brother, William, served under me before he was killed," the major said. "Had such a brilliant military career ahead of him. I know your father took it hard."

"Yes, he took it hard, sir." David closed his eyes. Even after all these years, he could hear his father shouting at him: *Three sons and you're all I've got left! Why couldn't it have been you? Why did it have to be William and Joseph?*

David studied the ragged Indians standing silently nearby. A thought crossed his mind, a thought too frightening to contemplate. He looked around the room at the others. "Sir, Mrs. Halstead is missing."

"Mrs. Halstead?" The major paused and scratched his bald head. "Oh, yes, that divorcée who runs the store." His tone seemed to be dismissing that as inconsequential.

David felt a flare of emotion; he was slow to anger, but it was building in him. "Is it— is it possible, the Cheyenne took her?"

"Aye, her horse was found grazing loose this morning," Muldoon volunteered.

"I've heard gossip about her," the major said. "The ladies of the fort say she does all sort of things like ride alone; foolhardy, if you ask me."

David clenched his fists at his sides. "Surely the major doesn't listen to idle gossip of a bunch of women—"

"She doesn't seem to care what people hereabout think of her," the major said.

"Well, sir," David admitted sheepishly, "that may be true. She's a bit headstrong and stubborn—"

"Not a good thing in a horse or a woman." The commander dismissed him. "Besides, Lieutenant, this talk is nonsense; those savages wouldn't dare touch a white woman."

David and the old Irishman exchanged glances, remembering the incident involving Two Arrows. David took a deep breath. "Ask them, sir."

The commander glared at the two Indians. "I don't speak their damned chatter."

"Beggin' your pardon, sir"—Muldoon fumbled with his cap—"I speak a little Cheyenne. If you'll allow me—"

"Yes, yes, get on with it." The officer made an annoyed dismissal with a beefy hand.

Muldoon said a few words that David didn't understand.

The pair of Indians looked at the floor and shuffled their feet, mumbled something.

"What'd he say?" David blurted, his fear for Glory's safety outweighing everything else.

Muldoon hesitated. "They may not know anything, sir."

David felt a sudden dread. "That one, American Horse, I recognize him; he speaks a little English." David confronted the man. "Tell me what you just told the corporal."

American Horse cleared his throat. "Some say," he muttered, looking out the window, "Two Arrows hungered for her. Maybe he take."

"Oh, my God!" It was more of a prayer than a curse as David put his hands out in front of him, sagged against the top of the major's desk. In his mind, he heard a woman screaming as a savage raped her; only this time, the woman had dark hair blowing as wild as a mustang filly's mane.

The major asked several more questions of the Indians, but their words were a blur to David. *Two Arrows hungered for her.* Yes, David had seen the way the scout looked at her. He closed his eyes, not wanting to think of all that hinted at. He would do more than whip the Indian when he caught him this time, he would kill him slowly and painfully if he'd dared to touch the woman David loved. He hadn't realized how much he'd cared until she was in danger. *Oh, Glory, my darling Glory.*

"Lieutenant? Lieutenant Krueger?"

"Sir?" David snapped to attention.

"Send Captain Rendlebrock to me. With any luck, we can find Mrs. Halstead and get those stinking savages back on this reservation before word gets out they're gone."

His reputation and his promotion, that was all the officer cared about, David thought bitterly. "Begging your pardon, sir, don't you think we ought to telegraph ahead for troops to cut them off, too?"

"And have them know what happened here?" Major Mizner snorted as he glared at David. "Let's contain this thing, keep this embarrassing news from spreading."

"But sir, Mrs. Halstead's safety—"

"Much as I hate to say it"—the major dismissed his words with a curt gesture—"we all know what might happen to her."

David didn't want to think about that, his worst fears. The commander's words forced the image into David's unwilling mind; his beloved Glory lying helpless and naked while dark savages took turns possessing her ripe body. It was Susan all over again; with one major difference; he had not loved Susan, more's the pity. And he had no more brothers to lose.

Bile rose up in David's throat, and his hatred of all Indians deepened. "We can have the troops mounted in less than thirty minutes."

"Good! Captain Rendlebrock will be in charge. You're dismissed." The major began to shuffle papers on his desk.

Rendlebrock. Once David would have led this expedition, before he'd been broken in rank. He had no confidence in Rendlebrock.

"Yes, sir." David saluted, but he had a sick, helpless feeling in his gut as he and Muldoon left the office. "Muldoon, get over to the telegraph and then get the boys moving."

"The telegraph?" His old friend eyed him as he walked. "You tryin' to end up as a private? You'll be finished if the old man finds out you ignored his order—"

"I care about Glory, I don't give a damn about anything else." David shrugged. "That's an order, Corporal. Maybe the troops ahead can cut them off, but I intend to catch them first. When I get my hands on that Two Arrows . . ." He gritted his teeth until they hurt.

"Now, don't worry, laddie, we'll get her back."

"I'm going to kill him with my bare hands," David promised. "I'm going to show him what real savagery is!"

It was past high noon, David thought with annoyance as he sat before the mounted troops, ready to ride away from the fort on his fine chestnut stallion. There was no telling when the Cheyenne had left last night; one thing was certain, they had a good head start and a way of melting into the landscape so that the soldiers might ride within a few yards of them and not know they were there. Out in the rolling hills and gullies of north-western Indian Territory, there were lots of places to hide. More than that, Two Arrows had spent years as an army scout; this was no simple savage. He would be wise to the ways of the soldiers, what they might think and do. Except for his growing dependence on whiskey these past few months, Two Arrows was as formidable, cunning, and tough as any professional soldier. David had whipped him like a dog, and now Two Arrows had David's woman. There was no telling what the Indian would do for revenge.

Corporal Muldoon galloped up to him and saluted.

David snapped him a salute. "Ready, Muldoon?"

"Sir, the telegraph line's down; be a while before we can get word up ahead."

"Two Arrows," David sighed through gritted teeth. "The others might not think of it, but he'd be smart enough to know we'd wire ahead. Probably tied the break together with rawhide somewhere, where it'll be hard to find and repair."

"Aye, sir"—the ruddy Irishman nodded—"that means there'll be no help from outside the fort for a while. 'Til then, laddie, if anyone's going to stop the Cheyenne and rescue the lady it'll have to be us."

Mustachioed Captain Rendelbrock rode up just then, frowning at being sent on this duty.

David and Muldoon saluted, but the officer hardly seemed to see them. He nodded absently and David got a whiff of liquor. "Troops ready, sir."

The captain cursed under his breath. "Damned Injuns. Why do I have to be the one sent on this miserable assignment? Mount the troops, Lieutenant."

"Yes, sir. Mount the troops, Corporal Muldoon." David squared his shoulders, his voice low with anger. "I'll teach that damned Cheyenne scout a lesson he won't forget!"

As they rode away from the fort, Captain Rendlebrock stroked his mustache. "Lieutenant Krueger, take a detail over to the Cheyenne camp to see if you can find out anything, then rejoin us on the trail."

"Yes, sir." David saluted, then rode back at a lope to choose his detail. He took Muldoon, of course. They had first ridden together during the Civil War, and he counted on the man. The old Irishman was both loyal and brave; his only weakness was that he gambled.

The patrol galloped out to the northern Cheyenne camp and dismounted, walked around. It was deserted, all right, but tipis and other valuable things were lying about, giving the look of being occupied. *Damned clever of Two Arrows,* David thought grudgingly. "Everyone look around, see if you find anything."

Young Private Tanner scratched his head and his black brows knitted together again. "Where do you suppose they went?"

Muldoon pointed north. "Anyone want to bet it's to the land of the big lobo wolf? That's their country."

"Muldoon, remember, no gambling," David reminded him as they began to search through the tipis.

"Aw, now, laddie boy, it was just a figure of speech; I swear on me poor mother's grave that I've not held a hand of cards or a pair of dice since they took my stripes."

David didn't believe it, but he didn't say anything because his attention was suddenly taken by the sound of a soft moan.

The blond hair went up on the back of his neck and he wondered if he had imagined the sound?

David ducked and entered a nearby tipi. Inside, in the gloom, he abruptly realized he was staring down at a shriveled old Indian woman lying under a buffalo robe. She breathed shallowly, but the air was close, and the place smelled of impending death. He stuck his head outside and took a deep breath. "Muldoon, come here; they've left someone behind."

The big Irishman came running, looked inquiringly at David, knelt quickly beside the pallet, asked something gently in Cheyenne.

Her eyes flickered open slowly. She looked from one to the other.

David frowned. "Good Lord, they really are savages, aren't they? Imagine them going off and leaving a dying old woman!"

Muldoon reached out and patted the old woman's wrinkled brown hand, said something gently in her language. It seemed to take all her strength to say a few words in return.

Muldoon swallowed hard. "This is Ancient One. Her daughter, Moccasin Woman, and the others left her behind at her insistence. She did not want to slow them down."

"Ask her about Glory." David leaned closer. "Ask her—"

The old woman's eyes flickered open and she smiled ever so

slightly, triumphantly, as she looked up at them. She said something in her language, her voice scarcely more than a sigh.

Muldoon blinked rapidly and swallowed hard. "She—she says we won't catch them; the wolf sang them the Cheyenne song; he's leading them to freedom."

In spite of himself, David was moved by the defiant tone of the dying woman's voice. "Get a canteen, Muldoon, and rig a litter so we can take her to the infirmary—"

"Too late, sir." Muldoon let go of the frail hand and pulled the buffalo robe up over the wrinkled brown face slowly.

David pushed his hat to the back of his blond hair. "God, what kind of barbarians are these people, to leave her like that?"

Muldoon cleared his throat. "They're desperate people, pushed to their limits, like my people against the damned English. We never should have brought them down here in this heat, and I'll wager they'll die before they'll let us force them to return."

David was a little more than annoyed with Muldoon as they went outside. "Get a detail of men to bury her and look around some more. So far, there's no evidence Glory's with them. Perhaps she did get thrown far from the fort and is walking back right now." The thought encouraged him.

"Yes, laddie." The corporal strode away to deal with the order while David walked about the camp, kicking the smoldering embers of fires, wondering just how long the Cheyenne had been gone? The camp looked more ragged and poor than David had thought it would be. He'd never been out here; but then, neither had most of the soldiers.

He turned and looked toward the north, wondering if the Cheyenne were crazy enough—or desperate enough—to think they would actually be able to make it all the way up to the Dakotas? With no more horses and supplies than they had, it would be almost impossible, even if the army weren't going after them. A day or two, and they'd have those savages back on this reservation where they belonged. And in the meantime, did they know anything about Glory's disappearance?

"Lieutenant," Muldoon called from the far side of the camp.

"Yes?" David whirled, started toward the returning burial detail.

"We—we found something." The old Irishman hesitated, then held out something, a small scrap of cloth.

"What on earth?" Numbly, David took it, staring in disbelief. Flowered blue calico. In his mind, he sat at the piano while Glory leaned on it, smiling at him in the lamplight, her beautiful profile softly lit. . . . *in the gloaming. Oh, my darling, when the lights are dim and low. . . .*

He grabbed the scrap of cloth, his fingers crumpling it as his hand clenched, remembering his beloved wearing this flowered dress last night as he sang to her. Oh, God, if there had been any uncertainty in his mind before, there was none now.

The Cheyenne had Glory.

Six

When they rejoined the waiting Indians, Two Arrows dismounted, reached up to pull Glory from her horse.

What was he going to do to her? "What—?"

"Be silent!" His face was a cold mask as he grabbed a long piece of rawhide to tie her hands in front of her, threw the other end up to loop over his saddle. "By the end of the day, I promise, Proud One, you will be too weary to attempt escape!"

As Glory watched with disbelief, he handed the reins of the bay horse back to its owner. Then Two Arrows remounted his paint. She stood there a long moment, realizing she was tied like a dog on a leash. The other Indians had already started moving north again. Two Arrows smiled grimly back at her, then nudged his horse into a walk.

"You can't do this!" she shrieked at him.

"Watch me."

The rawhide leash tightened and she dug in her heels, but her strength was no match for the big paint horse. The rope tightened, but only for a moment, then she was jerked forward. *Damn him!* Glory stumbled, then regained her balance as she was pulled along behind the horse.

"Stay on your feet, lying white girl," he yelled over his shoulder, "or I'll be forced to drag you!"

She was afraid to defy him. Fuming, she took one slow step, but the rope tightened again, and she had to quicken her step to keep from falling.

"You need to walk faster," he ordered. "We're already falling behind."

"Lieutenant Krueger will execute you for this!" she screamed at him as she stumbled along the dusty prairie.

He glanced back and favored her with an insolent grin. "He'll have to catch me first, Proud One."

She was breathless and hot already. "How dare you punish and humiliate me like this."

"You make a fool of me," he snapped, "other warriors laugh behind their hands. Now I make sure you're so tired, you won't try again."

She wouldn't beg if he dragged her to death. She had never in her entire life begged for anything, not even when Howard beat her. Her pride meant more to her than even her life. At the worst of times, her pride was all she had.

She could deal with this. Her head came up and Glory squared her shoulders, began a long-legged march. So he thought she was some weak, whining woman who would be groveling and asking for mercy within a few hundred feet. Well, damned if she was going to give him that satisfaction! She hadn't begged Howard not to beat her, and she wasn't going to beg this savage not to make her walk. She was in better physical shape than most white women because she was athletic and rode often. Glory made her plans. She would march along with dignity until the army came to rescue her, while watching for another opportunity to escape.

As the minutes turned into hours, the autumn sun grew warmer. Perspiration ran down her breasts and thighs as she walked.

Several times, Two Arrows looked back at her, concern on his dark features. "Perhaps if you would say you are sorry, I might be persuaded to give you a horse or let you ride double with me again."

Glory glared at him without answering. So this was going to be a battle of wills. She was not sorry, and she was not going to apologize if she had to walk clear up into Kansas.

He shrugged and turned to watch the trail. The welt marks on his broad, muscular back still gleamed along with his rippling muscles. "Step carefully," he said, "there's probably a few rattlers still out on this warm day."

"Rattlesnakes?" Glory hesitated and glanced from the arrogant savage to the dusty ground around her. She pictured stepping on a huge diamondback. Folks around the fort said a big one could kill you in a couple of hours and there was no medical help out here. No matter, she would not beg; she would not bend to this man's will.

He glanced back at her again, then reached for his canteen, shook it, opened it, took a drink and let some of the water run down the sides of his mouth and drip on his brawny bare chest. "If you asked nicely, I might give my slave a drink."

"I'm not your slave," she spit back, "and I wouldn't put my mouth on that canteen after you've been drinking from it."

"I forgot; I'm a savage, and you're a lady." His voice was grim and full of sarcasm. "All right, go thirsty then, Proud One."

He nudged the paint to walk a little faster and the leash tightened on Glory's wrists. The rawhide jerked her forward as she stumbled and struggled to walk faster to keep from falling and being dragged. Oh, it was so tempting to beg, be put on a horse again. How she wanted that water. She ran her tongue over her dry lips and thought about water, cold water. She yearned to swim naked in a creek so cold it would make her skin tingle. She wanted gallons of it to splash on her dusty face and drink and drink and drink, but by God, she wasn't going to let this dominating male break her pride; she'd die of thirst and exhaustion first.

As the hours passed, the afternoon sun grew hotter, but she kept walking. Her little riding boots had rubbed blisters on her feet and her wrists were red from the rope, yet she set her mouth with determination and kept walking, glaring at his dark, muscular back. The other Indians were strung out along the horizon, most of them far ahead of Two Arrows and his captive. Her boots raised a cloud of dust, and the grass whispered against her blue-flowered skirt as she staggered across the rolling hills. The landscape looked much the same except for an occasional tree or bush.

Oh, would the Indians never stop moving? Probably not until they camped for the night, she thought with a sinking heart. *David, where are you?* Surely by now the army knew she was missing and would be coming to rescue her. She glared at Two Arrows riding ahead of her. She must not think of thirst and heat and dust. To keep her mind occupied as she walked, she thought of appropriate ways to punish this arrogant savage.

She would watch as the soldiers tied Two Arrows up as she was now tied, then she lashed the horse into a gallop and dragged the Indian across the prairie through ant beds and cockleburs. She smiled at the thought.

No, that wasn't painful enough. She would help tie Two Arrows between two horses, then whip them up so that their running tore the scout limb from limb.

No, that still wasn't enough. She would have him tied to a tree, helpless and thirsty, while she drank slowly from a canteen. While he begged for a sip, she'd pour the rest of the water out on the ground while she watched. *Then* she would tie him between two horses to be torn apart. She stumbled and came back to reality. Only trouble was, he seemed as stubborn and proud as she was; he wouldn't beg for mercy, either.

Time and the sun marched across a sky the color of faded blue denim as the Indians kept moving north. *Where was the army?* She listened for the sound of galloping horses or a bugle charge. She listened in vain. Ahead of her, an Indian baby cried faintly from its cradleboard, a hawk made a lazy circle overhead, and somewhere in the prairie grass, a quail called *bob white; bob bob white.* How many hours until a merciful sundown, she wondered? Her skin seemed to be on fire. More and more often,

Two Arrows glanced behind him as if giving her every opportunity to beg for mercy.

She was not going to give him that satisfaction if she died out here of heat and exhaustion. Besides, anytime now, the army would come galloping across the rolling plains behind her, shoot that savage out of his saddle, and save her.

"Don't you want a drink?" Two Arrows reined in his horse and looked back at her.

She chose to ignore his question and keep marching forward. Her spirit had never been broken, and, God knew, Howard had tried.

"You are the damndest woman I ever met! Don't you know when you're licked?"

"Never!" She was so tired, she didn't know how much longer she could keep moving, but she was not going to give him the satisfaction of asking for mercy. No doubt he wouldn't grant it anyway; he just wanted to watch her grovel so that he could laugh with amusement. Her feet were rubbed raw by her boots, and each step was painful as she approached him. Red dust clung to her perspiring body. Her disheveled black hair hung limp around her narrow shoulders.

It was almost sundown, surely the Indians would be camping soon. The Cimarron River ought to be somewhere up ahead. "You aren't going to make it," she snarled at Two Arrows. "The army'll send a telegraph up to Kansas, you'll be caught between two forces."

Two Arrows looked down at her with a smile. "I took care of that. Your precious captain may spend hours trying to find where I cut that telegraph wire and tied it with rawhide back there at Turkey Springs."

Damn him, his years with the army and his background as a tough dog soldier made him a formidable foe. She ignored his words, keeping her head high as she approached.

"All you've got to do is ask," he said. "I might give you a horse and some water."

Mercy! It was so tempting, but her proud spirit was all that had sustained Glory's miserable life with a widowed, unloving father who had wanted a son instead, and a brutal, unloving husband.

"Go to hell," Glory said, and kept walking.

"I thought white ladies didn't swear?"

"I'm not a lady; ask anyone at the fort." Her voice was icy as she stumbled forward.

He grimaced and rubbed his hand across his mouth. He needed some whiskey, Glory thought; this was probably the longest he'd been sober in months. Now he shrugged, turned, and began walking his horse again.

Oh, would this day never end? She wasn't sure how much more of this she could take before she collapsed. It was almost dusk, and the Indians up ahead were yelling to each other. She understood just enough to know it was the river. Well, thank God for that. She might have enough strength to walk another few hundred yards . . . or maybe not. At that point, she swayed and fell, closed her eyes. The paint dragged her a couple of feet through stiff buffalo grass before Two Arrows reined in sharply.

She heard him dismount and stride toward her. She didn't move; not caring if he killed her as long as she didn't have to walk anymore. On the other hand, maybe she could take him by surprise, sink her sharp little teeth in his ankle, grab his horse, and escape, leaving him afoot and yelling after her.

"Proud One?" He knelt and half lifted her in his arms. She could feel his warm breath dangerously close to her lips.

She kept her eyes closed. "I— I am not begging."

"I know, I know." She heard the sound of him opening his canteen and then the feel of cold water on her hot, sunburned face. She opened her eyes and looked into his. There was a grudging admiration there as he held the canteen to her lips.

"I—I'm not begging."

"Shut up and drink it," he snapped. "You are the most stubborn woman I ever met."

She let him give her a drink and it tasted so good. She sighed.

"Are you all right?"

"Hah! You tie me up, drag me along behind a horse all day, make me do without water, and now you ask if I'm all right?"

"Stupid female. I told you, all you had to do was bend to me." He cut the rawhide from her wrists and she saw him wince as he looked at the marks there before he poured a little water in his big hand, wiped her sunburned face very gently.

"I don't bend to any man," she managed to whisper, although her throat was parched. "I wouldn't beg to save my own life."

"You're too much woman for Lieutenant Krueger, too spirited," he said, and there was just the slightest hint of admiration in his tone as he swung her up in his arms.

"I didn't ask your opinion of my fiancé," she gasped. His bare, muscular chest was against her face. She knew she ought to pull away, fight to get out of his arms, or at least sink her teeth into his chest, but she didn't have the strength. Besides, she had never dealt with a man like this one before; she wasn't certain what he'd do to her for that.

He must have read her thoughts. "You bite me, and I'll make you wish you hadn't!"

"You can't scare me." But she knew her voice shook. "I'm used to being beaten."

She couldn't read his expression. "I thought all white women were treated like pampered little pets."

"Not this one." Glory couldn't keep the anger out of her voice. She tried to pull out of his arms, but he held on to her easily.

"They're going to camp up ahead at the river," he said, and began to walk, carrying her, his horse following along behind. "I was beginning to think you were going to let me drag you to death."

"Sorry to disappoint you," she snapped. "Maybe you can drag me to death tomorrow."

"Don't tempt me! I've still got marks on my back because of you."

"I didn't tell the lieutenant."

He looked down into her eyes, his expression troubled. "Yesterday I thought you did."

He licked his lips, and she knew by his expression he was thirsting for whiskey.

"If you'd go back to the soldiers, they'd give you a bottle," she suggested. "You could probably trade me for a whole case. Think about that, a whole case of liquor all for you. You could get very drunk."

"Shut up, damn you. I—I'm done with whiskey." His tone told her he wasn't so sure.

Two Arrows carried her to the river and sat her down on a rock near the water. As he took off her boots, his face mirrored both surprise and regret. "How could you walk with your feet rubbed raw like that?"

"It was walk or be dragged by your horse," she reminded him.

"You could have stopped it the first hour by asking."

She thought of Howard slapping her and pummeling her, demanding she get on her knees and beg or he'd beat her some more. "I've got pride."

"Our prissy lieutenant has his work cut out for him if he marries you."

"David isn't prissy. He's a gentleman."

"That's what I said; you need more man than that."

She started to say something, decided he was goading her.

"Proud One, stay here until I get back. You know better than to try to escape again."

She was too tired to run, and there weren't any horses close enough for her to grab anyway, Glory decided. She watched him walk away—big, broad-shouldered, battle-scarred. He almost seemed to swagger when he walked. A wild, mustang stallion and as dangerous and unpredictable as one, too.

Around her, the Indians were hobbling horses and turning them out to graze. Women went about everyday tasks, building small cooking fires, nursing babies. Some cast curious glances her way, but evidently, they all accepted Two Arrows's ownership of the captive because the only one who came near her was little Grasshopper.

"Ah, Candy Lady, are you all right?"

Before Glory could reassure her, Two Arrows returned, carrying water and a small pot of ointment. "Of course she's all right, little one," he said gently to the child. "Her shoes rub her feet and white women are delicate as flowers, you know."

"Not this one," Glory retorted, surprised at his gentleness with the child.

"I did not give the captive permission to speak." He gave Glory a cold look, then smiled at the child again. "Run along, little one, and tell your grandmother I will come get some of her delicious stew soon."

Grasshopper laughed and ran off to play.

Two Arrows knelt next to Glory, picked up one of her small feet in his big hand. "It is stupid to be so stubborn that you would walk on stubs rather than bend to my will."

She tried to jerk her foot away, but his other hand was on her slim ankle. "It's your fault. Why are you suddenly so concerned for my health?"

He shrugged and poured the cold water over her foot. "I take good care of my horse, too, and everything else that belongs to me."

The cold water on her sore foot felt so good, she relaxed in spite of herself. "I do not belong to you; I belong only to myself."

"Proud One, you ignore the facts." He began to rub ointment into her foot. "As a hostage, you're valuable to us. The chiefs will be upset if I let anything happen to you."

She leaned back against the rock and closed her eyes while he massaged her bare foot with strong, supple hands. It felt good. She reminded herself that he was just a heartless savage after all. Why had she hoped he might be showing concern because he had a heart or conscience?

He put ointment on her foot and shook his head. "If I had a horse this sore-footed, I'd have to shoot it."

"How reassuring!" Glory snorted. "Anyway, I'm too valuable as a hostage, remember?" She was apprehensive, but not terrified anymore. Of course they weren't going to kill her, they needed her, and killing her would bring the army's vengeance down on them.

He licked his lips again.

"Need a drink bad, do you?" Glory asked.

He frowned. "How do you know that?"

"My husband drank. When he got drunk, he was crazy. I used to pour out all the liquor I found and pray he wouldn't buy more."

Two Arrows looked at her a long moment. "I've taken a vow not to drink again. It made me a white man's Injun. My people have given me a second chance; I can't let them down."

She shook her head. "My people won't give me a second chance; they gossip about that scandalous divorcée."

"I know; I've heard the talk," Two Arrows said. "I'll get some food."

She watched him walk away, staring after him; his muscular dark body, the welts she had caused on that broad back.

It was growing dark rapidly now, with night birds calling. She stared at the river. The sluggish Cimarron ran swift and deep in spots, and they said around the fort it held treacherous stretches of quicksand.

She looked around, wondering if she might get another chance to escape tonight?

Two Arrows returned with a big bowl of stew, sat down cross-legged, and began to eat. She watched him. He glanced at her, obviously waiting for her to ask. Not if she starved to death, Glory vowed.

He ate a few more bites, muttered a curse, and handed her the bowl.

She dug in. The rabbit stew tasted hot and delicious. "I didn't ask," she reminded him.

He looked at her a long moment and she saw admiration war with anger in his dark eyes. "I know, Proud One; I know."

She ate all the stew and set the gourd aside. Around them, the Indians were settling down in the darkness, except for a few sentries. "I—I'm not sure I'll be able to get my riding boots back on in the morning," she said. "My feet are swollen."

"So maybe I'll make you walk barefooted."

"I'll see you in hell!" Glory vowed, lifting her chin even higher in the air.

"You would, wouldn't you?" In the moonlight, he sounded both annoyed and amused.

"You damned betcha!"

Two Arrows threw back his head and laughed. In spite of everything, it was a hearty man's laugh, and she liked it. "Like I said, you're too much woman for Lieutenant Krueger."

"I don't remember asking your opinion." She kept her voice haughty.

"Okay, but I know it, and you know it, too." Two Arrows made a rude noise.

"You don't have much respect for David, do you? He says you never salute him."

Two Arrows shrugged. "He doesn't respect me either. He hates Indians, even the friendlies, and we all sense it."

She felt she had to come to David's defense. "He's got good reason to hate Indians."

"And I've got good reason to hate whites; that makes us even. Now shut up, hostage." His voice had grown as cold as his face. "I've got a couple of blankets. We've got a long day ahead of us tomorrow."

"You'd better enjoy it," Glory fumed. "It's your last day on earth; the army will catch up to us by then."

He tossed her a blanket. "Anything's better than starving to death slowly on that reservation." He reached for a strip of rawhide.

"What—what are you doing?"

"Now what does it look like I'm doing, Proud One? I wouldn't put it past you to stick my own knife in me during the night."

"If you won't tie me up, I'll promise—"

"I won't be that stupid a second time." He grabbed both her wrists in one big hand and she was acutely aware of the strength and power of him. He crossed her wrists and tied them in front of her, then spread his blanket next to hers.

Mercy! Surely he wasn't going to lie down next to her. Why, it would be like sleeping in the same bed.

About that time, the warrior she knew as Broken Blade sauntered over, carrying a knapsack. He nodded to Two Arrows even as his lustful gaze roamed up and down Glory's body in the moonlight. There was no doubt what he had in mind. She shrank back against the blanket.

Two Arrows glared up at Broken Blade with dislike. "What is it you want?" he asked in Cheyenne, although the man's expression made no secret of what it was he desired.

Very slowly, Broken Blade squatted down, pulled a bottle of cheap whiskey from the knapsack. "I have kept this as a gift; now I want to give it to my friend, Two Arrows."

Whiskey. Two Arrows stared at the bottle and licked his lips. This was the longest he'd been without a drink in almost a year.

Broken Blade smiled as he took the cork from the bottle, tipped it up, took a long drink, allowing the whiskey to drip from both sides of his mouth. "Ahhh! Good!" He wiped his mouth with the back of his hand. "Here, my friend, this whole big bottle is for you." He held it out.

Two Arrows ran his tongue over his dry lips again. Even from here, he could smell the whiskey. He had never wanted anything so much as he wanted to grab it from the other's hand and gulp it all down. His very soul cried out for whiskey. Two Arrows had dreaded tonight, attempting to sleep, cold sober. He knew in his dreams the old ghosts would come again, and he would awaken screaming. "To accept your gift means I must follow our customs and give you one."

Broken Blade grinned with sharp, crooked teeth. "Give me only the loan of your captive for an hour."

"What?" Two Arrows said.

"It's not as if she is a virgin," Broken Blade wheedled. "Has she not had a husband?"

Two Arrows nodded.

"And she is not a very young girl." Broken Blade smiled again and held out the bottle. "Among our people, do not older women who have no man anymore avail themselves of the warriors who have no wife?"

"Customs of the whites are different," Two Arrows snapped. He couldn't take his eyes off the whiskey. Already, he could taste the flavor, feel the brain-numbing spirits inside his belly, dimming the reality of Two Arrows's lonely existence. Broken Blade was right; Glory was no young virgin, and well he knew the custom of the Cheyenne. Perhaps she should be used to pleasure any warrior who wanted her; they might all be killed tomorrow.

"It is a fair exchange," Broken Blade wheedled, and held out the bottle again, "and also, a fitting revenge for the lieutenant's woman. Let us share it and her ripe body."

Whiskey. How he needed that! More than that, Two Arrows had thought of nothing but lying on this woman's belly with his mouth on her full breasts since the first time he had seen her. It would be a fitting vengeance for the whipping he had endured. Like most white women, she would be ashamed to tell the white soldiers what had been done to her.

Next to him, the Proud One asked, "What—what is it he wants?" Her voice sounded small and frightened.

Two Arrows turned his head to look at her in the moonlight. "I think you know what it is he wants."

He saw her delicate features go taut. She didn't look proud and haughty anymore; her dark eyes were wide as a hunted doe's. She reached out with her small, bound hands and laid them on his muscular arm.

Her wrist looked so fragile wearing little Grasshopper's bracelet. Two Arrows stared at her two hands grasping his arm, and into those lovely eyes that asked more than any words could.

"Why do you hesitate?" Broken Blade snorted in disgust.

"You have reason enough to hate all whites, and she's only a captive, meant to be used for a man's pleasure. Here, take the whiskey." He thrust it into Two Arrows's hands.

Two Arrows took a deep breath, and the scent of the liquor came to his nostrils. Already, he could taste it on his tongue. Broken Blade reached for the woman, and she dug her fingers into Two Arrows's strong arm.

She did not beg, only her tense fingers gave away her fright; that and her dark, terrified eyes.

In his mind, he was kneeling again in the cold snow at the river the whites called the Washita. The snow was smeared red with warm blood, and his dying wife, Pretty Flower, clutched his arm and looked up at him, terror in her eyes. "Two Arrows, the children . . ."

Dark, terrified eyes; a small hand clutching his strong arm. He had sunk down in the snow and held Pretty Flower close, rocking back and forth as he held her, not telling her the children were dead. Yellow Hair and his soldiers had attacked the sleeping camp at dawn. And Two Arrows had not been there to save her. He had been off on a hunting party and had ridden in too late, to find wailing women, burning tipis, and bloody snow. Around him, many of his relatives were dead or dying, the others fleeing in confusion. Almost ten winter counts ago, his woman had died in his arms. Ten long winters. He hated the white soldiers, and yet Two Arrows scouted for them because the old days were no more.

"Two Arrows?" Broken Blade said. "The white woman for the whiskey?"

Two Arrows forced himself to thrust the bottle back at Broken Blade, but it was a hard thing to do. He put his muscular body between him and the woman. "I say no. Take your whiskey."

Broken Blade came to his feet. "We have a bargain." His voice rose in anger. "I will use her!"

Two Arrows jumped up, pushing the other man backwards as he threw the bottle against a far rock and it crashed into pieces.

With a curse, Broken Blade stumbled after the bottle, grabbed up the shattered glass neck. "I will have her yet though you break our bargain!"

The Proud One screamed even as Two Arrows crouched to meet the charging warrior. They meshed, both as tall and powerful as stags. Two Arrows saw the murderous glint of the other's eyes. Broken Blade was past reason, more than a little drunk, forgetting the taboos about killing another Cheyenne.

"Broken Blade, you forget the taboo!" Two Arrows went into a fighting crouch, and Glory screamed behind him as the other advanced on him, the moonlight reflecting on the sharp glass in his hand.

Around them, horses neighed and reared, dogs began barking, people came out of their blankets rubbing their eyes sleepily.

Broken Blade's eyes gleamed with lust and fury as he stalked Two Arrows. "You poor excuse for a Cheyenne, you drunken soldier scout! I will geld you with this bottle, and then you can watch me rape your white captive!"

Seven

Two Arrows braced himself as the other ran at him, the broken glass gleaming in the moonlight. Broken Blade was past reason, lusting for Glory. The man yelled triumphantly as the two clashed.

Two Arrows caught the other's wrist and held on. The pair meshed like fighting stags in the moonlight. Around them, babies cried and people shouted as the camp came awake.

Abruptly, Broken Blade slipped a leg behind Two Arrows and tripped him. They went down with a crash, rolling across the ground, locked together, Two Arrows struggling to wrench the weapon away from the other.

Dogs barked frantically and people came running to form a circle around them. As the pair rolled over and over, Two Arrows stole a glance at Glory's terrified face, remembering for a split second how she had placed her two small hands on his arm in silent appeal.

He was a fool, he knew that, fighting to protect a white when he had every reason to hate whites himself, especially the lieutenant's woman.

Broken Blade tore free and raised the sharp glass again, his hard eyes gleaming in mirthless triumph, his sharp, crooked teeth bared like an animal's. "I will cut you up for crossing me!"

Two Arrows threw up his arm to protect himself, crouched to take the broken bottle away from the other and use it on him.

Two Arrows could not kill a fellow Cheyenne without being exiled from his people forever, but he was prepared to do it to protect his enemy's woman. He must be as big a fool as Broken Blade said he was.

Again, they locked and strained, one powerful man against another, struggling for possession of the shattered bottle.

Broken Blade put his ugly face close to Two Arrows's. "I will put my seed in her, drunken Injun scout, and you will watch me do it!"

Not while Two Arrows lived. Fury at the image the other's words brought to his mind gave him added strength. They were both damp with sweat as they struggled. Two Arrows gritted his teeth, tasting his anger as they fought.

He was a better fighter than Broken Blade; dog soldiers were always the bravest, best fighters of their tribes. He forced Broken Blade to his knees, trying to jerk the bottle from his hands.

"Enough! I order this stopped!" Old Dull Knife strode into the circle, his voice grim as thunder.

The sound of this chief's voice seemed to get through to Broken Blade's lustful brain. He hesitated, and Two Arrows jerked the broken bottle from his hand, tossed it away with a disdaining gesture.

Little Wolf strode over to join Dull Knife. "What has happened here? You know the taboo!"

Tangle Hair, leader of the dog soldiers, joined them, too.

Two Arrows hesitated. He did not want to bring trouble to Broken Blade.

Broken Blade coughed and staggered to his feet. "I—I caught this man stealing the whiskey I had kept for medicine. When I tried to stop him, he attacked me and broke the bottle. I only tried to defend myself."

The two chiefs and the others turned stony, disapproving glares on Two Arrows.

Tangle Hair spit at Two Arrows's feet. "And to think you were once a dog soldier!"

Two Arrows could not believe Broken Blade would dare

speak to the chiefs with a forked tongue; to do so was to bring
down all sorts of bad medicine to the tribe and to the liar. Yet
he had too much dignity to call the other a liar. Besides, the
way the people were glaring at Two Arrows told him they were
remembering only that he was a white man's Injun, a drunk
who would do anything for a bottle of whiskey.

Two Arrows hesitated. He had a right to demand the ceremony of the buffalo skulls, where each would touch the skulls
and speak and no one would dare anger the power of the ceremony by lying. Yet in the crisis surrounding the tribe, he dare
not ask for the time it would take for the ceremony.

All the Cheyenne knew how many of the tribe had been killed
up on the Crazy Woman fork of the Powder River when Broken
Blade's brothers had demanded that instead of fleeing Three
Fingers Mackenzie's soldiers, the whole camp stop to dance
over some fresh Shoshoni scalps. Mackenzie had caught these
very Cheyenne and defeated them—and Two Arrows had been
one of the scouts who found the camp for him. "If Broken
Blade can live with the words he speaks, I wish him good fortune."

Dull Knife looked toward Glory. "I suspect there is something more here; trouble over this captive. Perhaps her worth as
a hostage is not worth the trouble she can create."

Two Arrows clenched his fists at his sides, knowing he could
not bring himself to follow his chief's orders if he were told to
kill her. "I will see that she causes no trouble, Great Leader. I
will be responsible for her."

A disapproving murmur ran through the crowd. Obviously
many agreed with the chief that they would regret having the
captive in their midst.

Dull Knife looked at Little Wolf. "What say you?"

The other shrugged. "I say we have a long day tomorrow,
and we are not yet out of Indian Territory. Anyone who wants
to fight will have plenty of chances when the army comes!"

Two Arrows heaved a sigh of relief as the group began to
break up and return to their blankets. Only Broken Blade gave

him a malicious grin that promised he was not ready to forget this incident.

Glory had held her breath, watching the fight. As the chief spoke in his language, the others turned to look at her, and she felt a shiver of apprehension. Obviously some of the discussion was about her. If she was too much trouble, they might think it better to kill her than keep her as a hostage.

Whatever was happening, she could tell from the way that the others glared at Two Arrows that they thought the trouble was all his fault. She wanted to scream at them, tell them he was only protecting her, but of course, she didn't speak the language.

Now everyone was returning to their blankets, and Broken Blade looked at her and grinned with his sharp, crooked teeth. He wasn't finished with her; his cruel eyes betrayed that.

Two Arrows returned and flopped down on the blanket next to hers, not looking at her.

"Thank you," she whispered.

"Forget it. I only did it because you make a valuable hostage; wasted some good whiskey." He ran his tongue across his lips again and she knew his soul cried out for a drink.

Was that disappointment she felt at his retort? Of course that was the only reason he had done it. This afternoon, he had made her walk until she had blisters on her feet, why would she feel that tiniest bit of protective tenderness in the man? He was just a primitive savage. Tomorrow, David would arrive with the troops to save her and probably kill her kidnapper. Being caught in the middle of that battle would be dangerous. If she could possibly escape before the soldiers got here, she would.

Damn Two Arrows. She looked at her tied hands and lay back down on her blanket. The night was turning cool as it deepened. Gradually, the camp grew quiet, except that a baby wailed somewhere.

Were these people insane? They couldn't walk more than a

thousand miles before the first snows fell, not even if the army wasn't chasing them. The Nez Perce had tried the same thing last year with tragic results, Glory remembered, except they were attempting to escape across the Northwest to the freedom of Canada. Only a handful of Chief Joseph's people had made it; the rest had been killed or captured. She had read about it in the newspapers.

She didn't want to feel sympathy for her captors, yet it was difficult not to when one saw how ragged, starved, and desperate most of them were. Why didn't the stupid government in Washington let these people live in their own country? David had told her he was only an officer, carrying out orders, and the Indians must do as they were told.

She wasn't too good at that herself; she liked to make her own decisions. What was tomorrow going to bring? Mercy! Whatever it was, she was too weary to think about it now. She curled up into a little ball on her thin blanket and closed her eyes. Every muscle in her body hurt, and now she was cold. If she could just get to sleep, she would forget about her discomforts. At least, the scout wasn't going to let anyone rape her . . . yet.

Two Arrows awakened in the middle of the night, turned his head to see the source of the warmth against his big body. The woman was asleep, but in that sleep, her small body had sought the warmth of his. She lay shivering up against him.

Two Arrows hesitated. If he touched her, she would probably come awake screaming. No, he shook his head; she wasn't the type to scream or whimper; in some ways she was like an Indian girl, strong and enduring. He didn't want to admire her, but the way she had defied him and walked until her feet were sore made him ashamed he had treated her so.

He studied her; the soft curve of her dusty, ragged dress over her full breasts and rounded hips. He felt a stirring in him that he had not felt in a long time; not since his woman, Pretty Flower, had been killed at the Washita.

Two Arrows frowned and reminded himself that the Proud One was the woman of Lieutenant Krueger and, as such, Two Arrows hated her and all she stood for.

She shivered and burrowed even closer, seeking warmth. Very gently, he slipped his arm under her head and turned on his side to pull her closer, giving her the heat and protection of his powerful, muscular frame against the dangers of the cold dark night.

Her body was soft and just fitted the curve of his shoulder as if she belonged there. While he had taken a few whores or loose Indian women in drunken lust, it had been ten years since he had lain next to a woman and merely held her, liking the scent of her warm skin, listening to her breathing. She mumbled something, and he froze in place, afraid she was about to wake up and cry out, but she only lay her face against his bare chest and settled against his warmth. He could feel her gentle breath against his flesh and had to fight the urge to stroke that tangle of black curls. She was dark enough to have Indian blood herself and with her skin tan from the sun and different clothing, no one would recognize her as a white woman.

He needed a drink; his very soul cried out for a drink. He hadn't always sought peace in the bottom of a bottle; it was the Nez Perce capture that haunted him and drove him over the edge. Those hapless people had been less than forty miles from the border and freedom when he had spotted them as he scouted for the soldiers. He had even picked off one of their leaders with his rifle. The soldiers had rewarded Two Arrows for his find, but the sad eyes of the captured Nez Perce accused him of being no better than the bluecoats who had killed Pretty Flower.

Whiskey. Two Arrows ran his tongue over his dry lips. He'd give anything for a big bottle of whiskey, anything except the woman. He both hated and desired her, nor did he know what he was going to do with her. Perhaps the soldiers would parley

and let the Cheyenne go their way in peace in exchange for this
hostage. Maybe she would go back to Fort Reno and marry the
blond lieutenant. Krueger would be the man to put a son in her
belly. With a sigh, Two Arrows thought of his own small sons,
dead with their mother on that cold November day; dead in the
bloody snow; dead at the hands of soldiers.

And now he had the white officer's woman at his mercy. It
would be tempting to pleasure himself with her ripe body except
that it made her less valuable as a hostage.

She shivered again, and Two Arrows held her close, his hand
on the curve of her hip, feeling her warm breath against his
bare chest. Her breast pressed against him, and he imagined
how it would feel to mate with her. He had seen the muted
passion in her dark eyes; perhaps she didn't even sense she was
capable of it.

His manhood came up hard and throbbing with urgency. It
had been a long time since Two Arrows had had a woman, and
then it had been a quick, drunken tumble with an Indian whore.
His muscles tensed as his flesh became ever so aware of her
flesh, and he needed the release her ripe body could give him
almost as much as he needed a drink.

He was tempted. She was small and weak in comparison to
him. It would be nothing to roll over on top of her in the darkness, put one big hand over her mouth, tear open her dress so
that he could stroke and suck those fine breasts and force her
thighs apart. He could easily hold those small, bound hands in
the dirt above her head until he could get between those warm,
silken thighs.

Just the thought of it made him take a deep shuddering breath,
imagining the feel of thrusting deep inside her, riding her hard.
As badly as he needed a woman, he would be finished in half
a dozen hard, deep thrusts. He would leave her belly full of his
virile seed, give her a Cheyenne baby. He smiled at the thought
of such a revenge on the lieutenant.

It wasn't as if the Proud One was a virgin; she had had a
husband. Besides, it was taken for granted captive Indian

women were used for the pleasure of their captors. Why should this one be any different because she was white?

Because of the whites' anger and vengeance against his people, Two Arrows thought with a resigned sigh. He would fight this terrible need like he was fighting the need for whiskey, and, hopefully, he would win. Tomorrow's temptations would have to wait until tomorrow . . . and tomorrow the soldiers might kill them all. He had tonight. Tonight, he could hold the woman in his arms and enjoy the scent and the warm softness of her without her even being aware of it. Because of his duty to his people, that would have to be enough.

Glory awakened gradually. She'd been having the strangest dream about being kidnapped. A leaf dropped on her face, and she brushed it away, gradually opening her eyes.

Horror came over her as she realized she lay on a blanket under the protective arm of that Cheyenne scout. Mercy! It hadn't been a dream after all. How had she ended up asleep in his grasp? Oh God, maybe the savage had . . . no, she certainly would have remembered that!

Slowly, she began to crawl out from under his big arm. It was nearly dawn, and the camp didn't seem awake yet. Maybe she still had time to steal a horse and—

"Going somewhere?" He lay there looking at her.

"You renegade. You were only pretending to sleep." She was as angry as she was disappointed.

"After yesterday's trickery, I'll be on guard around you." He sat up, yawned.

"Do you suppose you could untie me for a little while?"

"Why should I?"

She felt her face flush. "There's—there's some things too personal to discuss."

"All right. There's some bushes over there you can use." He nodded toward some sand plums a little distance from the camp. "By the way, there's a sentry watching the horse herd."

"Just untie me. You can watch me walk to the bushes."

He leaned on one elbow. "Perhaps I'd better come along and make sure you don't try to sneak—"

"No! I'll not have you spying on me while I—never mind."

The camp was coming awake now as he untied her, and she went to the bushes to relieve herself. Her feet were so sore, she could barely walk; how on earth was she going to walk all day? She wasn't even sure she could get her boots on.

When she came out of the bushes, women were starting small fires and cutting up dried meat. Toddlers ran about, and children like little Grasshopper looked after them. The men sat about, polishing weapons and talking. All stopped and stared at her as she passed. The look Broken Blade gave her sent shudders through Glory. It was only a matter of time until that one tried to molest her again. Surely David and the troops would arrive in a few hours, parley with the leaders, and free her.

Glory looked down at her blue-flowered dress; it was torn and dirty. Old Moccasin Woman handed her a gourd of cooked maize with a nod. "You kind to my granddaughter," she grunted. "Most whites mean."

"Little Grasshopper? She's a lovely child," Glory said, thinking Indian women were much like white ones after all.

"Sorry for your trouble," the old woman said. "I not forget you give my granddaughter food."

Glory swallowed hard, looking at her bracelet. "My trouble isn't your fault." She knew whose fault it was. Glaring in Two Arrows's direction, Glory took the gourd of food and sat down on a log to eat.

The others watched her curiously. The men, including Two Arrows, gathered in a circle, drinking steaming coffee from tin cups and smoking. There seemed to be a lot of discussion between them, perhaps about what route to take, because they were drawing in the dirt with sticks, and Dull Knife pointed again toward the north.

They were wasting their time, she thought; the army would surely catch up with the runaways today and herd them back south to Fort Reno. Walking north more than a thousand miles was an impossible dream; especially across barren plains with several railroads that could transport troops crossing their path. The Nez Perce hadn't been successful attempting the same thing, and they'd had plenty of horses to ride and mountains and dense forests to hide them.

Glory looked about at all the weary old ones, the women and children, feeling a little sympathy for them in spite of her own plight. They looked thin and ragged, some were ill and coughing. No wonder they wanted to leave the reservation.

The women were busy with chores now, some packing up the camp, some nursing babies and putting out campfires, scattering the ashes.

Maybe she could at least soak her sore feet in the cold river water for a few minutes before Two Arrows put her back on her leash, Glory thought wearily. She sauntered down the bank, moving slow so that the stubborn scout wouldn't think she was trying to escape and come running after her. Then she noticed little Grasshopper playing all by herself near the water. As she watched, the child tiptoed out on a log that floated halfway out in the swift-running stream, laughing with glee at the way it bounced.

"Grasshopper, no!"

The little girl looked up at Glory at the very moment she lost her balance. Glory saw the sudden fear in the child's eyes as she fought to regain her feet, then the Indian child went off into the water with a splash.

"Help!" Glory screamed, and, jerking up her skirts, she ran as hard as she could toward the water. Her swollen feet hurt as they hit an occasional stone, but all Glory could see was the small head bobbing in the water as the current swept her downriver.

The water was cold as Glory splashed out into it, but she didn't hesitate. Grasshopper's frightened eyes and the dark head bobbing in the current lured her on. Then Glory was up to her breasts in the cold water herself, thrashing clumsily to reach the child as her sodden long calico dress began to pull her under. Behind her, she heard Moccasin Woman's anguished shouts and the excited buzz of people yelling to each other. Glory was the only one close enough to reach her before the child drowned, she thought, and she wasn't sure she was up to the task.

"Candy Lady, please!" The child held out chubby arms, little hands reaching frantically as Glory pushed farther out into the water, casting aside all caution. She had her now, holding Grasshopper close as the current carried them, Glory's sodden dress pulling them both under.

"Hang on, honey!" She wasn't sure the child knew what she was saying, but the girl hung on to her tightly, coughing and choking on the water she'd swallowed. *We aren't going to make it,* Glory thought as she went under, then came up, paddling frantically. She might save herself if she'd let go of the child, but that wasn't an option. She couldn't let a child die; not even an enemy child. And then her foot touched bottom. Oh thank God!

The sand seemed to turn to jelly beneath her feet and the water around them seemed to thicken. What the—? She was sinking in the muck of the river. Quicksand. Now her struggles were pulling them under.

"Proud One!"

She looked toward the bank, saw the scout's tense face. "Hold still, stop struggling. I'm coming!"

As the others watched, he stripped off his clothes save for a skimpy loincloth, wrapped a length of rawhide around his lean waist, dived into the river and came up swimming strongly and smoothly toward them. Behind him, men were organizing, tying tree branches together in a makeshift raft.

Glory followed his orders, fighting her panic to stay calm, determined to keep the child's head above the ooze until help came, even if she sank in the quicksand herself, never to be found. From here, she could see old Moccasin Woman's strained face as she helped with the lashing of the tree limbs into a raft.

He was coming, but it was going to be too late, Glory thought as she went under, took a gulp of the thick ooze and struggled back to the surface. She wasn't afraid to die, but she hoped Two Arrows at least managed to save the child.

He paused a few feet out. "Try to spread out flat," he shouted, and threw her a length of rope from his waist.

Glory did the best she could, but her wet dress sucked at her. Grasshopper did better because she was small and light. Two Arrows threw the rope. Glory grabbed for the end, but it was too far out. She went under again as he retrieved the line, tossed it again. Relief spread through her as her fingers clutched it. "I've got it!"

"Good. Tie it around you both, I'll pull you out."

He was going to save them. Somehow, she had confidence that he could do it. She passed the loop around them both and watched as he put his mighty strength into dragging them toward him. Behind him, two men had gotten the raft into the water and maneuvered through the current to aid him.

In minutes, Glory and the child lay spent and wet across the makeshift raft as the men paddled toward the riverbank.

"Are you all right, Proud One?" Two Arrows knelt next to Glory as they touched shore, and Moccasin Woman reached for her granddaughter with a glad cry.

"I—I think so." Glory didn't have the strength to move. He swung her up in his strong arms and carried her gently to set her under a tree. She realized with sudden embarrassment that he was all but naked, although he didn't seem to notice as he pushed her hair from her face.

"That was a brave thing to do." His voice held grudging admiration. He was staring down at her.

Glory glanced down. Her wet dress seemed almost transparent. Her nipples clearly showed through the fabric. She crossed her arms and began to shiver.

"Here," he said, and wrapped a blanket around her. Water glistened on his wet and almost naked body. Glory tried not to look, but he was more man than she had ever seen; tall, sinewy, a few old battle scars on his muscular brown body. That skimpy loincloth didn't hide much; his prominent manhood was clearly outlined under the bit of wet leather. Howard had been built small, not at all like this Indian stallion. What on earth was she thinking? Her face burned with guilt and embarrassment.

"You could just leave me here for the soldiers to find," Glory suggested.

He shook his head. "You're our insurance that the soldiers won't attack us. They'll be afraid of hurting you."

"Why don't you all surrender and go back before some of these women and children die out here?"

He looked at her a long moment. "They're dying back at the reservation, that's why they're willing to take the risk. If they're going to die anyway, it might as well be trying to reach freedom."

She looked down at her feet. "I don't think I can get my boots on, and I don't know if I can walk."

Old Moccasin Woman came running just then, holding little Grasshopper's hand. The child was all smiles. *"Hahoo,"* the woman said, "thank you, white woman, thank you."

Glory nodded, and smiled at the child. "I always wanted a child of my own," she said, then felt foolish, realizing the woman probably could not understand.

The grandmother said something in Cheyenne to Two Arrows.

He turned to Glory. "She wants to give you a gift."

Glory shook her head. "I didn't do it for a reward."

"You must not insult her," Two Arrows ordered. He said something to Moccasin Woman, and she smiled and nodded. She and the child hurried away.

In a moment, she returned with a pair of small moccasins in soft doeskin with intricate beadwork, held them out to Glory.

"Why, they're beautiful," Glory said, "oh, I can't—"

"Take them," Two Arrows ordered, "and say *'hahoo,'* it's a word all the tribes use for thank you."

Glory accepted the delicate footwear with a smile and a nod. *"Hahoo,"* she said to Moccasin Woman.

Little Grasshopper hugged Glory's neck. Two Arrows's expression softened, and he looked away, clearing his throat. "We have to get started. We need to get the river and as much distance as possible between us and the soldiers. There's a shallow place we can ford a ways down."

He said something to the old woman, and she and the child smiled again and went off to gather their things. Around them, the people were packing travois and mounting their ponies. Those who had no horses walked toward the river.

Glory put the moccasins on, pleased with the workmanship and their softness. They felt good on her sore feet.

"Come on, Proud One," he gestured, "we've got a lot of miles to cover."

Was he waiting for her to beg him not to make her walk? She put her chin up and took a deep breath. He could go to hell first.

Two Arrows strode over to his saddled paint, mounted up. "Well, are you coming?"

She looked for the leash. Instead, he held out his hand. "Come on, you're delaying us. The others are already crossing."

She was not going to beg. She marched over to him. He hardly seemed to notice her defiant air as he reached to grasp her hand. His seemed to completely enclose her small one. She hadn't realized how strong he was until he lifted her easily to sit behind him on the big paint horse. Straddling the horse pushed her wet dress up past her knees.

She was up against his hips. She could feel the heat of him through her wet clothes, and he wore nothing but that rawhide thong.

He glanced over his shoulder, and their eyes caught and locked. He seemed as aware as she was of her body up against his. She saw the sudden desire in his dark eyes. She didn't know what to do with her hands.

"You'd better hang on in case the horse steps in a sinkhole out there in the water," he suggested. "Tonight, maybe we can dry your clothes over a campfire or maybe later, Moccasin Woman can find you a deerskin dress."

She didn't intend to be here tonight, Glory thought. Surely David would rescue her today.

"Hang on!" he ordered as his horse went into the water, "I don't want to fish you out of the river again."

She seemed to have no choice except to put her arms around his waist. His belly was hard and flat and warm. Her hand brushed over that big knife he wore in his belt.

"You can forget about that," he warned as he nudged the horse forward. "You won't get a chance to use it."

She didn't intend to forget it. Sooner or later, she might need a weapon, yet to get that knife, she was going to have to cause Two Arrows to let down his guard. How to do that? Glory thought about it as the horse splashed through the shallow water toward the other side. She'd seen the desire in the warrior's eyes. Suddenly, she knew how she was going to get her hands on a weapon. There was one thing his stormy eyes told her he wanted worse than whiskey.

That one need might distract him enough so that Glory could escape. The question was: Would she be willing to make the sacrifice of letting him mate with her?

Eight

The straggly small group crossed the Cimarron and moved north in the autumn afternoon. The sun dried Glory's wet dress as she rode behind Two Arrows on his paint horse. She kept her hands on his waist, plotting how she could get that big knife from his belt and how she might escape.

In the early afternoon, they finally paused under the shade of a lone cottonwood, its leaves already turning golden yellow. Two Arrows sighed and rubbed his hand across his mouth.

He needs a drink, Glory thought, watching him. There might come a time when the temptation would be too great. Someone along this trail or in this band would have whiskey. If he succumbed to temptation and got roaring drunk, there was no telling what her fate would be—or maybe it would be an opportunity for her to escape.

He dismounted and reached to lift Glory down. His powerful hands almost encircled her narrow waist, and he slid her down the length of his almost naked body very slowly as he stood her on her feet. She was tempted to grab the knife from his belt, but decided this was not the best time to make a break for freedom, not in broad daylight and surrounded by Indians.

The others reined in, too, to rest and eat the little bit of food they had left. Above them, a flight of geese headed south, making a long, wavering vee against the pale blue sky.

Two Arrows looked up. "Soon the cold winds and the snow

will come," he said softly. "If we are not in our own country by then—"

"You won't make it. This is madness," Glory snapped, "a couple of hundred children and old people against the whole U.S. Army?"

"All they can do is try," Two Arrows said, shrugging wide shoulders. "So far, we've eluded and outwitted the bluecoats; maybe we've got a chance."

"I don't know whether you're brave or just simple fools," Glory said as she turned and looked toward the south. "You know soldiers must be on our trail this very minute. They won't stop until they rescue me."

Little Wolf rode up and grunted agreement. "The woman is right. Better we should have killed her."

She felt a chill of apprehension and looked appealingly at her captor.

Two Arrows said, "They must know we've got her. As long as she's alive and unharmed, they'll hesitate to attack. The lieutenant sets much value by her."

He frowned at Glory, and she knew he was recalling how he'd been beaten like a dog for accosting her. He took a small piece of smoked meat from his paint's saddlebags and handed it to Glory. She grabbed it eagerly.

Dull Knife rode up then on a thin bay pony that looked exhausted, its head hanging. "We need horses," he said. "We'll have to raid ranches and passing settlers for food and mounts."

"That will only bring us more trouble," Little Wolf argued, "because then we'll have armed cowboys hunting us down."

Glory pretended not to listen while she ate the meat, relishing the smoky, salty taste, thinking she was beginning to understand a little of the Cheyenne language. For the first time, she noticed that Two Arrows wasn't eating. "You didn't give me your share, did you?"

He snorted and made a dismissive gesture. "Of course not, Proud One. I—I'm not hungry; that's all."

Little Wolf said, "There's little enough food for our own people; captives can go hungry."

Two Arrows appeared anxious as he looked at Glory. "The army will take vengeance if she is starved."

"You are right, but they did not care that our own women were starving." The old leader watched her with eyes dark and hard as obsidian.

She was ashamed for her people then; ashamed no one had done anything for the hungry Indians. Some of the officers had tried, but between the crooked Indian agent who cheated the Cheyenne and Washington politicians who either didn't know or didn't care what was happening to a handful of the Custer killers thousands of miles away, not much had been done.

"We will have to send out raiding parties once we are certain the bluecoats aren't close on our trail," Dull Knife said. "We must have more food and horses."

He and Little Wolf now rode off to confer with other leaders.

Glory turned and looked south. Where were the soldiers? This pitiful little band had covered at least a hundred miles, and still the soldiers hadn't caught up with them. She glanced up, realized Two Arrows knew what she was looking for.

"The prairie is a vast place," he said. "With such a small group as this, the soldiers might ride within a few miles of us and never see us, especially in the hills up ahead."

Glory looked north. The terrain was changing into a more hostile, desolate land of hills and gullies. True enough, this little group could hide there and the soldiers might ride past and never see them—unless Glory managed to alert them or ride out to meet them.

"Time to move on." Two Arrows swung up on his horse easily. "My horse is about spent; wish I had that fine-blooded stallion of the lieutenant's."

"Mercy! You might as well wish for the moon!" Glory scoffed. "Second Chance is his future herd sire. He thinks more of that horse than almost anything."

"Except you?" He held out his hand to her.

"That's taken for granted." She kept her voice frosty, hating to accept his helping hand, but she couldn't mount without it. "You'll see how much he cares for me when he hangs you for kidnapping."

"He'll have to catch me first." Two Arrows grinned. She could not remember ever having seen him smile before. Why, he was almost handsome when he smiled, with those white, straight teeth in that dark, high-cheekboned face.

"I wish I had Misty; she's the second finest horse on the plains." Glory put her small hand in his big one and he lifted her easily up behind him. She was so very tired, but she didn't complain. If she became a burden, they might kill her. Still, she couldn't stop her weary body from relaxing against him as she slipped her arms around his lean waist again, sagged against his naked back. At least the whip marks were almost gone from his skin if not his soul.

Glory considered the sharp knife only inches from her hands, but she knew he was as quick as a striking snake. Sooner or later, he'd let his guard down, and the time had to be just right and in her favor. It was a matter of survival, and Glory was a survivor. Lord knew she'd been through enough with Howard. She'd never told David about the final incident involving Howard's brother, Nat. That had been the final horror that had galvanized her into filing for a divorce with all the condemnation and social scorn that went with it.

Two Arrows nudged his tired paint forward. Near them, a bony gray horse fell and died. The old man who had ridden it stumbled to his feet, his features sad as he patted the dead horse.

"Oh, the poor thing!" Glory stared at the horse, pained because she loved animals. "Oh, the poor thing!"

Two Arrows shrugged without looking. "Save your pity for my people. The Indian agent cheats us out of grain along with flour and cloth." His voice was bitter. "Our horses are not all that is thin and poor."

Glory didn't say anything, remembering now that the army's

horses were fat and sleek. Two women ran toward the dead pony with butcher knives. "What are they going to do?"

Two Arrows shrugged. "We've got to have meat; these people are starving."

"Oh my God." She closed her eyes and swallowed hard. The odds against these people were impossible and getting worse with each mile they covered.

Around them, the band moved slowly across the rough ground. Some of them looked so weary; the people were barely moving. Little Grasshopper rode in her grandmother's travois, but that horse didn't look too strong.

She must remember that these savages were breaking the law in fleeing, that they had kidnapped her and might kill her. Yet despite all that, Glory felt her heart go out to them. "Most of them won't make it," she said, almost to herself.

He nodded. "But some of them will, and they're willing to take that chance."

On a ridge far to the north, Glory noticed the silhouette of a giant timber wolf watching them. She gestured. "What do you suppose he wants?"

Two Arrows looked toward the distant animal, now turning to lope toward the north. "Good medicine," he grunted. "He leads the way for us. The Lone One sings a song my people know well; a song of all wild things—of hope and freedom."

She remembered the lonely howl floating on the wind in the darkness last night. Mercy! Only ignorant, stupid savages would think the wolf was singing to them or leading them. In reality, the beast was probably watching for a chance to raid the little band of ponies, take down a colt or steal a pouch of dried meat.

They must be in northern Indian Territory now, desolate and arid plains. Straggly gray clumps of buffalo grass and prickly pear cactus grew in the arid soil. Her legs ached from straddling the paint horse, and she was so tired. She daydreamed of a clean dress and a chance to comb her tangled black hair, put it up in curls on top of her head the way David liked it.

Behind them, a warrior appeared over the horizon, lashing

his horse to move faster. He shouted in Cheyenne, gesturing behind him, then galloped on toward Dull Knife and Little Wolf.

Glory felt the sudden tension in Two Arrows's big frame. "What is it?"

"Soldiers," he grunted. "You may get rescued yet."

Relief flooded her. Mercy! She had thought they would never arrive. She didn't have to plot her escape now; all she had to do was wait for the soldiers to kill this damned scout and save her.

"Hang on!" Two Arrows urged his horse into a lope up a canyon.

Glory clutched him tightly, burying her face against his bare back, afraid of falling under the running hooves. Around them, all was confusion as women gathered up children and old people, sent them scurrying into a deep gully.

Two Arrows followed them into the narrow wash, reined in, dismounted. "Get down!"

Maybe if she stalled; she could gallop away—

He reached up and jerked her off the horse, carrying her as he ran deeper into the gully. "I can't risk the chance that you might escape in the confusion or alert the soldiers."

Even as she protested, he reached in his belt for a strip of rawhide, tied her hands behind her and then tied her slim ankles together.

She had hoped she could slip away while his attention was diverted. He wiped his hand across his mouth again and licked his dry lips. Then he squared his shoulders proudly and stood up. "I am no longer a white man's drunken Injun," he whispered, as if reassuring himself. "I am a dog soldier, bravest of the brave!"

He turned to his horse, and, in spite of her hatred, she thought how magnificent he was, a man born to be a warrior. He opened his saddlebags almost reverently and took out a long leather band, intricately decorated with fine beadwork. A wooden stake, painted red, hung at its end.

He stared at it a long moment as if saying silent prayers, then draped it across his broad shoulder, around his muscular body.

She was mystified. It was obviously of some importance. "What is that?"

He paused, looking down into her eyes. "Do you know what dog soldiers are?"

She shook her head. "Only that even David admires them in spite of himself—"

"We're also what whites would call a suicide force." Two Arrows's face was set, emotionless. "We bring up the rear when the tribe is on the move. If we are attacked, it is our duty to protect the retreat at all costs." He touched the leather reverently. "An old custom, almost forgotten now. Only four honored warriors carry a *hotamtsit*."

In truth, he had turned from a trembling scout battling a need for a drink into a magnificent man among men before her very eyes. "David doesn't even know you own this, does he?"

Two Arrows shook his head, looked away, shame on his chiseled features. "For almost ten years, I have not been worthy to wear this, even to call myself a dog soldier. If attacked, a holder of the *hotamtsit* is expected to drive that stake into the ground, fight and die on that spot rather than retreat."

He paused, looking down at her as if loath to leave her, then smiled. "I forgot something."

He strode back to her, pulling a piece of rawhide from his belt. Now he knelt, ran his fingers across her cheek ever so gently, his face so close, she could feel the warmth of his breath. She pulled away, alarmed that his closeness and the touch of his fingers stirred something deep inside; something she wasn't sure she understood. This was not any emotion she had ever felt in her thirty-four years.

Abruptly, before she realized his intent, he raised the scrap of rawhide, forced it into her mouth while she fought to keep him from gagging her.

"Sorry, Proud One," he whispered. "I can't risk your alerting the soldiers to your hiding place." He smiled. "You're still too much woman for the lieutenant to tame!"

Damn him! Glory struggled against her bonds and glared

with murderous eyes. She tried to scream that she hoped he was killed, but her words were muffled by the gag, although there was no mistaking her tone.

Two Arrows put his hand on the back of her neck, tangled in her mane of hair, and twisted her face up to his, looked into her eyes for a long moment. "Good-bye, Proud One. In a couple of hours, either I will return for you or the soldiers will."

Glory fought to pull out of his strong hand, but he held her, his other hand coming up to stroke her cheek. Then he sighed, stood up, and strode toward his horse, checked his rifle hanging from the saddle ring. She tried to shout at him again that she hoped the soldiers killed him, but of course, with the gag in her mouth, all she could do was mutter and twist against her bonds.

Two Arrows swung up on the paint horse, the September sunlight glinting on the big knife in his belt and the beadwork on the magnificent leather band of honor. He looked like a dog soldier, she thought, arrogant, proud and brave. He gazed toward her again, nodded, and loped his horse over the crest of the hill.

Glory looked around her. Hiding in the brush of the canyon were women and children and the very old, their eyes wide with fear, their faces gaunt from hunger. Moccasin Woman and little Grasshopper gave her an encouraging nod, but she could see the resigned fear in their eyes. Glory looked away and tried not to think of the Cheyenne as people. These savages had kidnapped her and they might get her killed. Yet, in their place, would she have done anything differently? When they all returned to the fort, she would talk to Major Mizner herself and explain why they had fled the reservation, ask for mercy for these helpless ones. As for that damned, arrogant scout who had caused her all this trouble, she hoped to live to see him hanged. She was especially furious over those unidentified and unaccustomed feelings he had begun to arouse in her.

Two Arrows's heart was heavy as he rode over the rise to join the other warriors, knowing the handful of warriors were not only outnumbered, but had only a few ancient weapons between them and almost no ammunition. He was probably riding to his death, but such was the fate of most dog soldiers. He should be thinking of battle, but instead, he was remembering the woman's soft curves against his back, the feel of her slim arms around his waist. He smiled as he recalled how she had looked when he had lifted her from the river, her sheer wet dress clinging to her nipples. He had desired her then as he had never desired a woman before. No, not even with Pretty Flower had he felt such a hunger.

Despite himself, he was having more and more trouble hating the Proud One even if she was the haughty lieutenant's woman. Her valiant effort in saving the child at risk to her own life went against everything he had always believed about weak, whining white women.

He thought of the wolf and began to sing a warrior's song as he rode, a Cheyenne song of freedom and brave deeds. He had no respect for the lieutenant and would never willingly salute him, but he hungered for respect himself from these very people he had led Mackenzie's soldiers to back in the winter of '76. Two Arrows knew that the warriors were outnumbered and would probably die today; but he was not afraid. For the first time in ten years, he felt like a man again, and he would die defending his woman.

Two Arrows joined the small group of warriors on the hilltop, just out of rifle range, and looked around, still softly singing his song of valor to hearten the others.

Soldiers sat their horses in the distance. The landscape looked like a sea of blue cloth and shiny brass buttons. Had Washington sent the whole U.S. Army against this little group? Did they not know it was mostly women and children who had fled?

Two Arrows could see the plump, mustachioed Captain Rendlebrock out in front of the troops, the late-afternoon sun reflecting on the brass and blue of his uniform. Even at this distance, he recognized Lieutenant Krueger reined in next to the captain. No one could mistake that spirited, thoroughbred chestnut stallion the lieutenant rode.

The warriors were whispering among themselves, staring at the honored Dog Rope Two Arrows wore. He knew many of the younger men had never seen one. He squared his shoulders, fierce and proud as in the old days. Once he had been a warrior of many coups, respected and brave. Why had he given up in defeat, thrown in with the whites, drowned his sorrows in their whiskey? It felt good to be a man again; even if he must die today. He had a sudden wish that the Proud One could see him now as she had never seen him—not as a white man's drunken scout, but a dog soldier of many coups, a man respected and feared by his enemies.

From the halted troops, a courier party, including one of the Arapaho scouts, the old soldier called Muldoon and Lieutenant Krueger, galloped forth carrying a white flag and paused in the vast expanse of dry buffalo grass between the two sides. Krueger's light hair gleamed in the sunlight under the blue hat, and the spirited chestnut stallion danced as he reined it in. What a fine animal! The lieutenant was a very lucky man, Two Arrows thought. He owned both the finest horse and the most beautiful, desirable woman. Only right now she was in Two Arrows's possession.

The lieutenant was also a brave man, Two Arrows thought with new respect. The little group with their white flag was within rifle shot, and Krueger must know that. Or maybe he cared so much for the woman that he laid his fears aside. For the love of such a woman, any man would dare much. The Blue Cloud, as the Arapaho scouts were called, was certainly aware of the danger; sweat gleamed on his brown face, and his gaze darted from one side of the hill to the other.

Dull Knife, Tangle Hair, and Little Wolf conferred, then rode up to Two Arrows.

Tangle Hair, leader of the dog soldiers, nodded with approval. "You give heart to our warriors; I had forgotten that you had ever been a carrier of the *hotamtsit.*"

Two Arrows felt his face burn with shame. "I have disgraced it and my people, but perhaps the great god, *Heammawihio,* will give me another chance to prove my worth."

Dull Knife looked at the couriers waiting between the two sides. "Two Arrows, you speak the white man's tongue. See what it is they want."

"You know what they want, Great Leader," Two Arrows said. "They want us to give them the girl and return to the reservation."

"The girl they can have, if they will let us ride on in peace."

Two Arrows opened his mouth to protest, startled to realize that he did not want to give her back, no matter the soldiers' bargain. She was nothing, he reminded himself, just a hostage, a female meant to warm a man's blankets and give him sons. To the chiefs, he said respectfully, "And what if they will not let us go in peace?"

"This is not the place to stand and fight if we can avoid it," Little Wolf said. "What matters most is moving on north. We will fight only if they give us no other choice."

Two Arrows reached up to touch the leather band hanging from his broad shoulder. "If need be, I will carry out the pledge of the *hotamtsit* holder, to fight and die pinned to one spot, to cover the retreat and delay the soldiers."

The two old men looked at him, new respect on their lined brown faces. "You are your father's son after all." Little Wolf nodded.

Dull Knife turned to raise his hand to the handful of warriors on horseback or crouched behind boulders. "Hear me, men of the Cheyenne! We have a carrier of the honored Dog Rope with us today! We will show the white men how to die bravely and what freedom is worth!"

A murmur ran up and down the line as his words spread. Hope came alive on dark faces and shoulders squared as men waved their weapons with renewed vitality. "Yes, we are Cheyenne warriors, and we know how to die! We will do these soldiers as we did Yellow Hair and bring honor to our people!"

A chant arose in their throats, a wild, defiant shout of freedom that echoed across the plains and reechoed in the narrow canyons. The sound carried to the Arapaho scouts, who looked at each other uncertainly, and to the soldiers, who shifted uneasily in their saddles, their pale faces mirroring fear. They had thought they were coming to round up beaten, starving redskins. But these were men—proud, defiant men!

The chant went up from the warriors, ringing clear like the call of the lobo wolf. "No, we will not go back! Better to fight and die! We have a holder of the *hotamtsit* among us!"

Two Arrows's eyes went moist, and he blinked the wetness away.

Dull Knife smiled. "Two Arrows, you have heard the warriors; go tell that to the soldiers."

"Wait!" yelled Broken Blade, galloping his black horse over to join them. "How do we know we can trust Two Arrows not to sell us out and make a deal for himself? He has been the white man's scout for many years."

The spell was broken; the chanting trailed off as the warriors looked at each other uncertainly, remembering him again as a drunken, soldiers' scout.

Two Arrows sighed. "I speak with a straight tongue," he reassured the chiefs. "All I ask for is another chance to prove my worth. Send others with me to the parley so all will know I want the best for my people."

"I will go," Broken Blade volunteered promptly. "Two Arrows and I are not friends, so you know I will be listening well if he tries to betray us. He might trade our people's safety for a little whiskey."

The chiefs frowned. It was clear they did not like Broken Blade, but they were no longer sure of Two Arrows.

"So be it." Dull Knife gestured for the two to ride out to meet those who waited patiently with their white flag.

Two Arrows kept his shoulders square, his head high and proud as he nudged his horse to ride out to meet the truce party. The lieutenant seemed to recognize him immediately because the muscles in his jaw jerked and his hand on his saddle clenched into a fist. He looked as if he were about to grab his pistol from its holster, no matter that he rode under a flag of truce and had come without a weapon. His spirited chestnut stallion snorted and stamped its hooves, and there was no other sound save the white guidon snapping in the breeze.

Two Arrows felt the thick tension in the air as he and Broken Blade approached the waiting soldiers. The blond captain glared at Two Arrows with murder and pain in his square face. Two Arrows was surprised to realize that he would feel the same if he was the Proud One's man and thought another had mated with her.

The Arapaho raised his hand, began to speak Cheyenne, but Two Arrows made a gesture for silence. He wanted the lieutenant to understand what was being said. As a scout, he should salute the lieutenant as a sign of respect, but he did not. *"Hou. Why does the army follow us? All we want is what we were promised, a chance to return to our own country since we do not like the Indian Territory."*

Lieutenant Krueger's blue eyes were bright with anger. He ignored the question and blurted out, "You have the woman?"

Two Arrows smiled ever so slightly. "I have the woman."

He saw the muscles in the other's jaw work convulsively, and almost, his hand clenched as if he would reach to jerk Two Arrows from his horse, but Muldoon raised a hand as if to restrain him.

"Easy, laddie," he said under his breath, and the officer paused, though his hand shook.

Glory was right, Two Arrows thought. The officer loved her past all reason, more than any man had a right to value a woman. Good. That made her even more valuable as a hostage.

Two Arrows gestured in warning. "Keep your hands where I can see them, Lieutenant." There could be no mistaking the cold insult of his words as if the officer might be carrying a concealed weapon. David Krueger was too much of a polished gentleman to break the officer's code . . . or was he?

The other seemed to curse under his breath. "Is she? I mean, have you—?"

Broken Blade threw back his head and laughed. "We will all enjoy her, sooner or later, Bluecoat Officer. Right now, only Two Arrows gets the pleasure!"

The lieutenant's face paled, and he swallowed hard. He glared into Two Arrows's dark eyes. "I will kill you for touching her. Remember that promise."

Muldoon frowned, and the Arapaho took a deep breath, sweat dripping down his brown face. Evidently, he expected to be caught in a cross fire at any moment.

Two Arrows did not deny Broken Blade's lie. The white officer had whipped him like a dog before the other Cheyenne scouts. Now let Krueger suffer. Two Arrows threw back his head and laughed. "I know you won't want her back after a savage has used her!"

"God damn you!" Krueger snarled through clenched teeth. "I'd want her back, no matter what. Name your price!"

So he did value her above everything. Two Arrows's respect for the officer suddenly increased. "The Proud One is our hostage," Two Arrows said. "Let the Cheyenne go to their own country in peace, and when we are safe, we will release her."

There was a long pause, broken by the song of a scissor-tailed flycatcher flying up out of the grass. Metal jingled on bridles as cavalry horses stamped their feet and swished their tails against flies.

The lieutenant suddenly looked much older and very weary. His shoulders slumped. "I—I don't have that authority. I will not give my word if I cannot guarantee it." He nodded toward Captain Rendelbrock, waiting safely with the troops behind him. "I'm told to order the Cheyenne to return to the reservation or we'll attack."

"If you attack us," Two Arrows said, "you risk hitting the woman."

Krueger's handsome face turned abruptly pale. "I—I have no

authority to let you go." He looked at Two Arrows in frustrated, mute appeal. "If I could, I'd give you anything, anything."

He loved her, Two Arrows thought, and was almost ashamed that he had stolen the woman. Then he reminded himself of the whipping he had endured, and his heart hardened. "Let us go in peace, or risk the consequences."

Broken Blade grinned. "Think, Bluecoat! If you crowd us too close or trick us, you will hear her screams floating on the night wind as we torture her."

The lieutenant had eyes only for Two Arrows. He glared at him with pure hatred, his eyes like hard blue glass. "I hold you personally responsible for Glory's safety. Sooner or later, I will hunt you down and kill you without mercy."

Two Arrows studied the man, knowing he meant it. He had not realized such a civilized man was capable of such fury and passion. But then, Two Arrows was beginning to suspect the Proud One could arouse such intense feelings in a man.

He must not think of desire or the woman's soft body; he must think of his people. "You have heard Broken Blade," Two Arrows said sternly. "If you value her, go back and tell the captain her life rests on our being allowed to go in peace to our own country. When we get there, we will free her. Chase us at her peril."

The officer trembled, seemed to be fighting for control. For a moment, Two Arrows braced himself, thinking the man would throw himself at Two Arrows, attempt to kill him with his bare hands.

Two Arrows watched the old Irish soldier out of the corner of his eye. The man was tense in his saddle, ready to put himself between the two, so devoted was he to his officer. However, the lieutenant's shoulders slumped, and his tone was futile. "I will give my captain the message."

"Perhaps you can persuade him," Two Arrows said. "In the meantime, she is mine. Think about that tonight as you try to sleep." He could not resist this cruel jab, knowing the officer would lie in the darkness, staring sleeplessly in the night, thinking that the warriors were enjoying Glory's ripe body. It was a fitting revenge for the whipping, yet he felt ashamed when he saw the other man's tormented face, saw love for the woman in the blue eyes.

He watched the trio wheel their horses, riding back to their own lines. He knew the stubborn Major Mizner thought only of his military record and what Washington would say if the Cheyenne escaped. The captain and his troops were no doubt under orders to sacrifice the captive in exchange for a military victory.

He glanced down at the decorated band of honor across his mighty chest. Once, he had been a great warrior; perhaps he would have a chance to be so again. It was a good day to die, but Two Arrows had not had time to make proper medicine, paint himself with the war signs.

He and Broken Blade nudged their ponies and galloped out of rifle range and back to the chiefs. Up ahead, he could see war shields and a pitiful handful of weapons as the small group of warriors made ready to die fighting rather than be returned to the reservation.

Nine

Two Arrows bent low over his paint's neck, riding hard. Behind him, he sensed the soldiers would open up with a volley the moment the army couriers were safely back to their lines. He had ridden a long time with the soldiers; he could almost read their minds.

"Hokahey!" he shouted to the warriors, waving them to spread out, take cover as he and Broken Blade galloped up to report to the chiefs. There was no need to speak, the soldiers were already shooting. He glanced back over his shoulder in time to see the Blue Cloud scout crumple from a Cheyenne bullet and fall from his horse.

Two Arrows joined the leaders out of range behind a boulder. "As you can see, I made no deal for myself!"

Broken Blade grinned and nodded. "The lieutenant would like to kill Two Arrows very slowly, I think."

"And I, him!" Two Arrows touched his Dog Rope band. "Will you try to lead the people away? A few of us might be able to stay and hold them off."

Old Little Wolf frowned. "What say you, Dull Knife?"

The other scratched his pockmarked cheek. "We have only a handful of warriors and cannot sacrifice any; we will need them more later."

Two Arrows listened to the echoing rifle fire and looked toward the late-afternoon sun. "If we can hold them at bay until after dark, we can do as we did before, leave campfires burning and slip away."

"Would they fall for that foolishness twice?" Dull Knife asked.

Two Arrows shrugged. "We can only try. If they don't come looking until dawn, we can be many miles farther north, swallowed up in that rough country."

Dull Knife mused, "We are almost out of the Indian Territory; maybe when we cross into that place they call Kansas, they will stop chasing us."

"As long as we have the woman," Two Arrows promised, "the lieutenant will come after us."

Broken Blade grinned. "Then why don't all the warriors pleasure themselves with her tonight, then cut her throat?"

Two Arrows put one big hand on the hilt of the knife in his belt and glared at Broken Blade. "Are you a loco one? If she is hurt, he will chase us even harder. She is all that protects us from an all-out cavalry charge."

"Two Arrows's words make sense," Little Wolf grunted. "We will use a few bullets to keep the soldiers at bay. When it is very dark, we will slip away and leave them sleeping. Pass the word."

Rifle fire cracked and echoed, ricocheting against the boulder as the warriors returned the fire. Two Arrows cautioned, "Tell the warriors not to waste bullets; we have very few. We only need to hold them at bay until dark."

A brave galloped up the hill to tell the others, and they slowed their shooting, keeping up only enough firing to discourage the bluecoats from rushing the slope.

Two Arrows crouched, checked his rifle, and aimed, taking a bluecoat off his horse. If he could just kill Lieutenant Krueger, he could rest easy. He had no doubt the officer planned a terrible personal revenge against him because of the woman. He looked around at the other warriors shooting, keeping the soldiers at bay as the afternoon turned into dusk.

A bullet struck Little Wolf's thin horse and the poor animal died almost before its body touched the ground. The old leader stumbled to his feet, unhurt. "We must have more horses and supplies," he shouted to Two Arrows. "When we get into that land called Kansas, we will plan some raids."

Two Arrows nodded. There was no love lost between the Cheyenne and the ranchers and hide hunters of Kansas. In 1875, white ranchers and buffalo hunters had joined with soldiers to slaughter many Cheyenne at a place called Sappa Creek.

Dull Knife gestured. "Two Arrows, make sure your captive is secure. If she escapes, all is lost."

The noise of the shells rang in his ears, and the smell of acrid gunpowder burned his nostrils. But worse yet, his soul cried out for a drink of whiskey. He had thought about that as he rode out to meet the lieutenant, thought about how they might welcome him back with open arms because he'd know the Indians' plans. They would have given him all the whiskey he could drink in exchange for betraying his people. No, he shook his head stubbornly. His people were giving him another chance; he must not waste it. "From now on, we'll have to live off the land, steal horses and supplies from ranches."

Broken Blade laughed. "They stole all that from us first; maybe it's a fair exchange."

Two Arrows rode back to check on his prisoner as Dull Knife had ordered. He spread the word as he went: *Make ready to pull out when it grows dark, leave fires burning to fool the stupid soldiers.*

Glory was still where he had left her. He took the gag from her mouth. "If you scream now with all the gunfire, no one will hear you."

"I won't scream, damn you! I don't have any circulation left. Is Lieutenant Krueger with those troops?"

Somehow, her interest in the white officer annoyed him. "And what if he is?"

"Did you tell him I was all right?"

"The more miserable Krueger is, the more satisfaction I feel.

The fact that he thinks I'm using you for my pleasure is little enough revenge for the humiliation of that beating."

"How could you—?"

"Don't lecture me, Proud One, I've got more important things on my mind than your virtue."

She held out her wrists. "Won't you untie me?"

He considered a long moment, looking at her in the growing twilight, at the delicate beaded bracelet still on her wrist. Her dark eyes were so imploring as she looked up at him and held out her hands.

"Do you know the word 'please'?"

"I don't beg."

"I know." Two Arrows hesitated. If she did try to trick him, how far could she run on foot in that long calico skirt?

Her torn dress slid off one shoulder, revealing a swell of breast as she held out her hands again.

He could see her nipples through the thin fabric, and all he could think of was how they would taste. She couldn't go far on foot if she did run, and besides, he would keep a close watch on her.

Tears formed in her big eyes and ran down her suntanned face. She blinked them back defiantly.

He hadn't known the Proud One knew how to cry; so she was a woman with a woman's weaknesses after all. "As soon as darkness falls, we are going to do what we did before, fool the soldiers into thinking we are bedding down, then move out again."

Behind him, there was only the occasional echo of rifle fire. If only the soldiers knew how little ammunition the Cheyenne possessed!

Glory almost panicked. The soldiers were here to rescue her; so near and yet so far. She had to take the risk of eluding Two Arrows, steal his horse, and ride out to meet the army. The moon was coming up, a big harvest moon the color of a ripened orange.

First, she had to talk him into freeing her. She let the tears she had been fighting run unchecked down her face now and drip on her breasts. She held out her hands again, imploring him with her eyes. The movement of her arms caused her dress to slip even farther. In the pale moonlight, desire showed in his smoldering gaze. If she had to let him between her thighs to get him to free her, could she do it and would David love her enough to understand? The warrior was a bigger man than David; probably bigger there, too. Mercy! Glory felt her face burn. What was she thinking?

She held out her hands again, her dress completely exposing one breast now, her lips shiny and half-open.

"All right." He reached to cut her bonds, stuck the knife back in his belt. Then he handed her his canteen. "You must be thirsty."

She took it and drank, smiling gratefully at him, watching the knife glint in his belt. "I—I don't know if I can walk. I think I've picked up a pebble in my moccasin."

"Let me see." He slipped her moccasin off, ran his hand over her foot gently, massaged the instep. There was something about the way he touched and stroked her foot that felt so good. He was rubbing her ankle now, his big, capable hands soothing her tired muscles. "You have such small feet."

How could such a powerful warrior be so gentle? Abruptly, she saw him as a man; holding a woman close, stroking her body with those callused hands. How could she have such an outlandish thought? She must concentrate on what was really important—escaping.

The knife. Could she get that knife? He was intent on rubbing her bare ankle and looking at her with a troubled, aroused expression.

Glory smiled at him and leaned a little closer, so that he got a better view of her almost naked breasts. Once, she would have been too modest to expose herself like this; but if nothing else, she was a survivor, and her life and freedom were at stake. She heard a quick intake of breath, and his hands paused, tightening on her trim ankle. She closed her eyes and leaned forward a bit. "Thank you for being so kind to me and saving me from Broken Blade."

"You thank me?" He sounded startled. "Wonders never cease." He reached out and put his hands on her bare shoulders. She could feel the raw strength and virility in that grip. Glory leaned even closer, brushing her breasts against his bare chest.

"Damn you," he muttered, "I've been wanting to do this from the first moment I saw you!"

Before she could react, he pulled her into his embrace, covering her lips with his, sucking her tongue deep into his mouth as he clasped her close, her almost naked breasts pressed against his hot, naked chest.

She had never been kissed like this. Never! For a split second, she forgot everything else but the way this big man was holding her, bending her body to his will, tasting her lips, crushing her taut nipples against his strong body. For a moment, she wanted nothing so much as she wanted to lie back on the soft grass of the gully and surrender to him. She hungered for his hot mouth all over her skin, stroking and kissing her breasts; she wanted him lying on her belly, ramming deep inside her with his hard, throbbing manhood.

Was she crazy? The distant sound of gunfire brought her back to reality as his breathing deepened. Two Arrows seemed to have forgotten everything but this moment, his pulsating desire to mesh with her. She must forget about what her body cried out for; she must think of saving her life. The cavalry was only a few hundred yards away. Who knew if she would ever have a better chance to escape?

Two Arrows's hands still gripped her shoulders as he crushed his powerful body against the swollen tips of her breasts, oblivious to anything else. Glory glanced down. The pale moonlight gleamed on the big knife in his belt.

Desperation made her fast as a striking little rattler. Glory dived under his arm, grabbing for the knife.

But he was fast, too. Two Arrows swore and grabbed for her, but she managed to get the knife free, came up slashing. She gashed his forearm even as he twisted the knife from her hands, his blood running freely as they struggled.

She cried out as he jerked the knife from her grasp and tossed it away with an oath. "You lying white—!"

Oh God, he'd kill her now! She was fighting to get away from him as he attempted to get a grip on her in the darkness. His blood dripped wet and hot on both of them; she could smell the coppery sweet scent and feel its warmth.

"Let me go! Let me go!" Glory fought with the strength of a terrorized wildcat, knowing that if she did not escape, he would kill her for stabbing him. They were both slippery slick with his blood and he tried for a better grip, caught the front of her dress, tore it away.

In that split second, she saw the hot desire in his dark eyes as he stared at her pale, blood-streaked breasts in the moonlight. She struggled to get to her feet so she could run, but he reached out, caught her trim ankle, jerked her feet out from under her. They fought in the growing darkness, the distant rifle fire broken only by the sound of their heavy breathing and dislodged pebbles as they rolled across the ground.

With his superior strength, he ended up on top. Her dress was soaked with his blood as he pinned her arms above her head with one strong hand, lay glaring down into her eyes, his big body half on top of hers. She bucked and fought to no avail. There was a terrible passion in his eyes, the kind of emotion she had never seen in a man's face, and it scared her.

"Damn you, white wench! You tease me with your body, plotting to kill me all the while!" He snarled in anger as he bent his head and devoured her mouth, forcing her lips open, cutting her lips with his teeth as he held her head so she could not pull away from him.

She tried to bite him, but he only exerted more pressure against her mouth, forcing it wider still, his tongue going deep in her throat as he pressed her head back in the age-old gesture of total surrender. She could not move, she could only lie there and let him do as he would. His other hand went to cover her breast, cupping it possessively as he devoured her mouth.

She tried to protest, but his tongue went deeper still. She struggled to twist away from the hand cupping her breast possessively, squeezing her nipple. She arched her back, attempting to buck him away from her, but he threw one leg across her slim body. She felt his manhood, aroused and throbbing.

They meshed and battled like two wild things in the dirt. No man had ever held her in such a frenzy of emotion, no man had ever kissed her as if he couldn't get enough of the taste of her. His strength was too much for Glory. She stopped fighting and lay there breathless, letting him suck her tongue into his mouth, letting him explore her breasts thoroughly with his big, callused hand. Despite herself, she felt her nipples go turgid. To her surprise, she could not stop herself from arching against his demanding hands. Glory had never known passion; her husband had only expected her to lie there and let him make his feeble attempts at mating her. David was too much of a gentleman to touch her before they were wed.

This barbaric savage's seeking hands and mouth were demanding a response. If she stopped fighting and let this virile male have her body, would he free her?

Was she out of her mind? What would David think of her for submitting to a savage? Even as she thought it, Two Arrows forced his tongue deeper into her throat, exploring the velvet of her mouth as she gasped and stopped fighting.

Then his mouth went lower, kissing down the column of her throat. She breathed hard, aware of the heat of his breath and the touch of his fingers. Her hands were still pinned above her head by his strong grasp. Now that he'd taken his mouth off hers, all she had to do was scream loudly now and hope David heard—

Abruptly, his hot mouth covered her breast and sucked hard. Glory gasped aloud. She had never experienced any feeling like this before. Howard had seldom touched her breasts, yet this big savage was teasing them with his hot, wet tongue, sucking each of them into a pink, hard-tip mound. She must get away, she must scream for help. Yet all she could do was lie helplessly while he kept her pinned with his leg. She closed her eyes and tried hard not to react to his insistent, greedy mouth, and the throbbing of his insistent manhood against her body. She was only a toy to be used for his pleasure . . . and for hers. Any moment now, he would spread her thighs and ram his swollen male sword deep inside her. And all the while he was sucking her breasts as if he couldn't get enough of the taste of her.

"You tease me, now I will have you," he whispered hoarsely against her ear. "I will have you if it costs me my life!"

At that moment, the big wolf howled somewhere in the darkness, and it echoed across the hills. The sound seemed to bring Two Arrows to his senses. He sat up suddenly, turned loose of her. She realized she was trembling, but not with fear, as she tried to pull the bloody, torn edges of her bodice together.

He made a noise of disgust. "What kind of fool am I to put my hunger for a woman ahead of my people?"

He glared at her in the moonlight and she was afraid of the terrible passion in his dark eyes. "You bewitch me, Proud One, until I think of nothing else but lying between your silken thighs!"

"I was only trying to escape!" No doubt he would kill her now.

Instead, with a curse, he stood up and looked from his bloody arm to Glory. "You did this, so you can bandage it. My blood you can wear as a reminder of your treachery."

At least he wasn't going to kill her for stabbing him. *Of course not,* she thought bitterly, *I'm too valuable as a hostage.* She began to tear a strip from her hem, realizing her lips were swollen from his hard kisses, her nipples throbbing from his greedy sucking.

She inspected his arm, thinking she had cut him worse than she had known. She saw the grimace of pain on his stoic face as she began to bandage his arm. The bodice of her dress felt wet with his blood.

"I ought to let Broken Blade and the others have you for the night as punishment," he grumbled through clenched teeth.

That thought scared her. "I will submit to you if you won't let them touch me," she blurted.

He threw back his head and laughed. "You try to strike a bargain? Did you not realize just now that I am strong enough to take you anytime I wish? I don't need your permission."

"If I tell the soldiers you protected me, it will go easier with you—"

"You will tell the soldiers nothing!" He almost spit it at her. "You will not get the chance!" He grabbed her and gagged her as she struggled. Then he twisted her hands behind her and tied them. That rubbed her bare nipples against his muscular chest, and he reached out and caught one of her breasts in his hands. "The pleasure you give a man makes him forget everything else," he muttered.

Glory closed her eyes against the terrible need in his, forcing herself not to press her nipple against his fingers as he stroked there. What was it about this big, virile animal that brought out such a reaction in her very depths? At least she could be thankful that David need never know how she had almost let herself be swept away in a mutual rush of desperate need with this savage.

Around them in the darkness, Indians were mounting up, riding out. Two Arrows lifted her easily, looking down into her eyes as she dangled helplessly in his powerful arms. "The lieutenant is a very lucky man," he whispered. "Someday, when he lies between your thighs and breeds you, remember that I wanted you more than he ever could!"

Glory tried to curse at him, but the gag muffled her words. She attempted to twist out of his arms, frightened of the terrible desire in his smoldering eyes and knowing that the army was close by if only she could reach them.

"No wonder he doesn't want to lose you." Two Arrows stared down at her half-naked body, writhing in his arms. "There is surely not another like you."

He walked with long strides, carrying her to his paint horse, ignoring her helpless struggles. He put her on his mount and swung up behind her, pulled her close against him. Her bound hands now rested against his aroused manhood in the skimpy loincloth. He put his arms around her possessively, pulled her even closer. One of his hands went to rest on her bare thigh in the torn dress. It seemed to burn into her naked flesh. His other cupped her breast possessively.

Glory held her breath, feeling the heat of his hand on her thigh and his palm brushing across her nipple as if he owned her. How she hated him for that and for the unexpected reaction she experienced when he touched her!

With a sigh, he picked up the reins and nudged his horse forward. "A woman like you could make a man forget his duty," he said, "and you are no more to be trusted than other whites. You will not tempt me again, Proud One, because as a hostage, you will have no value if you are violated."

They rode away into the night, silent as shadows, heading north with the others. This warrior hungered for her as she had not known a man could want a woman. His throbbing manhood against her bound hands told her that. That was Two Arrows's weakness beside liquor. If she could seduce him, he might set her free. It would be worth it to escape, and David need never know. She relaxed against him, her hands against his aroused manhood. The soldiers couldn't find her to rescue her; she was going to have to save herself. Glory was a survivor; whatever it took, she would do it. The question was: would she ever get the chance again?

Around them rode or walked the others. Behind her was the army, but by the time they realized the Cheyenne had melted away into the hills, it would be hours too late. She had missed a chance to be rescued; she'd have to make her own opportunities now. She would do anything, *anything,* she promised herself.

The night winds blew chill as they rode farther north, and she shivered. When she did, he pulled her against him as if shielding her half-naked body from the cold and anything else that would harm her. He held her as if she belonged to him, like his horse or his rifle. Such arrogance! She was so very weary, that in spite of herself, she found herself nodding off to sleep, cradled against Two Arrows's broad chest as the paint loped into the night. The last thing she remembered was the way he cradled her gently and possessively against his big body.

Ten

Michael Muldoon returned from guard duty in the cool darkness, walked toward Lieutenant Krueger. The young officer sat by the campfire, staring off at the endless hills to the north. Muldoon's heart went out to him. David Krueger was more than his commanding officer; he was like the son the old Irishman had never had. He pitied him now. "You ought to get some sleep, lad." He looked around at the quiet camp. "Most everyone else is."

The younger man glanced up. "I can't sleep. Those savages killed three good men today, and Glory's still a prisoner. Who knows what's happening to her now?"

Muldoon was a keen judge of people; it had stood him well in a rough life. Whatever the truth, the lieutenant needed comforting. He rubbed his aching, arthritic hands together. "Aye, by the Holy Mother, it's a dirty shame about the troopers. Who would have thought the Indians would stand and fight against such terrible odds? As for the lady, I'll lay you two to one that feisty miss will win."

"That's what I like about her, Muldoon." The firelight gleamed on David's light hair as he took his pipe out, filled it. "That damned scout called her the Proud One. She's that, all right." His hand shook as he lit his pipe from a burning branch, sending the sweet smell of tobacco drifting on the still air.

Muldoon reached for a tin cup, poured himself strong coffee from the big pot on the campfire. He regretted now that he had told the lieutenant about the encounter between the lady and the scout; it had led to dire consequences. "She'll be fine, lad; she's too valuable as a hostage to harm her."

"That's right, isn't it?" David's square face lit up with hope, and he tapped his pipe against his teeth.

Muldoon nodded, warming his aching hands around the steaming cup. He did not say that he had looked into Two Arrows's eyes, recognized passion glowing there when the woman was mentioned. The Indian might want her badly enough to throw all reason, all caution aside. "My rheumatism is givin' me fits again; I'll wager we're in for some cold weather soon."

"You ought to retire and go someplace where it's warm," David scolded him affectionately as he smoked and stared toward the horizon again.

"Retire?" Muldoon snorted at the joke, masking his quiet desperation. "Unless I get me rank back and a sergeant's pension, I'll not have enough to live on, and who'd hire an old bloke like me?"

"You're the best with horses I ever knew," David reminded him.

"That does me no good," Muldoon scoffed, and sipped his coffee. "None be offerin' me a job. I used to be pretty good with the dice or cards, but with my hands so stiff—"

"Then I hope you've learned your lesson. If you're reckless enough to play cards with a captain, you ought to be smart enough to let him win."

Muldoon remembered the incident, grinned in spite of himself. "Aye, the captain was a poor loser. I meant to let him win some, but the gamblin' fever got the best of me."

David shrugged and smoked. "His complaint cost you your stripes. I guess maybe neither of us will ever get our rank back. My heart never was in the army, even though it's been a family tradition for a hundred years."

"That long, huh, lad?"

The other nodded. "Going way back to a Hessian officer who brought a troop of hired mercenaries over to fight in the Revolutionary War. Expert horsemen, all. The interest in horses is all I seem to have inherited, but Father would be in a fury if I quit the army."

Muldoon sipped his coffee, saying nothing. He had served under Colonel Krueger before that stern officer's old wounds had forced him into retirement at the beginning of the Civil War. Fritz was a hard man who thought David could do nothing right. More's the pity, Muldoon thought, because David was the only son Fritz had left. "I always wanted a son; but it's hard to afford a wife on enlisted man's pay."

The lieutenant's face grew serious as he smoked. "I just realized how little I know about you, Muldoon."

"Aw, nothin' much to tell." Muldoon shrugged. "Me, I'm a Mick immigrant, came as a boy during the potato famine."

"Was it as bad as I've heard?"

"Worse." Muldoon didn't elaborate. He wasn't sure David would believe tales of people dying of starvation. He and his father and younger sisters had scraped up the money to come steerage class. Then almost to America, the dreaded typhus had struck the ship. The authorities wouldn't let the ship dock until the disease ran its course. By then, all Michael's family was dead. "You know what a coffin ship is?"

"No." The other shook his head.

"Floatin' coffins, those quarantined ships were—unable to dock."

But the sailors had taken a liking to the plucky lad, sneaked him off. A poor Irish lad, alone in the teeming tenements of New York without a single relative or friend, learned to survive by his wits and gambling. A certain Irish ward boss was a sore loser, and Michael Muldoon had joined the army to get away.

David turned to look toward the distant hills again. "We're a pair, aren't we, Muldoon, both needing a second chance?"

On the nearby picket line, the big chestnut stallion raised his magnificent head and snorted.

Muldoon chuckled. "The rascal heard you say his name."

"He's looking for a treat." The lieutenant knocked the ashes from his pipe, pocketed it. He stood up. "I've got some sugar for you, Chance." David walked over to the horse, stroked his velvet muzzle, fed him the sugar.

"Aye, that one got a second chance, all right."

"Yes, that's how he was named." David frowned, stroking the stallion's head. "The colonel had high hopes for this colt, but when Chance was foaled, his little hooves were so curved under because of flexor tendons, he couldn't stand up to nurse. In spite of his fine bloodlines, the colonel ordered him destroyed."

"Your father has no patience with weakness or mistakes," Muldoon said.

"Don't I know it!" The lieutenant sighed. "For only the second time in my life, I disobeyed Father. I hid Chance, and kept working with him until I corrected the weak tendons so he could stand."

The stallion snorted and nuzzled through the man's pockets.

"Everyone says he's the finest horse on the plains," Muldoon said.

David fed the horse another sugar lump. "Second Chance, you rascal! Someday, you and Gray Mist will be the beginning of my fine herd when Glory and I—"

He paused and frowned. "Oh God, I hope she's all right."

"Don't think about it," Muldoon said gently, and threw the dregs of his coffee into the fire, where it hissed. "You need some rest, lad."

"How can I think of anything else?" he snapped, returning to the fire. "I've been praying for another chance, all right; just one chance to get that scout in my gunsights!"

Muldoon winced at the raw anger and hatred in the blue eyes. "Easy, lad."

David said nothing, staring at the Cheyenne campfires in the distance. He had failed Susan and his younger brother, Joe, by leaving the inexperienced pair to run the ranch while David was away at war. He never should have left them with the Comanche so restless, but his father wanted David to follow the family tradition as an officer. David hadn't been much of a soldier, but to please the colonel, he had stayed in the military after the war. Almost two years ago, against the northern Cheyenne, he had given a mistaken command that had cost men their lives. His father had been so disappointed and let David know how his middle son had failed him again. Now David had failed Glory.

"Let's get some sleep." Muldoon yawned, standing up. "We'll have a long day tomorrow."

The fire had burned out, but David was still sitting staring toward the north as daylight broke over the plains and the bugler sounded reveille. Soldiers scrambled to grab hardtack and strong coffee, roll up blankets, and saddle their horses. David fed Second Chance and reached for a bridle.

Muldoon joined him, riding his buckskin gelding. "Aye, I'm gettin' too old for this." He rubbed his stiff hands together.

David looked toward the hills. "Muldoon, there's something wrong; I can feel it. We haven't heard any drums from that camp or even an occasional rifle shot."

The Irishman turned to look toward the hills. "Hmm, now that you mention it—"

There weren't any Cheyenne in the camp to attack. Just as David had feared, when he led a patrol to investigate, the Cheyenne were gone, their fires now only smoldering ruins. He dismounted and looked around in frustration. "Damn it to hell! They pulled the same trick again, slipped through our fingers and took Glory with them."

Muldoon dismounted, examining the ashes of a campfire. "Stone cold. They've been gone a long time."

David kicked at the ashes in frustration, cursing the lost opportunity. "It's that damned, arrogant scout teaching them clever tricks! First, he refuses to salute me, now he steals my woman and thumbs his nose at me. I won't rest easy 'til I put a bullet in his brain!"

Captain Rendelbrock rode up just then with the rest of the column.

David saluted. "They're gone, sir."

The officer looked relieved and pulled at his mustache. "Well, maybe the Kansas troopers will intercept them. Those savages will be raiding all over Kansas now, and if the newspapers get ahold of this before we round them up and put them back on the reservation, I'll be the laughingstock—"

They heard the drumming of hooves and looked around. A cavalry patrol galloped in a cloud of dust and with them was a natty dude in a suit and derby hat.

The dude dismounted, tipped back his derby, grinned as he pulled out pad and pencil. "I'm Pollard, with the—"

"I know who you are," Captain Rendlebrock snapped, "how'd your newspaper hear—?"

"Never mind," Pollard grinned, his pencil poised. "Is it true what the telegraph's saying? Blood-thirsty Cheyenne are marching unchecked across the prairie?"

Sweat gleamed on Rendlebrock's pale face. "It's not worth a single line in your scurrilous papers, Pollard."

"Ah, so it is true!" Pollard grinned and began to write. "My nose smells a great story; anyone care to make a statement?"

"No"—David glared at the man—"the less publicity the better until we rescue Mrs. Halstead—"

"A kidnapped woman?" Pollard scribbled. "This gets better and better!"

The other three exchanged glances. David knew he'd made a terrible blunder by mentioning Glory.

The captain wiped sweat from his face. "Give me a break. We're trying to recapture them before Washington hears they've broken out and are headed for the Dakotas."

Pollard kept writing. "I can see the headline now; *'Blood-thirsty Savages Ravage Countryside!'* " He looked up from his pad, eyes wide with delight. "Oh, that should sell lots of papers across the country. Who's the woman?"

"Don't bring her into this," David warned, thinking how this publicity would finish destroying Glory's reputation.

The newsman gestured with his pencil. "Hey, I'm not to blame if the public hungers for details. I can guarantee that in a couple of days, newspapermen will be coming from all over to follow this outbreak."

Rendlebrock's face turned paler. "This isn't the army's fault. Besides, we'll have them back on the reservation before the newspapers pick it up."

"Will you now?" Pollard grinned. "That's not what soldier gossip tells me; I hear three soldiers were killed yesterday. Sounds like the Cheyenne are makin' fools of the army; think I'll ride along."

"No, you won't! Not unless we get other orders," Rendlebrock snapped. "We won't trail them much past the Kansas line; they'll be out of our jurisdiction. Isn't that right, Lieutenant Krueger?"

Before David could answer, Pollard gave him a shrewd, inquiring look. "Krueger? Any relation to the famous Colonel Krueger?"

"My father," David answered reluctantly.

Pollard's beady eyes lit up. "I remember now; you were busted a couple of years ago over a mistake you made at Powder River against these very same Cheyenne. Care to make a statement, Lieutenant?"

"You couldn't print what I'd like to say to you."

Pollard laughed. Nothing seemed to offend the man. He turned back to Captain Rendlebrock. "Where are these Indians headed?"

"They say they're going home," the officer answered, "but of course, with few horses and supplies, they don't have a chance—"

"I can already see my next headline," Pollard began to scribble again: " 'Cheyenne Ravaging Kansas! Settlers Beware!' "

"Don't print that!" Captain Rendlebrock blurted. "You'll have Washington investigating—"

"And the commanding officer more interested in saving his

rank than in massacred settlers," Pollard noted. "Oh, this is going to be great drama, newspapermen gathering like flies on a dead horse! If you'll excuse me now, gentlemen"—he tipped his derby—"I've got to get a message to the nearest telegraph."

The trio stared after him as he hurried away.

The captain took out a handkerchief and wiped his sweating face. "There goes my army career."

"Join the crowd," David said under his breath.

"What?"

"Nothing, sir." David saluted smartly. "May I suggest, sir, that we pick up the pace? I'm concerned about catching up to those Indians before they harm Mrs. Halstead."

"Hmm? Oh yes, you're right, Lieutenant. Dismissed."

David and Muldoon saluted, turned to stride back to their horses.

"You know, lad, I think there's yellow down Rendlebrock's back; he don't want any more fighting."

David felt his heart sink. "I know. He's hoping troops from Fort Dodge take up the chase so we can return to Fort Reno, but I intend to catch that damned scout! I hope to save the government the time and expense of hanging him!"

Muldoon swung up on his buckskin. "You think there's any chance those Cheyenne might make it all the way across Kansas and Nebraska?"

"Of course not!" David snorted as he swung up on the chestnut stallion. "Think, man! They've little ammunition or fighting men, and not nearly enough horses. There's three railroads running across the prairie between here and the Dakotas, which means the army can have fresh troops on their trail within minutes anytime they're spotted."

"Aye, you're right, lad. The poor devils don't have a snowflake's chance in hell!"

It had been a long day, Glory thought wearily, glancing up at the September sun. The Cheyenne reined in under a few straggly, pin oaks to rest the horses. She had pulled the torn, bloody dress together as best she could, but Two Arrows's blood had dried dark and stiff over the torn bodice.

As they started to ride out again, Glory noticed a very pregnant Indian girl on a bony bay horse. The woman suddenly grabbed her belly, wincing, but she did not cry out. The girl slid from her horse, her features creased with pain.

"Redbird's time may be here." Sympathy showed in Two Arrows's dark eyes.

Glory stared at the girl, who had sat down under a tree, her features grim. "So we'll be camping here until she gives birth?"

The scout shook his head. "She'll have to do the best she can; if we linger long, the army might catch up to us."

Glory forgot she was a prisoner, with every reason to hate Indians. "You mean, it's a choice of her trying to ride or being left behind?" She stared at the girl who now wrapped her arms around herself, evidently in labor.

"It doesn't look like she can ride on," Two Arrows said.

They would leave Redbird behind to do the best she could, Glory thought in horror. "The poor thing!"

Before Two Arrows was aware of what she was doing, Glory slid from the horse and went to the girl's side.

"What are you doing, Proud One? The column's already starting to ride out."

"I'm going to try to help her; tell her that," Glory said, and her chin came up stubbornly.

Two Arrows looked around. "Here comes Moccasin Woman; she'll help her."

Glory stared up at him in disbelief. "You're just going to leave them here with no men to look after them?"

"Glory, we don't have men to spare," the scout said patiently. "We've got to put distance between us and the soldiers. You saw yesterday they'd just as soon shoot at women and children as not."

"I'm staying to help; tell her that."

He paused, reining in his pinto, and she thought she saw a

trace of admiration in his dark eyes. "You don't know what you're saying; there will be hungry coyotes after dark, and if the soldiers come in the night, they might mistake you for an Indian and kill you before you can tell them."

She ignored him, nodding toward Moccasin Woman, who was already kneeling next to the suffering girl. "You will help?"

Glory nodded, and Moccasin Woman yelled something to the other women. They seemed to look at Glory with new respect. The others were looking at Redbird with sympathy, but then they looked north with longing. To linger behind was to face death or capture, with the army only hours behind them.

Glory looked from Moccasin Woman to the silently suffering girl, then to Two Arrows. "I'm going to try to help. If you say no, you'll have to tie me up and drag me out of here."

He stared at her a long moment. "I know we seem hardhearted to you, Glory, but the welfare of the whole group has to be placed above one girl in labor."

"Where's her husband?" Glory demanded. "He could stay and guard—"

"He was killed by soldiers a few weeks ago for stealing a beef to feed the starving people," the scout said.

Glory felt her mood plummet. She looked from the suffering girl back to Two Arrows. "Go on; we'll manage."

Two Arrows leaned on his saddle horn, looked down at her a long moment. "I'll stay," he said finally.

"You!" she said, surprised. "If the army gets here before Redbird gives birth, they might show mercy to one of the other men, but not to you."

His dark face was stoic and expressionless. "I know much better than you, Proud One, what the lieutenant and his soldiers will do if they catch me."

She felt a sudden surge of admiration for him as he dismounted and tied his paint to a nearby tree. Of all the men, she wouldn't have thought he would volunteer. The column was already moving away from the resting place, heading north again.

Moccasin Woman helped Redbird to a blanket under a bush and built a small fire. "There not time to do proper ceremonies," she muttered.

Glory knelt by the girl's side and took her hand. "How can I help?"

The old woman looked at Glory with respect. "Redbird is nothing to you; why do you care?"

"She's a woman and she's in pain," Glory said softly. "What did you do with little Grasshopper?"

"Gave her over to care of another friend," Moccasin Woman said. "If we run into trouble or soldiers catch us, I want child to have chance."

Tears came to Glory's eyes, and she looked at Two Arrows standing there. "I hadn't realized how desperate these people were."

Two Arrows said, "All they want is freedom; is that too much to ask?"

She was abruptly ashamed of her own people for what they had done to the Cheyenne. Mercy! *Are you crazy, Glory?* she scolded herself. *These Indians have kidnapped you to use as a hostage, and you're feeling sorry for them?*

Redbird moaned very softly, and Glory reached to wipe the sweat from her brown face. Women felt a kinship with each other at times like this, and nothing else mattered.

"This going to take a while," Moccasin Woman said to Glory. "See if you can find water."

Two Arrows said, "There's a spring in those trees."

Glory nodded. She gathered up canteens and started toward the spring, Two Arrows following her. Surely he didn't think she was going to try to escape right now.

She filled the four canteens, struggled to get the straps over her shoulder.

"Here, let me carry those," he said gently.

She handed them over, feeling a sudden spark when their fingers brushed. "You are courageous to stay, knowing what the soldiers will do to you if they catch you."

He shrugged. "I was once an honored dog soldier, bravest of the brave," he said. "I had lost that pride for a long time, drowned in a bottle of whiskey."

She thought about what she had heard around the fort about his past. "I am sorry about your family."

For a moment, his strong jaw worked, and he swallowed hard. "I should not have kidnapped you," he said finally. "I was angry; thought you had told the lieutenant about me grabbing your horse that night."

She paused and looked at him. "I would not have begged a man for help."

"I know that now, Proud One." He glanced down at his bandaged arm where she had stabbed him. "How well I know!"

She remembered then the way he had pulled her into his embrace, the passion of his kiss. She was almost ashamed that she had tried to kill him. "I was desperate to escape, and then you were ripping my dress, trying to—"

"I know. I forgot everything but that you were a woman I had desired since the first time I saw you galloping near the fort with your hair streaming out like a wild mustang's mane, your chin so high and proud."

She paused and looked up at him, seeing him as a man, not a savage, remembering the warmth of his arms, the taste of his mouth.

One of his big hands reached out slowly and cupped her chin. "I would never hurt you, Glory."

His gentle fingers felt warm on her skin as he looked down into her eyes. Her emotions were in turmoil, remembering yesterday and the way he had taken her in his arms, the way his mouth had dominated hers and the hot feel of his lips on her breasts as they meshed and struggled, both smeared with his blood.

Moccasin Woman yelled for the water, breaking the spell. Glory and Two Arrows turned and hurried back to where Redbird labored, great beads of sweat on her pretty face.

"She isn't crying out like white women do," Glory marveled.

Moccasin Woman shook her head. "Even our children know they must be silent as deer so as not to endanger us all."

"This is not a place for a man," Two Arrows said. "I will go up on that little rise and stand guard. As soon as she gives birth, we must move on; try to catch up to the others. I'll rig a travois behind her horse."

Glory watched him walk away, trying to sort out her feelings. He had kidnapped her, handled her, and kissed her like no other man had ever kissed her, making her blood pound in a way she had not thought possible. Yet he had such a gentle side she had never expected in such a virile warrior.

Redbird made a soft noise, and Glory took her hand, patted it. "It will be all right," she whispered.

Moccasin Woman shook her head. "There are ceremonies for a birthing, but here, we cannot do them." She looked at Glory. "You have little ones?"

Glory shook her head. How she had wanted children, even if they were to be sired by Howard Halstead, but in those five years of marriage, there were none. She had gone to see a doctor secretly. The doctor found nothing wrong with her. When she told Howard, he had beaten her, screaming that it could not be his fault; she must be barren. Then there had been that terrible scene involving his brother, Nat, who was visiting from his ranch in Kansas.

She didn't want to think about that now; there was too much to do here.

Dusk fell while valiant Redbird labored to give birth. Somewhere in the distance, a pack of coyotes yapped. The sound unnerved Glory. She looked toward Two Arrows silhouetted up on the little rise. He nodded reassuringly and patted the rifle in the crook of his arm. She was surprised at how secure she felt, knowing he was on guard.

Glory held Redbird's hand, wiped the sweat from her pretty face as she labored, watched with admiration as Moccasin Woman assisted. What brave women, these two are, fighting bravely to bring forth a new life under such terrible circumstances and with none of the medicines and amenities white women had.

Finally, after dark, Redbird gave birth to a fine, squalling daughter. Moccasin Woman wiped her off with dry grass, wrapped her in a scrap of blanket, and handed her to Glory.

"Oh, she's beautiful!" She held the baby close, crooning to her a long moment before she laid her in the crook of the mother's arm.

"Hahoo," the girl whispered to Glory, and smiled as she spoke her own language to Moccasin Woman.

"Redbird says 'thank you,' " the older woman translated. "She did not expect help from a white woman. She say you must be Indian in heart."

Glory smiled. "Tell Redbird all women are the same, and I was happy to do what little I could to help."

Moccasin Woman translated, then said to Glory, "We go soon." She turned and looked toward Two Arrows. "He is brave man, even if he scouted for bluecoats; I used to think him nothing but a drunken white man's Injun."

"Yes, it was brave," Glory agreed in spite of herself. "He knows what would happen if the lieutenant caught him."

"We must eat," Moccasin Woman said. "See if you can find something to make some broth."

Glory dug in a knapsack as the woman directed, soon had a rich broth bubbling from dried meat.

In the meantime, Moccasin Woman was busy with her patient. "Redbird, there is no male relative here to name this child."

Tears came to the girl's eyes and she shook her head and motioned toward Two Arrows, said something in her language to the old woman.

Moccasin Woman nodded, evidently, greatly moved. To Glory, she said, "She asks if he will do the naming? Would you ask him?"

Glory swallowed hard. Somehow, she knew this was a great

honor. She walked out to where the scout sat on guard. "It is a fine, fat girl."

"Good." He smiled.

He was handsome when he smiled, Glory thought. "Redbird asks if you will choose a name?"

"Me?" He touched his chest in surprise.

"Why not? You have done something brave to stay behind and risk soldiers catching you."

His shoulders squared as he stood up. "I will be pleased. It is too bad we cannot do it the old way, with all the ceremony, but nothing is the way it used to be when the Cheyenne ruled the prairie and the buffalo ran."

Together, they walked back, Two Arrows evidently deep in thought. As they reached the tree, behind them they heard a faraway sound echoing through the prairie night. They both turned to look. Far to the north, the big lobo was silhouetted against the moon on a hill, singing to the sky.

"It is a good sign?" Redbird held her baby and looked up at them hopefully.

Two Arrows squatted to look down at her and her baby. "It is a very good sign," he answered. "Our untamed brother sings to the new child the song of our people."

He reached out and took the baby, held her a long moment, looking down into the small brown face. Something in the man's expression pulled at Glory's soul, and she wondered if he were remembering his own dead children? Two Arrows placed the tips of his big fingers ever so gently on the baby's forehead. "You're destined for great things," he whispered, "because your mother dared to dream of freedom. Little woman of the Cheyenne, I name you Brave Dream."

Moccasin Woman nodded her approval. "It is good name."

Redbird smiled and held out her arms for her daughter. "Her father would have been pleased."

Glory found herself blinking back a sudden mist.

"Now," the older woman took charge briskly, "this broth Two

Arrows's woman has prepared, let us eat of it and be on our way."

"I am not his woman, I am his captive," Glory corrected.

Two Arrows frowned and the good feelings of the baby naming were broken. "I will go saddle my horse."

The women stared after him, a tall, muscular figure in buckskin striding through the moonlit night.

"Take him some broth," Moccasin Woman ordered.

Glory filled two gourds and walked over to where he checked the girth of his saddle. "Brave Dream is a fine name. It is a good thing to have children."

He didn't say anything, only cleared his throat and looked away.

"Tell me about your children," she said.

He shrugged. "Dead at the Washita along with my woman. Yellow Hair's soldiers hit the sleeping camp in the early dawn. I was away hunting when I heard the distant gunfire and saw the smoke rising on the horizon as the camp burned. Pretty Flower died in my arms in the snow."

"I—I'm sorry." She felt awkward about the personal things her captor was telling her.

He swallowed hard and did not speak for a long moment. "It has been a long time; ten years the way whites count time. All my family is dead or scattered; some I know not where. I know only that my nephew, Storm Gathering, rides with the Lakota." He took the steaming gourd from her, began to eat.

She ate her broth in silence, imagining the bloody scene that haunted him. No wonder he drank. The night had turned chill, and she shivered.

"We must find you something to wear tomorrow; your dress is torn and bloody." He took off the buckskin shirt he wore, put it around her, his hands lingering on her shoulders. It was a strange thing to do for a prisoner, Glory thought. Despite herself, she was moved by the gesture.

Moccasin Woman called out to them. "Help with travois. We go now."

Glory looked at Two Arrows. "It's a shame to move that girl."

"There's no help for it," the scout said. "We must catch up with the column. They'll probably be camping next up on the Arkansas River."

We're almost into Kansas, she thought. It was amazing all those well-equipped soldiers hadn't managed to catch this ragtag, hungry little group of Indians. "That's near Dodge City, isn't it?"

"Yes. If we don't change course, the trail will take us out of Indian Territory and west of that town."

If she got close to Dodge City, the possibilities for escape would increase, Glory thought. Perhaps if she planned carefully, she could yet escape. First, she would have to win his complete trust—or do something even more extreme. She would not consider that possibility right now. One thing was certain; things between them had changed. She was no longer seeing him just as a drunken Indian and dangerous kidnapper. Despite herself, because of everything that had happened over the last several days, she was beginning to respect and admire him and this valiant little band of Cheyenne.

"I hope your people make it," she blurted, and was surprised to find that she meant it.

"I could almost believe you're sincere." He reached out and caught her hand, pulled her to her feet. He didn't let go, and it was a long moment before she pulled her fingers from his grasp and hurried away.

She reminded herself that he was her kidnapper, and she should hate and fear him. Frankly, she wasn't sure how she felt anymore. She didn't look back at Two Arrows, but she knew he walked behind her, leading his horse.

Between them all, they got Moccasin Woman's bay gelding hitched to the travois and helped Redbird and her nursing baby into it. The old woman mounted then.

Two Arrows sat his paint looking down at Glory. "Will you ride behind Moccasin Woman?"

"Her horse is already overloaded with the travois and all," Glory said.

Wordlessly, he held out his hand and she let him lift her up before him on the paint stallion. Somewhere on the prairie behind them, the man she planned to marry was coming hard with a troop of soldiers, determined to rescue her and kill her abductor. She would not think about that right now, or what might happen tomorrow.

Glory reminded herself that she must win Two Arrows's trust if she was going to escape. She leaned back against the warmth of his big frame and his arm went around her protectively. Funny how she just seemed to fit against him that way. They rode out across the rolling land into the darkness, heading north. Somewhere ahead of them, the big lobo wolf sang in the September night and it suddenly seemed to Glory he was singing to her.

Eleven

The five of them caught up with the main Cheyenne band late that night, where they were camped on a creek. Many gathered around to greet the new baby, Brave Dream, and nod with respect to Two Arrows and even Glory. Evidently, the fleeing Cheyenne had not expected to see the little group again, thinking they had been killed or captured by the pursuing soldiers.

Those already camped shared what little food they had, and then Two Arrows tossed her a blanket. "Get some sleep. Tomorrow will be a long day; we are almost out of supplies. The council meets at dawn to make some tough choices."

"You could surrender," Glory suggested as she took the blanket and lay down near the fire. "The army will feed you."

"If the army had fed us, these people would not now be trying to walk clear back to the Dakotas," he said wryly.

He spoke the truth, she thought, ashamed now of her own people. All these Indians looked so desperate and thin.

Two Arrows paused, then leaned over to pull her blanket up over her shoulders. "What you did, helping Moccasin Woman with Redbird and her baby; that was more than we expected."

"It seemed a decent thing to do," she said truthfully.

"Most white women wouldn't have bothered, especially since you're a captive."

A captive. She had almost forgotten that. "I'm so tired of

being dirty and hungry," she said, "and my hair is just tangled and awful."

He surveyed her in her filthy, torn dress, stiff with his dried blood. "To me, you will always be pretty, Proud One. Tomorrow, I'll try to find you something to wear."

He lay down nearby and pulled his blanket over himself. Glory sneaked a furtive look around. The exhausted Indians lay asleep around her, and in the center circle burned a tiny campfire. She realized there were guards watching the horse herd, so there wasn't any chance of escaping tonight. Besides, she was exhausted, and who knew what dangers lay out there on the dark prairie? She thought about the mysterious wolf that the Cheyenne said was leading them home. They thought it was big medicine, but more than likely, the beast was just waiting for a chance to take down a horse or anyone who ventured too far from camp unarmed.

Anyway, the army must be gaining on them and might rescue her tomorrow or the next day, so she'd better not take the risk. Broken Blade might be the one who recaptured her. The thought of him made her scoot a little closer toward Two Arrows. He reached out and patted her. "You'll be all right," he whispered.

So he hadn't been asleep after all. No doubt, he was lying there watching to make sure she didn't try to escape. Well, at least he hadn't tied her up. Was he concerned about her comfort, or did he figure she'd given up the idea?

Before dawn, she awakened to the sound of men speaking Cheyenne over the muted movement about the camp. She opened her eyes and saw the men sitting cross-legged around a council fire, smoking a ceremonial pipe they passed from hand to hand. Two Arrows sat in the circle now as an honored warrior, not hanging around the perimeter as a drunken outcast. Somehow, that pleased her. He had said some important things had to be discussed this morning. She wished she spoke more of the language so she could understand. She wondered if they were discussing her fate?

Two Arrows sipped the strong, sweet coffee. The craving for whiskey had slacked off and he was relieved. He looked around at the other warriors. All looked weary and hungry, Many were old; too old for a hard journey like this. Some of the ancient ones like Sitting Man seemed to keep going on sheer bravery.

Dull Knife said, "This is the last of our little bit of sugar and coffee."

"We are out of meat, too," Tangle Hair, leader of the dog soldiers said, "and even if we eat all our horses, the meat will not last long, and then how will we carry the sick and very old ones?"

They looked at each other and didn't speak, all knowing that unless they got fresh mounts soon, those people too weak or old to walk would be left by the trail to die.

Little Wolf scowled. "This is the way it was with the Nez Perce last year, except they had forests and mountains to hide in as the army chased them. We are on flat prairie."

"We must not stand and fight," Thin Elk said. "We are almost out of ammunition, too."

Little Wolf glared at Thin Elk and Two Arrows remembered the gossip that Thin Elk was paying unwanted attention to Little Wolf's daughter. Even if he did not like it, it was considered beneath a chief's dignity to notice or criticize Thin Elk for this personal affront.

Two Arrows considered the tribe's desperate situation as he looked around the circle. "Somehow, we must get more horses and supplies."

Little Wolf frowned and stared into the fire. "We had hoped to slip through this Kansas, silent as shadows so the settlers and hunters would not join the army in chasing us."

Broken Blade's cruel eyes lit up. "We will raid these settlers and take beef and horses and scalps!"

"Then the settlers and ranchers will hunt us, too," Two Arrows noted. "Every fight slows our march, and we must not be caught on the trail when the snows come."

Tangle Hair nodded. "The dog soldiers are ready to give their lives to protect the retreat as always, but Two Arrows is right—time is our most deadly enemy."

"Food and horses," Dull Knife mused, "these we must have. If we can take them without killing whites, that is good; but we will do what we must." He looked toward the creek, where, even now, gold and scarlet leaves fell from the trees and whirled toward the water to float downstream like tiny boats.

The pipe passed to Two Arrows, and he held it a long moment, almost overwhelmed to think that he was once again accepted as a warrior of the people after all these years of scorn. He took a puff, savoring the sweet tobacco, and passed the pipe on. "Perhaps we could go on a hunt this morning before we begin our march. We might get a few deer or even find some buffalo."

"Hah!" Broken Blade sneered. "The hide hunters have killed all the buffalo! How long has it been since any of us saw even a small herd? Besides, we would still not have enough horses, and the ones we do have are mostly poor old nags. I say we begin raiding ranches! Half the horses these Kansas settlers own were stolen from Cheyenne herds. Besides, we owe them vengeance because of the massacre on Sappa Creek."

"Ayeee! Let us paint ourselves for war!" shouted younger braves, and a murmur of agreement passed around the circle. Faces grew hard and angry as warriors remembered the slaughter of Cheyenne women and children more than three years ago at Sappa Creek.

Many of those here had lost a loved one in that massacre in northern Kansas, Two Arrows thought. Ranchers, settlers, and cowboys had joined the soldiers in the attack. Afterward, the soldiers had set the tipis ablaze and thrown the dead bodies on the fire. Moccasin Woman's husband had been one of those killed.

"Let us be calm," Dull Knife cautioned, "and listen to Two

Arrows, who knows how the whites think, since he has ridden for them as a scout. To raid settlers is to bring thousands more soldiers on the Iron Horses that run through this country. Do we not have enough soldiers hunting us?"

"They hunt us because of the woman," Broken Blade complained, glaring at Two Arrows. "If we killed her, they would stop following us."

Two Arrows felt sudden alarm. Automatically, his hand went to the big knife in his belt, and he was shocked to realize that he would use it to protect her if need be, even against his own people. "On the contrary, the soldiers will chase us even harder if we harm her; hunt us down like rabbits and take revenge."

Little Wolf nodded. "Two Arrows is right." He looked around the circle at the others. "First, we hunt. Later, we will spread out, try to steal horses and supplies, but if we must, we will kill any who try to stop us. Nothing must keep us from reaching the freedom of the north. What say you?"

There was a chorus of agreement and nodding heads around the circle.

"Good," Dull Knife said. "We know some of us will not make it, but it is glorious to give our lives to try. Let us make ready to hunt. We must be finished and on the move again before the soldiers catch up to us."

"Dodge City lies only a few miles to the north," Two Arrows said. "If we time it right, we can slip past after dark. Dodge City will be full of cowboys itching to join the chase."

"Agreed," Dull Knife responded, nodding that the meeting was ended. But as some got to their feet, Broken Blade demanded, "What about the white woman?"

"Does Broken Blade want to make her his business?" Again, Two Arrows's hand went to the knife in his belt. He would kill any man who tried to harm her, even though murder of another Cheyenne was a terrible taboo, and a man would be exiled for it.

Little Wolf shrugged. "She belongs to Two Arrows, and may yet be useful as a hostage. Watch yourself, Broken Blade; you think too much about her."

Heads nodded in agreement as the men began to scatter. Two Arrows drew a deep sigh of relief.

Glory sat up in her blankets, absently playing with her beaded bracelet and watched the council leaving the fire. Everyone was stirring now, going for water from the creek, cooking what little food they had. She felt concern when she noticed the children seemed too weary to play, and many of the horses' ribs showed as they grazed.

Two Arrows came over to her, knelt. "The men are going hunting, spreading out, hoping to get a couple of deer or buffalo before we take the trail again."

"Why don't they just give up?" Glory asked. "Some of these people will surely starve and die on this trip. The army would feed them if they would only surrender."

"Food or freedom?" he asked bitterly. "Cheyenne weren't meant to live like that. Besides, if we surrender, the army might hang our leaders. Dull Knife and Little Wolf would rather die like warriors, from a bullet, than to be throttled by a rope. To die that way is shameful for a warrior."

"Lieutenant Krueger will hang you if he catches you, won't he?" Glory realized suddenly.

He grinned at her. "And give you a seat in the front row, no doubt."

She looked away so he would not see the fear she felt for him in her eyes.

He began to gather up his weapons.

"Where are you going?"

Two Arrows paused. "We are going to spread out and hunt for a couple of hours, see if we can find some fresh meat." He slipped her a small piece of smoked jerky. "Here, this is for you so you won't be hungry while I'm gone."

Glory grabbed it, pulled off a bite, chewed it greedily. The salty, smoked taste was the best food she could remember eating. Abruptly, she paused. "Where's yours?"

"I have eaten mine already." He busied himself with his bow and rifle.

"You are a poor liar."

He shrugged. "Indians don't get as much chance to practice as whites do."

"I can't take this meat," she insisted, "knowing you are hungry, too."

He looked at her a long moment. "So the Proud One's heart softens toward me."

"No. I want you to live to be caught and hanged!" she snapped, the words sounding false even to her own ears.

"Such spirit!" he said with admiration. "What fine, brave sons you would give a man; but what type of weak sons will the lieutenant sire?"

"Now that's hardly any of your business, is it?" She felt an angry flush rise to her cheeks.

"We will see." He finished gathering up his weapons. "I will return in a few hours."

In spite of herself, she felt alarm. "You're—You're going to leave me here alone?"

"You are safe enough. The women admire you because of your helping Redbird, and most of the men will go on the hunt. Besides, no man will touch you, knowing you belong to me."

She gritted her teeth, thinking she might be wrong about not wanting the army to hang him. As she watched the arrogant way he strode away, she thought she might even want to be the one to spring the trap. He saddled his big paint and rode out at the head of the hunting party.

She had eaten a little of the smoked jerky, but now she felt guilty. That both annoyed and surprised her. Why should she feel guilty? These savages were her enemies, her kidnappers.

As she paused uncertainly, somewhere on the edge of the camp, a baby cried. Redbird would need food to be able to nurse her baby and certainly little Grasshopper and her grandmother were hungry, too.

Glory took the meat and sought them out. The little girl ran to her, throwing her small arms around her legs with a glad cry. The two women smiled and nodded to Glory. She leaned over to peer at the small, dark-haired baby wrapped in a ragged scrap of blanket. She had some baby things back at her small store; she wished she had them here, and all those other things, too, for these pitiful people. By now, her creditors were probably taking the place over.

Little Grasshopper smiled with delight. "You still wear my present I gave you?"

Glory nodded and touched the delicate beaded bracelet. "It is beautiful like you. Every time I look at it, I think of you, my little friend."

Funny, Glory thought, it was getting more and more difficult to think of these valiant people as savages. All they wanted was freedom and a chance to return to their own homeland. That didn't seem so unreasonable. "I have a little bit of meat," she whispered to the older woman. "Perhaps you could make a broth for all."

"Isn't it food Two Arrows gave you for yourself?"

"I—I have already eaten my fill," Glory said.

"You lie bad as any Cheyenne." Moccasin Woman smiled. "You must be Indian in heart. All right, I make broth and we all share."

Afterward, the old woman looked at Glory with a frown. "Your dress is ruined. I have a very fine dress I would like to give you. That is, if you do not mind dressing like a Cheyenne woman."

Glory's heart went out to her. "I would be honored."

Moccasin Woman dug around in the things on her travois, very carefully brought out a dress of the most delicate doeskin, heavily fringed and delicately beaded and decorated with elks' teeth.

"Mercy," Glory said in awe as she felt the butter-soft leather, "this is too beautiful! I can't accept this. You should wear it yourself."

For just an instant, Glory thought she saw sadness in the

older woman's eyes, but then Moccasin Woman said, "Now look how broad I am. You think I fit this small thing?" She held it up, and sure enough, it was made to fit a much smaller woman.

"Where did it come from?" Glory took it in her hands, admiring it.

The other hesitated. "Same place those moccasins on your feet came from. Not polite to question gift. I be pleased if you wear it."

"You are so kind." Glory hugged the magnificent dress to her body. "I'll be happy to get out of this calico rag."

"In hour or so, sun will warm creek," Moccasin Woman continued. "Then you wash yourself and put on dress. Maybe we comb the snarls from hair, too. Here, I saved pounded yucca root, which we use for soap."

Glory nodded as she accepted everything, remembering the right word. *"Hahoo,"* she said gravely, *thank you.*

She sat down under a tree and watched Redbird nurse her baby while little Grasshopper and the other children played about the camp. The women and old men sat patiently, waiting for the hunting party's return. Glory was touched by the hope in the weary brown faces. She looked toward the south, wondering where the soldiers were? She was surprised to discover that she didn't want the army to come riding in and attack these people. If they would just leave her here for the cavalry to find, and ride on north. . . .

Glory wandered about the camp, waiting for the sun to warm the creek and autumn air so she could bathe. The children had no qualms about the cold water, and laughed and dived like sleek little otters. As she watched, Glory was appalled at how thin the little brown bodies were. The white people and the soldiers around Fort Reno probably didn't realize, or didn't believe how close to starvation these Cheyenne really were. A few, like Mrs. Frost, probably just didn't care.

As she wandered about the camp, nodding to the women who

seemed almost friendly to her, Glory realized that all the men but the most ancient ones had gone on the hunt. Perhaps this was the ideal time to steal a horse and gallop away toward the south, where she would surely run into the pursuing cavalry. However, once she looked over the two or three bony old horses that grazed on the prairie, she gave up that idea. The hunters had ridden the few good horses, and these old nags probably wouldn't get very far without collapsing.

Eventually, the sun warmed the earth. *Indian summer,* Glory thought, that last brief time of glorious weather before winter's cold winds blew in from the north to cover the world with snow until spring. She studied these weary, gaunt people as she gathered up the fine doeskin dress. Time was running out for them to travel. Soon, a blizzard might sweep down and catch them on the trail with little food and no shelter from the cold. She winced at the thoughts of the children, little Grasshopper, Brave Dream, and yes, Moccasin Woman and Redbird, miserable and dying on the vast prairie.

"Moccasin Woman," she called, "I'm going down to the creek to bathe."

The other nodded, preoccupied with helping Redbird with her darling baby.

Most of the children had left the river and were lying up on rocks sunning themselves and resting.

Glory found a secluded cove along a bend that was sheltered by sumac bushes. The sumac leaves were turning scarlet and above her, tree leaves swirled toward the earth, all scarlet and gold. She wouldn't have to worry about anyone seeing her naked in this area.

Very carefully, she laid the beautiful, beaded dress and her moccasins in the fork of a bois d'arc tree, and added the dainty beaded bracelet to the pile.

She looked down at the blue-flowered calico she wore and wrinkled her nose with distaste. It was not only grimy and tattered, it was dark with Two Arrows's blood. She remembered the moment she had stabbed him. A lesser man might have killed her in a fury. Abruptly, she recalled something else, the taste of his lips on hers, his tongue exploring the depths of her mouth, the strength of the man as he had held her against him when she struggled and tried to get away, the hot wetness of his mouth on her breasts as he tasted them. And last, the throb of his pulsating manhood against her and the intense desire in his dark eyes.

The memories made her face burn, and she inhaled sharply, then let out her breath with a shuddering sigh. Mercy, what was wrong with her? The sexual relationship with her husband had been hurried and without feeling. She could not ever remember her pulse pounding when Howard kissed her.

She looked around, making sure no one watched her before pulling off the filthy dress, chemise, and pantalets. She stared at them in distaste. What to do with these? Certainly as ragged and bloody as the fabric was, no one could wash and wear them again. She might leave them hanging on a tree limb as a clue to the soldiers, but she was certain some sharp-eyed Indian would spy them and tell Two Arrows what she had done. Then his guard would be up again, and she would never get another chance to escape. Glory thought about it a minute, finally put the torn clothes under a rock near the water and waded out into the hip-deep stream.

It was warm, she thought with pleasure. She looked down at her reflection in the water, appalled at the tangle her long black hair had become. Her breasts reflected in the water, and she stared at that, remembering Two Arrows holding her down with her hands above her head, twisting to get away while he sucked those pink nipples into swollen, throbbing points. *You are always pretty to me.*

Again, she felt her face flush and splashed water on herself. Only then did she note how much the sun had darkened her exposed skin the last several days while her breasts and belly were still creamy white.

"Why, my skin is as brown as Redbird's," she thought aloud.

"With my hair in braids, I could probably pass for an Indian myself."

She remembered then that her long-dead mother had been from the Dupree family; French Cajun and perhaps a trace of Seminole or Creek Indian. She barely remembered her mother, and her father never wanted to discuss her.

Glory submerged her body in the water, washing herself with the pounded yucca root Moccasin Woman had given her. She even washed her hair. "White women don't know what they're missing," she said, as she rinsed the soap out and began to dive and play in the water. She wasn't much of a swimmer, but the water wasn't very deep.

Glory thought she heard excited voices in the camp, but paid it little heed. She went under the water and came up, laughing aloud, standing in the hip-deep water.

She heard a slight noise and glanced toward the bank. Two Arrows stood there, staring at her without speaking. Glory looked down, abruptly aware that she was naked, the water only hip deep. Immediately, she squatted so that the water came up around her bare shoulders. "How dare you spy on me!"

"I wasn't spying," he said matter-of-factly, but he was still staring, his eyes dark and intense. "Moccasin Woman told me you were here. I came to tell you we killed two deer. The women are cooking them now."

Roasted deer. That sounded good. "All right, you've told me, now go back to camp until I get something on."

His brow wrinkled. "You aren't going to put on that bloody—"

"No, Moccasin Woman gave me a beautiful dress. I'll put it on when you go away."

"It's a good thing Broken Blade never saw you naked." Two Arrows seemed to be thinking aloud. "I would have had to kill him to keep him away from you."

The thought of Broken Blade possessing her made her shudder. "Where is he?"

"Up at the camp—I think." He must have seen the expression

on her face because he added, "Don't worry, I'll watch out for you. That water looks inviting."

"You aren't coming in now, are you?" She backed up, her hands covering her breasts.

He shook his head. "If I did, I don't think I could keep myself from . . . never mind. I'll be down around the bend washing if you need me."

She watched him walk along the bank with long, easy strides and disappear into the bushes. Glory stayed sunk in the water up to her shoulders until she heard the definite sound of splashing from farther down. Only then did she wade out, stand a long moment, letting the breeze dry her skin, before she put on the moccasins and the fine dress. It was a perfect fit, Glory thought. Whoever this dress had been made for was just about Glory's size, and the beadwork and fancy elk teeth were beautiful. Too bad she didn't have any under garments, but hidden by the doe-skin, who would know? She slipped on the little moccasins, and last of all, the bracelet the small girl had given her.

Glory leaned over the bank and looked at her reflection with wonder. In this dress and with her skin tanned by the September sun, all she would have to do to pass for Cheyenne was braid her long black hair. At the very least, maybe Moccasin Woman could help Glory comb out the tangles.

She paused, listening. No longer did she hear splashing from around the bend. Had Two Arrows sneaked up to watch her swim? The thought embarrassed and angered her. If she caught him doing that, she'd see that he paid for his impudence when the army finally captured him. She crept quietly through the brush and blundered out onto the riverbank and almost bumped into Two Arrows, who was just tying his breechcloth.

He froze and stared back at her, water streaming down his powerful, almost bare body. "If you wanted to see me naked, you came a little too late."

"I beg your pardon!" She felt an angry flush and looked away. "I'm returning to camp and thought I'd tell you."

"What an obedient captive. Next thing I know, you'll be learning to say please and beg when you want something."

"That'll be a cold day in hell when I beg a man for anything!" she snapped. "I'm too proud for that."

"Don't I know it!"

She seemed rooted to the spot as he took a step toward her. She ought to turn and run for the camp, but to do so might make him think she was afraid. But this time, his attention was on the dress. "Where'd you get that?" he demanded. "Did you steal it from Moccasin Woman?"

"How dare you! I don't steal." She was overwhelmed by how close this wet, almost naked man stood to her. "She gave it to me." She looked up into his eyes, wondering what he knew about this dress.

His big hands came up to clasp Glory's shoulders. "You have been paid a great compliment," he whispered gently. "She must like you very much."

His fingers seemed to burn through the doeskin of the dress, and she couldn't make herself pull away. She glanced down, then back up at him. "There's something special about this dress, isn't there I knew it the moment I saw it that it's no ordinary—"

"Glory," he whispered, "it's one of the finest dresses among all the Cheyenne. When our people see you in it, they will know Moccasin Woman loves and respects you. It was her dead daughter's wedding garment."

"Oh my God." The tears welled up then and filled her eyes, realizing what a great compliment she had been paid.

"Don't cry, Glory, I'm sure Gentle Rain would have wanted you to have it." Slowly, he pulled her close, bent his head, and kissed her lips. It was a tender kiss, almost a caress across her mouth.

For a moment, she was too surprised to move. Then, though she didn't mean to, she reacted instinctively, her arms going up around his neck as she kissed him in return. At this encouragement, he pulled her hard against him, his arms embracing her, holding her so close that she felt the heat of his wet, powerful body and the swell of his manhood against her while his tongue teased her lips into opening for him to kiss her deeply, thoroughly.

She didn't think, she only reacted, clinging to him, pressing against him, returning his passion with her own. No man had ever kissed her like this, and she had never responded with the fire she now felt deep in her very soul. The passion blazed higher, consuming her, and his big, muscular body seemed to envelop her, his heart pounding hard against her breast.

Somewhere in the distance, she heard little Grasshopper calling, "Two Arrows, Proud One, where are you? We have meat ready; plenty of meat!"

They jerked apart abruptly, Glory both appalled and stunned that she had returned his kiss with such ardor.

"No wonder the lieutenant wants you back," Two Arrows whispered. "A man would move heaven and earth to keep you!"

"I—I must be losing my mind!" She pulled away from him, turned, and ran for the camp. She didn't look back, horrified that she had done such a thing. What kind of a woman was she to go into some savage's arms, especially *this* savage's arms— her kidnapper. Again she remembered the bloody knife fight where they had struggled and he had held her down, ravaging her mouth with his own; the unfamiliar feelings that blazed in her when he had kissed and fondled her breasts. This time, she wasn't a prisoner of his strength, and she had returned his fiery passion with her own.

She ran all the way back to the camp, recalling the desire burning in Two Arrows's dark eyes that had ignited a spark she had not known existed. Something primitive and intense in her own soul had responded eagerly; no, more than eagerly—with abandon. She must be insane from the stress of captivity!

She resolved that she would keep her mind on her rescue. David would lead the soldiers to free her soon, and he must never suspect that she had reacted this way to the Indian scout. Certainly he would be as shocked as she was herself. Two Arrows's dark eyes told her he ached for her with a passion more intense than she had ever seen in David's blue ones. The longer she stayed among the Cheyenne, the more danger she was in from starvation, the coming cold weather, Broken Blade, or being accidentally shot by some attacking soldier. She couldn't just wait to be rescued anymore; she must escape and make her way back to the advancing soldiers!

Glory smiled as she walked into camp because she had just made a decision. She wanted to escape; her captor wanted her body. Was it possible that Two Arrows could be bribed into letting her go? Bribed with what?

She only had one thing to offer in trade. Once the thought would have horrified her, but David need never know. Desperate situations called for desperate solutions. Tonight, or the first chance she got, she would offer to make love to the dog soldier. She would exchange a passionate night in Two Arrows's arms for her freedom!

Twelve

Lieutenant Krueger stood at attention, saluting smartly.

"At ease," Captain Rendlebrock said to the handful of officers and noncoms gathered under the lone tree on the vast stretch of prairie. "Men, that courier who rode in just now brought a message from headquarters. We've reached the limits of our jurisdiction, so this outbreak is no longer our responsibility."

David blinked in disbelief. "You—you don't mean, sir, that we're returning to Fort Reno?"

"That's just what I mean," the other responded. "After all, no one knows exactly where the renegades are, somewhere in Kansas or even western Colorado, and—"

"But they've got Glory Halstead!" David blurted, realizing as he did so that he had just interrupted his superior officer, but he was too distressed to care. "We can ride a little faster and harder, catch up to them—"

"Lieutenant Krueger"—the captain favored him with a sympathetic smile—"I understand your distress, knowing about the lady, but we must be realistic; orders are orders. Troops from Fort Dodge, Kansas, under Major Lewis, are on the lookout for the renegades, and I hear Tip Thornburgh is being brought in, too."

David saluted. "In that case, sir, may I request permission for a temporary assignment with the Kansas unit?"

The other pulled at his mustache. "They don't need you, the Kansans can handle this."

David managed to keep his voice level and calm, although his nerves were taut with frustration and anger. "You don't understand, sir. One of the ringleaders, and the one who kidnapped Mrs. Halstead, is one of my former scouts, Two Arrows."

"Oh yes," the captain mused, pulling at his mustache. "Insolent devil, as I recall, and drank too much."

"That's the one," David said. "Never would salute me; arrogant and disrespectful. I want to be there for the kill!"

"He might be captured, not killed," the officer reminded him.

"If I'm there, he'll be killed." David's tone was a promise, not a threat.

"All right, since you feel so strongly, I'll take care of the paperwork when I get back to the fort."

"Thank you, sir." David saluted.

"Hmm." The captain pulled at his mustache again. "A little unusual, but we can all appreciate your feelings. However, Lieutenant, you ought to face reality."

"Sir?"

"These Cheyenne have been moving at an incredible pace, staying ahead of our cavalry."

David nodded. What was the man's point? "All the troopers know that, sir. We've seen the evidence: worn-out horses dead along the way; old people who died and were left along the road without taking time for proper burials. Much as I hate to admit it, we've all begun to admire their spirit and their fighting skills."

"The point I'm making, Krueger, is that these desperate people are setting a killing pace, one most white women couldn't survive."

David realized with horror what the captain hinted at. "No," he said, "not Glory. She's feisty and spirited; a survivor, sir. She's alive out there somewhere, knowing I'll come rescue her. I hope to marry her, sir."

"Umm." He chewed his lip. "Lieutenant, there's something else you might not have thought about."

"Sir?"

"She might have killed herself by now, as any self-respecting white woman would if those savages have—well, if the brutes have . . ." Captain Rendlebrock cleared his throat awkwardly and flushed red, "may have had their way with her. Under those circumstances—"

"Glory is not the type to kill herself, sir." David's hands clenched into fists at his sides. He was considered a calm, dependable officer, but right now, it was all he could do to keep from screaming at the man and attacking him. "She won't be dead, sir, and I want to marry her, no matter what she's endured. I love her more than any man possibly could."

The others looked at the ground, avoiding his earnest gaze. David tried not to think of the arrogant scout mating with Glory, enjoying her body as David never had. "I want to be the one to catch Two Arrows; it's a personal thing."

It was a personal thing, all right. David almost smiled as he imagined putting a pistol to the scout's head, blowing his brains out without mercy.

"All right, Lieutenant, permission granted."

The big Irishman stepped forward and saluted smartly. "Permission to speak, sir?"

The captain nodded. "Go ahead, Muldoon."

"Requesting permission to accompany Lieutenant Krueger on his special assignment."

The captain frowned. "Are you sure you want to do that, Corporal?"

"Aye, sir. The lieutenant and I have been together a long time. I share his concerns."

"Permission granted. The rest of the troop will make ready to mount up and return to Fort Reno. Troops from Fort Dodge will be taking up the chase soon. Dismissed!"

"Thank you, sir." David and Muldoon saluted smartly and the group broke up, the others walking toward their horses.

Most of the troop looked back, and David saw pity in many eyes as the troops mounted, before the order was given and the column started south.

David watched them ride out, addressed the other. "I appreciate the gesture, Muldoon, but you didn't need to come along. You could have been back at the fort enjoying a warm bunk and some hot food."

"Aye, lad, but I've gotten sort of used to your company." The corporal turned to look toward the north, where the skies had turned gray and the wind had picked up across the prairie. He rubbed his gnarled hands together. "Me rheumatiz is hurtin' again; must be colder weather ahead."

David sighed as he swung up on the fine chestnut stallion. "That means more hardships for Glory. I'll see that damned scout pays for his insolence!"

The other didn't answer as he swung up on the fat buckskin, but David saw the expression on the weathered, ruddy face. Muldoon thought she was probably already dead, too. He was coming along out of loyalty to David.

"Let's move out," David said, and nudged Chance forward, "so we can join up with those Kansas troops. I won't quit until I rescue her." He gritted his teeth as he urged his mount into a lope. "And when I catch that Two Arrows, I'll kill him without mercy!"

Relentlessly, the Cheyenne moved on northward. Sometimes Glory saw just the shadow of the big lobo running ahead of the weary riders and sometimes she began to imagine that she heard him singing to the sky. The Cheyenne lookouts spread across a thirty-mile front, always on the alert for fresh horses. As a horse wore out and died, the starving Indians ate it. In desperation, when they passed a ranch, warriors raided, taking what they needed to survive and kept moving. If cowboys or settlers resisted, the Cheyenne killed them. Dull Knife had given orders not to kill any whites, but sometimes they had to, knowing all

Get 4 FREE Books!

We created our convenient Home Subscription Service so you'll be sure to have the hottest new romances delivered each month right to your doorstep—usually before they are available in book stores. Just to show you how convenient the Zebra Home Subscription Service is, we would like to send you 4 FREE Kensington Choice Historical Romances. The books are worth up to $24.96, but you only pay $1.99 for shipping and handling. There's no obligation to buy additional books—ever!

Save Up To 30% With Home Delivery!

Accept your FREE books and each month we'll deliver 4 brand new titles as soon as they are published. They'll be yours to examine FREE for 10 days. Then if you decide to keep the books, you'll pay the preferred subscriber's price (up to 30% off the cover price!), plus shipping and handling. Remember, you are under no obligation to buy any of these books at any time! If you are not delighted with them, simply return them and owe nothing. But if you enjoy Kensington Choice Historical Romances as much as we think you will, pay the special preferred subscriber rate and save over $8.00 off the cover price!

We have 4 FREE BOOKS for you as your introduction to
KENSINGTON CHOICE!
To get your FREE BOOKS, worth up to $24.96, mail the card below or call TOLL-FREE 1-800-770-1963.
Visit our website at www.kensingtonbooks.com.

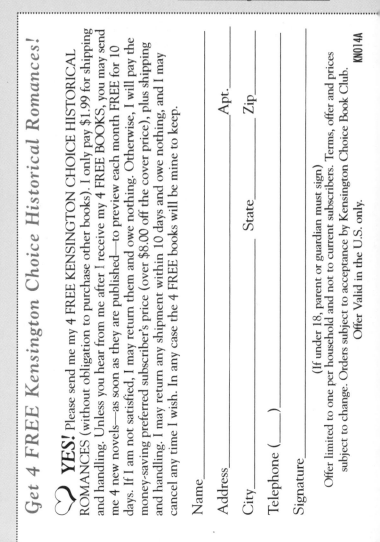

Get 4 FREE *Kensington Choice Historical Romances!*

YES! Please send me my 4 FREE KENSINGTON CHOICE HISTORICAL ROMANCES (without obligation to purchase other books). I only pay $1.99 for shipping and handling. Unless you hear from me after I receive my 4 FREE BOOKS, you may send me 4 new novels—as soon as they are published—to preview each month FREE for 10 days. If I am not satisfied, I may return them and owe nothing. Otherwise, I will pay the money-saving preferred subscriber's price (over $8.00 off the cover price), plus shipping and handling. I may return any shipment within 10 days and owe nothing, and I may cancel any time I wish. In any case the 4 FREE books will be mine to keep.

Name _____

Address _____ Apt. _____

City _____ State _____ Zip _____

Telephone (___) _____

Signature _____
(If under 18, parent or guardian must sign)

Offer limited to one per household and not to current subscribers. Terms, offer and prices subject to change. Orders subject to acceptance by Kensington Choice Book Club.
Offer Valid in the U.S. only.

KN014A

llı.lıllıı...lll.lılı.ılı..ılı.llı.ılı..llılı.llıı.l

KENSINGTON CHOICE

Zebra Home Subscription Service, Inc.

P.O. Box 5214

Clifton NJ 07015-5214

PLACE
STAMP
HERE

the while that the raiding only increased the number of armed ranchers and renegade whites joining the soldiers to hunt down and kill the escaping Cheyenne.

It seemed to Glory that they were always on the move, as the people crossed into southern Kansas. Often, Two Arrows cut the telegraph wires that stretched across the prairie skies. It sometime delayed the military messages, but the wires could be repaired, and besides, who could miss the hundreds of foot-prints and hoof marks on the dusty prairie?

During one rest period, old Moccasin Woman had combed Glory's hair with a porcupine brush and braided it. When Two Arrows saw Glory, his sharp intake of breath told her what he thought. "You could pass for a Cheyenne girl now," he said, and there was admiration in his voice.

"You're right," Glory said. "The hot sun has browned my skin."

Two Arrows frowned, staring up at the scudding gray clouds blowing in on a chill wind from the north. "There will soon be times you would be pleased to feel a hot sun."

She looked to the south, wondering how far behind them the soldiers were? It was beginning to seem as if the soldiers were not going to catch them. In that case, it was up to her to save herself; but how?

Two Arrows seemed lost in thought.

"What's the matter?"

"Up ahead lies Dodge City," he said. "We've got to get past it without all those whites spotting us."

This was going to be her chance to escape, Glory thought. "How do you intend to do that?"

"I just don't know. Some are saying it's impossible; we should send a peace party to Dodge and surrender."

"That doesn't sound like you," she said before she thought. "The other warriors admire you now. I have seen the way they come to ask your counsel."

"It is a weighty responsibility, this being given another chance." He ran his tongue across his lips.

"Do you ever think about whiskey?"

He laughed without mirth. "I would be lying, Proud One, if I said I didn't, but what I have in exchange, respect, a return to my people's confidence; that makes it worth it."

A camp crier rode through the weary people, shouting and pointing north.

"Are you ready to move on?" he asked. "It is time."

"Two Arrows, your leaders can't keep driving the people this way; the old ones and the young need rest. We're losing some every day."

"You think I don't know that?" His temper flared as he confronted her. "They'll get plenty of rest if the army catches us and throws us all in prison."

He strode over to his paint horse, led it to her. "This whole ordeal may end at Dodge City. The Arkansas River is there, and our scouts tell us it's running at almost flood stage. There's also train tracks. The telegraph can bring hundreds of soldiers on that train within hours."

Someone at the front of the column yelled a signal, and the people got to their feet and began to move forward again; some walking, some riding. As always, she noted, the dog soldiers were waiting to ride at the end of the column so as to protect the retreat, if need be.

Two Arrows mounted up and held out his hand. She hesitated, knowing that she was putting even more distance between her and her rescuers if she cooperated.

"Do you want to walk again as you did that first day?"

"Mercy, no." She put her hand in his big one, looking up at him with moist, half-open lips.

"Then come on, Proud One." He pulled her up on the horse behind him. Could she bribe him with her body to let her escape when they rode close to Dodge City? Thinking that, she put her hand on his thigh and leaned into his back, pressing her breasts against him as she slipped both arms around his waist. She felt him go tense, and then he reached down almost absently and patted her hand. His touch was so gentle, it surprised her.

He nudged his paint horse and they swung into the end of the moving column now, bringing up the rear with Tangle Hair and the other dog soldiers.

"This is an impossible undertaking," Glory muttered. "The army is going to catch you anytime."

He laughed, and she liked the deep, rich sound of his voice. "The army had better hurry! We never expected to make it this far with all those hundreds of soldiers hoping to catch us."

"But they will," she insisted.

"Glory, as starved and tired as we all are, it's what whites would call a miracle that we've made it this far. Anything beats dying by inches back on that reservation."

She could sympathize with their desperation, *even if I am a prisoner,* Glory thought. She turned her head, laid her face against his broad back, and watched the landscape. As they moved farther north, the prairie was turning into sand hills. Many of the trees they passed now had already lost their leaves. This was madness, she thought. The Cheyenne people were dying along with their few horses every day. It was unthinkable that they might walk all the way to Montana with winter coming on. Such a brave, resilient people. She didn't want to admire them, but it was difficult not to.

Two Arrows was only too conscious of the softness of the woman pressing against his back. He should be thinking of his people and his next action, but all he was conscious of was the feel of Glory's breasts against him, the warmth of her small arms around his waist. He ought to take this woman, satisfy the hunger that had been building in him since the very first time he had seen her. It would be a good joke on the rich lieutenant to return his woman with her belly swollen big with Two Arrows's son. And then he faced the truth; he did not want to return her at all, not even when her use as a hostage was ended. He wanted her to warm his blankets forever. Of course, that was impossible. How she would laugh if she knew that!

In the late afternoon, way up ahead, he saw an old woman stumble and fall by the trail. The column kept moving, passing her by. Nothing must delay them; to do so increased the threat of the soldiers catching them and then all might die.

"Two Arrows," Glory protested as they rode abreast of the old woman, "can't we do something? We can't just leave her."

He didn't want to leave the woman, either, but it was evident the old one was dying anyway, and the march could not be delayed. "It is the way of things, Proud One. She would be the first to protest us stopping the people, knowing we have to stay ahead of the soldiers."

"No, we must help her!"

He reined in and dismounted, looking up at Glory with new appreciation. "You have a good heart; as good as any Cheyenne girl. All right, I'll see what we can do." He took his canteen from the saddle, motioned the others to keep riding, then knelt next to the old woman. "Can you not make it a few more miles, Grandmother? Then we will eat and rest."

The old one reached one trembling hand to place on his arm. "My time is near; I know. I will not delay the people."

He held the canteen to her lips, and she drank eagerly. "Perhaps it is not your time yet. Here, you can ride my horse a while. I can walk."

"It is not fitting that a great warrior such as Two Arrows walk while I ride."

A great warrior. He had won the respect he had hungered for. "Let me decide what is fitting, Grandmother."

"Will the white girl mind?" She looked up at him, wrinkled and frail as a brown leaf whirling in the autumn wind.

"She is of good heart, old one, she will not mind." He helped the old woman to her feet and assisted her onto the paint. Glory held the old woman before her.

Two Arrows grinned up at Glory and turned back onto the trail, leading the horse. His heart felt good now; he had not wanted to leave the old woman behind.

Finally, in late afternoon, the straggly column stopped to rest in the lee of some low sand hills that shielded them from the wind. Two Arrows assisted Glory and the old woman down from the horse. "If we can get some food in her, it might strengthen her so that she can keep going."

"I'll give her my share," Glory said softly.

"No, Proud One, I'll give her *my* share."

The old one looked up at Glory, smiling with only a few teeth. "Thank you. You are surely one of the people and worthy to be this warrior's woman. Give him strong sons to make him proud," she said in her native language.

"What did she say?" Glory asked.

She would scoff or even laugh, probably, if he told her what the old woman's words meant. "She says to thank you for your kindness."

Glory patted the old woman's arm. "Tell her I will make broth for her while we rest. How long will we be here?"

Two Arrows's face turned grim. "We are only a few miles from Dodge City, but we can't risk passing near it in daylight. Some lawman or shopkeeper might see the dust rising from our horses and travois. We must wait for dark."

At least she could rest until then, Glory thought gratefully as she busied herself with the broth. All the time she labored, she tried to come up with an escape plan when they neared Dodge City.

Only now did Glory realize how frail and weak the old woman was and wondered how she had made it this far. Sheer willpower, she thought with respect, sheer willpower; just like most of the others. Even as the old woman enjoyed the broth and smiled up at her, she seemed weaker.

Glory sought out Two Arrows. "I don't think the old one will make it."

"I know, Glory, but we have done what we could for her."

Tears came to her eyes. "It is shameful that the army chases old women and children this way."

"We're savages, remember?" He put his hand on her shoulder, and she didn't pull away. "The army isn't worried about anything but keeping us on that reservation."

The old woman died just before dark; almost as if she knew that she was delaying her people and knowing they must move on. Glory did the best she could to prepare her for burial, but the Indians could not spare a blanket to wrap the body in with the cold winter coming. Two Arrows placed the thin, frail body in a tree because there was no time to prepare a burial platform.

Glory swallowed hard. "It doesn't seem fair that she walked so far and will be left out here, many miles from anything."

"She was not the first, and she won't be the last," he said, his face set, betraying no emotion. "All we want is to be allowed to return to our own country and live as we have always done, free as the great lobo wolf."

It was getting more and more difficult to think of these people as the enemy. "When I get back," Glory said, "I'm going to tell the whites how it was on this trip, how brave your people were. If the American people knew how the Indians have been mistreated—"

"Do you think they would care?" Two Arrows's voice was full of irony as he mounted up.

"Many would," Glory said. "They just don't know, but I promise I will tell them."

He smiled as he offered her his hand. "Is some of that sympathy for me?"

"Not you, you—you renegade kidnapper! You, I hope they hang!"

"They'll have to catch me first." He lifted her up on his horse behind him.

The Cheyenne started off again in the darkness.

"How close will we pass to Dodge City?"

Two Arrows said over his shoulder, "A couple of miles, maybe less. We are trying to time our passing very late, when most of the townspeople are asleep. There'll be a railroad to deal with and also the river."

Dull Knife and Little Wolf rode back to talk to Two Arrows.

She couldn't understand what was being said, but there was evidently some disagreement. After a few minutes, the two galloped back to the head of the column.

"What is happening?" she asked.

Two Arrows shrugged. "Nothing to concern you. They are in disagreement as to which direction to take when we reach Nebraska."

"Are these men insane?" Glory asked. "They're talking about a decision to be made hundreds of miles ahead of us? The army will never let them get that far!"

"They never thought we'd get this far, remember?" He sounded preoccupied and worried. No wonder. This getting past Dodge City without being seen and captured was an impossible task. But then, the Cheyenne had been doing the impossible ever since they had fled the Indian Territory and outwitted the soldiers these last few days.

However, weather and time were working against these brave people. Soon, snow would come swirling around the exhausted marchers and most of the horses were wearing out and there was always a shortage of food and weapons. Glory didn't intend to be around long enough to see the defeat and capture of these valiant people. Somehow, she was going to escape, but how?

Dodge City. There'd be lawmen, cowboys, and soldiers in town who'd help her if she could only give Two Arrows the slip and gallop to help. There'd also be a telegraph where she could wire David that she was free and unharmed. The thought of David didn't thrill her as it might have once.

Yes, this crossing near the town was going to be a big responsibility for Two Arrows. He might be distracted enough that she could slip away. By the time she was missed, she might be so close to Dodge City that the Indians would be unwilling to try to recapture her for fear of being seen.

Several hours passed, and then she saw the dim outline of buildings against the night sky, a few lights burning in the town. This might be her last chance to escape.

* * *

Two Arrows reined in and sent runners along the column when he saw the lights of Dodge City to the east. "Tell everyone to keep silent. We want no sound that might start dogs barking in that town that will wake a curious citizen. Tell mothers to keep their babies quiet if they have to put their hands over their mouths. Take anything that jingles off bridles or travoises."

Broken Blade sneered. "You are too cautious! I don't fear the whites."

"Then you are a fool," Two Arrows declared. "I was at Sand Creek and again at the Washita when Yellowhair attacked. I know better than you what the whites might do. No doubt, the local citizens of Dodge are already planning a display of our scalps in town like Colonel Chivington and his men did after Sand Creek."

Glory listened to the discussion, understanding only the hostility between the men. Broken Blade looked at her a long moment and smiled, telling her with his eyes what he would like to do to her. She snuggled closer to Two Arrows's broad back, knowing he would protect her.

Protect her? Was she out of her mind? In only a few minutes, she was going to try to outwit this scout and get away on his horse. If he caught her, there was no telling what he might do.

Broken Blade rode away, and the Indians moved forward through the night. Glory's heart began to beat faster, and she trembled, wondering if she had the nerve and the luck to hit Two Arrows across the back of the head, push the unconscious man from his horse, and take off at a gallop? Then she remembered she didn't have anything to hit him with. Since she had her arms around his waist, she might manage to get his big knife from his waistband, but somehow, she couldn't quite see herself stabbing him. She told herself it was because he would wrestle the knife away from her before she could use it anyway. No, she'd just have to think of another plan.

The three hundred rode as silent as ghosts, ever mindful of

the few lights to the east of them. Glory picked up the terrible tension in the air and held her breath, watching the silent, dark outline of the buildings as they rode closer. As outnumbered as they were, and with few weapons, the Cheyenne wanted to choose the time and place of their battles, and Dodge City wasn't it; not when the telegraph could bring hundreds more soldiers to the area in hours.

They were approaching the railroad, silver tracks gleaming in the moonlight. On this side of the tracks, Glory noticed several white hills shining in the darkness. "Snowy hills in the middle of Kansas?"

Two Arrows shook his head and his voice was grim. "Take a good look, Proud One, and know why my people fight!"

What was he so angry about? Glory stared at the white hills. "Why, they're made of—of—"

"Bones," his voice was bitter. "Now that they have slaughtered all the buffalo, the whites make a profit by gathering up the bones and shipping them back East for fertilizer. In the meantime, Indians starve for meat."

"Oh, my God!" She was horrified at the huge piles of bones looming on the horizon, thinking how many animals must have been slaughtered to make such white mountains.

"The buffalo were once like a great brown sea," Two Arrows said somberly. "Now they are gone. To destroy the buffalo is to destroy the tribes."

Somewhere in the distance, the Cheyenne's medicine wolf howled in a particularly haunting way, and the sound echoed and reechoed through the darkness. Two Arrows's big body went tense. "He warns us. Some danger—"

Abruptly, a sound pierced the still night, a long drawn-out whistle from the west.

"A train!" Glory said. "A train's coming into Dodge."

Two Arrows cursed under his breath as he turned in his saddle, waving to the people. "Get down! Hide yourselves! A train is coming!"

There was a murmur of terrified confusion and panic as hundreds of people dismounted. "The horses, Two Arrows, what about the horses?"

"Get the bone piles between you and the railroad! Get the horses to lie down if you can! Pass the word!"

A buzz ran through the column as the train whistled again, loud and long. Now they could see it chugging through the night from the west, its one bright yellow eye cutting through the darkness.

Around them, all was confusion as people scrambled to flatten themselves against the ground.

It was going to be difficult for several hundred people and horses to keep from being seen on this bright moonlit night if anyone looked out the train windows, Glory thought. There might be soldiers coming in on that train to Dodge. She might be rescued.

"Everyone get down!" Two Arrows yelled again and gestured.

Glory began to make her plans as the Indians rushed to lie flat, force the horses to the prairie. They were like frightened quail, she thought sympathetically, hiding against the ground, hoping the hunters passed on by. Two Arrows slid off the paint horse, yelling directions to the others. Glory peered around as the people flattened themselves into shadows. The dog soldier was everywhere, yelling orders. If he were spotted, he'd be easy to pick off with a good rifle. This was a brave man, Glory thought with admiration in spite of herself. He cared about his people.

In the meantime, Glory noticed, he seemed to have forgotten her completely. The train whistled again, long and lonesome, echoing across the prairie. In the distance, she could see its yellow eye growing larger and larger as it clattered along the steel rails.

Glory looked around. No one was paying the slightest bit of attention to her. She grabbed up the reins. When the train was abreast of her, she intended to whip up the horse to a gallop, ride alongside the train until someone in the crew saw her and yelled for the engineer to stop. She wouldn't tell the crew about the Cheyenne scattered about on the surrounding prairie, she would simply scramble aboard and ask the train to speed up before the startled Two Arrows could react.

The train whistled again, louder as it neared, the headlight lighting up the track before it. She could smell the smoke from its firebox, almost taste the cinders and ashes that blew on the wind. With her eyes, Glory measured the distance from here to the tracks. With any luck, she'd—

"Get down, Glory!" Before she could move, Two Arrows reached up, caught her hand, pulled her from the horse. Then he turned his attention to giving the signal for the well-trained horse to go to its knees.

What to do? Maybe she could flag the train. As it approached, engine chugging, throwing sparks from underneath, steam boiling from its smokestack, Glory hesitated, took one step forward even as Two Arrows reached up, caught her arm, yanked her to the ground. "Oh, no, you don't!"

"Damn you! Let me go!" She struggled to break away and run, he fought to keep her on the grass.

Low scudding clouds covered the moon suddenly, throwing long dark shadows from the bone piles across the prairie; shadows that hid the people cowering against the ground, hid the pair fighting and rolling as the train clattered past. Golden light streamed from its windows, rows of soldiers inside stared out at the night. She fought to escape Two Arrows, hoping to stand up, catch the attention of the train!

They rolled over and over, she fighting and scratching to scramble to her feet, he holding her down with the weight of his big body. As they fought, he ended up half on top of her and between her thighs.

Maybe she could shout and the soldiers would hear her! She opened her mouth and he put his lips over hers, his tongue deep in her throat. She pounded on his chest and bucked under him, but she could not dislodge him.

He kissed her the whole time the train was passing, his hand caressing her breasts, and, after a long moment, Glory forgot about the train, forgot about everything except the heat of this virile male lying between her thighs, the way his tongue teased her mouth. Her own pulse seemed to be pounding like a war drum in her head.

She could feel his hard manhood throbbing against her body as he held her down and caressed and kissed her. For the first time in her life, Glory knew what it was to ache with desire for a man. For too long, they had been holding back the fire, and now it blazed like flames across dry grass. *He's going to take me right here and now,* she thought in a hot haze. And she wasn't sure she could—or wanted to—stop him!

Thirteen

Despite her fighting, Glory couldn't get away from Two Arrows, and he overpowered her. The train was only a dot in the distant darkness, pulling into the Dodge City station when he raised up on his elbows, glaring down at her. His dark eyes shone both with fury and desire. "Glory, for what you just tried to do in alerting the soldiers, I ought to toss you to Broken Blade!"

She rolled out from under him, bruised and angry that she'd missed her chance. "Damn it, why don't you do just that!"

He hesitated, then whispered, *"Ne-mehotatse."*

"What?" She thought she'd heard that phrase before, but she couldn't remember what it meant.

He shrugged, stood up, and yanked her to her feet, while watching the train in the distant town.

"You could at least tell me what it means."

"It means you'd better not try that again. Let's get moving. I have a feeling all those soldiers unloading here may be meant for us." He whistled, and his horse got up, snorting.

Ne-mehotatse. Somehow, she didn't believe his translation. The tender tone he'd used was not the tone a man would use in barking an order. Her anger cooled. After all, he felt responsible for the safety of all these people, and her alerting the soldiers might have endangered them. She'd bide her time and hope she got another opportunity.

Two Arrows signaled the others. "Hurry!" he ordered. "We never know when another train might come. Some of you men get branches to wipe out our footprints near the tracks after we cross, so passing trains won't see them tomorrow."

"Everyone's tired," Glory protested. "You aren't going to make them ride all night?"

He swung up in his saddle, held out his hand to her. "We've still got a river to cross, and the scouts tell us it's at flood stage. We've got to put plenty of distance between us and the town full of soldiers before we rest."

If only the soldiers knew she was here! There was nothing she could do now but watch for another opportunity to escape. Still . . . she touched her lips absently, remembering the taste of his mouth, the muscular virility of his powerful body pinning hers down.

She let him pull her up on the horse behind him, rested her face against his broad muscular back. His big frame made quite a windbreak, and his body was warm as she fitted hers into the planes of his.

The column started out again, and she put her arms around his lean waist, remembering with trepidation her own sudden reaction to the feel of his big body lying on hers, the taste of his mouth, the caress of his hand on her breast. She had seen the hunger in his eyes and knew it could be used to her own advantage. Tonight, maybe she would get a chance to bargain with him. Perhaps she could trade her body for her freedom.

When she saw the Arkansas River running swift and deep, she knew they were in for trouble. "Two Arrows, you can't take these people across that; some of them will never make it."

He had dismounted, studying the water. "You think I don't know that?" He looked behind him toward Dodge City and then toward the east. "It isn't long until dawn. We've got to cross now, or we'll be trapped up against this river if those soldiers from the train see us and attack."

"I—I'm afraid; I can't swim."

"I didn't think you were afraid of anything," he answered wryly. "It's good to know in a few ways, you're like other women after all. Besides"—he lowered his voice—"you know I'm not going to let anything happen to you."

"Because I'm a valuable hostage?"

Annoyance clouded his handsome features in the moonlight. "Sure. What else?"

The leaders rode over to confer with him while the women and children waited. Their expressions were somber as they studied the swiftly flowing water, then looked back at the weary people waiting patiently for orders.

Two Arrows's high-boned face was a grim mask as he returned, reached to lift her down. Then he swung up into the saddle.

"Where are you going?" she demanded, suddenly apprehensive to have him ride away and leave her. She hadn't realized how much she'd come to depend on him the last few days.

He checked the lasso on his saddle, tossed the end to Tangle Hair, who began tying it off to a big rock. "I'm going to swim my horse across, attach the rope to that stump on the other side. That will give people something to hang on to as they cross, keep them from being swept away downstream."

"And what's to keep you from being swept downstream? Why doesn't Broken Blade do it?"

"Because he didn't volunteer," he snapped, his mind evidently already on the task at hand as he waded his horse out into the water.

"Two Arrows—"

He turned in his saddle and looked back at her. "Yes?"

"Be—be careful."

He looked surprised and smiled. "I will. Wait here, Proud One; I'll be back for you."

She nodded, surprised to realize she had complete confidence in his abilities. If anyone could get that rope across the swift current, Two Arrows could.

The paint waded out into the river, snorted, began to swim for the far bank at his rider's urging. The horse's head went under, and it came up thrashing the water into brown foam as Two Arrows clung to its neck, urging it on.

Glory heard a sharp intake of breath around her and looked up. All eyes were on the scout; all their hopes were pinned on him, she thought. If the Cheyenne were still on this side of the river after the sun rose, they would be captured; some of the ringleaders hanged. Of course she wanted that arrogant scout to pay the penalty. Then why did she find herself urging him on?

She saw Redbird holding her baby and old Moccasin Woman and her granddaughter close by. They all gave Glory an encouraging nod. She smiled, touched the little beaded bracelet for luck, and turned her attention back to the river.

For what seemed like an eternity, Two Arrows struggled against the fast-flowing water, then his horse touched bottom and scrambled up the bank to a sigh of relief from the waiting people. Glory realized then that she, too, had been holding her breath, concerned for his safety. That disconcerted her. She should be hoping he drowned, anything to delay the crossing until dawn, when someone from the town might spot her and come to her rescue.

He secured the line around the stump on the other side and signaled the warriors. They pulled the line taut on this shore and began guiding people into the water, one or two at a time, holding on to the rope to keep from being swept away. This could take a very long time, she thought, watching the east. Dawn would be breaking in an hour or so, and surely that many people couldn't cross so soon.

Fragile old Sitting Man, with a bundle of supplies tied to his back, was crossing now. The water pulled at the bundle, then it came loose and floated away downstream. There was a small cry from some of the others, knowing it contained food they couldn't afford to lose, but it could not be helped. The old warrior made it safely to the other side, Two Arrows reaching a strong hand out to help him.

Now Redbird crossed, her baby girl safely tied to her back.

Warriors began crossing, holding their few weapons over their heads to keep them dry.

Old Moccasin Woman and little Grasshopper started across, but halfway out into the churning water, the tired bay horse got into trouble and little Grasshopper was swept away. The grandmother cried out as the child bobbed in the water.

Promptly, Two Arrows dived in, came up swimming strongly, grabbing for the child.

Glory pushed her way through the people to the riverbank, determined to help; but he didn't need any help. He swam to the other side to place the little girl on the riverbank and helped the grandmother and the horse ashore. Glory heaved a sigh of relief and watched the others crossing. Finally, there were only the dog soldiers and Glory left.

Two Arrows motioned to her. "Come on, Proud One."

The water looked so deep and cold in the autumn night. "I—I don't swim well; I don't want to do this."

"White women," Broken Blade sneered, standing next to Two Arrows. "They are pretty but helpless; good only for a warrior's pleasure." He was speaking English for her benefit, she guessed.

"Proud One, I'll come after you." Two Arrows dived into the dark water, came up holding on to the line, struggled against the current to reach her on the other side. "You ready?"

No, she was terrified, but too proud to admit it. Her head came up, as proud as a spirited mustang filly. "I—I'm ready."

He led her into the water. It felt cold lapping around her legs. "Hang on to me, Glory."

She hesitated as she turned to him, knowing suddenly that she had complete confidence in him; that he wouldn't let anything happen to her. "Let's go."

She clung to him as he started across the river, molding herself against his lean, hard body. The water pulled them both under and they came up choking and coughing.

"Let her go and save yourself!" Broken Blade yelled, but Two Arrows never relaxed his grip.

Glory closed her eyes and hung on, feeling his hard muscles rippling under his buckskin shirt as he struggled. It seemed like an eternity before she felt his feet touch the river's bottom and he waded toward the bank, swinging her up into his arms. "Take it easy, Proud One, you're safe now."

He was still cradling her in his strong arms as he strode away from the river. "Are you all right?"

She realized then that she had her arms around his sinewy neck, her face resting against his hard, wet chest. "I'm all right."

He kissed her forehead in a quick, surprising gesture. "Good. Let's get out of here before it turns daylight."

The people were wet and weary, but Two Arrows insisted they put several miles behind them and the river before they stopped to rest in a little grove of trees. "Better not light any fires; the whites might see or smell the smoke, but try to dry your clothes somehow."

Glory let him lift her from the horse, sank gratefully to the ground out of the wind. Maybe she could wrap herself in a blanket, hang her doeskin dress over a bush, and let the wind dry it.

"Glory"—he knelt by her side—"the men are going on a quick hunt; someone spotted signs of buffalo. Maybe we can bring in some meat to replace what was lost. In the meantime, there's still a little smoked jerky to share around."

She caught his arm. "Thank you for saving me in the river."

He smiled. "Hey, you wouldn't have been in this whole mess if it hadn't been for me; I owed you that."

"Thanks anyway, and take care of yourself." She watched him nod and stride away, surprised to realize she meant it.

The hunters rode out, then she helped Moccasin Woman divide the jerky with some of the weary, hungry people as dawn broke, gray and chill. Glory paused as she thought a minute. "Moccasin Woman, what does *ne-mehotatse* mean?"

The other looked at her strangely. "It means 'I love you.' Why?"

I love you. She felt stunned, light-headed. Two Arrows had said that to her, never dreaming she would find out its meaning. "Nothing; I just wondered, that's all."

The people were spreading out to rest, getting out of the wind, trying to dry their wet clothes. Glory found herself an isolated place in a gully out of the wind, looked around. She was alone in this spot. After a moment's hesitation, she stripped off the wet outfit, hung it over a sand plum bush to dry, wrapped herself in a blanket, and settled down to nap in the autumn sun. She would think about Two Arrows and the words he'd spoken later, when she felt rested and clearheaded. After a few minutes, she dozed off.

Glory awakened with a start when a shadow loomed between her and the sun. She looked up, the blanket falling off one naked shoulder. Two Arrows stood looking down at her. "There was only one old buffalo, the women are cutting it up. Maybe later, we can build some small fires and roast the meat."

"That sounds good." She pulled the blanket up over her bare shoulder, too weary to move.

She saw him glance at the dress hanging on the bush. "Are you warm enough?"

She nodded. "I'm fine. You look tired and discouraged."

"You're getting to know me too well, Proud One." He sat down next to her, rested his elbows on his knees. "Getting all these people to the Dakotas is a heavy responsibility."

In spite of herself, she sympathized with the Cheyenne people and their plight. "You don't really think you'll get them there?"

He gazed at her a long moment. "Glory, I've got to try; they're counting on me. The problem is, Dull Knife and Little Wolf are disagreeing over our destination. I'm afraid they'll split the group."

"A smaller group would be easier to hide."

"Yes, but it divides the warriors, and we've too few as it is."

She laid her head on her knees. "I'm just so tired of being on the move all the time, watching people die, knowing some of them are going hungry or eating their horses."

He reached out and hesitantly put his arm around her shoulders. "I'm sorry I got you into this; I should have just tied you up and left you in the camp that first night."

"It has been a nightmare." Her shoulders shook as she tried not to cry.

"Here, here, Proud One, this isn't like you." He hugged her to him, and, without thinking, she put her face against his broad chest and let him hold her while he brushed a wisp of hair from her eyes. She turned her face up to him, tears running down her cheeks, and saw his love for her shining in his dark eyes. It was as if they both knew what was going to happen; what had been destined between them from the very first time they met. Very slowly, he bent his head and kissed her lips.

For a long moment, she paused, and then her arms went around his neck and she couldn't stop herself from kissing him in return. In answer, his arms pulled her so hard against him, she could scarcely breathe. His tongue touched the corners of her mouth, tasting and teasing as he embraced her, bending her to fit the hard curve of his body. They went down onto the prairie grass, his big manhood throbbing against her naked belly.

His breath came in gasps and he trembled as he pulled away, looked down into her eyes once more. "Glory?" He was asking, not taking.

"Yes! Oh, yes!" She kissed him with abandon, putting her tongue in his mouth and her hands inside his shirt, raking her nails across his powerful chest. The blanket fell away from her shoulders, revealing her nakedness.

With a low moan, he pulled it up over them both while he slipped his arm under her head and used his free hand to fondle and explore her breasts. She gasped and arched her back, pressing her nipples against his seeking hand as his thumb raked across them. "I've wanted you since I used to stand under the trees and watch you ride at night."

She pressed her naked body against him, feeling him throbbing against her as he kissed her again. "This is crazy," she gasped. But instead of pulling away, she pressed even harder, eager for his big callused hands to explore and tease her body.

They were touching and tasting and caressing in a frenzy of pent-up desire. She had never known passion before, and it surprised, even frightened her as she writhed in his arms and his mouth went to her breasts.

"Ahh!" She gasped and pulled his head down to her, wanting more; wanting him to suck her breasts harder as her hand went to grasp his manhood. It was rigid as steel, she thought, swollen with the seed he had to give as they writhed in a frenzy.

"I must have you!" he gasped against her ear. "I will have you!"

In answer, Glory rolled over on her back and spread her thighs, holding his face against her breasts while his fingers went down to explore her silken wetness. In a blaze of feeling she let her thighs fall wide apart while Two Arrows kissed down her belly.

Surely he wasn't going to kiss her there . . . and then he did.

Glory cried out at the unaccustomed flame that rose in her and clasped his face hard against her body while he explored and kissed there, his tongue thrusting deep. "You're wet," he whispered, "so wet; wet with desire for me!"

He came up on his knees, positioning her, and then he came down in a hard thrust that seemed to go deep into her very being at the same moment that his mouth covered hers again and she tasted her own essence on his lips. She had never known that mating could carry this frenzy, this heart-pounding emotion. He was riding her hard, his brown flesh slapping against her bare belly and thighs. She rode a crest of feeling she had not known existed, and she arched against him, meeting him thrust for thrust, her soul riding higher and higher as he plunged into her one more time, hesitated, trembled, and gave up his seed, gasping for air with the mighty effort.

At that moment, she wrapped her long legs around him, locking him to her as she reached her own pinnacle of pleasure, locking him to her so that he could not break away until he had given her what her body hungered for.

After a long moment, he collapsed on her, breathing hard. "Oh Glory, Glory, you're mine now; mine. No man could ever love you as much as I do!"

That was what David had said. David. His calm, dependable face came to her mind as her head cleared, and she lay there panting, a sheen of moisture on her skin from meshing with this virile warrior. Was she out of her mind; a civilized white woman lying naked on the grass, coupling with the Cheyenne brave who had kidnapped her? "Oh God, what have we done?"

"I knew you'd regret it." Two Arrows sighed, pulled away from her.

Did she regret it? No, and yet, this was a love that could never be. "Lieutenant Krueger—"

"To hell with Lieutenant Krueger!" Two Arrows flared. "I have so little respect for him, I won't ever salute him!"

He started to get up, but she reached out and caught his arm, not willing to give up the special intimacy they had just shared. "You don't understand."

He brushed her hand away. "I understand; he's rich and white. The ignorant savage was just a moment's entertainment!"

"No, it was so much more than that."

"Was it?" His voice was bitter as he turned and strode away.

She stared after him, confused and unhappy. She wasn't certain how she felt or even if her feelings really mattered. Sooner or later, most of these Indians would be captured or killed. Two Arrows would be punished for his part in this uprising; they would hang him or throw him in prison. No, he was too defiant to be taken alive; he would go down fighting. Once she would have looked forward to that; now she wished there was some way she could save him. It was inevitable. Two Arrows would be punished, the army would rescue her, and she would marry David Krueger. He need never know about this one Indian summer afternoon when a Cheyenne dog soldier had taught her passion such as she had not known existed.

She could hear the confusion as the people made leave to march again. With a sigh, Glory reached for her clothes. Whatever the army's action, she was still that warrior's prisoner, and the Cheyenne were on the move.

Fourteen

As September lengthened, the Cheyenne moved across Kansas, fighting two more engagements with the army, then fading from the scene like wisps of morning fog. Only their footprints, or the occasional remains of a worn-out horse, gave any clue that they had passed through.

On a cool morning, David and Corporal Muldoon, riding ahead of Major Lewis's column, which they had joined at Dodge City, found an abandoned campsite. They squatted by the scattered bones and stared at them. "Those Indians are starving," David said. "As much as the Cheyenne love horses, they're eating them now; that means they're desperate. Why don't they just give up?"

Corporal Muldoon rubbed his arthritic hands absently, stuffed them in the pockets of his fur overcoat, then looked back to the blue column approaching from the south. "Don't ask an Irishman that question, lad. Freedom's more important to men than food."

"You're right; damn them! They've got Glory, and they can't win, yet I can't help but admire their spirit." He stood up and fumbled in the pocket of his buffalo fur coat, found and lit his pipe, remembering everything that he loved about her. "Oh God, there's no telling what she's enduring."

"She's a valuable hostage, lad. They'll treat her well."

His old comrade was trying to comfort him, he knew, but it was useless. David had not known a moment's peace since she'd been kidnapped. "That damned Two Arrows. I'm going to kill him personally; nothing else will satisfy me."

"Aye, but you may not be here for that. Remember, General Sheridan has sent for you."

"I don't know what insight I can give him," David grumbled, as he prepared to mount Second Chance. "I don't really understand Two Arrows; except that he's arrogant and disrespectful. I can't predict what he'll do next."

Corporal Muldoon pulled the collar of his thick buffalo coat up around his red ears. "You know him better than any man."

David put his pipe between his teeth, staring toward the north, wondering where his love was and how she was faring? "I wish I'd never laid eyes on him," he answered bitterly. "And I intend to make him wish he'd never been born!"

General Sheridan was in a nasty mood, David thought as he came into the general's temporary office at the frontier fort, snapped to attention, saluted.

"At ease, Lieutenant—?"

"Krueger, sir."

"Krueger? Oh, yes, I remember your brother, William; fine soldier; too bad he was killed so early in the war; know your father, too." He combed his fingers through his beard thoughtfully, and David flinched, knowing the officer was thinking how shameful it was that a family of military men had spawned one who had been broken in rank. Sheridan turned back to the maps spread on his desk before him. "You know something about these Indians, Lieutenant?"

"Yes, sir." David walked over to the map, studied it. "Unfortunately, they've got one of my ex-scouts with them, so he knows army thinking, what move we might make next."

His frustration and fury must have shown in his face and voice because the general said, "I hear you have a personal stake in this, Lieutenant."

"There's a lady, Glory Halstead, who was kidnapped and taken along as a hostage."

"Hmm." The older man leaned on his desk with both hands, staring at the maps. "Judging from past history of white women captives, you know what's probably happened to her."

He didn't want to think about it. "She's spunky, sir. If anyone could survive an ordeal like this, Glory could."

"I didn't mean just survive, Lieutenant." The general hesitated. "You know what savages usually do to female captives."

David closed his eyes, swallowing hard, and when he finally managed to speak, his voice was little more than a whisper. "I love her. I want her back, nothing else matters, so I'm requesting a return to the field as soon as possible. I want to be there when she's found; I want to be there to deal with Two Arrows!"

"Easy, son." The other man's hard face softened, and he went over to a sideboard. "Here, have a drink, then look at these maps and tell me what you think. I've got to do something to get President Hayes off my back!"

David accepted the brandy gratefully. It was the best, bracing and smooth. "I thought Major Thornburgh was closing in on them?"

"Thornburgh!" Sheridan snorted as he sipped his drink. "Good fellow, excellent shot; we go bird hunting together. Unfortunately, all Tip's done on this assignment is get his command lost in Kansas. The wires tell me he's been wandering around out there for days without finding anything."

An aide stuck his head in the door. "Excuse me, sir, but I've got the latest papers. You said to let you know when they arrived."

The general set his drink on the desk as the aide brought in the newspapers. Sheridan took them, reading as he returned to the desk. "Damn it, I've got to end this Cheyenne thing; the papers are crucifying us!"

David wasn't sure whether he was expected to comment. He ran his hand through his light hair and waited as the older man spread the newspapers on the desk, scanning them.

Now the general's ruddy face turned redder still. "The press is laughing at the army; look at this one and this one!" He rapped his fingers across the papers. "They all want to know why a handful of ragged, starving savages are outwitting the finest army in the world!"

"Like I said, sir, the Cheyenne have one of our best scouts advising them."

Sheridan paced the office. "That shouldn't enable them to just disappear like ghosts! Last year, when the Nez Perce took flight, they had forests and mountains to hide in and still, the army caught them. These Cheyenne are moving across flat prairie that mostly wouldn't hide a quail."

"Yes sir, but the Nez Perce didn't have Two Arrows."

"You sound like you're beginning to admire the red devil, Lieutenant."

"Not likely; although he's done a superb job of leading his people and avoiding capture."

"Where the hell do you think they're headed?"

"Back up to the Dakotas where they're from."

"Impossible!" Sheridan snorted. "They can't walk fifteen hundred miles across flat plains without being intercepted. There's three railroads across their paths that can transport troops anywhere in a few hours. We've got telegraph wires galore to alert every fort and lawman at the drop of a hat. Walk fifteen hundred miles? For God's sake; they can't do this!"

"Begging your pardon, sir," David countered gently. "So far, they're doing a pretty good job of it."

Sheridan didn't seem to hear him. The officer was staring at the newspapers again. "Oh damn, here's the *Chicago Times* and listen to this quote about Major Thornburgh's fiasco: 'It wasn't that anyone expected Thornburgh to capture the Cheyenne, they're just happy the Cheyenne have not captured the major.' And here's one in the *New York Times* commenting on the jealousy between General Miles and General Gibbon and that the Indians have outgeneraled the generals. Damn newsmen to hell, and I hope they take the Cheyenne with them!"

David watched the officer pace up and down in a fury. "Those stubborn Indians are not going to ruin my career! The army will stop them, no matter how many men I have to put in the field." He paused and looked at David.

"Sir, I respectfully request an assignment back to the front. I want to be there for the kill."

"Yes, you're going back to the Plains, Lieutenant. I want someone who can identify this Two Arrows when we finally corral those Indians. If he's not killed in the fighting, we'll hang him. We can't allow the American public to sympathize with this so-called noble redman."

"My sentiments exactly, sir." He thought of his beloved Glory, wondered again if she were alive, and if that savage had raped and tortured her?

The general paused to light a cigar, stare at the map again. "Before the month's out, I want the hostage freed, this Cheyenne scout dead, and the other ringleaders in prison."

David smiled without mirth. "Believe me, General Sheridan, Two Arrows is going to die. I promise you that!"

It seemed to Glory as she rode behind Two Arrows that the Cheyenne had been on the trail forever instead of several weeks. Her expectation of being rescued had faded with each encounter with the army. Whether the soldiers were just being outwitted or outfought was something she hadn't decided.

"The bluecoats fight for money." Two Arrows shrugged. "We fight for our freedom and our very lives. It makes a difference."

He had been cool and distant to her ever since they made love in a frenzy of feeling, only to realize it could come to nothing. For herself, she had never experienced such an emotional high, yet she didn't encourage him, knowing it could come to nothing, and she was uncertain how she felt about him.

It was almost dark somewhere in northern Kansas when the Cheyenne found a small arroyo that offered some protection from the chill wind and possible sighting by the army or ranchers. Two Arrows conferred with the chiefs and they called a halt for the night.

He dismounted and held his hands up for her. She slid off the horse, too weary to speak and stood there a long moment, feeling his hands on her shoulders.

"Proud One, you're very quiet. What is it you are thinking?"

She wanted to lay her face against his broad chest, but she did not. "The skirmishes with the army, this constant riding; will it never end?"

"Maybe not," he admitted, stroking her hair, "but Dull Knife believes the whites will let us live in peace once we return to our own country."

"How can he be so naive?" She looked up at him.

"Man lives by hope, and that's all the Cheyenne have right now." He shrugged and began to unsaddle his horse.

"If you don't believe you can win, why do you go on with this fool's errand?"

"Because my people have confidence in me; they've given me another chance. I'm probably leading them to their deaths or a prison cell, but I can't look them in the face and tell them freedom is not a possibility, only a dream."

"The wind's getting cold," Glory said, wrapping her arms around herself.

"There's a good place over there under that little bluff that should be warm enough with a campfire." He turned his face toward the north. "Time is our enemy; winter may unleash heavy snows and bitter cold before we can make a permanent camp."

More people would die then, she thought. She avoided his eyes, knowing he watched her; seeing anger and hurt there. Worse yet, when she looked into his face, she remembered their frenzied, passionate coupling that day after they had crossed the river. She was not going to allow herself to care for this man; to do so would only add to the heartbreak and tragedy that waited at the end of this road. "I'll start a fire."

"Keep it small," he said. "I don't want the north wind to

carry the smell of smoke if there are soldiers anywhere south of us."

"We haven't seen a sign of soldiers for days."

"They're out there somewhere. Lieutenant Krueger is not going to give you up easily."

David. She felt guilty because he hadn't crossed her mind in days. "This rivalry and hatred between you two isn't about me," Glory said as she broke up twigs. "It's something between you two—a personal rivalry, about winning."

"That, too," he answered, checking his rifle.

"If it were just about me, the army would stop pursuing your people if you'd turn me loose."

He shook his head. "You're our insurance, Proud One. They won't risk a full-fledged attack as long as they fear hurting our prisoner."

Glory looked around at the bony horses, the thin, exhausted people. "Some of these can't go much farther."

"We will keep moving as long as a single one of us can stand on his feet." Two Arrows shrugged. "And pray that maybe the great god, *Heammawihio* will give his people another chance like he did me."

It was a doomed flight, they were all going to die, she thought, whether from army bullets, cold, or starvation. At least, she had a rabbit to cook. Two Arrows was an excellent shot with a bow. Bullets were now too precious to waste on something as small as a rabbit. Glory made a soup and shared it around as far as it would go with Moccasin Woman, little Grasshopper, and Redbird. Two old ones and a warrior who had been wounded in the last skirmish with the army had died yesterday.

At least, she had a good, snug camp up against this bluff out of the wind. "I saw you talking to the leaders earlier."

Two Arrows nodded, his face shadowed with concern. "I thought I saw soldiers in the distance this morning, but no one else did. Broken Blade convinced them that my eyes are playing tricks on me. Little Wolf and Dull Knife are disagreeing again. The group may split up and go two separate ways."

He hobbled his paint, and turned it out to graze in the buffalo grass along the shallow canyon. As darkness fell, he sat down before the fire watching her. "You look like a Cheyenne woman in that buckskin dress and braids. Be careful, Proud One. If the soldiers should see you, they might shoot you before they realized who you are."

"Soldiers don't shoot women."

His lip curled with derision. "Sure they do; I've ridden with them for years, remember?"

Glory didn't know how to answer that. "I don't intend to get killed; I'm a survivor; otherwise, I never would have ended up in Indian Territory." She reached for her blanket, wrapped it around her, and settled down by the fire.

Two Arrows stared into the flames. "I made a mistake, bringing you with me," he said in a voice so low, she had to strain to hear him.

She shrugged, playing with her beaded bracelet. "You needed a hostage, I guess, and I happened along."

"That's what I said; what I told my people, but I spoke with a forked tongue, even to myself. I kept seeing you riding at night, your head up like a wild mustang filly running into the wind, your hair loose and blowing. I wanted you as I have never wanted a woman, not even my wife, Pretty Flower."

"So that's why you tried to drag me off my horse?" She wrapped her arms around her knees, staring at him.

"I didn't try to drag you off your horse," he protested. "I caught the filly's bridle to keep her from rearing and throwing you."

"I'm sorry you got whipped, but I didn't go to David begging for help. I'm too proud to beg anyone for anything."

"It's a trait I like."

Glory shivered and scooted closer to the fire.

"You're cold; take my blanket." He held it out to her.

She shook her head. "Then you'll freeze." He was her captor, and yet, he had been tender and protective of her.

"I've put you through a lot of misery, Glory; I'm sorry."

She was touched by his words, by the tender expression on his face. "No more misery than the Cheyenne are enduring."

"But you're not one of us."

She didn't answer, looking into his eyes. For an hour one afternoon, she had felt like one of the people because for a brief time, she had truly been a dog soldier's woman. She would never forget the precious moments in his embrace. Without thinking, she reached out and put her hand on his muscular arm.

He put his other hand on top of her hand. "I've given this a lot of thought, Glory. The next time the soldiers are within sight, I'm going to give you a white flag so they won't shoot, send you away."

She blinked in surprise. "Mercy! After all these miles and all this time, you'd free me? Why?"

He didn't look at her. "You are much trouble. Besides, maybe then the lieutenant will go easier on me if he finally captures me."

"You lie! After all this, you'd send me back; what's the real reason?"

He looked at her a long moment, and she was not sure he would answer. "I took you because I lusted for you; I'll return you because I love you. I don't want anything to happen to you."

"I—I don't think I can go." She began to cry.

"Don't cry, Proud One." He seemed awkward in dealing with her tears. "The lieutenant will want you back; he need never know you've been in my arms. I wouldn't tell that if they tortured me."

"Don't you think I've considered how David would react if he knew? That's not the reason. I—I don't want to go. I don't want to leave you."

He shook his head and made a gesture of dismissal. "Don't do this to me, Proud One. You'll change your mind later, regret it, and that would tear me apart. Be realistic. With him, you'll have money, a life of ease as an officer's wife. You know what you can expect with me."

"Can I expect the kind of passion you gave me that one afternoon? *Ne-mehotatse,* my dearest," she whispered. *I love you.*

"If you only knew how much that day meant to me," he whispered, "but when the lieutenant comes—"

"I'll send him away." She went into Two Arrows's embrace, cutting off his protest with her lips. For a moment, he held himself rigid as if afraid to believe the choice she'd made.

Then he groaned as he took her in his arms, holding her tightly, returning her passion with his own, kissing her lips, her eyes, her throat. "If you're lying, I don't want to know it."

"Dearest, next time the soldiers catch up to us, I'll go out and tell them to stop chasing us; tell them I don't want to leave."

"You think the lieutenant would listen?" Two Arrows held her close, kissing her with wild abandon. "He would think you had lost your senses; he would take you away by force."

"Then from now on," she declared, "I am no longer Glory Halstead, I am Proud One, a Cheyenne Woman."

He kissed her deeply; passionately. "When I am finally killed by soldiers, it will been worth it to say the Proud One was my woman!" He pulled her down on the blankets by the fire and began to unlace her doeskin dress.

"Don't talk about being killed," she protested, taking his bronzed face between her two small hands. "But whatever happens, I want to be your woman."

He began to undress her, kissing her all the while. "Tonight, I'm really going to make you my woman," he whispered, "because we have all night to make love."

She slipped her arms around his neck, looking up at him as he brushed a lock of black hair back from her forehead. Then he kissed her deeply, stabbing his tongue deep into her mouth, teasing hers to caress the insides of his mouth.

She reached up to open his shirt, splaying her fingers across the sun dance scars on his powerful chest. In the glow of the small fire, she could see the high-boned planes of his dear face, feel the corded muscles of his virile body. She kissed his throat, working her way down until she raked her teeth across his nipple.

He groaned aloud and held her mouth against his chest while he reached to finish unlacing her dress. Then he rolled over on his back, pulling her on top of him. Her breasts spilled out of the open bodice like ripe fruit hanging down to be enjoyed by his greedy mouth. Glory arched her back, her hands on each side of his head, offering her breasts for his pleasure. She sighed heavily as his hands massaged and caressed them. "Kiss them," she demanded, "I want to feel the heat of your mouth on them."

He complied, sucking hard at her nipples while she closed her eyes, arching her back. He reached up and clasped her back, pulling her down against his face so that he could bite and tease her breasts.

"I'd like to kiss you all over, too," Glory breathed hard at the feel of his hot mouth on her.

"As the Proud One wishes." He stood up, stripped off his buckskins. He stood there in the firelight, scarred and powerful, virile as a magnificent stallion, his manhood big and hard as steel. Now he looked down at her with smoldering eyes. "Do what you will; tonight, I'm here to please you."

"And I'm going to please you!" She came up on her knees, embraced his naked, lean hips, kissing his manhood in a sign of submission. He was hot and hard and throbbing with the seed he had to give. As she explored him with her mouth, he gasped and tangled his fingers in her dark hair, holding her face against him, her naked breasts against his sinewy thighs. His manhood was pulsating with the seed he had to give, and she caressed it with her tongue as he pressed her down on him hard and she relaxed her throat and took it while he writhed against her mouth.

His seed was on her lips as he fell with her to the blankets by the fire. "Have you ever put your mouth on another man?"

"You know I haven't! I've only submitted without emotion to my brute of a husband."

"My Proud One," he whispered, and pulled her on top of him. "Pleasure yourself with me; ride me; ride your stallion."

Hesitantly, Glory lay on him, feeling his rigid maleness

against her belly. Then she spread her thighs and mounted him while he fondled and caressed her breasts.

Her velvet sheath slid down to envelop his sword, taking all of it and gasping that he was so big. He seemed to be spearing her deep inside. She splayed her fingers across his mighty chest, stroking his nipples while he writhed under her. He was here for her pleasure, she thought as she began to ride him slowly.

"You feel so good around my manhood, Proud One. I want to be deeper still." He reached up and put his hands on her small hips, grinding her down on his hard rod. Then she lay on him and kissed him, putting her tongue deep in his throat, while he twisted with need under her, and began to move her up and down on him with sheer strength. "Ride me, Proud One," he begged. "Ride your stallion!"

She felt him pulsating deep inside her and she had a terrible need to have his seed within her wet velvet depths. It was a need as old as womankind. She wanted him to breed her and pleasure her, leave her satisfied.

"Ride me, Proud One, ride me!" He was arching under her, his hands grinding her hips down on his dagger as she built a rhythm, harder and deeper, harder and deeper; the intensity and the emotion building at the slap-slap-slap of flesh slamming violently against flesh.

"Take it, Proud One, take all I've got!" And at that instant, he arched so that he gave her his full length even as she ground herself down on him and felt him shudder and begin to explode within her.

At that precise moment, her body began to convulse, squeezing his maleness, wanting every drop he had to give. When she could reach no higher crescendo of feeling, she cried out and pitched forward into his arms, her breasts flattened against his chest.

For a long moment, they clung together, gasping, their bodies locked onto each other's; his giving, hers demanding.

For what seemed an eternity, the only sound was the crackle of the campfire and both of them gasping for air.

Finally his hands reached up to embrace her and stroke back her tangle of hair while his lips brushed her eyelids. "Proud One, I never had anything like this, not even with Pretty Flower. God help me, I care for you more than my life, more than my people, more than anything on earth!"

"And I'd give up everything for you, my love." She lay spent and satisfied in his embrace, listening to his heart pound in her ear, feeling loved and protected.

He reached to pull the blankets over both of them, but they did not disengage their bodies.

She lay on him, warm and happy, staring into the fire. "I never knew it could be like this. My husband took me mechanically and brutally. If I objected, he hit me until I was senseless and then took me anyway."

She felt his body tense with anger. "Why did you marry the beast?"

She shrugged. "At that time, Howard was an older man of wealth. He offered to pay off the debts on Father's struggling little store in Virginia. Father insisted I marry him. I guess Howard always thought of me as something he had bought and paid for and could treat any way he wanted."

He rolled her into the hollow of his shoulder. "How could any man not love you?" Two Arrows whispered, and kissed her forehead with tenderness.

She didn't answer, lost in the bad memories. When Howard began to lose his fortune through bad business deals, his temper got worse. He beat her for the slightest infraction. "I was too proud to tell anyone that Howard beat me," she said, "and it wouldn't have done any good anyhow."

"My poor Proud One." He leaned over and brushed his lips across hers. "I wish I had this cowardly husband of yours here; I'd show him what a beating was."

"I don't need you to protect me; I've been looking after myself a very long time."

"I take care of what's mine"—his voice was soft but firm— "and now you belong to me."

She **didn't want** to admit it, but it felt good to snuggle down against that **powerful** chest and know he would look after her. "Father lost the store and came to the Territory to take over the sutler's trading post at the fort. He never forgot how I had humiliated him by filing for divorce. Men sometimes ask for a divorce, but not women."

"But if he mistreated you—"

"No one wanted to hear that. The sheriff said he didn't want to get involved in a domestic dispute; the preacher said I must not be obeying my husband like the Bible said, the ladies of the town gossiped about me and expected me to put up with it because men have always beaten wives if they needed it. Since I was too proud for my own good, I probably deserved it, they said."

He ran his fingers across her cheek in a gentle caress. "So you left that state?"

Glory nodded. "No one would give me a job, and Father needed free help at the sutler's store. I thought I'd get a fresh start, a second chance, but the scandal about the divorce followed me. I met David, and it didn't seem to make any difference to him, but I think it would to his father."

"You had no children?"

She shook her head, not wanting to remember that last terrible night before she had fled the house with the little bit of money she had saved from her household funds. Howard had wanted a son, but Glory hadn't produced one. She thought if she gave him a child, Howard would change and be a good husband. She went to a doctor in another town who said there was nothing wrong with her; it must be her husband. She didn't tell Howard, knowing it would throw him into a rage.

Then his brother Nat, a Kansas rancher, had come to visit. Glory shuddered at the thought.

"What's the matter, Proud One?"

"I—I was remembering that final night. My husband's brother was visiting, trying to talk Howard into joining him as a partner on his ranch, since Howard's business was failing. I—

I can't tell the rest; it's too awful; I never told anyone; not even my father." She choked back sobs.

He kissed the tears from her eyes. "No one will ever hurt you again."

She had to tell someone; she had kept it bottled up too long; and there had been no one to tell who would not have been shocked or pitied her. "They—they were both drinking, and Howard began to complain to his brother that I hadn't given him a son. That's when I blurted out that it was his fault, not mine. That enraged him."

He held her very close, saying nothing, waiting.

"His brother, Nat, said maybe he could get the job done. Howard laughed and said at least they'd be keeping it in the family." She was weeping now, weeping as she had never done in her whole life; not even in the worst days of her marriage. She had pushed these memories from her mind although sometimes late at night they returned as bad dreams.

"Oh my Proud One, don't tell it if it hurts that much." Two Arrows held her against him, kissing her gently.

"No, I need to tell you. They—they ripped my dress almost off while they were laughing and trying to hold me down so Nat could rape me. I grabbed a heavy brass candlestick and knocked both of them unconscious. Then I took the little bit of money I'd been saving for years from household funds and ran out into the night. I went to another town where he couldn't find me and filed for divorce."

"It's too bad you didn't hit them harder; if I'd been there, I would have killed them for you."

She buried her face against his chest. "I had a letter a few weeks ago from Howard saying he had lost everything, was leaving Virginia, and would I want to put the marriage back together?"

"What did you tell him?"

"I never answered it, but I've always feared he might come after me. My father would have let him take me."

"You're safe now, Proud One." He cuddled her close against

him. "No wonder you struck out when I grabbed your filly's bridle."

"I reacted without thinking, remembering Howard."

"I will never hurt you." He bent his head and kissed her.

"You won't make me go back?"

"The arrogant, uppity lieutenant will have to kill me to get you back."

She thought a moment, running the tips of her fingers over his high-cheekboned face. "Am I your revenge then?"

"No, you're my love; for whatever time I have left before the soldiers kill me. I'm going to make love to you all night, Proud One, and if the soldiers kill me tomorrow, or the next day, I'll count the moments I spent in your arms well worth the cost!"

He kissed her throat and she reached up, pulling him down on her as her passion began to burn again.

The fire turned into glowing ashes before they were finally sated and dropped off to sleep.

The dawn was only a pale lavender light on the eastern horizon when the pair was awakened by the camp crier galloping through the camp. "Ayee! Make ready! Make ready to fight! The soldiers are coming!"

Fifteen

David chewed his pipe stem in frustration as he looked toward the low hills and gullies barely visible in the coming dawn. Major Lewis's forces had cornered the escaping Cheyenne, and the only thing holding the army back from full attack was the possibility that Glory might be up in those rocks somewhere. He glanced over at Muldoon, hunched on his fat buckskin gelding and rubbing his swollen hands. "Your hands hurting you again?"

"Aye, gettin' where I can hardly hold a handful of cards and—"

"Muldoon, your gambling's going to be the death of you yet." He scolded, looking from the Irishman to the rolling land ahead of them.

"Nah, not the gamblin', but this blasted cold. Ah, even the fires of hell sound good on a chill day like today."

David's mind was busy with thoughts of Glory, the inevitable confrontation with Two Arrows. "You stubborn old coot, you ought to retire."

"And what would I live on?" He blew on his hands and rubbed his red ears. "I've naught kith nor kin, know nothin' but horses, and have nothin' put aside."

David didn't answer, watching the movement along the north Kansas ridge as the Indians seemed to realize the soldiers had moved into position during the night. Was Glory up there somewhere waiting to be rescued? She had to be; she just had to be.

White-haired Major Lewis cantered his bay horse over to the pair. They both saluted, and the major returned the gesture. "The men are in position to attack, Lieutenant. See if you can negotiate with the red devils since you know this scout so well."

David tapped the cold pipe against his saddle, scattering the tobacco, tucked his pipe in his pocket. "Yes sir, I'd like to try to talk them into giving up their hostage, surrendering."

"Pardon me for being so blunt, Lieutenant"—the older officer cleared his throat—"but the possibilities that the woman is still alive seem slim and none."

Glory. The thought of her seemed to make his soul ache. No man could ever love a woman as much as David loved her. "Beg your pardon, sir, but Glory Halstead is a survivor; I think she's alive and waiting up there in the rocks for me to save her."

The major's blue eyes reflected doubt. "Excuse me for mentioning such an indelicate subject, Lieutenant Krueger, but in most of these cases, the woman's been . . . outraged, so she might have already killed herself as any self-respecting woman would have done—"

"She would never kill herself," David snapped, and closed his mouth in a tight line to keep from shouting at his superior officer. *Outraged.* A polite euphemism for rape. David had a sudden vision of Glory spread out and held down while virile bucks took their turns on her beautiful, ripe body. He flinched, thinking it was all too easy to imagine Two Arrows's dark, virile body entwined with hers. He'd seen the way the Indian looked at Glory as if he had never wanted a woman as much as he wanted her.

"Lieutenant, are you all right?" David realized with a start that the major leaned forward on his horse, staring anxiously at him.

"I—I'm fine," he lied, "if I can just have a guidon and a white flag, sir, Muldoon and I will try to parley."

The major signaled for the yellow cavalry banner, and a private galloped forward with it and a white banner. "Lieutenant, you don't have to volunteer. They might shoot instead of sending out riders."

David shook his head. "No, Two Arrows has too much pride for that; he'd rather kill me in some honorable hand-to-hand combat."

"Honor? A savage?" The major threw back his head and laughed. "Surely you jest!"

"No, he wants the pleasure of looking me in the face when he kills me for the same reason he kidnapped Mrs. Halstead; I whipped him like a dog, and he hasn't forgotten it. On the other hand, if I get the chance, I'll put a bullet in his brain without a second thought."

"Now, Davie lad," Muldoon protested, "you don't mean that; you'd not even give him a fightin' chance?"

"None!" David's voice was as cold as his heart. He saw the senior officer's eyebrows go up, no doubt both at David's comment and Muldoon's familiarity. "We're old friends, served together since the Civil War," he explained.

"Still, highly irregular," the major grumbled, casting an icy stare at the red-faced Irishman. "All right, Lieutenant, if you want to give negotiating a try, go to it. Mind you, it's against my better judgment. With the newspapers and telegraph spewing all this ridicule about how the whole army is being outsmarted and outfought by a handful of ragtag savages, I'll not take a chance on them giving me the slip. If you can't get them to surrender, I intend to blast them all to hell about the time that sun peeks up over that far hill." Major Lewis nodded toward the horizon that was now pale lavender with just a hint of new gold and rose.

"Thank you, sir." David and Muldoon saluted, joined by the soldier carrying the two flags, and turned to canter out into the bare, half-frozen prairie, the cloth flapping in the cold morning air.

In the distant rocks, Glory stood by Two Arrows's side and watched the soldiers in the distance, wondering whose troops these were? "Look, there's a trio riding out."

Two Arrows frowned. "Want to parley, no doubt. Get down,

Proud One. The soldiers have no qualms about shooting women." He put his hand on her shoulder, pushed her gently down behind a boulder.

She tried to peek over the edge of the rock, but could see little. She had an uneasy feeling in the pit of her stomach, but she had to know. "You're not going to be the one they send out again?"

He nodded. "We're only buying time; there's no honest negotiating with the whites. They'll insist that we return to the reservation, and our people will die fighting first."

"They chase you because of me."

"No, they would chase us anyway." Two Arrows hesitated as he reached for his horse's reins. He turned his head and looked at her with an emotion in his dark eyes that warmed her to her very soul. "Proud One, I can no longer hold you against your will, I care too much for you. If you want to return to the whites, I will take you with me when I ride out under the white flag."

"No!" She caught his arm. "I don't want to leave you. Besides, no matter what they say, I fear once they have me, they will attack the Cheyenne without mercy."

He patted her hand absently, nodding toward Wild Hog, and Tangle Hair, leader of the dog soldiers, who waited a few yards away carrying dirty, ragged white banners. "I must go now, Proud One. You might want to rethink your choices. Look at who is in that truce party."

She peered up over the rock, staring at the trio of bluecoats cantering out into the middle of the prairie. One she didn't recognize; but the other two were David and old Muldoon. She felt no emotion, no rush of feeling. Instead, she tightened her grip on Two Arrows's arm. "If I rode out, met with them, and told them I was staying of my own free will, perhaps they would stop chasing us—"

"If you rode out there and said that," Two Arrows frowned, "they'd think you're temporarily insane, grab you, force you to go back with them. I'll ride out."

"No!" she protested again. "David is liable to shoot you on sight—"

"I don't think so." Two Arrows shook his head. "The lieutenant hates me, but he's an old-fashioned officer who plays by the rules. He would think it dishonorable to kill me as long as I ride under a flag of truce."

"You're beginning to sound like you admire David."

Two Arrows put his hands on her shoulders, looking down at her. "I can respect the lieutenant and still dislike him. Choose carefully, Proud One; this may be your very last chance!"

Their gazes locked for a long moment, and she knew in her heart that she had found the man destined for her, the man she loved more than life itself. She reached up and put her arms around his sinewy neck. "No, I want to stay with you, my love. Never again do I want to be Glory Halstead, the white woman. From now on, I am Proud One of the northern Cheyenne!"

"Ne-mehotatse," he murmured and pulled her close, kissed her. "I'll tell the lieutenant that his woman is now mine."

She reveled in the strong warmth of his embrace. "Come back to me soon, my warrior."

"Nothing can keep me from your arms," he whispered, "not after the love you gave me last night." He kissed her again, swung up on the paint stallion and galloped to join Tangle Hair and Wild Hog, riding out to meet the soldiers under the ragged scrap of white cloth.

When David realized who was riding toward him, he took a deep breath and laid his hand on his holster, then remembered he was unarmed. Truce parley or not, he intended to kill this scout.

The Indians rode up and reined in, Two Arrows holding up his hand in the age-old sign. *"Hou."*

David fought for self-control. "The proper sign from you is a salute."

The other's lip curled in disdain. "I salute only those I respect."

How he wished he had his pistol! However, besides the fact that it was dishonorable, to kill these envoys under a white flag would endanger Glory. The other two sat like stone, impassive and expressionless. Perhaps they spoke no English. "You—you still have the woman?"

Two Arrows nodded. Was that just a trace of triumph in his dark eyes? "I have her. She says she does not wish to return to the whites."

"You lie!" David shouted, losing control. "She would never say that! You're holding her against her will!"

The other's face darkened with anger. "One thing I do not do is speak with a forked tongue; I leave that to the whites."

Two Arrows looked cold sober, David thought, then remembered there was no place the scout could get liquor out here. "I have no proof except your word that she is all right. Bring your people in; the soldiers have plenty of food and supplies, whiskey for you."

Two Arrows spit in disdain. "I do not want the liquor, and my people are not willing to trade freedom for food."

Muldoon cleared his throat. "Two Arrows, you and me was always on good terms."

The other nodded, and his expression warmed. "Your heart understands the Cheyenne, Muldoon."

"Aye, your people and the Irish have both been mistreated; we both know what it is to hunger for freedom. Still and all, you know how the lieutenant cares about the lady. Can you not find it in your heart to return her?"

"I would if she would come," the warrior said gravely, "but she will not."

It was all David could do to keep from throwing himself at the arrogant brave, grabbing him by the throat, choking the life from his lying lips. He glanced up at the white flag flapping in the cold wind over his head. He was bound by honor. "You offer no proof that she's alive, that she's well cared for?"

"She's all right," Two Arrows said firmly. "Believe me. I have protected and cared for her myself."

"What does that mean?" David said, suddenly upset by the expression in the other's eyes.

Two Arrows shrugged. "Exactly what I said. I will not trade her for food or even weapons and ammunition. For her sake, will you stop pursuing my people?"

"You know I have no authority to agree to that!" David snapped.

He saw a new, grudging respect in Two Arrows's dark eyes. "You could promise with no intentions of keeping it as other white men have always done. Yet you do not. Why not, Krueger? After all, no one expects you to keep your word to a savage."

"I am an officer in the United States Cavalry," David said through clenched teeth, "and I am honor-bound, even though I have vowed to kill you, and make no mistake, I have made that vow." David glared at him, imagining Two Arrows groveling on the ground, begging for his life, while David coldly put his pistol barrel against the black hair and pulled the trigger.

In that long moment, the big chestnut stallion stamped its hooves and the banners snapped in the wind overhead. In the distance, the first orange edge of the sun peeked over the horizon; blurring in the early-morning fog. David shifted uneasily in his saddle, more than a little aware of the mounted soldiers behind him and the armed warriors up in the rocks ahead. "Let Glory ride out here and tell me herself she doesn't want to return to the whites."

"The Proud One offered to do that," Two Arrows said, "but I told her the whites had no scruples, they'd grab her and force her to return to the fort."

The Proud One, David thought; what a perfect description for Glory. Even if the Indian was mistreating her, she wouldn't beg; she'd never begged anyone for anything in her whole life. It wasn't in Glory to bend to anyone for any reason.

David took a deep shuddering breath. "Is this your final word then, you will not return the woman or let us speak with her?"

"I told you it was her choice."

"I will not believe that unless I hear it from her own lips," David snarled. "You leave me no alternative but to report to my major; he will order an attack; many will die!"

Two Arrows shrugged. "We all die sooner or later. It is only important how we die and what we are willing to die for. Freedom and the love of a woman are worth fighting for." Two Arrows turned and looked over his shoulder at the rising sun that bathed the frosted landscape and the drifting fog with a pale orange glow. "It is perhaps a good day to die."

"Listen to me!" David shouted. "Do you people not understand you cannot walk all the way to the Dakotas?"

Two Arrows smiled ever so slightly. "We seem to have no other choice except to starve in the Indian Territory."

"Be reasonable"—David looked around at the three warriors, knowing the other two probably did not understand a word of English—"frost already coats the ground every morning; soon the snow will be too deep, and you will all freeze to death. I don't want that to happen to Mrs. Halstead."

"I don't want it to happen to her, either," Two Arrows said softly, "but time is our enemy, and the soldiers waste our time."

"Damn you, Two Arrows, you know I can't just let your people ride out! We'll have to try to stop you!"

"Then it is a good day to die," he said gravely, nodding to the other two silent warriors with him. They wheeled their horses and cantered back toward the rocks. It almost seemed to David that the arrogant Cheyenne was deliberately offering him the target of his broad back.

David gritted his teeth so hard, his jaw hurt. "That arrogant son of a bitch! I ought to—"

"Aye, but you won't," Muldoon said softly. "Well, lad, I ken there's naught to do now but report to the major. I was hopin' in my heart of hearts we'd find a way out of this."

"Don't tell me you're going soft on me, Muldoon."

"No, but I'm like the rest of the men, lad. We hate the killin' of women and small ones, and see no harm in lettin' them go home."

"Damn, Muldoon, you're an Indian lover sure enough. Well, let's report." With a heavy heart and a sense of dread, David wheeled Second Chance and galloped back to his own lines, followed by the other two. Glory. Oh God, Two Arrows still had her, and Major Lewis would insist on launching a full assault! David loved her more than life itself, and he was going to have to fire on her.

With a sense of relief, Glory watched Two Arrows returning. To judge from his set features, the news hadn't been good, but then nobody had expected the army would let the Cheyenne ride out in peace. She had recognized David out there. Almost, she had been tempted to call to him, tell him she didn't want to return to her own people, that she was where she wanted to be, with Two Arrows and his people.

Behind her, she heard a soft chuckle, glanced back. Broken Blade stood just behind her, and he was bringing his rifle to his shoulder. "We're going to fight the whites anyway, pretty white girl, I might as well begin the battle now!"

Only then did she realize he was aiming for Two Arrows. "No!" She screamed out and grabbed up a rock, running at him even as he pulled the trigger.

Her shout seemed to startle Broken Blade as he fired. She glanced back just in time to see Two Arrows react; whether in surprise, or because he'd been hit, she couldn't be sure. Firing broke out from both sides; each side obviously thinking the other had begun the fight. She ran at Broken Blade, her heart full of murder. "Trying to kill your own warriors! I'll—"

"You'll do nothing, white girl!" Broken Blade caught her, twisting the stone from her hand as he dragged her into the rocks. "The two of us will escape while the cavalry and my people fight it out!"

Glory raked her nails across his ugly face as they struggled.

"Two Arrows will stop you! Wait 'til Dull Knife finds out you're a traitor!"

"Everyone else is too busy fighting!" He clapped his hand over her mouth, his other pawing her body as they struggled.

Glory fought with all her strength, but Broken Blade dragged her toward two horses tied in the shadows and the fog. Around her, confusion reigned, while shots and shrieks echoed through the coming dawn.

Two Arrows felt the bullet rip through his shirt and automatically shied, swearing under his breath as he fell from his horse, rolling behind a boulder.

That white coward! He would have sworn David Krueger was too honorable to shoot him from behind. However, the lieutenant was looking back, his expression as shocked as Two Arrows felt. Did he think Two Arrows had fired at him? Yet if the soldiers hadn't fired prematurely, who had?

All hell had broken loose after that first shot shattered the dawn; both sides firing wildly. Two Arrows hunched behind the rock, assessing the situation. He was pinned down here for the time being. His first thoughts were for Glory's safety, but he'd left her up in the rocks; maybe she'd be safe enough until warriors diverted the bluecoats' bullets so that Two Arrows could escape. Until then, he was powerless to move.

David galloped back into his own lines, swearing mightily. "Damn it, who fired that shot? I'll see that man court-martialed! Who fired on a flag of truce?"

Muldoon galloped up to him, shouting, "It came from the other side, lad! I'd swear it wasn't aimed at you but at the scout!"

"Impossible!" David answered over the thundering rifle fire, his fine chestnut stallion snorting and stamping its hooves. "The Cheyenne wouldn't shoot at their own!"

Quickly, David looked around in the gray dawn, assessed the situation. Major Lewis was down, the soldiers firing in confusion. In the distance, the Cheyenne seemed to be pulling back into the foggy gray light of dawn. By the time full daylight came, they would have faded into the distance if someone didn't stop them. He had to stop them and save Glory.

David hesitated, trying to make a plan. David didn't see Two Arrows anywhere, but he had seen him fall when that first shot rang out. Maybe the big scout was dead.

David held his stallion in, looking over the Cheyenne lines with an experienced eye. There was a weak place in the Cheyenne defense to the left. Maybe, just maybe, he could get behind the warriors. If Glory was in that camp somewhere, this might be his only chance to take them by surprise and save her. He spurred the great stallion to one side, giving Second Chance his head as he galloped along a low string of bushes. Behind him, he heard Muldoon cry out in protest at his foolhardy action, but David paid him no heed, thinking of nothing but Glory's safety. Several times in the past, Indians had killed captives when the army tried to recapture them.

Hunching low over his stallion's saddle, David swung wide and galloped to one side of the Cheyenne lines. Maybe because it was a foggy dawn, no one seemed to notice him. Good! He'd get behind the Cheyenne, and—

What was that in the distance? A Cheyenne warrior struggling with an Indian girl. Puzzled, David slowed. Why would the brave be trying to drag the girl away and why would she be fighting him? Once she broke away and the warrior brought his knife up as if he intended to kill her. David brought his rifle up and fired instinctively. The warrior whirled, firing just as David fired. David saw the sudden spurt of blood, and the warrior crumpled even as David felt the bullet tear into his own shoulder. Almost in a daze, he watched the Indian girl running away from the dead warrior. David brought the rifle up again, hesitated. As much as he had reason to hate the Cheyenne, he couldn't kill a woman. He swayed in his saddle, fighting the pain as the rifle fell from his numb fingers. If he didn't make it back to his own lines, the Cheyenne might torture him if they captured him alive.

"Take me—take me back, boy," he whispered to his horse, and struggled to rein the horse around. Second Chance was the best and fastest horse on the plains, David thought, reeling in the saddle. His shoulder seemed to be on fire and he could feel warm blood running down his arm. Around him, shots echoed and reechoed; horses whinnied, and men screamed and died. He wasn't going to make it; he was losing consciousness.

It seemed almost from a long way away that he heard that rough Irish voice shouting encouragement. "Hang on, lad, I'm coming!"

Muldoon. Good old Muldoon. In a daze, David hung on to the saddle. He had never been in such pain and his blue uniform seemed wet with blood. Gritting his teeth, he forced himself to stay conscious and keep moving back through the line of fire. Then that ruddy Irish face was close to his as the other grabbed David's reins. "Hold on, lad!"

"No, got to go back . . ." he protested, "Glory! Got to save Glory!" He swayed in the saddle as Muldoon led the chestnut stallion back toward the soldiers.

The next thing he remembered was the ground coming up to meet him and Muldoon by his side, lifting him. "You'll be all right, Davie lad. Major Lewis is hit, too."

David opened his eyes. Around him, shots still rang out and men screamed. "Muldoon, she—she must be there somewhere."

"Did you see anything of her?" The old Irishman bent over him, stifling the flow of blood.

He was slipping into unconsciousness, but he shook his head. "Killed a warrior, only saw an Indian girl. . . ." He wanted to say more, but he couldn't keep his eyes open.

"Take it easy, lad," Muldoon whispered. "Cheyenne are riding out, but we've too many men hurt to follow!"

Glory. Two Arrows still had her, and David hadn't rescued her. "Got to save her," he whispered, "got to—"

"You and Major Lewis are both in a bad way, lad." Muldoon held a canteen to his lips. "You aren't goin' anywhere except to the nearest fort hospital!"

The next several days were a blur to David as he floated in and out of consciousness. When he awakened in an iron bed in a sparse room, a plump, frowning man leaned over him. "Good to see you coming around. We thought we'd lost you like we did poor Major Lewis."

"Where—where am I?"

"Fort Dodge infirmary. I'm Dr. Bell," the other said. "You're lucky to be alive."

David moved, then moaned aloud.

"Be careful of that shoulder, young man."

David remembered the fight with the Cheyenne then. "Major Lewis didn't make it?"

The doctor shook his head.

"How—how long have I—?"

"Almost a week, Lieutenant."

Glory. What had happened to her in that week? He wanted to ask about her, but he couldn't seem to speak. David licked his cracked lips, and the doctor bent, held a cup to his mouth. David drank gratefully. The water tasted cold and good. He stared at the window and saw the frost there. "Corporal Muldoon?"

"He's here and worried as an old mother hen about you." The other grinned. "I understand you two are both up for promotions and medals for your bravery against the Cheyenne."

Glory. "I—I have to get back," David muttered, and tried to sit up which sent a spasm of agony through his body that made him cry out.

The doctor grabbed him. "Sorry, Lieutenant, you're not going anywhere for a few more days. Maybe by then, you'll be in shape to travel."

David sighed with relief. "Good, maybe we can still catch the Cheyenne and—"

"No." The doctor scratched his bald head. "I meant home. You're a lucky young man, son, you're getting holiday leave so that shoulder can heal. We've already notified Colonel Krueger to be expecting you."

David tried to get up, but he was too weak to move. "You don't understand. I—I've got to get back. Glory; the Cheyenne have her."

"Easy, son," the surgeon soothed him. "Would you like to see your corporal?"

David nodded. "He's—he's here?"

The doctor was already walking toward the door. "Hey, Corporal, he's finally awake and asking for you."

"By the Holy Mother, it's about time, I'd say!" Muldoon came bursting through the door, leaning over the bed. "Hey, Davie lad, I was worried you wasn't going to make it. In fact, I was takin' bets—"

"I thought you swore off gambling." David grinned, glad to see the older man.

"Ah, I still can't pass up a sure thing." The Irishman rubbed his hands together and grinned. "It's colder than hell here, lad, I wish we was down south."

"Thanks, Muldoon"—he reached out and took the other's big, rough hand—"thanks for coming after me."

The other blinked rapidly. "Got something in me damned eye; makes a man tear up." He cleared his throat and looked embarrassed. "We're heroes, did you hear? We're goin' get our rank back, and medals besides."

Only one thing mattered to David. "Glory?" he whispered. "When the Cheyenne pulled out, did you find any trace of Glory?"

The other hesitated, shook his head. "The Cheyenne have disappeared like ghosts again; nobody knows where they are."

"We—we've got to look for Glory," David insisted.

There was something tragic in the other's eyes. "Me, I'm

bein' sent to Fort Robinson up in northern Nebraska, wouldn't you know? And me with my rheumatiz hatin' the cold and all?"

The plump, bald doctor had moved to stand by the bed, listening.

"Where am I being assigned? I've got to find—"

"Davie, don't you understand?" The old Irishman spoke gently. "You've been bad hurt; nearly died. You'll be lucky to be back on duty by January. They're sending you home for the holidays to mend."

"I don't want to go home," David insisted stubbornly. "I can't stop looking for her as long as there's any hope."

Muldoon sighed. "Then, lad, there's something you should know."

The doctor shook his head, "I think that information can wait, as weak as this man is."

David saw the looks that passed between the other two men. He reached out and caught Muldoon's hand. "What is it?"

"The Doc's right," the corporal said, and smiled a little too cheerily. "We'll talk later."

"Now, Muldoon, now. Oh, please, if you know something!"

Muldoon looked desperately up at the doctor, back to David. "Aw, lad, you're puttin' me in a bad spot."

He knew then, knew from the looks that had passed between the other two. "It's bad news, isn't it? You—you know something? She was killed in that last attack?"

The doctor sighed. "You might as well tell him, Corporal; I have a feeling he won't settle down and rest until he knows."

Muldoon swallowed hard and reached in his coat for a small bundle. "Lieutenant, a rancher found something floating in a creek down in Indian Territory, no telling how long it's been there or where it came from; could have washed for many miles."

He was afraid to ask. Briefly, David closed his eyes, waiting. "I—I can take it."

"Mother of God, forgive me," Muldoon muttered and opened the bundle ever so slowly. Tears trickled down his weathered, ruddy face. "The rancher heard about the missing captive and brought this in."

Very slowly, Muldoon held up a torn, stained rag. David stared at it. It was difficult to know what it might have been, but he recognized the dark stain as blood.

David reached out and took it between numb fingers. In his mind, it was that night he had been invited for dinner. Afterward, Glory leaned on the piano while David sang to her. He would always remember her lovely profile silhouetted against the glow of lamplight as she played with a beaded bracelet an Indian child had given her. *In the gloaming, oh, my darling, when the lights are dim and low, when the flickering shadows falling, softly come and softly go. . . .*

"Where—where did you get this?" David whispered, not wanting to believe what this damning evidence must mean.

"Floating in a creek."

Glory was dead, David thought in dazed confusion; she had been dead for weeks. That villainous Two Arrows had tricked David into believing she was still alive so the army wouldn't attack full force, and all the time, she had been lying dead back in Indian Territory. No doubt they had murdered her only a few days after they abducted her.

"I'm going to kill him for this!" David vowed. "I'm going to kill Two Arrows very slowly and painfully!"

He tried to get up and fell back onto the bed, too weak and ill to move, the blue rag clenched in his hand as he drifted off into unconsciousness. The last thing he remembered was Glory's beautiful face on the night he had sung to her and how lovely she had looked in that blue calico dress.

Sixteen

Glory was relieved when Two Arrows crawled back through the rocks to her amid the thunder of gunfire. "Thank God you're alive! I was afraid Broken Blade—"

"That sorry—! Are you all right?" He pulled her against him protectively.

She nodded. "He—he's dead." Glory buried her face against Two Arrows's powerful chest. "Broken Blade tried to kidnap me when a soldier shot him; it might have been David. The soldier had a chance to kill me, too, but he hesitated."

Two Arrows brushed a lock of hair from her forehead. "He's more honorable than I gave him credit for," he murmured, grudging respect in his voice. "I saw him take a slug, and Muldoon risking his life to rescue him."

"Oh dear God!" Glory winced. "I hope he's not hurt badly. I don't love him, but I don't want anyone killed."

The din of battle swept over them. Two Arrows turned to survey the fight. "I don't know if he's dead; maybe not. There's confusion on their side; I think their commander's been hit. That gives us a chance to clear out." He threw back his head and howled softly, a signal that could be heard in spite of the thunder of guns. It echoed across the lonely northern Kansas plains; that song of freedom, the call of the wolf and the Cheyenne. Immediately, another warrior picked up the signal and passed it on. Within minutes, the Indians were melting into the fog, slipping away, one or two at a time until the confused and disorganized soldiers were firing at shadows, not even realizing the Cheyenne had disappeared, heading north again.

For the next few days, no one interfered with the Cheyenne as they moved near the Kansas-Nebraska border. Now and then, an old one or a child died, but the stoic Indians hardly paused for a quick ceremony. Nothing must stop the northward march because winter was coming hard now. Most mornings, when the people took the trail, the frost crunched under their moccasins. There was never enough food, and horses were worn out from the relentless pace. When a horse fell, the Cheyenne built small fires and gobbled the half-raw meat.

Two Arrows saw to it that Glory and her little group of friends was fed. She dare not ask where the supplies came from because she knew the warriors were fanning out as the group moved, taking what they needed from any ranch they crossed and killing anyone who tried to stop them.

Although she was sometimes hungry and cold, Glory was satisfied to be alive and relishing the free life that was Cheyenne; riding with her warrior, and spending her nights asleep in his strong arms. They had not been attacked by soldiers again, but Glory knew it was only a matter of time before the army picked up their trail and tried to head them off. She learned to live for the moment, not expecting that they would make it to the Dakotas, but the dream and the love her man gave her made it all worthwhile.

There were days that Glory was so exhausted, she could hardly move, but she kept going, determined that she wouldn't hold her adopted people back. And on those nights when Two Arrows took her in his arms and made love to her in their blankets out under the stars, nothing else seemed to matter.

"Proud One, I have done wrong by you," he whispered against her hair.

She felt a sudden alarm. "You've decided you don't love me?"

They lay naked, wrapped together in his blanket. "You know better than that." He kissed her face tenderly. "But I've let you in for hardship when the lieutenant could have offered you so much more."

"Not more love." She slipped her arms around his neck and held him close, feeling his great brave heart beating against her breast. "I am glad I made this choice, and I would follow you anywhere, my love, anywhere, no matter the danger."

"Ne-mehotatse," he murmured against her hair and began to stroke her naked body.

She arched herself against his seeking hand, reveling in his touch and the heat of him. "Maybe the soldiers have given up and won't chase us anymore."

"You know better than that," he murmured. "We've made fools of the government, and so they'll stop at nothing to catch us. But until they do, we have all these nights together."

"And I wouldn't trade whatever time we have left for all the luxury as a respectable white wife." She pressed bare flesh against bare flesh as he kissed her and made love to her for the long, chill night while the big lobo wolf sang from his hilltop. "It is a good sign, Proud One, that he is still with us." His hand stroked her breast.

She arched herself against his touch, her pulse pounding faster as he molded her against him. "Surely some of us will make it."

Even in the moonlight, she could see the wistfulness in his dark eyes. "If I could hope for anything, it is that the army would let us go in peace and that next year, you would give me a fine, strong son."

She held him close, thinking of the children he had lost on the Washita so many years ago. "Oh, my dear one, I hope so, too. You and the others have suffered enough at the hands of whites. It doesn't seem too much to ask for; there are so few of us, and we want so little out of life."

He began to kiss her breasts. "No man could ever love a woman as much as I love you."

David had said those very words to her, she remembered. She thought of David then, a little sadly, and wished him well, but she was in the arms of the man she loved. She never wanted to be any place else but in Two Arrows's embrace. For him, she had turned her back on David's money and social position, but she didn't regret it.

"Tomorrow," Two Arrows murmured, "tomorrow, we'll be near Sappa Creek."

Sappa Creek? What was the significance of that? She started to ask, but when she opened her mouth, he put his tongue inside, caressing her mouth even as his hands caressed her body. At his touch, she forgot about everything else except the way he held her and made love to her. Then Two Arrows placed himself inside her body and began the slow rhythm of passion. Now she had no time to think anymore, only to feel his hard, throbbing maleness inside her, his hot mouth dominating hers, the warmth of his powerful body protecting hers as he mated with her.

Glory arched against him, excitement building, and loving him as she had never loved anyone else. When he poured his seed into her and she went into spasms of pleasure, clasping his maleness with her own body, she was doubly certain she had made the right choice. She did not know if they or any of the Cheyenne would survive this relentless trek, but these glorious moments in this warrior's arms made her choice worthwhile.

She caught the excitement the moment her eyes opened before a cold, brisk dawn. "What is it?"

Two Arrows was painting his face red and blue and yellow, putting on a magnificent feather bonnet. "I told you last night; the Cheyenne attack Sappa Creek today; we have waited a long time for this revenge, more than three years as the white man counts."

She looked around and saw the other warriors polishing their weapons, painting their faces. "This is crazy, we must keep moving north. This delays us."

"We owe it to them." Two Arrows brushed her hand away and reached for his war shield made of tough buffalo hide and painted with magic symbols. "In the spring of '75, the soldiers attacked our camp on the creek and slaughtered our women and children without mercy. Then they threw our wounded into the fires they built to burn our tipis and supplies."

Glory put her hand to her mouth, almost sick at the thought. "But this will alert soldiers," she protested. "They'll be after us again."

Two Arrows frowned. "I knew you were too soft to be a warrior's woman. I should have returned you to the lieutenant."

"It's only that I love you," she said. "I'm afraid for you."

"The warriors have not forgotten they promised vengeance," Two Arrows answered. "A hundred years from now, the white settlers will remember that the Cheyenne returned and evened the score for Sappa Creek." He turned and raised his bow, shouting out to the others.

As Glory watched, he swung up on his paint horse, so resplendent in war paint and carrying his bow and rifle, his fine war shield hanging from his saddle. The war party rode out at a gallop, shouting their war chants. Only after they disappeared into the cold dawn did she remember that Howard's brother, Nat, lived near Sappa Creek. She gritted her teeth, remembering. Maybe she should welcome revenge, too. Nat deserved whatever he got for what he had attempted to do to her.

Howard Halstead stood by his brother, smiling as he watched the glowing flames consuming the homesteader's cabin. "You find anything else to steal?"

Nat laughed and held up a small bag. "A little gold, that's all. This was a great idea, brother, paintin' ourselves up like Injuns, killin' and robbin'. Those damned Cheyenne who are on the loose will get the blame for it."

Howard wiped at the war paint on his face. "And in the meantime, we've hit a dozen ranches and homesteads this past week, gathering up gold and horses. The women weren't bad, either."

"You finish with the woman inside?"

Howard nodded and held up a blond scalp. "She had nice tits on her; too bad we couldn't keep her."

Nat sighed. "She was a pure pleasure for a man to lie on, wasn't she? 'Course we couldn't leave her alive to tell on us. Never mind, brother, there'll be more homesteaders' wives and daughters. We can expect to play hell for another month and let the Injuns take the blame."

"You take care of the man?"

Nat looked over his shoulder toward the barn and held up a scalp. "Sure did. Another poor homesteader killed by those damned Cheyenne!" He laughed as he tucked the scalp in his belt.

"Well, then, let's round up the horses and clear out before anyone sees the smoke from this burning cabin and comes to investigate."

"Right!" Nat wiped his bloody knife on his pants and stuck it in his belt. "You'll be rich again, brother, and the Injuns will get the blame."

"Then I'm going down to Indian Territory and get my woman back," Howard grumbled. "Glory was a real challenge; I always thought if I beat her enough, I could break her; she was too damned proud. She might not be proud anymore; I heard her pa died, and she's strugglin' to make a livin.' "

"She won't want to come with you." Nat kicked through the rubble for anything else worth stealing.

"Aw." Howard made a gesture of dismissal. "Nobody's gonna stop a man from taking his own wife with him so he can talk some sense into her." He pulled the small oval, daguerreotype from his pocket. "See, I still carry the uppity little bitch's picture."

"She was uppity all right," Nat agreed. "Imagine her squawking just because we wanted her to take us both on; after all, we're brothers."

They started toward their horses.

"Damned bitch," Howard complained, "humiliated me to death with that divorce. When I get her back, I'll make her wish she hadn't of done that."

They strode through the burning rubble, kicking things out of the way, the bloody scalps hanging from their belts.

"And then we'll share her?" Nat asked.

"Hell, why not?" Howard laughed. "If I can't breed her, maybe you can and we'd keep the whelp in the family."

"You are a good brother!" Nat laughed, too, as they swung up on their horses. "Hey, Howard, I know of a fine farm a couple of miles north of my place we could hit tomorrow or the next day. Farmer's got two pretty young daughters, one for each of us."

"But after that," Howard said, "we're going down to Indian Territory and get Glory; after all, I think if she sleeps with me, that makes the divorce null and void."

"You gonna share her?" Nat asked as he spurred his horse.

"Well, now, of course; share and share alike, that's the Halstead brothers." He spurred his horse and they began gathering up the snorting horses and cattle grazing in the yard of the burning house.

Abruptly, riders appeared on the horizon.

Howard reined in. "Oh God, it's soldiers, I reckon. Quick, Nat, dump them gold pieces and throw away the scalps, we'll tell them we got here just in time to run the Injuns off."

Nat's ugly face lit up as he wiped at the paint on his homely face. "We'll be heroes; that's almost as good."

As they wiped away the paint, Howard got a closer look at the riders coming in through the foggy cold dawn. "Wait a minute," he whispered, "I don't see no blue uniforms."

"Maybe it's buffalo hunters." Nat peered at the figures. "The way they hate Injuns, they'll believe our story."

In the split second that passed, Howard suddenly realized the riders were dark-skinned, painted, and half-naked. "Oh God, Nat, ride and ride hard! It's Injuns!"

"Maybe it's Injun scouts from the fort—"

But Howard was already lashing his surprised horse, swearing as he took off at a gallop. "Maybe we can outrun them!"

"Brother, wait for me!" Nat yelled, but Howard didn't look back. He was concerned with saving himself; his brother would have to do the best he could.

He heard the sound of his brother galloping after him and the sudden shriek as Nat's horse stumbled and fell. Nat's shriek floated on the air after him. "Brother, come back for me! We can ride double!"

Howard glanced behind him, saw his brother holding up his hands, running after him. The Indians on the horizon were coming hard now, Howard could see them gaining on him. He might get away, but not if his horse had to carry double.

Abruptly, riders materialized out of the brush ahead of Howard, cutting off his escape. Howard swore and reined his horse to the left, trying to avoid the painted warriors. Behind him, he heard Nat shrieking for mercy.

Cheyenne. Real Cheyenne. Howard tried to dodge past the big painted warrior coming at him on a pinto horse, and, as he did, the warrior swung his rifle and caught Howard across the chest, knocking him from his saddle. Pain seemed to explode in Howard's chest, and he cried out as he flew through the air and hit the ground.

Even as he groveled, the big Cheyenne dismounted, stood towering over him. "So you play at being Cheyenne and cause us more trouble."

"You speak English?" Howard babbled, crawling toward the other man on his knees. "We didn't do anything, honest! Look, I have gold, you want?" He took the sack from his pocket, held it up.

In answer, the tall savage glared at him and knocked the gold from his hand.

"Look, what can I give you? We have scalps! Look at this pretty blond one!" He held it out with shaking hands. "You want scalps?"

The Indian glared at the bloody thing. "What happened to the woman?"

Oh, the Injun was interested in white women. Howard's hand shook as he reached into his pocket for the daguerreotype. "You want a woman? Maybe I can get this one for you! How'd you like this one?"

The other frowned suddenly, jerked the oval frame from Howard's trembling hand. "Your woman?"

Howard nodded frantically. "She's down in the Territory; I'll make you a present of her if you'll just let me go!"

The other smiled ever so slightly, as if he knew something Howard did not. Abruptly, the warrior tucked the small picture into his waistband, grabbed Howard by the neck, and began to drag him back to where the others surrounded Nat.

Nat was groveling and begging, sweat running down his paint-smeared face. He smelled as if he had soiled himself. "Howard, tell them we ain't done nothin', we'll share what we got; give them anything they want. Tell them, brother."

Howard looked around the circle on stern, unsmiling faces. "We—we have a ranch on Sappa Creek," he gasped. "Let us go and—"

"Ask your brother if he was at Sappa Creek three years ago!" the big one demanded.

"Sure he was, what difference—?" Howard paused, realizing what the Indian was asking. He remembered too late how Nat had laughed about the buffalo hunters and the ranchers joining forces to attack the Cheyenne camp, slaughter the women and children. "Look, I wasn't there," he implored the silent Indians. "He was there"—he gestured toward Nat—"but I wasn't. Take your revenge on him and let me go!"

Horror etched Nat's ugly face. "Why, brother, you dirty—!" Then he fell on his knees, groveling and begging, "Don't kill us!" He gasped. "We'll give you all the stuff we've stolen the last few days!"

The tall warrior smiled without mirth. "Those things we will take anyway. We are about to do the settlers of this county a favor, whether they realize it or not." He turned and barked an order to the others. "They have robbed, tortured, and killed. Give them the sentence their own law would give them." He glared down at Howard. "I only wish I had the time to repay you fully for what you did to Glory."

"Glory?" How did this savage know Glory? "How—?"

Two Arrows didn't bother to answer. He turned and strode toward his horse, listening to the two white men begging and groveling behind him. Even though Howard Halstead deserved to die, he didn't want the coward's blood on his hands. He heard the man scream and looked back. Howard lay pinned to the earth by a lance, kicking like a speared rabbit. His brother, who had admitted to being at the Sappa Creek massacre, was grabbed by two of the warriors and dragged kicking and screaming toward the burning house. Women and children had been thrown into the flames of their own tipis at Sappa Creek.

"No!" the white man screamed. "Oh, please!"

The expressions of the Cheyenne did not change as they grabbed him and threw him bodily into the flames. The man screamed and tried to run out, his clothes on fire. The men grabbed him to throw him back into the fire.

At that moment, Two Arrows sickened of the torture, raised his rifle, and shot the man between the eyes as the braves threw his body back into the fire. "We show you more mercy than you showed our people," he said softly.

The other white man moaned and moved, still pinned in the dirt by the lance. He could live a long time this way. Two Arrows took out the precious daguerreotype he had taken away from Howard and stared at Glory's lovely face, remembering the pain and terror she had described to him she had endured as Howard Halstead's wife. She would always be afraid as long as this man lived. The man deserved torture, but Two Arrows had no stomach for it; not even for this beast. "End his pain!" Two Arrows ordered.

Wild Hog stepped to the white man, grabbed his hair, and jerked his head back, then cut his throat.

Tangle Hair frowned. "Soldiers may be drawn by the smoke, they will hold us responsible."

Two Arrows stared at the dead men. "These two deserved to die, but you are right; we would get the blame. Gather up food and weapons!"

"There's good horses and fat cattle those white men were stealing," Tangle Hair noted. "We feast tonight!"

"Remember there are others who deserve our revenge!" A warrior brandished his rifle as he swung up on his lathered horse. "Soon the whole of Sappa Creek runs red with blood as it did three years ago when my woman died there!"

The warriors yelped in triumph and rode out at a gallop, leaving the homestead burning behind them. Two Arrows breathed easier, knowing that never again would Glory have to fear that her husband might come after her. Two Arrows would protect her forever; he loved her so!

The people were grateful for the horses and fat cattle the warriors drove back to them. The war parties also picked up a few weapons and blankets when they attacked other ranches along Sappa Creek. In some cases, perhaps innocent whites suffered for Lieutenant Henely's massacre of Indians at Sappa Creek three years earlier, but there was no way to tell the innocent from the guilty as the Cheyenne went on a rampage.

Two Arrows took very little part in the killings, wanting only to get meat and supplies back to the little group of marchers so they could move on.

When Two Arrows dismounted, Glory ran into his arms, trembling. "I was so afraid for you."

He would not tell her about Howard yet; maybe he never would. "We are all alive; but we've left the valley ablaze. There's no doubt the army will be on our trail again, but at least we have fat beef and fresh horses now."

The people found a little draw out of the wind and cut up a

beef. Then they gorged themselves on the fat meat and settled down to rest for a few hours.

Two Arrows wrapped Proud One in his blanket and held her close, kissing her face. The wind had picked up and it smelled like snow. "We will move out in the middle of the night," he whispered, "before the soldiers start to look for us. Nebraska is only a few miles away, and in those sand hills up there, we can easily lose our pursuers."

"Is it going to snow?" She put her warm face against his bare chest.

He nodded, and brushed her hair from her eyes. "Perhaps that is good, Proud One, it will cover our tracks."

"It will make it harder going," she said, "and so many are worn-out and can't go any farther."

"All we can do is try, my love," he whispered. "We'll keep moving, even if we have to wade through snowdrifts. After all, no one ever thought we would get this far across the Indian Territory and Kansas."

Her warm mouth nibbled at his chest and licked across his nipple, sending spasms of pleasure through him.

"It is a good night to make love," she murmured against his chest.

He held her face against him and reached down to squeeze her full, soft breast. "With you, every night is a good night to make love."

"I can never get enough of you," she sighed.

He kissed his way down her belly and then her thighs until she was writhing under him, clawing his back and holding his mouth against her. He stroked her with his fingers and she arched against him, silky wet and ready.

He was throbbing with his own need when he rolled over on her and slowly thrust his manhood into her. "You're so hot, my woman," he said against her mouth. "I'm going to take you tonight until my seed runs down your silken thighs."

"Then do it," she challenged him, and began to move rhythmically under him. "I want your son."

Her words set his desire and his body on fire. Yes, he wanted to breed her, make her belly big with his child, cause her breasts to swell with milk for his son. He was aching with need as he came down into her hard, thrusting deep while she dug her nails into his back and tilted her hips, meeting him thrust for thrust until he reached one final plateau of pleasure and went deep, clasping her to him, pouring his seed into her very depths.

Even as he did so, he heard her gasp for breath and felt her nails clawing his wide shoulders. "Oh, love," she gasped, "oh, love, you are so wonderful!"

He swept her into his arms, protecting her, covering her, kissing her face while he surged deep in her and felt her eager body squeeze his seed into her eager womb.

She was asleep in minutes, while he was still in her. He could feel the warm breath of her mouth and the softness of her small face against his broad chest while he held her close, keeping her warm with his big body.

For these few precious moments, he lay there, meshed with the woman he loved above all others, loved more than his own life. In an hour or so, they would have to be on the trail again, and the north wind was picking up. Two Arrows used his muscular body to shield the sleeping girl beneath him from the icy wind. He was cold, but he would not move and disturb her rest. He felt something touch his face, looked up. Snow fell from the cold black night; only a few flakes at first, and then the flakes grew larger and fell faster. He tried to shield her lovely face but a snowflake fell on her eyelashes and he leaned over, kissed it away. She smiled in her sleep and murmured to him.

"It's all right, Proud One," he whispered, "I will take care of you, always."

The snow fell faster, and the wind picked up. The Cheyenne had lost the battle against time, Two Arrows knew. The winter had come, and with it, the blizzards, before the people could make warm, snug camps up in their homeland valleys. Many sleeping here tonight would not survive the cold that was to come. Proud One would survive, he vowed, if it cost him his own life.

In the middle of the night, the wolf roused the camp with his echoing howl. Two Arrows could see him poised up on a bluff in the moonlight, his breath drifting like frost as he began to run, looking back to see if the people were coming with him.

Two Arrows wrapped his woman in a buffalo fur and then roused the camp so they could make ready to move out.

One old man could not be roused; he had died there in his sleep. One less free Cheyenne to be returned to captivity, Two Arrows thought bitterly as he took his own blanket to wrap the frail body in. It was shameful to leave an old and honored warrior lying in the snow with not even a blanket to cover him. However, there were no trees here in this windswept place to build a burial platform, and the little band could not spare the luxury of killing a horse to carry him on his way up the *Ekutsihimmiyo,* the Hanging Road to the Sky. Two Arrows asked the man's spirit and the gods for forgiveness as they left the ancient one on the ground and piled a few rocks over him to keep away the coyotes.

The snow fell thick and fast now, covering the bleak brown prairie with a pristine white blanket. Two Arrows saddled up and placed Proud One on his horse, still wrapped in his buffalo fur. Then he swung up on the horse and she snuggled against his broad back, protected against the cold north wind by his muscular body as they rode out of the camp, breaking trail for the weaker ones behind.

They had lost the race against time, he thought, yet the snow would cover their tracks when the bluecoats came looking, and it was good to feel his woman warm against his back. When he glanced down, her slim arms were locked about his waist. He reached down to caress her small hand and smiled to see Proud One still wore the beaded bracelet that little Grasshopper had given her.

The group of Cheyenne started north into the howling blizzard. Things looked hopeless, Two Arrows thought, with Dull

Knife and Little Wolf arguing over what they should do next, but nothing much mattered to him but that his woman was against his back, warm and protected. Moccasin Woman and the child were mounted on a fresh horse, as was Redbird, her baby snug in its cradleboard. Two Arrows had seen to them. They might not all make it, but Two Arrows would do what he could.

Seventeen

It seemed to Glory that the Cheyenne had ridden for days through the cold weather as they crossed into Nebraska and kept moving. They were running short on food and horses were worn-out and faltering under the relentless pace. People died in spite of everything the women could do. Sometimes, a stubborn old one decided she was holding the people back and sat down along the trail, awaiting the inevitable, despite the others' cries and protests.

If there was one thing about the October cold that was good, it was that the snow covered their tracks and discouraged soldiers from coming after them. The Cheyenne crossed two more railroads, holding their breaths, expecting trainloads of soldiers to appear out of the chill, their brass buttons gleaming. So far, they had seen no soldiers in the bleak sand hills. Two Arrows recognized the terrain and brightened, saying they were in north-western Nebraska and soon, would be safe in their own country.

The chiefs had called a halt for the day. Glory had built a snug little windbreak and lit a tiny fire to cook the rabbit Two Arrows had shot. She smiled now as he joined her. "Good news?"

He sat down on the blanket cross-legged. "Perhaps."

She took a look at his frowning face. "It is not good news, you only try to spare me from worry."

He sighed. "Little Wolf and Dull Knife have had another disagreement at council just now. Little Wolf thinks we should veer off and lose ourselves in the wilderness; the farther north, the better."

"And Dull Knife?" She didn't care much where they went, as long as she was not separated from her lover.

"He wants to take us to the Red Cloud reservation of our friends, the Lakota. He thinks that since the Lakota are allowed to stay there, once we get there, we will be allowed to stay, too."

She tore off a bit of the roasted rabbit and held it out to him. He caught her wrist playfully, nibbled the meat until he had eaten it, began to kiss the juice off her fingers. "I have more meat," she said.

"I don't want more meat, I want you." He began to kiss his way up her arm.

"Aren't the people almost ready to move out again?" She didn't want hurried lovemaking.

"No, because the two chiefs are still arguing." He was sucking her fingers in a very sensual manner.

"What do you think?"

"About what?" He continued to suck her fingers, pulling him against her so he could put his other hand down the front of her dress and stroke her breasts.

"About what? About whether they will split up and which way we will go."

"Proud One, I have offered an opinion; we have all offered our opinions." Two Arrows was abruptly serious. "There are pros and cons for both destinations, and no one knows who is right. Some say splitting up would be a good thing; the army would have to chase two groups then."

The army. She didn't want to think about the army. "We have seen no soldiers for a long time."

"They are out there somewhere and when they find us . . ." His voice trailed off, and he stared into the fire.

Glory played with her bracelet, thinking. "Don't talk about that. Despite the hardships, these have been the most wonderful weeks of my life."

He put his arm around her shoulders. "For me, too."

She laid her face against his broad chest and closed her eyes. "Maybe we shall make it all the way and live wild and free; after all, we have made it this far."

He grunted and stroked her hair. "That is true; no one ever dreamed we could travel almost fifteen hundred miles with all those soldiers trying to stop us. The soldiers must be the most surprised of anyone."

"Desperate people can be very determined. If the group splits up," she asked, "which one will we go with?"

"Does it matter to you?" He looked down into her eyes.

Glory shook her head. "As long as we are not separated; I don't care, my love. The only thing that ever worried me was that Howard might come after me."

"Proud One," he hesitated, "there is something I should have told you; I didn't know how."

She caught the reluctance in his voice, looked up, startled. "Mercy, he's looking for me, isn't he? You found out somehow. He's coming after me and—"

"Proud One, he's dead."

Of all the things he might have said, this startled her the most. "How—?"

"Back at Sappa Creek. We caught him and his brother killing homesteaders and robbing them, evidently laying the blame on Cheyenne. I was not the one who killed him."

No, this couldn't be true. "How—how do you know it was my husband?"

Wordlessly, he reached into his waistband for a small, gold-framed portrait.

She took it, recognizing it, then handed it back. Funny, she didn't feel anything except relief. "Howard would have killed me eventually because I wouldn't beg; he liked his women groveling."

Two Arrows smiled. "Have you ever begged for any reason in your whole life?"

"Never!"

He put his fingertips under her small chin and tilted her face up to his. "Whatever happens, Proud One, I want you to know, I wouldn't change places with any man in the world." He bent his head and kissed her.

"Me either," she breathed, then opened her lips, taking his tongue into her mouth in a slow, languorous way, sucking it deeper as she caught his hand and placed it on her breast.

His big hand covered her breast, raking his thumb back and forth across her nipple until she gasped for air and reached to pull his face down, offering him the gift of her breasts and smiling with contentment as he pleasured himself with them. His free hand went to slip her doeskin skirt up. He laid his head in her lap, kissing her bare thighs, then he turned his head ever so slightly and kissed something else while his hand caressed and squeezed her breast.

She gasped at the sensation of his warm tongue.

"You like that?"

"You—you know I do," she whispered, and spread her thighs slightly apart.

His mouth moved against her body again. She reached down and held his dark face against her, insisting that he continue to kiss and caress her with his tongue.

When she could stand no more, she gasped and began to breathe loudly, going rigid under his seeking mouth. Now he reached to take her hand in his, bring it across his lips. "You are my woman," he said solemnly, "and I will always look after you and protect you, Proud One, no matter the danger."

She yearned for nothing so much as to be carrying his child. If only that could happen. *"Ne-mehotatse,"* she whispered.

He gathered her into his arms, holding her close to his heart while he kissed her breathless. *"Ne-mehotatse,* my Proud One."

Little Wolf and Dull Knife were going their separate ways. It had cleared a little, but it was still cold and snowy, so that everyone's breath hung on the air like ghostly shadows. Now the Cheyenne gathered around their leaders, each man making his own decision.

Two Arrows thought this was the hardest choice he had ever made; this choice between which leader to follow because after crossing the Platte River, the fleeing Cheyenne were finally going to part.

Old Moccasin Woman and her little granddaughter, Grasshopper, decided to go with Dull Knife's group because she had friends in the Lakota camp.

On the other hand, Redbird had distant relatives among the few Cheyenne camping somewhere in the wilderness that she hoped to find, so she elected to take her baby, Brave Dream, and go with Little Wolf. Two Arrows sat cross-legged and smoked the last bit of precious tobacco he possessed, thinking over his choices. "Proud One, you will go wherever I choose?"

She nodded. "It makes no difference to me as long as we are not separated. You make the choice, my love."

He studied her, loving her because she trusted him enough to put her very life and future into his hands. He noted suddenly that she looked very weary and drawn. "Are you ill?"

She shook her head, "No, of course not. I may be a little tired, but I'll be fine once we settle in for the winter and stop this constant travel."

He stared at her; marveling at how Indian she had come to look with her black hair in braids and her skin browned by the past few weeks of relentless sun. If the Cheyenne didn't find a place soon where the people could rest and eat plenty of good, warm food, Proud One might sicken and fall along the way as others had. "I have made my choice," he said gravely. "We follow Dull Knife."

She nodded, not questioning his choice or asking why he had chosen thus.

He was glad because he did not want to tell her that he made his choice because with Dull Knife, they would pass near Fort Robinson. There would be an infirmary at that northern Nebraska post. If Proud One should fall ill, Two Arrows wanted to be able to detour to the fort, where medicine and a doctor were available. The soldiers would capture him if he did so, maybe throw him in prison, but nothing mattered but her welfare. Besides, no one could ever take away the memories of the weeks he had spent in her arms.

The day the Cheyenne split into two groups was a cold, windy day in the Moon When Water Begins to Freeze on the Edges of Streams that the whites called October. They divided the food and supplies, even the guns. There were scarcely two dozen guns in the whole lot, Two Arrows knew, and most of them were old relics. Even for these, the Cheyenne had only one or two bullets each. With these few outdated weapons, a handful of determined, brave people had outfought and outmaneuvered more than ten thousand of Uncle Sam's best soldiers. No wonder the army was embarrassed and angry!

So Two Arrows and Proud One went with Dull Knife's little band, and for the next several days, Two Arrows began to hope they really were going to make it all the way to the Red Cloud reservation. He could only pray Little Wolf's group had been so lucky.

With Proud One riding snug against his broad back, Two Arrows reined his horse in and looked for the wolf that had led them all the way from the Indian Territory. No one had caught a glimpse of the great furry beast in days. "I'm afraid it has deserted us. That is not a good omen."

She put her arms around his waist and hugged him. "Maybe it is a good omen; maybe the wolf thinks we're safe now. How many more days do you think it will be before we're safely with the Lakota?"

"With this weather?" He turned his face up, feeling the tingle of delicate snowflakes melting on his brown face. "Who knows? The drifts make very hard going."

He looked around the landscape that was white in every direction, the north wind howling like a sulking coyote. "No soldiers would be crazy enough to be out in this, so if we can make it a few more miles, we can lose ourselves among the Lakota."

Two Arrows reached to place his big hand to cover her small ones.

"I am so glad it's almost over. To tell the truth, I don't know how much more of this hard travel I could take."

Two Arrows looked down at her arms and felt remorse that she was so thin. She's not well, he thought. If I weren't so selfish, I should take her to the fort. Lieutenant Krueger, if he were alive, would want her back, no matter what. Giving her up would be like tearing Two Arrows's heart out. He didn't want to think about that—at least, not yet. "I love you, Proud One."

"Then that's all that matters," she whispered, her breath warm against his back.

He nudged his thin, tired horse forward, following the trail Dull Knife's band had left. As was the custom, the dog soldiers were bringing up the rear, ready to fight and die, if necessary, to cover the retreat in case of attack. The wind stirred up the northern Nebraska snows, and he turned his horse into the arctic blast and kept riding, glad for the warm feel of his woman against his back. "Within a week, we should be safe among the Lakota."

The way she tightened her grip on his waist and pressed her face against his muscular back let him know how happy she was. "We're going to make it," she said, and her voice was full of hope. "We're going to make it all the way!"

October 23, 1878

Captain J.B. Johnson, leading two companies of the Third Cavalry, hunched his broad shoulders against the northern Nebraska cold and looked back at his troopers. Damn, if they could just make it to shelter. "Hey, Lieutenant?" he reined in and pulled off his gloves, blowing on his numb fingers a long moment and pulling the fur of his coat collar up against his red ears, "this is a helluva time to be out on maneuvers, isn't it?"

The other laughed, frost on his dark mustache. "Nobody was

expecting this blizzard to blow in; it isn't fit for man or beast out here."

"Well, you know what the poem says: *'Ours not to reason why, ours but to do and die.'* God, I can hardly wait to get where it's warm!"

They began to ride again, the wind whipping up the snow so that visibility was poor. The horses were having a hard time of it, Johnson thought, the drifts were deep, and the sand hills of this prairie state seemed endless. It would be easy for a man to get lost out here.

A grizzled old scout came out of the fog, urging his black horse forward; its legs churned up the white snow as it moved. "Hey, Captain Johnson!"

"Hey, Zeke! Beginning to think you were lost!" The captain reined in, watching the scout making his way to him through the snow.

"Captain, there's something out there, moving toward us, thought it was ghosts at first."

Johnson felt a chill go up his back, but he laughed. "Only crazy ghosts, I presume; no sane one would be out in this blizzard unless he was under government orders."

The other brushed snowflakes from his ragged beard and gestured. "You'd better come up on this rise and have a look, sir."

Johnson nudged his bay gelding forward and rode up on the snowy rise and reined in. For a long moment, he saw nothing and was annoyed. That old coot had been drinking bad booze again, he thought, and was seeing things that weren't there. He stood up in his stirrups, angry with the scout. "I don't see a damned thing, Zeke, and you wouldn't either if you'd quit drinking that white lightning."

The scout spit a stream of brown tobacco juice into the snow. "I saw something, sir," he insisted.

Captain Johnson cleared his throat, leaning forward in his saddle to stare into the blinding snow. "Maybe it was a small herd of buffalo or wild horses."

Zeke shook the snow from his beard again, staring into the vast distance. "Buffalo's all killed out by hunters, probably not a couple of hundred left in the whole West. Hey, look!" He pointed.

Captain Johnson strained his eyes, looking in the direction Zeke pointed. For a long moment he had a sudden, chilling feeling that he was seeing specters moving silently through the blowing snow. Or maybe it was nothing at all. He chided himself for his own active imagination, or perhaps he was going loco from living out here on the Plains; the West would do that to a man. Maybe it was only shadows or snowflakes whirling up in the relentless wind.

The gale whipped the snow into a fury, taking the very breath from his throat. Somewhere in the distance, a wolf howled, or maybe it was only the north wind. Whatever it was, it sent the hairs on Captain Johnson's neck rising as he remembered every ghost story he had ever heard about werewolves.

There was no sound save the warning wail that drifted on the cold air. Then out of the snow in the distance rode the specters. They were so faint on the horizon that he was not sure for a long moment what it was he saw—or if he saw.

Then Zeke gasped. "Injuns; God Almighty! Injuns!"

Abruptly, Captain Johnson knew what he was seeing; this small band of riders slumped on thin, stumbling horses moving north. He looked a long moment, torn between pity and admiration. "Fifteen hundred miles," he whispered. "And we thought they were dead out there somewhere to the south."

Then he remembered his duty. "Zeke, get to the fort at once; we may need reinforcements."

"Yes sir." He stared into the blizzard just before he wheeled his horse to ride out. "Anything else?"

"Tell headquarters," Captain Johnson said, and he didn't know if he was sad or jubilant, "tell them we've found their missing Cheyenne. They're almost out of Nebraska, heading north!"

* * *

Glory had been half-dozing, riding against Two Arrows's warm back as they rode through the blizzard. When she felt him stiffen, she came immediately awake. "What's the matter?"

"Hush, Proud One," he said softly. "Perhaps they do not see us in this blinding snow."

Cautiously, Glory peeked around him. In the distance on a little rise, she saw the outline of men on horses. She rubbed her eyes, not sure she hadn't imagined them. Blue uniforms. *Oh, please no, dear God. Surely we haven't come all this way, only to be caught just before we reach our destination.* "What—what are we going to do?"

His hand went to his rifle and his voice was resigned. "They—they've seen us."

Glory felt the tears starting in her eyes and blinked them away, knowing they would freeze on her face. "I don't want to be separated from you, my love."

The soldiers rode out of the mist now, rifles at the ready, swinging to surround the ragged little group. She could see the shock on the young officer's face. "Good God!" he said. "Is this pitiful little starving bunch that wild, dangerous horde of bloodthirsty savages the telegraph lines have been humming over? Why, there's probably not more than a hundred or a hundred and fifty, most of them women and kids."

Two Arrows smiled ever so slowly. "Scared white men make us much more than we are."

"You speak English?"

Two Arrows nodded.

The officer and his soldiers looked around at the other ragged, shivering people. "Who leads this band? Let us eat and talk."

Two Arrows nodded to Dull Knife, who rode forward, his dark face set and tragic.

So near and yet so far, Two Arrows thought; *we almost made it, just like the Nez Perce, we almost made it. Perhaps there is still hope, there weren't that many soldiers.*

Dull Knife spoke in Cheyenne to Two Arrows, who rode forward. "My chief says he will talk. You have coffee and food?"

The young officer grinned, his face red from the cold. "And tobacco and sugar, too."

The soldiers relaxed, evidently pleased they wouldn't have to fight today.

The people dismounted. Two Arrows reached up for his Proud One, helped her down. "Keep silent," he said in Cheyenne. "Do not give yourself away."

She nodded, keeping her head down. Two Arrows quickly erected a shelter against the wind from some blankets and motioned old Moccasin Woman and little Grasshopper to join Proud One. "Build a little fire. The soldiers will bring food."

The old woman made a face. "It chokes me to eat the soldiers' food."

Two Arrows looked around at the soldiers who were dismounting and building a big fire. "There are not all that many of them. Perhaps tonight, as they sleep, we can slip away like ghosts."

Glory smiled. "There's still hope. The wolf tried to warn us, and it's still out there, wild and free as a Cheyenne's heart. Get some hot food for all the children and old ones."

"And for you, too," he said softly, and reached out to touch her face as he turned to go. *October; our freedom ends in October.* Only a year ago in October, Two Arrows had been the one to spot the escaping Nez Perce as Chief Joseph's people struggled to make it to the Canadian border and freedom. Because of him, the army had surrounded the luckless Nez Perce and stopped them just short of their goal. Only a handful had escaped in the darkness to freedom. Now Two Arrows, who had helped capture the Nez Perce, was in exactly the same fix. Perhaps this was only justice.

Two Arrows strode proudly through the snow toward the big fire. The other warriors were gathering there in the lee of a bluff, out of the wind. They were all ragged, their moccasins full of holes, their ribs showing. Ah, but they were proud! Their heads were up as if they had just returned from the Little Bighorn or the fight on the Rosebud or a dozen other battles where they had whipped the white men.

The young officer sat down cross-legged on the blanket and offered tobacco all around, staring at the tired, cold Indians. "Fifteen hundred miles," he whispered in a tone of awe. "Fifteen hundred miles on sheer guts. This will be something I can tell my grandchildren."

Two Arrows watched the soldiers from the corner of his eye as he accepted the tobacco with half-frozen fingers. Bluecoated sentries watched the whole proceedings. There would be no chance to overpower this bunch; but perhaps tonight, as the whites slept . . .

They smoked in silence, Two Arrows relishing the taste of tobacco. The smell of strong hot coffee blew on the wind as the iron pot steamed on the fire. For only a moment, he remembered his life as an army scout and the half-forgotten taste of the good food and the fine blue jacket that had been his. There had been money in his pockets and thick blankets. There had been whiskey, plenty of whiskey.

The thought crossed his mind as he smoked and stared into the fire that even now, he could probably rejoin the army scouts. He could tell them he had been forced to ride along against his will, tell them where to find Little Wolf's band. For this, the soldiers would give him his blue coat again and a bottle of whiskey.

But he would not do that. His people had given him another chance, and with that chance went respect and pride. He had the Proud One for a mate, and he would die before he would give her up.

They all sat and smoked while the soldiers cooked beef. It had been several days since Two Arrows had eaten, and then it had been only a few bites of half-raw horse meat. The scent of the food drifted, but even those faint from hunger gave no sign. They might be ragged, thin, and half-frozen, but they were

Cheyenne warriors, and, besides their freedom, they had only their pride.

This was a good officer, Two Arrows thought, watching him. The young man signaled for the coffee to be poured and plenty of lumps of sugar to be added. He did not begin to talk unceasingly like a magpie, he acted as if he were serving honored guests and that he had all the time in the world to drink coffee and smoke.

Two Arrows took the steaming cup, warming his cold hands around it. The other warriors accepted theirs as if they were doing the soldiers a favor. They would not shame themselves by gulping and showing their hunger.

Two Arrows cleared his throat. "If the captain please," he said with dignity, "our women and children."

"Of course." The officer nodded to his sergeant who brought out more cups and began to circulate among the families. "Please do me the honor of sharing my food."

He had forgotten how good beef was; not as good as buffalo, but then, most of the buffalo had been slaughtered by white hunters long ago. The chiefs accepted tin plates of beef and hardtack and began to eat.

Two Arrows saw the soldiers relax visibly, and he did, too. The only thing that worried him now was that one might recognize the Proud One and demand her return.

The wind lessened, and the soldier chief passed out more tobacco and more coffee. At least this white man understood Indians well enough not to be rude and rush to the subject. It was not polite among Indians to rush to the point of any discussion. Finally, the captain said to Two Arrows, "Tell your chief he would honor me by coming to Fort Robinson."

No one said anything for a long time after Two Arrows translated. The wind whistled through the camp, and the Indians smoked and stared into the horizon as if they had not heard.

The captain repeated his words.

Two Arrows turned to Dull Knife. "Once we get to the fort," he said in Cheyenne, "we have no chance of escaping."

Dull Knife nodded to show he understood, but his grave expression did not change. "Tell the soldier chief that we are almost to our own country and while we have enjoyed his feast, we must now be going to join my friend, Red Cloud."

Two Arrows translated.

The officer's red face mirrored concern. "Ah, but what is the hurry? Let us talk more. It will soon be dark and no time to ride. Let us eat more meat and smoke, tell stories into the night."

Two Arrows looked out at the sentries with their rifles at the ready, and translated again.

Dull Knife considered, then spoke in Cheyenne. "Perhaps we can get away in the darkness."

"We can try," Two Arrows answered. "Perhaps we had better hide our weapons." However, to the officer he smiled, and said, "The meat and coffee are good. We will linger and smoke and talk."

It was late before everyone finally settled into their blankets, but the soldier chief, wise to the ways of Indians, posted a guard on the cavalry horses. Two Arrows found his way to Proud One and crawled in under the blanket.

"What is going to happen?" she asked.

He pulled her close against him, relishing the warmth of her soft body. "Did you get plenty to eat?"

"Yes, and them, too." She nodded toward the old woman and little girl curled up by the fire nearby. "I hadn't realized how hungry I was."

He felt sorrow and shame. Perhaps a white woman was too frail for this harsh life. "All you have to do is identify yourself, and you'll be on a train and out of here."

"Mercy! And leave you, my love? I think not." She put her arms around him and pulled him close. "What's going to happen now?"

He kissed her face and held her close. "We're hoping we can slip away before morning or maybe even overpower them if we must."

She curled herself against his chest. "Let me know when it's time to move out."

But when Two Arrows checked in the middle of the night, there were still sentries guarding the horse herds, and the soldiers had their rifles at the ready. Before morning, their other plan was dashed, too, as reinforcements rode into the encampment.

Two Arrows felt his hope sink when he saw the additional soldiers. "The officer must have sent a rider to the fort."

She put her hand on his strong arm. "We have no chance of getting away then?"

"Not unless we can convince him to let us ride on." That wasn't likely, Two Arrows decided. Several times over the next two days, the chiefs met with the officer, who insisted they must ride with him to Fort Robinson.

Old Dull Knife's faith was touching and childlike. "Surely they will not send us back to Indian Territory," he said to the others over and over, "now that we have walked all this way. Surely they will understand and let us go on to our own country."

Wild Hog, Tangle Hair, Crow, Sitting Man, and Two Arrows exchanged looks. "Just in case they don't," Two Arrows suggested, "maybe we should hide our weapons before they demand we give them up."

Dull Knife looked alarmed. "We will not give up our weapons, we will fight them instead."

But the next morning when they awakened in that encampment, more soldiers had arrived during the night, and the new ones had brought cannons.

When Dull Knife saw the cannons, he said, "Yes, it is time to hide our weapons."

The soldiers did not notice anything—Two Arrows saw to that. Stealthily, the Cheyenne dismantled all but the most ancient and useless of their weapons. Over several days, the dismantled weapons went piece by piece into the women's clothes. Here and there went a cartridge or a spring or a trigger, used as a hair ornament or earring among the old ones or the children.

Even Proud One had a rifle barrel tied with a thong and hanging down her back under the doeskin dress.

Finally came the moment the soldiers demanded that the Cheyenne give up their weapons. The warriors argued and stalled, as was expected. There was much discussion and smoking around the fire. The soldier chief insisted. Finally, the Cheyenne gave up a couple of the ancient, useless guns and pistols. Some would no longer fire or they had no cartridges to fit them anyway. It was a very small pile of weapons they laid on the blanket before the officer.

Even he looked surprised. "There is no more?" he asked Two Arrows.

Two Arrows shook his head. There were no more they were willing to give the soldiers. It did not seem to occur to the soldiers to search anyone; or perhaps they knew the warriors would not take kindly to white men putting their hands on the Cheyenne women. Cheyenne women were very modest and even wore chastity belts; they were not like the Pawnee sluts, who were free with their favors.

Again and again, the Cheyenne argued with the young officer that they should be allowed to travel on north, but with patience befitting an Indian, he shook his head and said he could not make that decision, only Washington could, and the Cheyenne must go with him and wait.

On that last night, Two Arrows was sorely tempted to steal a good horse and get away. He would be able to find his way to Little Wolf's band. Having tasted freedom, it was difficult to contemplate that the warriors might be sent away to prison in Florida as the army had done in the past. Since he was an ex-army scout, the penalties for him no doubt would be worse.

Even as he thought that, he looked into Proud One's face and knew she was weary and almost sick from the hunger and the long journey. She might not survive if he tried to take her with him, and he would not go without her. This woman meant everything in the world to him, he loved her so!

Finally, on a cold morning, the officer asked the warriors to council. "We must go back to the fort and wait for Washington's decision. There will be plenty of food and hot coffee there."

Dull Knife looked from Two Arrows to the officer, hope in his weary, lined face. "Perhaps Washington will see how much we've sacrificed, how many have died to reach our country, and turn us loose to follow the wolf."

The officer started to say something, hesitated. "Perhaps," he said, and he sounded as if he wished it were true.

The Indians looked at each other, and Two Arrows was glad they had hidden most of the guns. Later, he thought, as he helped Proud One up on his horse, later, they were going to need weapons. The Cheyenne had pledged to die fighting rather than return south to Indian Territory!

Eighteen

Glory remained silent and kept her head down so she would not be noticed as the growing number of soldiers surrounded the Cheyenne.

Now they rode toward Fort Robinson surrounded by soldiers. At least they would be out of the cold, she thought with relief, as they were assigned to an empty army barracks at the fort. The first thing the Cheyenne did was hide the weapons they had sneaked in under the floorboards of the barracks.

To Two Arrows, she said, "Maybe Washington will decide to let the Cheyenne stay in the north."

"I doubt that, but we can hope," he answered. "In the meantime, it gives our people a chance to rest and gain weight; some of them were so worn-out, they couldn't have traveled another mile."

She looked out the window at the soldiers on guard duty. "No one seems to have noticed that I'm white."

"The way you're dressed and with your coloring, you look Indian," he said. "Just be careful not to speak English in front of any of them."

"I wouldn't let them take me away from you," she protested.

"You might not get a choice." He kissed her forehead, holding her close. "They would think any white woman who wanted to stay with Indians had gone insane, and they'd ship you to some asylum."

Glory shuddered at the thought and laid her face against his chest. "I have to admit I'm glad to get a warm place to sleep for a while."

"Are you all right?" He took her small face between his two big hands, staring anxiously down into her face. "Maybe the camp doctor—"

"Would find out I was white and separate us," she reminded him. "I'll be fine. While we wait to find out what the government is going to do with us, we'll simply make the most of whatever time we have."

He looked troubled, but nodded. "You're right, Proud One, we won't borrow trouble by worrying about tomorrow, we'll just treasure every minute we have together."

The weather warmed intermittently, and the army treated their Indian charges reasonably well, saying they were waiting for Washington to make a decision. The Cheyenne relaxed, hoping for the best. The barracks were comfortable enough, the army provided rations, and the new commander, Captain Wessells, decided the Indians were no threat. He allowed them to hunt and roam away from the fort as long as everyone was back inside the barracks and accounted for every night.

Life fell into a pattern over the next few weeks. The men hunting and women and children sewing buckskin or sitting in front of the barracks, enjoying the chill, sunny days. In the evening, the people sang and talked, and the men smoked far into the night.

Glory had never been so happy as she was now. During the day, she worked with the women and learned more of the language and skills she would need if she were ever to live as a Cheyenne wife. Moccasin Woman taught her about beading and fancy quill work. Glory delighted in the children, especially little Grasshopper, who seemed to be everywhere, charming even the toughest of soldiers. She stayed away from the whites, afraid someone might realize who she was, but she could tell some of the soldiers were sympathetic to what the Cheyenne people had been through in traveling this far. At night, curled up in a bunk with Two Arrows, she was more than content.

"This is heaven to me," she whispered against his ear, "even if we are crowded into a barracks."

He pulled her against him and kissed her. "As long as you are in my arms, Proud One, anywhere is heaven."

She sighed contentedly as he stroked her body with his big hands. "Is there any chance we'll be able to escape this place?"

He nibbled on her ear. "We'll wait first and see what Washington does. You and I could sneak away easily, but you know the commander has this rule about the head count each night. If we slip away, he'll punish the rest."

"I love all these people." She embraced him and listened to those around her breathing rhythmically as the wind rattled the old building. "Someday, I'd like to have a child just like little Grasshopper."

He kissed her and sighed. "I dream of fine strong sons; but I would not want to raise them as captives."

"Someday, we'll be free as the wolf, free, as the Cheyenne were meant to be."

Almost in answer, from somewhere in the distance, the faint howl of a wolf drifted on the cold wind.

"See? He hasn't deserted the people; he's calling us, singing the Cheyenne song," she said.

"I'm afraid right now, he calls in vain."

She did not want to think about tomorrow or next year. All that mattered was this moment in time and being in this man's arms. "Someday, we will go with the wolf."

He held her very close and stroked her hair. "That's too much to hope for."

She laid her head on his arm. "As long as we aren't separated, I can deal with anything else."

"I should never have stolen you, Proud One. The last several weeks, you were so ill, I feared for you. David Krueger would have given you a life of ease and plenty."

"I don't want Lieutenant Krueger."

"I would do anything to keep you from harm," he whispered, and kissed her, "even though it would tear me apart to think of you with another man."

"Oh, my dear one, don't ever regret me," she whispered against his lips. "I never knew what true love was until I became your woman."

He was strangely quiet for a long moment as he kissed her. "I will always put your welfare above everything."

"What do you mean?"

"It means I am tired of this discussion." He laughed softly and rolled her on top of him then, where he could reach her breasts. "Make love to me, Proud One; make love to me so I'll forget where we are and what tomorrow might bring."

"I'll make you forget everything but me," she vowed with a smile and began to kiss and caress his big, scarred body. "And then we'll do it again and again and be glad we have each other. Nothing else matters but our love."

"Nothing else matters," he echoed, and began to make love to her in earnest until she was gasping for air as she rode him, whimpering for more and digging her nails into his wide shoulders.

The weeks passed uneventfully. Things fell into a pattern for the Cheyenne as they waited for the decision from Washington. Every night, Two Arrows made love to his woman, and, as he dropped off to sleep with her in his arms, he was certain he could never get enough of her, no matter how long they were together. They might have only days or weeks, but that would have to be enough. Two Arrows was almost happy, concerned only that eventually, the soldiers would discover the Proud One was white and take her away from him, or that the Cheyenne would be ordered to return to Indian Territory. However, as one week passed into another and the white men's holidays came, Two Arrows began to hope that maybe Washington would be lenient, order Dull Knife's band turned loose to return to their hunting grounds. Nothing had been heard of Little Wolf's group, and he breathed a sigh of relief, glad they had avoided recapture.

Sergeant Michael Muldoon dismounted from his buckskin and strode through the crust of snow into the commander's office, saluted smartly.

"At ease, Sergeant Muldoon." Captain Wessells leaned back in his chair behind his desk, gestured to the chair across from him. His German accent was thick, but no worse than Michael's himself. "Is good to have you assigned here to Fort Robinson."

"Aye, thank you sir." Muldoon rubbed his aching hands together, stared at the cedar tree in the corner, with its strings of colored paper and berries. "To be honest, I'd hoped to spend Christmas in a warmer clime."

Captain Wessells pulled at his precise goatee and laughed. *"Ja,* northern Nebraska in late December isn't the warmest place. I hear you got a medal and promotion back there when Major Lewis was killed."

Muldoon shrugged and felt his ruddy face color modestly. "I was only rescuin' my officer; the lad and I been together since the Civil War."

"Well, I hear you were both brave. He should be happy with his medal and promotion. How is Captain Krueger?"

"Recuperatin' at his father's estate. After the first of the year, I suppose he'll be reassigned. His horses are at Fort Reno, waitin'."

The captain steepled his fingers. "I imagine with him being a hero and all, he gets an easy Washington post."

Muldoon shook his head. "That'd be best; but he's got a score to settle, and he won't forget it."

"Ja, I hope they don't send him here, then." The captain leaned back and put his shiny boots on his desk. "I heard about fraulein being kidnapped and killed. While I sympathize with Krueger, my job is to keep the northern Cheyenne corralled peacefully until I get orders."

Muldoon stared past the Christmas tree to the snow outside. "To tell the truth, I'd begun to admire the Indians; they're as tough as the Irish and up against about the same odds, but David has sworn to kill Two Arrows."

The officer frowned and fingered his goatee. *"Nein,* not while this officer in charge. I don't know even if that particular brave is here. Much as I understand Captain Krueger's pain, I can't allow him to declare hunting season and start Indian war."

"Sentiment across the country has swung to the Indians," Muldoon said. "Even the Omaha paper is askin' for mercy for them."

"Ja, they're valiant devils"—the captain nodded—"and you got to respect such bravery. Still, Washington's afraid that if Cheyenne are allowed to get away with this, all Indians will be walking from reservations and going where they please."

"Just like free men; well, now, wouldn't that be a pity?"

The other frowned and stared at the toes of his shiny boots. "As old soldier myself, I warn you to watch your mouth; you wouldn't want be labeled an Injun lover."

"Injun lover I ain't," Muldoon said. "Injun respecter, I guess I plead guilty. I feel terrible about what happened to Mrs. Halstead, but things happen in war."

The captain nodded, and Muldoon stood up. "I'll be findin' me quarters now, sir."

Wessells stood, too. "Rumor is Washington is going to ship Cheyenne back to Indian Territory."

Muldoon frowned. "Ah, it does seem a shame after what they've been through."

"Ja, I know, but that not up to us; we just follow orders. If they get wind of it, they try to escape, and I don't want trouble during the holidays at Fort Robinson!"

When Two Arrows first saw Muldoon at a distance, his heart almost stopped, but the soldier didn't seem to see him, so Two Arrows pulled the collar of his buckskins up and stayed out of Muldoon's way. He did, however, alert the Proud One that the

Irishman was on the post. "Be careful," he warned. "He of all people would recognize you."

"Is David with him?"

He shook his head. "From what I have heard, both of them were promoted and given medals. Krueger was wounded and sent home. He and Muldoon are both heroes."

"Good." She smiled. "He said he only needed another chance; looks like both he and Muldoon got one. Maybe it's a good sign, and the Cheyenne will get one also."

"Proud One"—he put his hands on her small shoulders—"this may be *your* second chance. If you have any regrets at all, you could go to Muldoon, get him to notify Krueger, and you'd be safe as his wife."

"Never!" She came into Two Arrows's arms, hugging him to her. "I have faith that Washington will find in our favor."

It seemed so important to her that he held her to him and nodded. "Maybe it will be as you say. I only think of how much you have given up for me."

"I haven't given up anything; I've lost nothing and gained everything." She laid her face against his broad chest. "If I have your love; I want nothing more except a chance to live with you in freedom and give you sons."

He held her very close, feeling her heart beat against his. It weighed heavily on him that she was enduring such hardships just to stay by his side. He loved her enough to want the best for her, no matter if he finally had to give her up. "I swear that no man ever loved a woman as much as I love you."

"Then nothing else matters, my dearest. I'll stay out of Muldoon's way. Now stop worrying and hold me a while. I forget all our problems in your embrace."

So he took her in his arms and made love to her, and, finally, she slept. But Two Arrows did not sleep and he could not forget the problems. The days were moving one behind another through the cold winter, and soon the white man's new year would be coming. Soon, Washington would certainly make up its mind about the Cheyenne. He had a terrible feeling the news would not be good.

David stood by the Christmas tree, smoking his pipe and staring out the window of the library at the snow falling across the Kentucky pastures.

His father limped through the double doors, still ramrod straight even as an old man. "Well, I saw Dr. Linder out; I know you're glad to have all those bandages off. I hope you'll be able to use that hand."

In answer, David flexed it. "I can."

"Good." His father's ice blue eyes were almost friendly in the stern, military face. "You've got a great future in the military now."

"Umm." He pretended to look at the Christmas tree while tapping his pipe stem against his teeth.

"I've heard from one of my old friends, Colonel Carter. He thinks he may have an opening on his Washington staff."

"I didn't ask you to do that, Father."

"What are fathers for if they can't help a son's career?" Fritz Krueger shrugged him off. "It will be good for you to be where the action is; not stuck out at some dreary, distant post where you'll soon be forgotten and overlooked for promotion."

"You might have asked me what I thought—"

"I knew you'd be happy about it, so I went ahead." The colonel smiled with satisfaction. "You make some good connections, get promoted to major, then colonel. President Hayes might find a spot for a young, ambitious officer."

David started to speak, then sighed. His father had always made his decisions for him, and he had tried all his life to please him without success.

"You don't seem very happy about it. Your brother, William, would be a general now, if he had lived, but then he had so much more potential and was so handsome!"

"Yes, Father, so you've told me many, many times."

"I don't understand you, David. You've been given a chance to erase the mess of your past, make me happy—"

"Just once, I'd like to make myself happy," David ventured, staring out at the snow, smoking and thinking.

"You're talking gibberish," his father snapped with a shrug. "You're following a long-standing Krueger tradition. We've been professional soldiers for more than a hundred years in this country, ever since your Hessian ancestor came to America to fight as a mercenary for the British in the Revolutionary War."

It took all his nerve to blurt it out, "You know, I really never wanted to be a professional soldier."

"Oh, poppycock!" The colonel paced the library. "I thought you were over that childish whim that caused you to take off for Texas to play cowboy—"

"Please don't bring up Susan and Joe," David asked, and put the tips of his fingers on his throbbing temples.

"Fine girl, good bloodlines. Susan would have made a great officer's wife, but no, you had to take her to Texas and then talk your younger brother into—"

"Joe didn't want to be a soldier, either."

"Poppycock! Of course he did! He was so smart, and I had made such plans—"

"Father, I am sorrier than you know about what happened to them both," David whispered and leaned on the window, looking out across the landscape. "I would give my life to change that, but I won't ever have that chance again." He hesitated, wanting to say that if he had been there when the Comanche attacked instead of off fighting the Civil War at Fritz Krueger's insistence, Susan and Joe might still be alive. He didn't say that, of course; he never argued with his father. Texas. It was warm along the Rio Grande right now, he thought, and felt an awakening urge to be on his ranch to see the bluebonnets bloom in the spring. The colonel didn't even know David still owned that land. He wondered where they'd assigned Muldoon, him with his poor, hurting hands?

"All right, we won't discuss all your past mistakes—the many times you've disappointed me. You're the only son I've got left, David; all my dreams and ambitions ride on you."

David didn't answer; there wasn't any use.

His father busied himself sorting through the pile of mail on top of the elegant grand piano. "You really should get your horses sent home," he said. "Second Chance and Gray Mist are worth a fortune, you know. I built my money on raising good horses for the cavalry. We can build a whole stable of fine cavalry mounts from those bloodlines."

In his mind, David saw himself on the chestnut stallion galloping along beside Glory on Gray Mist. Glory always had her head up so proud and defiant, her hair flying behind her as she raced across the prairie. He summoned all his courage. "Father, I—I don't know if I want to end up on this estate."

Old Fritz paused, evidently surprised at his son's sudden independence.

"I mean, I'd like to make my own choices for a change."

The older man shrugged, returned to sorting through the mail. "You made your own choices, and it almost wrecked your career."

Did he have the nerve to buck his father? "I—I didn't choose this career; you chose it for me, as you chose my school and my wife."

"Poor Susan." The colonel sighed and shook his head. "Such a perfect wife from such a good family—"

"I never loved her," David snapped. "You chose her, and I let you pressure me into marrying her—"

"David, what is the matter with you?" the old man confronted him, blue eyes blazing. His sons had always done just as he said. "You have behaved strangely ever since you were sent home wounded. At first, I thought it was just the trauma—"

"No, I came to an epiphany," David said recklessly, "and realized my whole life had been nothing but an extension of your life. I've never been allowed to live my own life, make my own choices!"

"Oh, how like a serpent's tooth is an ungrateful child!" The colonel began to pace, his limp considerably less now that he was angry. "David, everything I've done, I did for my boys, and now you are the only son I have left—"

"Why don't you say it?" David whispered. "Why don't you say how much you regret that it wasn't me instead of William who was killed in that cavalry charge at Gaines's Mill?"

"Shut up! You aren't even worthy to speak his name!" His father was shouting now, "William died a hero for a noble cause!"

"William and the Fifth Cavalry rode right into the blazing guns of the Confederate infantry; it was a terrible slaughter, and for what?"

"You are a soldier!" The older man's face had gone an ugly red. "The Kruegers have always been military men, always!"

He was not sure he had the nerve to defy his father, and maybe there was no reason to. "Father, I'm sorry, but I hate the army. I tried to tell you before you shipped me off to West Point, but you wouldn't listen." David leaned against the windowsill and stared out at the snow. "All I ever wanted out of life was to own a ranch where I could raise children and cow ponies—"

"You'll inherit this estate and raise fine cavalry mounts," the other reminded him with a scowl.

David shook his head and walked over to empty his pipe among the coals of the fireplace. "I don't want to raise horses to carry men into battle. I want nothing to do with war. I want to raise horses that a cowboy might—"

"Cowboys!" his father sneered. "You dare speak to me of the West? It was your crazy idea about Texas that got Susan killed, that got Joseph killed—"

"And you will remind me of that every hour of every day for the rest of my life, won't you?" David turned on him. "If I'd been there to protect them against Comanches, instead of off playing soldier—"

"So again, it is your father's fault?"

David closed his eyes and sighed. "No, it's no one's fault but my own, I guess, for not standing on my own two feet like a man should, making my own decisions. Ever since I survived this wound, I've been thinking maybe God was offering me another chance."

"Well, of course he is," the older man said firmly, as if God himself wouldn't argue with Colonel Krueger, retired, U.S. Cavalry. "You've gotten your rank back and a medal. Now with a little rest, you'll carry on the valiant tradition of the Krueger family as William would have done."

What was the use?

"Father," David sighed, too weary and heartsick to argue further, "you haven't heard a word I said."

"Of course I have." The colonel shrugged and smiled. "You said God has given you another chance, and so we're agreed."

David stared into the fire a long moment. Of course he was going to stay in the military. He had to track Two Arrows down and take revenge. *This is for Glory.*

The doorbell rang.

The colonel limped to answer it, grumbling, "Now, who can that be?"

At least, this confrontation was ended, David thought with relief as he went over, sat down at the grand piano, stared at the keys. The mother he barely remembered had taught him to play before she died. His father had thought it unmanly.

The colonel limped back into the library. "Good! Dr. Linder said it would exercise that arm for you to play again."

"I—I don't really want to play it."

"Poppycock!" his father snorted. "Of course you do. Play something for me; what about that song that was popular among the young people last year; what was it? Something about the gloaming."

That was the one song he would never play again. David closed his eyes at the memory it brought back. Before the older man could insist, he asked, "Who was at the door?"

"Oh, a letter for you." The colonel handed it over, his lined face bright with curiosity. "Who do you know in Nebraska?"

David took it, grinning. "Why, it's from Muldoon; bless his old heart!"

"I remember that rascal!" His father scowled. "Didn't he lose his rank for gambling—?"

"He also saved my life," David reminded him, ripping open the letter. He had forgotten how much he missed the Irishman. "Hmm, what do you know; he's been transferred to Fort Robinson."

"Nebraska. That's good enough for him, I suppose." The colonel sniffed. "The army has a tendency to forget men it assigns to distant posts. You're frowning, David; is there bad news?"

He didn't know himself. "The northern Cheyenne have finally been apprehended and sent to Fort Robinson." He reread the letter, but Muldoon did not mention Two Arrows. He thought about his dead sweetheart, and he gritted his teeth and silently renewed his vow. Even his dreams at night were full of images of putting his gunsights on the defiant Cheyenne's head and pulling the trigger. He would never find peace until he did that.

"Cheyenne? Ragtag savages!" The colonel snorted. "Not like fighting real soldiers."

"You haven't fought against them." David grunted. "Best light cavalry in the world, with no weapons, no supplies, nothing but raw courage."

Fritz Krueger's white eyebrows went up. "You admire them?"

David thought a minute. "I respect them," he answered finally. "They will fight with their bare hands, if necessary, for what they believe in."

"Poppycock! This isn't real cavalry; we're talking savages." His father made a dismissing gesture as if that ended the discussion. "Oh, David, by the way, I did tell you we're invited to that Christmas Eve ball tonight?"

"Another one?" He carefully folded the letter so he could reread it again later and put it in his pocket. "I don't feel like a party; go without me."

"That's what you said to the last three invitations," the colonel snapped. "Dr. Linder said you're well enough, and all the young ladies have been asking—"

"I'm not interested in meeting young ladies," David said, picking out a note or two on the piano.

"But Susan has been dead a long time, and it's time you remarried—"

"And I suppose you've got her all picked out for me?"

"Don't be smart-mouthed," the older man said, "although I have narrowed the choice down to two or three, all of whom will be at tonight's ball."

"That figures." In his mind, he pictured the girls his father would choose, pliant, meek, dull. He'd known a proud, defiant woman in Glory, and he didn't want another staid, proper Victorian lady. "Really, Father, if you don't mind—"

"Mind? Of course I mind." The colonel dismissed David's protest with an impatient shrug. "Senator Pierce Hamilton is going to be there, and these young ladies from the prestigious Carstairs Oaks Academy—"

"Carstairs Oaks is an estate."

"It was," the older man corrected him. "When old Elizabeth Carstairs died, she left her estate to be converted into a girls' school."

"Hmm." David began to pick out an old melody on the piano. Maybe if he dropped the subject, his father would, too.

"David, perhaps you don't understand," the colonel began again as if explaining to a balky little boy. "These young ladies I have narrowed the choice down to come from very well placed families. One of them is the niece of General—"

"Oh, please, Father, must we discuss this?"

"Of course not! I won't take no for an answer—"

The doorbell rang again.

"Why does the bell keep ringing on Jeeves's day off?" the older man roared and limped out of the room.

David sighed with relief as he watched his father leave the room. He wasn't going to take no for an answer about that party tonight, and maybe it wasn't worth bucking him over. But one thing was. David reached to touch the letter in his pocket and smiled. He was going to ask for a post at Fort Robinson so he could search out Two Arrows. He would have his pair of fine horses shipped there, too. Only twice before, when he had bought the Texas ranch and when he had saved the colt his father had ordered destroyed, had David ever defied old Fritz Krueger. The posting at Fort Robinson would be the third time. *Third time's a charm,* he thought.

The colonel limped back into the library carrying a large box, his face puzzled. "This came for you; something you ordered months ago, the deliveryman said."

"I don't know what it could be." Baffled, David stood up and took the box, laid it on the top of the piano, opened it, removed the tissue paper. *Oh my God.*

"What is it?" His father peered over his shoulder.

For a long moment, David could not answer; his voice choked up and his eyes blurred as he ran his hand over the fine fur. "It—it was to be a surprise Christmas gift for the woman I hoped to marry."

"Marry? You've said nothing about a woman—"

"She—she was killed by the Indians a few weeks later. I had planned to bring her home for the holidays to meet you." David blinked the tears away and stroked the fur, imagining Glory in this full-length coat, the fox-trimmed hood around her lovely, proud face.

"Oh, I'm sorry," the colonel said casually. "You should have told me; fine family, I presume?"

"Family? I really don't know," David whispered. *I am going to kill Two Arrows,* he vowed again. *I am going to stare down that gunsight into his dark eyes and say, "This is for Glory."*

"Well, time marches on." The colonel dismissed the coat and the information. "The best thing is for you to attend the ball tonight, meet all these pretty young things, choose one who might give your career a big boost, and give me some fine grandsons."

"Father, I don't really think I feel—"

"Oh, but you'll feel much better once you get there," his father said, "and you've disappointed me so many times in your life already."

David stared out the window, his hand still stroking the fur. There was no use in arguing; his father was determined to take David to the ball. Someday, he'd stand on his own two feet and make his own decisions, but for now . . . "All right, Father." He sighed in defeat. "I—I'll go get dressed."

Nineteen

It was a cold and lonely Christmas for Muldoon at Fort Robinson as only Christmas for someone with no kin can be. He broke his own vow not to gamble and his arthritic hands did well enough that he cleaned out the paychecks of half the soldiers in the company. With the money, he bought trinkets, toys, and peppermint sticks for the Cheyenne children. Muldoon was particularly taken by the charming little elf known as Grasshopper and her old grandmother, Moccasin Woman. On Christmas Day, he presented the old woman with a thick wool blanket and a small china doll for the child.

Moccasin Woman accepted the gifts with somber gratitude. "You are good man, Muldoon, you respect my people."

He felt himself color. "Ah, who could not respect such brave ones? And somehow, ye remind me of my own dear mither."

"Here is gift for you." Gravely, the old woman presented him with a package of smoked beef jerky. "I made this myself from our rations."

He started to refuse it, knowing the Indians had little food to spare, then remembered that to give a gift, one must accept one in return. "Thank you. I'm glad Grasshopper enjoys the doll."

The old woman sighed as they both turned to watch the little girl running through the snow with the doll in her arms. "What we would really like is to be turned loose. Will it happen, Muldoon?"

He hesitated. "I am only a soldier; I get no say in such things." He could not bring himself to tell her that rumors around the fort said that Washington had made its decision, and it didn't bode well for the Cheyenne.

Later that evening, he reread the letter he'd gotten from David Krueger and worried about him as he rubbed his throbbing hands. Muldoon had served with Fritz Krueger and knew there was not an ounce of give to the stern old man. Ah, what Michael wouldn't give to have a fine son like David!

He got a new letter from David the day after New Year's saying that while he hadn't yet gotten the nerve to tell his father, he'd applied to be transferred to Fort Robinson so he could serve with his old friend and already arranged to have Second Chance and Gray Mist shipped up there. This latest message gave the old sergeant even more cause for concern. When it came down to it, Muldoon didn't think the young officer had the nerve to defy his stern father, and he wasn't sure what would happen between David and the Cheyenne. What Muldoon hadn't told David in his letters was that he had recognized Two Arrows at a distance, and that the warrior was here at the fort.

Muldoon had mixed feelings about it all. But then, things happened in war, and these people had been desperate. He doubted David Krueger had anything but hatred for these people, and who could blame him? Muldoon could only hope fervently that if the Cheyenne were to be sent back to Indian Territory, they would be gone before David ever arrived.

Two Arrows sat on a wooden stool at the end of his bunk, restringing a hunting bow. He looked up at the sound of Dull Knife's step. One look at the set face told him there was trouble. "What is it, O Great Leader?"

"The white officer has called a meeting; I am to bring our most important men. I want you at my side, Two Arrows."

He nodded, his heart heavy. Once, Two Arrows's heart would have rejoiced at the honor, but the chief's grave face made him think only of the fate of his people. They talked a moment, then Dull Knife turned and left to confer with Tangle Hair and Wild Hog. Two Arrows began to make ready to go. Proud One ran up, alarm on her pretty dark features. "Everyone says a meeting has been called. Is it good news?"

"I don't know." Deep in his heart, he knew; Dull Knife's tragic expression had betrayed him, but Two Arrows couldn't bear to tell her yet. "I am to be part of the delegation that meets in Captain Wessells's office this afternoon."

She put her arms around him. "I am proud you are to be among the leaders."

He hugged her. "Once, having my honor returned, being accepted by the chiefs and war leaders would have been all that mattered to me; now you are most important." He kissed her forehead.

She looked so hopeful, smiling up at him as if she had something to share. "It must be good news; it just has to be."

His heart was so heavy, he hardly heard her. "Nothing has to be. Like a Cheyenne woman, you must learn patience and not to expect good things from most whites. Now, help me dress. I would not dishonor my people by not appearing as a warrior of many coups."

She helped him into his finest buckskins, which she had beaded herself, and put eagle feathers in his hair and hammered-silver ornaments on his arms and neck. When he finally strode through the admiring throngs of women and children and saw Proud One's pleased face, he knew that once again, he looked as an honored dog soldier was supposed to look, with his Dog Rope band over his broad shoulder, the ceremonial war shield on his arm.

Old Moccasin Woman set up the trilling for the victorious warriors that he had not heard in many a year. The other women picked it up as they surrounded the little group that was to be sent from the ragged old barracks to the captain's office. Dull Knife's shoulders straightened and Tangle Hair, Crow, and the others raised their heads high, remembering the old days when all feared the best and bravest warriors of the plains.

Tears came to Two Arrows's eyes as he looked out and saw Proud One, trilling with the others, looking as if she were born to be a Cheyenne wife. For a moment, he forgot that he was a virtual prisoner at a dreary, snowy location. At the sound of the women's trilling calls, he was once again a top dog soldier, returning from a raid against his enemies, the Pawnee and the Crow. He remembered and relived the glory days of the mighty Cheyenne; his cousin, Iron Knife, and his brother, Lance Bearer. How often they had ridden together against the enemy when the Cheyenne were as proud and free as the wolf. Now all his family was dead or scattered; he knew the whereabouts only of Storm Gathering, Iron Knife's son, who rode with the Lakota.

When he looked into Proud One's face, he knew he loved her more than he had ever thought possible, more than he had loved his Cheyenne wife. Proud One had erased the hurt and the bitterness from his wounded soul. He smiled at her, and she nodded to him in encouragement.

Dull Knife made a gesture to move out, and the group of warriors strode through the snow in their finest costumes, never mind that their moccasins were so thin they could feel the cold through the torn leather and they were all living crowded together in an old wooden barracks.

There were soldiers stationed around the captain's office, and they were armed and nervous-looking. The little group was ushered in, and the captain stood and shook hands with much ceremony. There were other officers there. Abruptly, Two Arrows recognized Muldoon. Sergeant Muldoon's eyes widened as if he almost didn't recognize this proud dog soldier as the drunken white man's scout he had known.

"*Ja,* sit down," the captain said and nodded to the sergeant to pass out big, steaming mugs of coffee with plenty of sugar the way the Indians liked it, and then passed around cigars.

Politely, each Indian took the coffee and a cigar, waiting for the sergeant to pass around the matches. For a long moment, Two Arrows inhaled the smoke, savoring it, and sipped the coffee, remembering the old days when as an army scout, he had always had coffee and cigars. But those good things were not worth the respect he now had among his fellow warriors. They sat and drank coffee and smoked a minute, but evidently, the captain did not really understand Indians because he immediately got down to business, and pulled impatiently at his goatee. "I have called you here to talk."

The atmosphere cooled, even Muldoon's ruddy face frowning some, and the Indians looked at each other. Anyone who knew about Indians knew they valued patience. It was good to sip coffee and smoke and talk around a subject a long, long time. It was rude to rush to the point as if in a hurry to end the companionship and be done with it. But then, white men were slaves to the thing they called a clock.

"We will have more cigars and maybe then we will talk," Dull Knife said with a nod, attempting to teach the white man proper manners.

"Sir," Muldoon, who did know Indians, said, "it would be good to pass around food and perhaps some lumps of sugar—"

"Nein, Sergeant, I didn't need you tell me what I should do next." The man's expression looked like thunder.

The Indians exchanged glances. It was not good that a leader humiliate one of his own men in front of others.

Captain Wessells stood up abruptly and glared at each one through the cloud of smoke. He reached in his desk for a paper and waved it about. Two Arrows had never been sure why white men set so much importance on the scribbling on paper. "Word has come from Washington. I'm sorry, Dull Knife, it is not my doing, but I am ordered to send your people back to the Indian Territory." He threw the paper down on his desk as if relieved to be finished with the announcement. "There's no use making a fuss about this."

Now he hesitated, as if uncertain. No one was making any fuss; they were all sitting there staring at him stoically. Two Arrows did not move or speak. He felt as if a knife had just been plunged into his heart. Even though he had been expecting this, it still was like a death sentence being handed down.

With much dignity, Dull Knife rose. "Does not Washington understand that to return us to Indian Territory and its hot weather is to condemn us all to death?"

The officer swore in an unknown tongue. "How do I know what Washington thinks?" The captain began to pace the floor in his shiny boots. "They don't tell me such things; *ja,* I only follow orders."

"We will not go," Dull Knife said, and turned to look at all his men. There was a murmur of agreement around him. "We will not go," he said again. "If we are going to die, we might as well die here."

The captain looked both confused and angry, pulling very hard at his goatee. "But you see, you cannot defy Washington; you must do as they order."

"Why?" asked Tangle Hair. "Why do we need ask someone in a distant place where we may go and what we may do? We have roamed this land long before the white man came."

The captain picked up the paper again. "This says what you must do; but I don't know exactly when you must do this."

The Indians smiled and nodded to each other. Two Arrows felt relieved. Washington usually moved very slowly. By the time they got around to deciding this, there might be a new man in this White House all the soldiers talked about, and he would countermand everything the other had said.

Dull Knife stared out the window at the frozen landscape and the deep snow outside. "We will not go back, no matter what Washington says." Then he stood up, and with great ceremony, strode outside, followed by the others. Two Arrows was in such a state of shock that for a long moment, he did not notice that Muldoon had followed them outside.

"I am sorry," Muldoon said. "I am sorry."

The others turned and walked away with great dignity, but Two Arrows paused. "Sergeant, you and I have known each other many, many moons."

"Yes, 'tis true," the other nodded, "but I did not recognize you just now."

"I saw a chance to change, and I took it." He decided not to mention it could all be traced to a much loved woman. "Is there any chance that Washington will change its mind?"

The other hesitated.

"Speak true to me, Muldoon, I know you have a good heart."

The other hesitated, looked away, and shook his head. "None, from what I hear; I'm sorry."

If he had some weeks to plan and some warm weather, maybe the Cheyenne could plan to walk away from Fort Robinson the way they had walked away from Fort Reno. "How long do you think before Washington tries to make us go?"

"Maybe soon, they say."

"Soon?" Two Arrows said in amazement. "But it would be loco to try to force old ones and children to start back through the snow and blizzards."

"Aye, it is a crazy thing indeed"—Muldoon looked chagrined—"but then, Washington has never been known to do the sane, logical thing, like wait for warmer weather."

"Muldoon, about the white woman—"

"I don't want to know how she died," Muldoon interrupted him. "I know things happen in war that men do not mean to happen. I should warn you that Captain Krueger has asked for a transfer to this post and you know what's in his heart. I think it will be a good thing if the Cheyenne are transferred elsewhere before he arrives."

Two Arrows stared at him in confusion. The whites thought Proud One was dead for some reason; no one would be looking for her. He could keep her forever unless someone recognized her. However, Muldoon was right; Two Arrows and Proud One needed to be gone before Captain David Krueger came to Fort Robinson.

Muldoon rubbed his hands together and frowned. "Damnable weather! Did you have something to tell me, Two Arrows?"

He could not bring himself to make this sacrifice yet; not when there was any hope. "No; nothing." He turned and strode away.

Back at the barracks, all was wailing and confusion. Proud One rushed up to him, and he could see great sadness in her dark eyes.

"You heard?"

For a moment, she could not speak and tears welled up in her eyes and she only nodded. "Is—is there nothing that can be done?"

He could not bear to see her so sad. "Perhaps Washington will change its mind," he said a little too brightly, "or perhaps, by the time they decide to do this thing, we will have managed to get away. After all, we did it once."

His words seemed to cheer the wailing women and children and they began to talk to each other. "Yes, we did it once. If Washington says go, perhaps we can slip away and escape like we did before."

But late that night, as he lay on their bunk, holding her close, listening to the steady breathing of the others sleeping in the barracks, he could only think that the whites thought she was dead and they would not be looking for her if she were careful. "I'm sorry the news was not good," he whispered, and held her close.

"They will surely change their minds." She sounded scared and desperate. "We will freeze to death or die of exhaustion on that long trail back."

But not you, my dear one, he thought as he held her close. *I am going to do whatever it takes to save you, no matter how much it breaks my heart.*

She snuggled against his big body. "What are you thinking?"

"How very, very much I love you," he said, and was glad it was dark so she could not see the tears in his eyes.

"Then make love to me," she whispered, and kissed him until he returned her kiss and began to make slow, tender love to her. "There are tears on your cheeks; what's the matter?"

"Smoke from the stove," he lied, and held her very close, knowing that soon all he would have would be the precious memories of moments like these. He began to make love to her as if by doing so, he could chase away the reality that he already knew; they were going to be separated, and he was going to see to it.

That night, the Cheyenne brave, Bull Hump, disappeared. Two Arrows knew the man had been longing for his wife, who had slipped away when the Cheyenne were first captured by Captain Johnson. Barracks gossip said that Bull Hump's love for his wife had overshadowed all and he had simply forgot Captain Wessells's ruling that each must be present and accounted for, or he would not have caused his people this trouble. Nevertheless, the next day, when the soldiers did the head count on the parade ground and there was one missing, Captain Wessells flew into a thundering rage and lectured the Cheyenne like naughty children. *"Ach!* One is gone! You are responsible!" he roared at Dull Knife.

Dull Knife stared back at the officer calmly. "Among our people, each man is responsible for himself. Bull Hump's woman is among the Lakota; he had a sudden urge to see her, so he went."

"I want hostages to prove no one else will leave," the captain said, marching up and down in his shiny boots.

"No other man has a woman among the Lakota," Dull Knife said with great logic.

In the background, some soldiers laughed, and the captain grew even more red-faced. *"Ja!* You are making me look the fool!"

Two Arrows said, "We do nothing; the captain needs no help."

The captain was so angry, he shook, and he waved a paper in Two Arrows's face. "You are all to be sent back immediately! Do you hear? *Ja!* Immediately!"

A murmur ran through the Cheyenne standing on the parade ground as the officer's words were quickly translated.

Two Arrows felt a chill run up his back. "Immediately? But the snows are very deep and the weather is the coldest it has been for years. Wagons cannot move in this—"

"You'll get back the way you came," the officer shouted. "You can all walk!"

In his mind, he saw his Proud One struggling through the snow and ice on the return trip. He wasn't certain she could survive that. "Many of the women and old ones will not live if they are forced to travel in this weather," he argued. "Many of them will die."

"That is not my problem." The officer shrugged. "I will follow my orders."

Dull Knife's stoic face did not change. "We will not go. If we are to die anyway, we might as well die here in our northern country that we love."

"By damn, you will do what I say!" the captain roared, then turned and stalked off in his shiny boots. The Indians stared after him a long moment.

"We will not go," Dull Knife said with a note of finality to the others.

The others nodded agreement and started back to the barracks. Two Arrows stared after them a long moment, sick to his very soul. More than anything, he had wanted to live free and proud, his woman by his side. If the long trip back through this terrible cold didn't kill most of the people, the hot, dry country of the Indian Territory would finish the job. He could not allow that to happen to the Proud One; he loved her too much, enough to think clearly about what was best for her.

That night, he prayed to the great god for guidance while holding his woman in his arms.

"Is it true, Two Arrows, are we really being sent back?"

"So they say; but perhaps the decision will change."

She stroked his face. "You try to remain hopeful for me, so I won't worry."

"As ill as you've been lately, I doubt you could survive that trip twice."

"I can make it," she said, her voice stubborn. "As long as we are together, nothing else matters."

The moonlight streaming through the window revealed just how tired and fragile the Proud One really was. He would not put her through that ordeal only to lose her in the cold and snow. He leaned over and kissed her forehead. "No matter what," he said, "know that I loved you more than life itself."

"Why do you talk like that?" she whispered. "We will both survive this, and, somehow, we'll be happy, even if we do have to live near Fort Reno."

He held her very close and made gentle, tender love to her because he had already made his decision about what he was going to do. The two choices open to the Cheyenne were terrible ones: either they could fight and die here resisting the order, or they could go back on that long fifteen-hundred-mile walk. Either way, Proud One would probably either be killed or sicken and die. Two Arrows made his decision; he would save her, even if he must lose her.

The next morning, he sought out Muldoon when no one else was around to see him talking to the soldier. "Muldoon, about Captain Krueger, he is coming here?"

The old Irishman nodded, his look puzzled.

"Did he love the white girl very much?"

Muldoon nodded. "He always said he loved her more than any man could. Why—?"

"She—she's alive." He loved her more than David Krueger ever could, he was certain of it.

"What? I don't understand—"

"Just listen." Two Arrows lowered his voice. "She is in this camp dressed as a Cheyenne woman, my woman."

Muldoon's blue eyes widened. "If this is some kind of a terrible joke—"

"I tell you she is here," Two Arrows insisted. "I have kept her away from you so you wouldn't recognize her."

"You've been holdin' her prisoner—?"

"Yes," Two Arrows lied. "She's been my prisoner, and she wants to return to Captain Krueger."

The other looked baffled as he blew on his hands in the cold and rubbed them together. "If she's been a prisoner, she's had plenty of chances to approach any of us in the past several months and ask for help, why—?"

"Muldoon, don't ask anything you don't really want to know."

"She's in love with you," Muldoon said suddenly, understanding in his pale eyes, "and she doesn't know you're doing this."

"She's not to know we talked." Two Arrows swallowed hard. "I—I want her to be safe."

"But the others," Muldoon said sadly, " 'tis a sinful thing to force little ones like Grasshopper and her old grandmother to walk all that way in the cold."

He did not dispute that. He would save them all if he could, but he only knew how to save one. "The Proud One has become a Cheyenne in her heart, but I cannot let her die, and I know Captain Krueger loves her."

"Proud One?"

"Glory," Two Arrows said. "I gave her her Indian name."

Muldoon smiled slowly. " 'Tis fitting. What would you have me do?"

He sighed and almost changed his mind, then he thought of how much she meant to him and knew he was willing to make any sacrifice that would protect her. "I—I want you to send Captain Krueger a wire, tell him she's here, so he'll come immediately."

"But he'll kill you on sight!" the old Irishman protested. "And—"

"I'll take that chance, if only he'll take Glory away from here, marry her, take care of her."

Muldoon looked at him a long moment. "You must love the lass very, very much."

For a moment, Two Arrows could not answer; he only nodded. "More than I have words to tell. She must not know I've done this; she won't understand. Once she's away from me, the captain can win her love again. She belongs with him, but she doesn't realize it."

"I see." Muldoon nodded. "I know the telegrapher here; I can trust him."

"You alone I trust," Two Arrows warned. "The soldiers must not realize who she is. If word gets out before Krueger arrives, they will take her out of the barracks. There is no telling how soldiers would treat a white woman who had chosen to stay with the Indians."

Muldoon didn't answer. They both knew drunken soldiers might consider Glory Halstead fair game for any man who wanted her. He held out his hand very slowly, and Two Arrows shook it. "Two Arrows, there's something that's been bothering my conscience, something I did back at Fort Reno."

"Yes?"

" 'Twas me that got you whipped," Muldoon admitted, coloring with shame. "I told the officer about you grabbin' her horse's reins; because, you see, I feared for her at your hands. I had seen the expression on your face when you looked at her."

Two Arrows nodded. "Deep in my heart, I don't think I ever believed she did that; she was too proud to beg any man's help."

"Aye, she's proud, all right; that's what always made her so different from other women I've known, proud and brave, too. I often wondered if she was Irish?"

Two Arrows stared at him, startled, and in that moment, he realized that Muldoon was in love with her, too, and wondered if the old soldier even realized it himself?

Muldoon cleared his throat awkwardly. "Aye, I'll send the wire. Maybe I can't save them all, but by God, I'll help you save her."

"Do it right away before I change my mind or Captain Wessells can act on his orders," Two Arrows said. "And thanks, Muldoon."

They shook hands solemnly again before Two Arrows walked away. What he didn't tell Muldoon was that the Cheyenne had already made their choice. He wanted to get Proud One out of harm's way—because rather than return to Indian Territory, the Cheyenne had decided to stand their ground, fight and die here!

Twenty

"I'll get it!" David hurried to the door when he heard the bell ring. He was expecting a letter that he'd been reassigned to the West, and he wanted to present it gently to his father, hoping perhaps he could still avoid a confrontation. All these years, David had hungered for his father's approval, and yet, he was going against Fritz Krueger's wishes by asking for a post in Nebraska. He had mixed feelings about that.

He opened the door to a lanky boy delivering two telegrams, one telling he was being reassigned to Fort Robinson. He sighed with relief and shut the door, starting to open the other as the colonel came down the stairs.

"Who was at the door?"

"It was a telegram, Father," David took a deep breath, "with my assignment."

"Ah, good! You'll like Washington!" The old man rubbed his hands together briskly with satisfaction. "Now, the next thing is out of all these girls you've met, to find you—"

"We've—we've got something more important to discuss," David stammered, annoyed with himself for feeling like a small child about to brave his father's wrath over a new toy. "Why don't we go into the library and talk about this?"

"All right." They went into the library, the old man beaming as he poured himself a whiskey. "This calls for a celebration."

"None for me," David said, wondering how to begin. He had avoided confrontations all his life, trying to please the old man.

He stuffed the telegrams in his coat and took out his pipe. Until he filled and lit it, he hadn't realized his hands were trembling. "Father, you know I wouldn't have much chance for heroic actions in Washington that might get me more medals and commendations."

"That's true," the old man said, sipping his whiskey. "Commendations do get a soldier noticed."

David tried to stop his hands from shaking as he took a deep puff of smoke and stared out at the snowy scene. Did he really want to buck his father? He'd only done so twice in his life; once when he'd gone off to Texas, and later, when he'd saved the colt his father wanted to destroy. "Perhaps we might reconsider my being assigned to the West for that reason."

"No," the older man shook his white head and sipped his whiskey, "that's not what I want for you at all, David."

He took a deep breath. "Father, do you ever think about what I want?"

"What a silly question! I want what's best for you; so what I want is what you want, too."

He couldn't decide what to say next. This was not going to work out; he could not reason with the stubborn old man. David thought about the other telegram in his pocket, the one he had not yet opened. It probably announced that General Carter was doing his father a favor and might have a post available for David in Washington. All that was left was to get his horses rerouted to Washington instead.

Fritz Krueger smiled with satisfaction. "It is going to be a great new year. I am glad we agree on everything, David."

Agree? He hadn't heard a word David said; no, not in thirty-five years. With a sigh, he laid his pipe in the ashtray and reached into his pocket for the other telegram while hating himself for being such a gutless coward. He opened the telegram and read it, then reread it, his mouth slowly opening in speechless amazement.

"David, what is it?"

David stared at the words: *Glory Halstead alive. Stop. Come at once to Fort Robinson. Stop. Signed Sergeant Michael Muldoon.*

"She—she's alive!" No, it couldn't be, how—? But then he cared nothing for logic or anything else, he stood up shouting, "She's alive, Muldoon says she's alive!"

"Who?" His father looked puzzled but annoyed that something seemed about to interrupt his well-laid plans.

"Glory! Glory Halstead!" Maybe it was a mistake; no, Muldoon would be careful about contacting him unless he knew for certain. A thousand questions came to his mind, but he was too excited to do anything but stare at the paper and blink, not certain whether to laugh or cry.

"Halstead? I don't remember meeting—?"

"Father, don't you remember I told you I was in love and wanted to bring her home to meet you? Oh, there's so much to do! I've got to get a train ticket—"

"David, what on earth are you talking about?"

"I thought she was dead, but she's turned up alive somehow," David babbled. "I've got to go to Fort Robinson." He strode to the door and yelled at the maid, "Sophie, please find Jeeves for me, I've got to send him to the train station for a ticket, and then I'll need some help packing. Oh, be sure and get that fur coat in the box upstairs!"

"David, you can't just run off like this." The colonel set down his glass.

"I'm sorry, Father, but I've got to get to her, and when I reach the fort, I'm going to marry her."

"But who are her parents? What's her background? I don't know if I can approve—"

"Father." David turned and faced him, took a deep breath. If he didn't take charge of his own life now and permanently, he never would. "I'm a grown man, I don't need your approval to get married. If I'm getting a second chance, I'm damned well going to take it!"

The old man blinked. His mouth opened, then closed again

as if he didn't believe what he was hearing. "Maybe once I met her and her family, I might—"

"I doubt it, Father." David shrugged. "You see, she's divorced."

"Divorced! David, you can't be serious!"

"I couldn't be more serious," David said and suddenly, he didn't care what his father thought anymore, it was like having a sack of iron lifted from his shoulders. "She's divorced, and I know little of her background, but I love her, and nothing else matters." He started out of the room, heading for the stairs to gather up his things.

His father limped behind him. "David, think what a scandal marrying a divorced woman would be; it will wreck your military career!"

"Would you believe I don't care?" David threw over his shoulder as he started up the stairs to pack.

"So you'll disappoint me again, will you?" the colonel raged, right behind him.

David paused and turned on the landing. "Father, I have always disappointed you; nothing I ever did was good enough. I wasn't as handsome as William, I wasn't as smart as Joe. You've been angry all these years that they died and I lived."

"How dare you say that when you got your younger brother killed along with your sweet wife—"

"Father, stop laying guilt on me; I won't take it anymore!" David was shouting now. "If I had been in Texas instead of off fighting in the War to please you, I might have saved them both."

"The War was a noble cause, your older brother died bravely—"

"It was a waste; a total waste of William's life. I was never cut out to be a soldier, I told you that, but you wouldn't listen. You've never listened, and you've never loved me! Like that colt, you wouldn't accept flaws in man or beast!"

"You are out of your mind!" his father shouted up at him. "I will disown you if you do this, David!"

David paused at the top of the stairs and turned around, looking at him a long moment. "Your money and this property mean nothing to me, but I would like your blessing, Father, on my forthcoming marriage and whatever I choose to do with my life from now on."

"You can never make it up to me for William's and Joseph's deaths!" The angry old man was shouting at him, his face a furious red.

"I know that, Father." David's voice was suddenly soft and soothing. "I am sorry, but I didn't kill them, and I'm so tired of feeling guilty for being alive."

"How dare you speak to me like that!" Fritz Krueger was raging. "William and Joseph would never—"

"I am not William or Joe; and that's the trouble, isn't it? I'm David, poor, bungling, not handsome, disappointing David." He felt suddenly free, and it was a good feeling. "Father, I hope someday, when you think this over, we can start again and maybe have some kind of relationship, but for now, I've got a train to catch!"

His father stood wordless, staring up at him as if he could not quite believe what had just happened.

David turned and raced up the stairs, his heart pounding with excitement. Glory! He wasn't going to ask any questions, and nothing mattered to him but getting her back safely. His revenge against Two Arrows for kidnapping her could wait. As soon as David could get to Nebraska, they would be married, with old Muldoon as his best man and the devil take the hindmost!

It was freezing cold, the temperature continuing to drop, as Captain Wessells called a meeting of the Indian leaders in his office. Two Arrows came and Muldoon was there, but this time, the officer did not do the good-mannered thing and offer coffee or tobacco. There was no ceremony at all.

"I'm sorry," he snapped, "but I've heard from Washington,

and they say you must be sent back to Indian Territory." He waved the paper in their faces.

There was a murmur of disappointment and disapproval from the Indians.

Two Arrows cleared his throat. "How many weeks before—?"

"*Ja,* immediately," the captain said, pulling at his goatee.

Even the soldiers in the room gasped.

For a long moment, Two Arrows tried to deal with the reality of the words as others translated for the old ones. "Immediately?" Two Arrows asked. "But the temperature is below zero out there and—"

"*Nein,* that is not my problem." The officer shrugged, staring down at his shiny boots. "I tried to convince Washington they should wait for spring, but they say the trip should begin now."

"This is loco." Two Arrows leaned on the desk, glaring at him. "Most of these people will freeze to death in this weather if you make them walk all the way back to Fort Reno!"

"Maybe we can get a few wagons," the officer offered, "or maybe not. Anyway, Dull Knife, you must go back to the barracks and tell your people. By tomorrow—"

"But there's even more snow coming," Two Arrows protested. "It is madness and murder to put children and old ones out on the trail in this weather."

"Maybe that's the idea," someone whispered, and it sounded like Muldoon.

"*Ach!* I heard that!" the captain roared. "Who said that? I'll put him on report!"

No one said anything, but Two Arrows looked over at Muldoon's ruddy face, and saw the disapproval there. Time. Time was the Cheyenne's enemy; if they only had more time to convince Washington, time until the weather warmed, time until they could escape.

Dull Knife made a stony-faced gesture of dismissal. "We will not go back to Indian Territory; it is hot and our people die there. If we must die, we will do it here in our own land."

Captain Wessells seemed to be barely holding his temper. "I

have asked Washington for the delay, but they say *nein,* and I must fallow orders. Go tell your people."

"There is nothing to say," Dull Knife answered with great dignity. "We will not go." At that point, he turned and marched out of the office. His warriors followed him out. Two Arrows paused outside, looking at the snowdrifts and worried as much about Proud One as about his own people.

Muldoon came out just then and stood next to him. They watched the old men walking back to the barracks.

"Aw, Two Arrows, I'm that sorry. I wish I could—"

"I know, Muldoon; it's not your fault." He looked down at his worn moccasins and thought about subfreezing temperatures and sickly people without enough blankets and warm coats. Most of them would die on the return trip. "Did you reach Krueger?"

"Yes, I suppose he's on his way, but with this weather, there's no telling when he'll get here."

"Good, then she'll be safe. Now I only have to worry about the rest of them."

"This is loco," Muldoon rubbed his hands together. "I've grown right fond of that wee child, Grasshopper, and her old grandma. They can't survive that long march."

"Muldoon, we aren't going; you heard Dull Knife. We'd rather die here and now than slowly in Indian Territory. I only hope Krueger arrives in time to get Proud One before—"

"I'm sorry," Muldoon whispered. "I'm truly sorry."

"You're a good man, Muldoon; there's going to be some soldiers killed if they try to force us; I hope you aren't one of them."

" 'Tis suicide to resist," Muldoon protested.

"And it's suicide if we have to walk through blizzards. You're a gambling man, Muldoon; looks like our odds are bad either way."

"By the Blessed Mother, I wish I could help you poor devils."

"Thanks for your kindness; just pray that the captain will at least get here in time to save my woman." Two Arrows strode away toward the barracks, lost in thought. It appeared he'd have to take desperate action to save Proud One if David Krueger didn't get here in time.

That evening, the Cheyenne decided they would no longer come out of the barracks. The captain sent a soldier to read an announcement that he was going to cut off food and fuel and that the women and children should come out and surrender. Only a handful came out.

Two Arrows urged Glory to leave, but she shook her head, stubborn as any Cheyenne woman. "We have talked it over," she said, "and the women have decided that Captain Wessells will not fire on the barracks as long as there are women and children inside; to do so would look bad in the newspaper, so as long as the women stay, our men are safe."

He put his arm around her shoulders, hugging her to him, wondering how many days it would be before David Krueger arrived on the post? The barracks was like a powder keg that would soon explode. Two Arrows did not want Proud One to be here when it happened.

She looked up at him, her dark eyes so large in her small face as she reached to touch his cheek. "What is it? I know you well enough to know something's wrong."

"I'm worried about the outcome of this, that's all." It was difficult to look into her eyes and lie to her. Instead, he took her in his arms and held her close, relishing each moment, knowing that he had only hours or maybe a day or two at best before she was taken away by David Krueger. The thought of her in another man's arms almost tore his heart out, but she would be safe, and that was what mattered most.

"I've got to help Moccasin Woman," she said. "The women are going to ration out the food, see how long we can make it last."

"You eat my share."

"No." She shook her head. "There's too many children and old ones; I couldn't take it with good conscience."

He nodded, his mind busy with the problems facing the people as he watched her walk away, relishing the look of her, the warmth of her. She would make David Krueger a better wife than he deserved. The thought made him swallow hard and his resolve weaken. He must not weaken, not if he loved her.

Dull Knife called a meeting of his main leaders to discuss what to do next.

Two Arrows sat on the floor with the others, knowing there were few options. "All I can suggest is that we try to break out when the soldiers least expect it, try to find and rejoin Little Wolf."

There was much discussion, each trying to find a less grim alternative; but there seemed to be none.

Dull Knife looked around at the silent women and children. "We can last a while without food and firewood; maybe in the meantime, Washington will change its mind."

Two Arrows said, "The women are rationing the food, and we can break up furniture and wooden beams of the barracks to keep the stove going a day or so more."

The others nodded with approval.

Crow said, "We have those few guns hidden under the floor we can assemble."

"How many?" Wild Hog asked.

"Maybe five old rifles and a dozen pistols," Two Arrows said.

For a long moment, no one said anything. Two Arrows watched his breath drift on the cold air of the dim light. Somewhere in the barracks, a baby whimpered, and its mother tried to shush it.

Old Dull Knife asked, "Do we have even one bullet for each gun?"

"Maybe one or two each," Crow answered, "but we can tear up the bunks and iron pieces from the stove to make clubs."

A handful of bullets and a few clubs against all those soldiers' rifles, Two Arrows thought, and knew the others were thinking the same.

Wild Hog said, "If we have to break out, we have a better chance getting away at night."

"We are in the midst of a full moon," Two Arrows said. "With the moon reflecting off the snow, it will be like daylight out there."

Old Dull Knife nodded. "If we could wait a few days more, the nights will be moonless."

A murmur of agreement went around the circle. They would wait until they were forced to act.

Tangle Hair, leader of the dog soldiers, said, "If we must break out, the dog soldiers will do as tradition calls for; we will be the last ones out and try to cover the others' escape."

It was the Cheyenne way, Two Arrows thought, the dog soldiers always covered the retreat. They would certainly die as the soldiers recovered from their surprise and began to fire on the escaping Indians. He did not question his fate; he was proud that his people had accepted him again. It was better to be an honored dog soldier than a drunken white man's scout.

Dull Knife got to his feet slowly. "It is decided then."

The meeting broke up, but as Two Arrows returned to his bunk, Proud One caught his arm. "What is this I hear about the dog soldiers staying behind to cover the escape?"

He shrugged. "It is the dog soldiers' tradition, just as we did on the march."

Her chin went up stubbornly. "Then if you stay behind, I will stay behind also. We will both go at the same time."

He put his arms around her and drew her close. "I promise that you will stay behind," he said, and was troubled that his words intentionally deceived her about what he intended to do.

Several days passed. The temperature outside dropped, and Captain Wessells came with another announcement to be read outside the barracks telling the Cheyenne that food, tobacco, and warm blankets waited for those who came out.

No one else came out.

Two Arrows watched the officer walk away, grumbling and kicking his shiny boots against the snow. All the soldiers wore their thick buffalo fur winter coats in this cold while the Cheyenne shivered and did without.

Would David Krueger never get here? His horses had arrived; Two Arrows had caught just a glimpse of the pair being led to the stables by Muldoon. His own exhausted paint horse now belonged to some bluecoat.

Inside the barracks, the temperature had dropped until the drinking water had frozen solid and children whimpered and cried as women tried to melt the ice over dwindling supplies of wood. In spite of all the people could do to ration it, the food was finally gone, and the firewood, too, but still the people refused to come out of the barracks.

Even Muldoon went to Captain Wessells's office to protest. "Sir, I know I'm overstepping me bounds, but those people are goin' to start dyin' in there. The soldiers are feelin' mighty bad about—"

"*Ja;* and what would you suggest, Sergeant?" The German officer leaned back in his chair and glared at him. "Should I have a squad charge the barracks and get a bunch of people killed?"

"I don't know, sir."

"Well, I do know. If they have no food or fuel, they finally surrender peaceful and come out."

"Beggin' your pardon, sir," Muldoon said, rubbing his aching hands together and silently cursing this cold country, "I've dealt with Indians much longer than you, and I think they'll die in there before they surrender and let you ship them back."

"*Nein.*" Wessells pulled at his goatee in frustration. "They will not let their women and children die that way."

Muldoon shrugged. "They figure if they're going to die anyway, they might as well die one place as another."

"Thank you for your comments, Sergeant, you're dismissed, but you may put a little more wood in the stove before you go."

"Yes, sir." Muldoon began putting kindling in the big iron stove near the desk.

"It is damnable cold." The officer hitched his comfortable chair closer to the stove. "I hear Captain Krueger is due here anytime."

Muldoon looked up from his chore. "So I hear, sir."

"I've got one final card to play to bring those Cheyenne out to surrender." The officer sipped his brandy and stared out the frost-covered window.

"I don't know what else you can do, sir." Muldoon glared at him. "You've cut off their food and fuel."

"Pass the word not to give them any more water."

Muldoon paused and stood up. "Sir?"

"You heard me!" the captain snapped. "No more water!"

"But sir—"

"Ach! Do you not speak the English? That is an order!"

Muldoon took a deep breath and gritted his teeth.

"Sergeant, I hope I do not have to remind you that you only lately regained your stripes. The next black mark on your record may get you drummed out of the corps!"

Muldoon swallowed hard. "Yes, sir. I'll see to it, sir." He saluted, managing to keep his face immobile, while his soul seethed with indignation. If David were here, maybe he could do something to stop this cruelty.

"Good. Dismissed." The officer threw him a halfhearted salute and put his shiny boots up on the stove nearer the heat. "We see now how long damned stubborn Injuns can last without water!"

Twenty-one

January 9, 1879

Glory had never been as thirsty as she was at this moment, watching little Grasshopper lick the frost off the inside of the windowpanes. The child did not complain, she only clutched the little china doll Muldoon had given her and licked at the frost. The children and the women were quiet and patient, waiting for whatever came next in the cold barracks as morning turned into afternoon.

It seemed to Glory that she had always been hungry and cold. She shivered uncontrollably, and Two Arrows took his own thin blanket and put it around her shoulders, held her against his warmth. "I am sorry, Proud One, for getting you into this."

"I'm with you, that's all that matters to me." She snuggled up against his big chest and fingered her beaded bracelet. "What happened at Fort Reno seems so long ago."

He kissed her forehead. "If I had let well enough alone, you'd be married to Captain Krueger now and warm and well fed."

"Perhaps." She smiled. "I didn't realize what I was missing until I found it in you."

"If something happened to me, you could return to the white way of life," Two Arrows said. "The captain would still want to marry you."

"Don't ever talk like that!" she scolded. "I am your woman. Do you regret me?"

"Never! Someday, maybe you'll realize how much I loved you."

She didn't like the finality of his tone. "You'll be there to tell me. We're going to survive this."

"I will see that you survive," he whispered against her hair. "I promise that."

Somewhere in the barracks, a child whimpered, wanting water, and its mother shushed it, explaining there was none. Glory ran her tongue over her dry lips and looked outside at the snow clinging to the bare trees and the icicles hanging from the barracks roof. "That looks so good and so cold."

"Don't think about it," he said. "Soon, you'll have plenty of food, water, and warm blankets."

"You think Captain Wessells is going to relent then?"

He didn't look at her. "I wish every white person in America could hear these little ones crying. We're slowly dying here, and no one knows or cares outside this fort."

Outside, it appeared the temperature was continuing to drop. Muldoon and a squad of soldiers came to the barracks. "Captain Wessells wants to talk to Dull Knife again."

Something about Muldoon's expression alerted Two Arrows that something was amiss.

Old Dull Knife stood up to go, but Two Arrows grabbed his shoulder. "Do not go; I think the German officer plots to get you in his clutches and lock you in the guardhouse."

"Yes," seconded Tangle Hair. "He knows that without you, the people are leaderless."

"Some of us will go," Two Arrows announced. "Who will go with me?"

The others hesitated a long moment, knowing that someone must go, but that they might become prisoners. Just such devious plotting as this had killed their Lakota friend, Crazy Horse, at this very fort a little more than a year ago.

"We will go with you, Two Arrows," offered Wild Hog and several of the others.

Proud One caught Two Arrows's arm, "No, not you."

"I must, dear one." He turned, and the little delegation left the barracks.

Surrounded by armed guards, the spokesmen strode through the snow toward Wessells's office. The frozen crust crunched under their moccasins, and Two Arrows licked his dry lips, thinking how good cold, wet snow would taste, but he was too proud to fall down and grab handfuls of it, stuff it into his mouth. He kept his head high, concentrating on the task at hand. The others did the same, although Two Arrows saw that they kept glancing down at the drifts they passed. Out of the side of his mouth, he whispered to Muldoon, "Is Krueger here yet?"

"Not yet; soon; maybe tonight or tomorrow."

He had to trust someone, Proud One's life depended on it. "He must get her out; we've gone as far as we can go."

Muldoon's red face was troubled as they walked. "Aye, I'll do what I can to help."

Then there was no more time to talk as they were at Captain Wessells's office. And again, he demanded that the Cheyenne come out of the barracks and surrender. The Cheyenne simply looked at him and said nothing.

He dismissed them, and they went out onto the porch. At that moment, out of the corner of his eye, Two Arrows saw sudden movement aimed at Wild Hog and shouted.

Wild Hog turned, screaming a warning to his comrades as a soldier's rifle blazed. Two Arrows and the others took off running, leaving Wild Hog crumpled in the snow behind them, rifles cracking like thunder as they ran. When he glanced back, he saw Muldoon diverting the soldiers' attention and Wessells shouting at him for being so clumsy and stupid. Good old Muldoon!

It seemed a million miles through the snow back to the barracks with the soldiers shooting at them. The late-afternoon sun threw distorted shadows across white drifts as the warriors raced for the barracks. The Cheyenne held the door open for them and waved them on. Any second now, Two Arrows expected the agony of a bullet cutting into his flesh or perhaps one through the brain so that he would never feel himself tumbling into the bloody snow.

Like a true dog soldier, he held back now, covering the others' retreat. Then they were inside, their breath coming in icy gasps like cold fire as they slammed and bolted the door behind them.

Proud One ran into his arms. "Are you all right?"

He could only nod and gasp for air, holding her warm body against him. "They got Wild Hog; Wessells wanted hostages, just as we thought."

She looked up at him. "Was Muldoon—?"

"No." He shook his head. "I think he was as surprised as anyone; he may have got himself in trouble for diverting their attention so we could make it to safety."

Outside, the moon came up full and round as a silver ball. Two Arrows peered out the window. "It couldn't be a worse night for us to try a breakout, it's as bright as daylight out there."

The men looked at each other silently.

Dull Knife sighed. "We can't wait any longer; the people are dying of thirst. Get the guns and assemble them."

Crow shook his head in disgust. "If only there was no moon. Against that white snow, they will see us running."

Proud One was holding little Grasshopper, who was wrapped in the wool blanket Muldoon had given the child's grandmother. Grasshopper clutched the small china doll. Proud One looked up at Two Arrows. "There's no other way?"

He shook his head. "We're out of time; it has to be tonight. We'll wait until late, when the fort has settled down to sleep."

She handed the sleepy little girl to her grandmother. "But there'll be guards."

"Yes," he nodded. "I suspect Muldoon will try to help us, but I don't know how."

Glory looked around. The Cheyenne were yanking up the floorboards, dragging out the old guns, reassembling them. Their dark faces looked set and grim in the moonlight that streamed bright as day through the dirty windows.

Two Arrows peered around the window jamb. "There are

many sentries posted now," he said, "marching around this barracks, ready to spread the alarm and shoot anyone who sticks his head out."

Little Shield said, "We have our few weapons and our clubs; maybe we could overpower some sentries and take their weapons."

Glory leaned against Two Arrows, and let him slip his arm around her. So this was what it was all going to come down to; a pitiful chance at escape when the deck was stacked against them.

"You're trembling," he said gently. "Are you afraid?"

"No, just cold. In your arms, I am never afraid, love."

He held her close. "Proud One, I have done what I could for you; I'm sorry I couldn't do more."

She smiled at him and put the tip of her finger on his lips. "No apologies, my love. I wouldn't trade one day of these weeks with you for a hundred years with anyone else."

He caught her hand and kissed that fingertip. "I want you always to remember, Proud One, that whatever I did, I did for love of you."

He was talking about kidnapping her, she thought, but his face was so grim, so tragic.

Old Dull Knife stood now, and even the children ceased their whimpering as he began to speak. "Late tonight, we will make our break. Remember, there are wooded bluffs along the creek about two miles from here. It is almost impossible to get a horse up those bluffs, so if we can reach those, we may outwit the soldiers."

Two miles, Glory thought, two long miles through subzero temperatures, running across the snow with a full moon lighting the scene as bright as day for pursuing soldiers on horseback. To Two Arrows, she whispered, "Some of these old ones and children are too weak; they can't make it that far."

Old Moccasin Woman, standing nearby, seemed to hear her. "We will make it," she said firmly, and held little Grasshopper with her china doll against her bosom, both wrapped in the wool blanket. "We will make it or die in the attempt. Listen, everyone, beyond the bluffs a few more miles, there is a big cave that few whites know. If you make it past the bluffs, go to the cave. We will be safe there while the soldiers search for us."

Two Arrows listened to her describe the cave and nodded. "I know that place."

Dull Knife looked around at the hungry, thirsty people. "There is nothing to do now except rest. Late tonight, when the soldiers are relaxed and most of them in bed, we will make our break for freedom. The dog soldiers, as is the custom, will cover our retreat."

"No." Glory shook her head, looking up at Two Arrows. "No, it's suicide to linger, you must go with me!"

He held her very close and kissed her. "Dear one, I am a drunken Injun scout no more; I am a dog soldier, bravest of the brave. That is their tradition, that they cover the retreat, delay the enemy, at whatever cost."

The tears came to her eyes then, and, almost, she told him her secret, but she knew it would not change his decision. "And I am a dog soldier's woman," she answered, "and I can die as bravely by your side."

"Let us not talk of dying," he whispered. "Let us talk of love and living and how it will be in the spring when the choke-cherries are ripe and the new fawns are born. Let us talk of freedom and riding at a gallop across the prairies with the wolf leading us up into the Buckhorn Mountains and buffalo, thick as a great brown sea, waiting for our bows."

Glory swallowed hard, imagining all that and wanting nothing more than to live to experience the spring with her lover. "And we will dance around the fire and eat juicy ribs," Glory said, and forced herself not to weep. "Then we will swim naked in the river and lie out on a rock in the sun like otters to dry."

"And when we are dry," he said against her ear, "we will make love and then swim again, and there will be plenty of food and all the cold water we can drink."

Around them, the Cheyenne were settling down to rest. Two

Arrows put his arms around her, and they both stood looking out the dirty panes of the window. Outside, the sentries marched, looking cold and miserable, the moonlight gleaming on their brass buttons. She watched Muldoon approach a sentry, stand and talk to him. Muldoon had a deck of cards in his hand. The one sentry paused and then motioned to another.

Beside her, Two Arrows chuckled. "Muldoon thinks to help us. I would not be surprised if after a while, most of the sentries are off in a card game with that old rascal!"

The barracks around them was so quiet, she could hear the gentle breathing in the darkness.

"We need to rest if we are to escape tonight," she said, leading him to their bunk. "Make love to me."

They lay down, and he took her in his arms and held her very close, sheltering and warming her with his strong body. "My dear one. If only I could hold you like this always."

"Don't sound so final," she murmured, and kissed him. "We'll get out of this together; we must get out of this; I can't lose you now."

"You won't lose me, Proud One," he reassured her. "No matter what happens, I want you to remember all the times we spent together. Memories are like golden coins in a bank; you can take them out and spend them over and over again."

"You talk as if you are going to die," she protested. "I don't want you to die; I'm afraid for you to die!"

"We all die, Proud One, each one of us; it is only important that we use whatever time we have, live it to the fullest. Someday, when you are an old lady with grandchildren around your knees, you will perhaps take out those gold coins and smile a little as you sift through those memories, thinking of me."

She was crying now, she couldn't help it. "We will leave this place together," she insisted fiercely. "We must make it out. We can't have come all this way only to die shot down in the snow like starving dogs!"

"Hush, sweet," he commanded, and kissed the tears from her lashes. "You wake the others."

"Make love to me," she said. "Make love to me as if it were the very first time."

"With you, Proud One, each time is as wonderful as the very first time." He gathered her into his arms, holding her as if he would never let her go. After a long moment, she reached to touch his face, and felt the hot tears there.

Around them, others slept the sleep of the doomed and the exhausted, but time was too precious to waste on sleep when these next few minutes might have to last a lifetime.

He opened the drawstrings of her doeskin dress, pushed up her skirt. They clung to each other, kissing in the darkness as if they would never get enough of the taste of the other's mouth and skin. His hands were warm on her body as he pressed her against the heat of him.

It was as if it were the very first time, she thought in wonder as he stroked and kissed her breasts. She remembered all over again what it had been about this virile, passionate warrior that had swept all her reason and inhibitions away.

She was glad to forget about the terror and death that awaited them outside. For an hour, time seemed meaningless, and they made volatile love as if it was both the first time and the last time, caressing each other's bodies, kissing and exploring every summit of experience.

She tilted her body up to meet his, meeting thrust for thrust, daring him, no, challenging him to go even deeper into her hot sweetness while she dug her nails in his broad back, pulling him down into her while his mouth sucked her breasts into two points of pulsing fire.

They made it last a long, long time, and when he finally buried himself in her and gave up his seed, it was with a sweet finality as if he never expected to make love to her again. Then they lay in each other's arms, quiet and lost in thought, content to be together. There was so much to say, and yet, nothing to say, that had not already been said.

She didn't want this night ever to end, knowing that death awaited some of them before morning. When she turned her head and peered out the dirty window, the full moon still lit the snow as bright as day and here and there a solitary sentry walked in the cold, the ice crunching beneath his boots. She felt the precious time slipping away in spite of everything she could do; not the richest or the most powerful could stop the sands of time, but she must try.

"Love me again," she demanded, and arched her back, raising her hands above her head against the steel frame of the bunk, offering her breasts to him. The little beaded bracelet gleamed on one wrist in the moonlight.

He smiled in the dim light and leaned over to kiss each nipple. "Almost, you could tempt me to stay; never leave."

"Let me tempt you then," she said, her arms still above her head, her wrists resting against the steel of the bunk.

He caught her wrists with one big hand, holding them against the iron as he kissed her breasts. "Remember, I did this to you as a captive."

She smiled in remembrance, liking the feel of his hard hands pinning her wrists above her head so that she was a helpless prisoner of his passion as his hot mouth kissed her breasts. "Keep doing that," she smiled, "and then taste all the way down my body."

Abruptly, she felt him run rawhide strips around her wrists. "What is it you're doing?"

"Tying you up."

"What kind of silly game is this?" She moved her arms and realized she was tied to the iron metal of the bunk.

"I'm sorry, Proud One." He leaned over and kissed her lips again. "I love you more than you know; so I'm leaving you behind."

"What?" She tried to jerk free, but the rawhide held.

"David Krueger is on his way here; I want you to be safe." He stood up.

"No! I want to go with you!"

"Be quiet, you'll alert the sentries and they'll kill us all." He leaned over and kissed her one more time. "Always remember that I loved you more than any other man possibly could." He took the little daguerreotype from his waistband, smiled gently, and slipped it back inside. "I will think of you every minute of every day of my life if I make it. You forget about me and try to be a good wife to Krueger, he's not a bad sort, and he loves you."

"No! You can't leave me behind! I—I've got something I've got to tell you!"

But he wasn't listening; he had already begun to rouse the people, and they were making ready to go out the windows and make a run for it, gambling that the sentries would be too startled and surprised to shoot. Maybe a handful could get away before the soldiers recovered from their shock and took up the chase.

Glory protested, yanking at her wrists, but the rawhide on the steel held. Little Grasshopper stared down at her a long moment, holding the little china doll close.

"Grasshopper, untie me!" Glory demanded, but Moccasin Woman grabbed up the child and shook her head. "You are Two Arrows's woman, and he loves you enough to leave you behind," she said. "Treasure the memory of such a man!"

They were opening the windows, gathering up the guns. Glory went into a panic, yanking at the rawhide until it cut into her flesh. Nothing mattered but going with Two Arrows, and the Cheyenne were making ready to slip out into the night. They were going without her! She pulled at her bonds until it was agony, but she hardly felt it. She would not be left here; she was going with her man if it cost her her life!

Captain David Krueger smiled with relief as the sleigh clipped along at a merry pace and slowed as it pulled down the parade ground among the silent buildings silhouetted against the bright moon in the darkness. "Thanks, soldier, for picking me up at the train."

The skinny youngster saluted. "Happy to do so, sir; hope you'll like Fort Robinson. I'll take your luggage to your quarters."

David nodded, his mind busy as he looked around at the silent post. He could officially present himself to the commander in the morning. "Did my horses arrive, soldier?"

"Yes, sir, finest pair I ever saw; besides that fat buckskin Sergeant Muldoon rides."

David grinned. "Ah, Muldoon! Can you direct me to the sergeant's quarters?"

The other pointed. "I see a light under the door; Muldoon may have a late night card game goin'."

David shook his head and started walking through the snow. Muldoon would never change. Here he had another chance and he still might sink his career if the commander caught him gambling. He wanted to find Muldoon right away, hear about Glory. He wouldn't rest until he held her in his arms tonight; assured himself that it was really the woman he loved and that she was safe and sound.

God, it was cold! David took out his pipe, lit it absently as he walked through the snow, thinking about Texas, and bluebonnets and a woman with black hair that blew behind her like a wild filly's mane.

He looked across the camp with a practiced eye as he walked. Strange, there were almost no sentries out. With those northern Cheyenne held prisoner here, the lack of sentries was very strange indeed. He wondered if Two Arrows were among them? Why hadn't Muldoon told him that?

David smoked as he walked, his anger at the thought of the Cheyenne burning deep in his belly. Yes, they had been a formidable foe, one had to respect them for that. However, he didn't intend that should stop him from executing Two Arrows. Had that savage touched her? David loved her too much to let it make a difference, but when he had Glory safely back in his arms, then he would seek out that damned savage and kill him if it cost him his captain's bars.

He strode over to the door with the dim light filtering beneath, rapped sharply.

"Who's there?" asked the startled, unmistakable Irish voice. There was also the sounds of a flurry of confusion and an ex-

cited murmur of voices as if the men were hiding the money
and the cards.

"Captain Krueger, newly arrived."

The door flew open and the old man jerked him inside in a
bear hug. "Ah, lad, I thought you'd never get here! Boys, this
here is the best captain in the cavalry!"

The men were falling all over each other attempting to stand
at attention.

"At ease, men." He tried not to grin. "You're all dismissed;
except you, Muldoon. It appears you're breaking some rules
here; we'd better discuss this."

"Yes, sir." Muldoon saluted, his blue eyes twinkling in his
ruddy face.

David liked to be saluted, it showed respect. The others tum-
bled over each other to get out of the room. David waited until
the last one was gone. Then they shook hands again and clapped
each other on the back.

"Ah, lad, I thought ye'd never get here."

"Muldoon, have you lost your mind?" David tried to sound
gruff. "If the commander caught this going on . . . hey, by any
chance, were those the night guards?"

The Irishman looked suddenly devious. "Well, now, they very
well might be."

"The Cheyenne are prisoners here, and you've got the whole
sentry force playing cards instead of guarding them?"

"Davie, things are terrible here—"

"Never mind about that." David knocked the ashes from his
pipe. "You said she's alive, where is she?"

"Aye, she's still with the Indians. Two Arrows—"

"Two Arrows?" David felt a rush of hot anger. "Is that red
devil here? I hoped he'd been killed!"

Before Muldoon could answer, all hell broke loose in the
camp.

Twenty-two

Glory yanked again on the rawhide, struggling desperately to break free as she watched the Cheyenne silently climbing out the windows. The dog soldiers were waiting until the last as was the custom, each carrying whatever poor weapon he had. Most of them had no more than one or two bullets.

Two Arrows looked back at her one more time as she fought to break free. "Remember always how much I loved you," he whispered.

"Two Arrows, please, don't leave me behind."

"Good-bye, Proud One. Pray that we make it." Then he, too, slipped through the window.

For only a split second, she stared after him, acutely aware that she was alone in the barracks. She yanked so hard on her wrists that she felt the rawhide cut into them and the flesh bleed, but she didn't care. All she cared about was going with her man.

Seconds counted, she knew that. Any moment now, some guard would spy the Cheyenne slipping across the frozen ground around the barracks. With strength born of desperation, she worked the rawhide down the side of the bunk toward the floor and rolled over so that she could reach it with her teeth. She'd heard an animal caught in a trap would chew its leg off to get away and that was just how she felt now. Glory sank her teeth into the rawhide, began to tear at it with her teeth. Her wrists were bloody and every pull hurt, but nothing mattered but escape.

At that moment, she heard a sentry shout, followed by gunfire. Even as all hell broke loose outside, she chewed through the rawhide, stumbled to her feet and ran to the window. A bluecoat lay crumpled in the snow, another was firing after shapes disappearing toward the trees a few hundred yards away. Somewhere, a soldier shouted the alarm, and lights began flickering on all over the fort.

She must not be left behind! Glory went out the window, but beneath her feet instead of the hard crunch of snow, she felt a warm, soft body. She clapped her hand over her mouth to stop her scream, looked down, realized it was the body of old Sitting Man, his brains scattered across the white snow. She felt both guilt and relief that it was not her lover.

Glory took off running for the trees, following the disappearing people. She thought she saw Two Arrows's big body far ahead of her, bringing up the rear of the escape, shepherding the others.

Her little feet went into the snow almost up to her knees and she gasped at the cold as it came up over her moccasins. For only a moment, she resisted the terrible need to quench her thirst by stopping to scoop up snow, realized her life was at stake, and kept running. In the distance, she could barely make out the dark forms of running people. They had fanned out along the terrain, evidently aware they'd be harder to hit that way. In the rolling terrain, she lost sight of Two Arrows.

Gunfire cracked here and there and she saw to her horror that soldiers were scattered in the shadows. Ahead of her, a Cheyenne woman paused to scoop up snow and put it in her mouth. In that moment, her thirst cost the woman her life as guns blazed and she went down.

Glory felt rising panic as she dodged those soldiers and went on. Behind her now, soldiers shouted and guns thundered. When she glanced back over her shoulder, she saw sleepy men running out of army barracks in their long handles, confused, and without boots. However, others fired at anything that moved and more lights came on all over the camp. "After them! They're getting away!"

She kept sloughing ahead, the snow deep as her knees in spots, which made it difficult to move. She gasped for air, her lungs felt as if they were full of cold fire, and her legs and feet grew numb. Ahead of her, she saw an occasional Cheyenne running, too. Each showed up clearly on the white, white snow, the full moon throwing long shadows across the drifts. It was as bright as noonday, she thought in horror, seeing her breath hanging on the cold air ahead of her.

Behind her, the soldiers seemed to be getting organized; at least there were more shots, more shouting and cursing. A young Cheyenne boy was running ahead of her, she could see and recognize him although she could not recall his name. The frozen stream of the White River lay up ahead; Glory could see its ice shining in the moonlight. The boy fell down on the bank, attempting to break the ice. There were other desperate ones there, too, she saw, stopping for water, no matter the danger.

She must not stop; to stop was death. She saw a woman break through a thin place in the ice as she struggled to cross and go into the water up to her waist. To get wet in this weather was to freeze to death. Glory took a deep breath and ran across the hard surface, slipping on the ice, expecting any moment to fall through. There were small trees along the bank on the other side. She ducked into the shadow of those even as several women who had stopped to drink attempted to stand and were cut down by a volley of shots.

Oh, God. She closed her ears to their dying screams and took off running again. Two miles. Dull Knife had said it was two miles, but she had no idea whether in her starved and weakened condition, she could run that far or even if she was heading in the right direction. Nothing mattered but that she keep moving. She was passing others now; those who were too weak to go on, those who had been wounded. Those who were dead. She recognized the body of one of the dog soldiers who had been covering the retreat.

Behind her, the soldiers' guns roared again like deadly thunder, and they sounded closer. Ahead of her, sprawled the body of an old woman, grotesquely spread across the white snow. Oh, please don't let it be Moccasin Woman! The old grandmother had held Grasshopper and her doll as she went out the window. Glory paused to lift the body, didn't recognize the woman who was already stiffening in death. The body's warmth had melted a little hollow in the snow.

She let go of the old woman, knowing she must keep moving. Her legs felt like lead weights as she struggled through the snow, and she wasn't sure she could feel her feet anymore. She could freeze to death out here. No, she shook her head stubbornly; she hadn't gone through all she had endured throughout her life only to die out in the Nebraska cold. Besides, Two Arrows might be wounded, and if he were, he would need her. That thought fueled her weary body, and she began to run again.

Ahead of her were desperate, running Indians of all sizes and ages and, behind her, soldiers were coming. She could hear their shouts and curses, and every few seconds a rifle cracked. It seemed she could feel the lead flying past her ears, and she braced herself, thinking any moment now a slug would catch her. Would she even feel the bullet that killed her? Or would she fall wounded in the snow to bleed in agony or freeze to death? She must not think of that now; nothing mattered but rejoining Two Arrows.

Then far ahead of her like an answer to her prayers, she saw him running through the woods. He looked like a strong, magnificent stag, she thought; he would make it to the tops of the bluffs and the safety of the cave beyond.

Glory redoubled her efforts; determined to catch up to him. She had waited all her life for a love like this, and she was not going to lose him; by God, she was not going to lose him!

The soldiers were gaining on her. She was afraid to look back, but she could hear them crashing through the crusted snow behind her, swearing and shooting at anything that moved.

An old man staggered almost abreast of her, and he gave her

an encouraging nod even as the guns boomed again. He cried out, threw up his hands, and was dead even before he hit the ground. The scent of fresh blood filled her nostrils and ahead of her, melting the snow, was a patch of blood from some wounded soul who must be still running. The dark blood looked so stark smeared across the white drifts. She watched Two Arrows's back as he ran, started to call out to him, knew he would be in danger if he returned for her, kept silent and continued to run. Ahead of her, Two Arrows paused to lift a fallen one, urge him on, still covering the retreat, even though he could easily outrun the others and make it to safety.

The soldiers were gaining on her. She must run faster, she told herself; but she couldn't run any faster. She had reached the top of a bare knoll, where there were no shadowy trees to hide her movements. She would be outlined against the full moon, an easy target for the vengeful guns.

At that point, she tripped and fell in the deep snow, struggling to get to her feet. The shock of the icy chill against her hands and face shocked her back into reality. She didn't mean to call his name, but he was her link to life, to everything good and true. "Two Arrows!" she screamed. "Two Arrows!"

He paused and whirled.

"No!" she shouted. "Go on! I—I can make it!"

His love for her was in his eyes as he turned and came running back, an old rifle in his hand. The soldiers' guns blazed at him, but he didn't stop. He swung the gun like a club, roaring like a bear at his enemies as he charged right into the gunfire. Even as she struggled to get up, he hesitated, dropping the old rifle, grabbing at his side.

"Oh, no! Two Arrows! My love!"

At the sound of her voice, he straightened, her small daguerreotype falling from his waistband as he ran toward her, his hand on his wounded flesh, the blood seeping between his fingers. He was charging right into the gunfire, right into certain death to save her. She held up her hand, reaching for him. If they were going to die, they would go down together, holding on to each other. He was all that meant anything to her, love and truth and courage!

"I've got you, Proud One! I've got you!" With tremendous strength, he bent and lifted her, swinging her up in his powerful arms.

"Leave me! You can make it alone!" she screamed, as he staggered. "Leave me!"

"Not in this lifetime will I ever leave you again!" He gasped and turned and began to run with her in his arms. She clasped her arms around his sinewy neck, feeling his great heart beating hard against her body and his warm blood wet on her doeskin shift as he staggered forward, the soldiers right behind them, guns blazing.

"Oh my dearest." She wept. "I've gotten you hurt! Leave me and go on!"

"Hush," he commanded, and kept moving forward.

In the moonlight, she saw the strain in his face, the sweat on his dark forehead from the pain. His lifeblood was trickling out but he staggered on across the snow, past dead and dying Indians. "We can make it! We can make it, my Proud One!"

Ahead of them, she saw the bluffs looming darkly through the snow. It looked like a thousand miles to the top and safety. He might make it alone, but not carrying her added weight. He was weakening and slowing, yet he hung on to her as if she were the most precious thing in the world to him; more precious than his own life.

At that moment, he stumbled and fell, and she went into the snow. "I—I'm sorry," he gasped.

She scrambled to her feet, caught his hand, and pulled him up, terrified of the bloody smear he'd left in the drift. "Come on, my dear one," she urged. "We've got to get to the top of the bluffs!"

"Yes," he murmured and stumbled ahead, his hand clutching his wounded side, "but if I fall again, don't wait for me. Go on and save yourself."

"Like you did?" She began to walk toward the bluffs, half-urging, half-dragging him with her. Up on the bluff, in the moonlight, the silhouette of the giant wolf appeared suddenly and it threw back its head and howled, a long lonesome sound that echoed and reechoed across the snow, a challenge to a hostile world. "Do you hear him, my darling? He's singing to us the Cheyenne song, a song of freedom!"

Two Arrows looked encouraged as he stared up at the wolf, staggered on. There was a trail through the rocks ahead, a path to the top of the bluffs. Two Arrows's wound left a trail of scarlet droplets on the white snow as he stumbled and paused. "Forget about me," he urged. "Go on!"

She ignored his command, gripping his hand and pulling him with her. Either they were both going to make it or neither would. "It's not much farther," she pleaded. "And the bluecoats are coming! You're a dog soldier, not a white man's Injun; don't quit on me now!"

Her challenge seemed to revitalize him, and he began to climb, following her up the twisted path toward the top of the bluffs.

"We'll make it," she promised herself, the wind cold against her face as she labored across the rocks, reaching back to keep him with her. "We're got to make it!"

Despite her brave words, she wasn't sure he could climb all the way before the bluecoats caught them. *Oh, dear God, please, we need this chance!* Behind them, the soldiers sprayed the rocky bluffs with gunfire, but the pair kept moving. Finally, they reached the summit.

"We're here!" She gasped and put his big arm around her, attempting to help him walk. She could feel his blood on her arm, hot and sticky as she half helped him, half carried him along, his tremendous size threatening to take her to her knees.

His face had gone pale. "Proud One, leave me and try for the cave yourself; I can't possibly walk that far."

"Oh, of course you can," she lied, looking around desperately. Maybe if he could rest a few minutes, and she could get the bleeding stopped. . . .

She started across the bluff, helping him along. A few hundred yards ahead, she saw a rocky outcrop. "We can get out of the wind there, rest a little."

He was protesting that she should abandon him and save herself.

Instead, she dragged him under the rocky ledge and knelt next to him. "Even if I would leave you, which I won't, I don't know where that cave is; I couldn't find it alone."

She inspected his wound in the moonlight. He had stopped bleeding, but he was too hurt to walk any farther, and they both knew it. Glory curled up against him, attempting to keep him warm. *If only we had horses,* she thought, *horses and coats and food, we could make it to the cave.* As it was, this was where they would die or be captured.

Two Arrows held her close. "I wonder if Moccasin Woman and little Grasshopper made it?"

"I hope so." In her mind, she saw the child, with her big brown eyes and the china doll. Glory noticed then with consternation that somewhere in this frantic climb, she had lost the beaded bracelet little Grasshopper had given her. She had felt the bracelet was a lucky charm, and now all their luck had run out.

Two Arrows touched her face very gently with a blood-smeared hand. "I want you to know how much I love you, Proud One."

"Don't talk like this is the end; we're going to make it," she lied, wondering whether to tell him her secret; she might not get another opportunity. Yet if she told him, he would insist that she try for the cave by herself, and she was determined not to leave him. He was hurt too badly to walk, so they could only wait for the soldiers to hunt them down and kill them—that is, if they didn't freeze to death first. They had done the best they could, and now, only a miracle could give them that chance they needed so badly. Glory did something then she hadn't done for a long time; she closed her eyes and prayed for that miracle.

Now all she could do was hug Two Arrows to her, attempting

to keep him warm while they settled down under the lee of the ledge and waited for whatever fate awaited them. She felt strangely at peace. Maybe nothing else mattered as long as they were together.

Back at the fort, confusion reigned. Captain Wessells was running up and down in his underwear, shouting and cursing. *"Gott!* What in hell happened?"

David saluted, trying not to notice the officer was barefooted in the snow. "Captain Krueger reporting for duty; the Cheyenne have broken out!"

The other swore in German. "Guards! Where were guards?"

David glanced over at Muldoon's sweating face, "Uh, temporarily diverted, I think."

"By *Gott,* the savages won't get away with this!" Wessells glared at Muldoon. "Sergeant, everyone be assembled in ten minutes with full gear!"

"Yes, sir." Muldoon snapped him a salute.

Wessells looked down at his cold, bare feet, seemed to realize for the first time that he was standing outdoors in his underwear while the other two men wore full uniforms and thick buffalo fur coats. He turned loose a torrent of German curses, headed back inside, yelling behind him, "Captain Krueger, pass word there's a promotion and reward to the man who gets the ringleaders!"

"Yes, Captain!" David saluted smartly and turned to run to the stable, Muldoon right behind him. "Did you hear that, Muldoon? A promotion and a reward; but I'd pay to kill that damned arrogant savage myself!"

In his heart burned a rage that threatened to choke him. Oh, he had looked forward to this moment, all right! In his mind, he put his gun against Two Arrows's head, and said, "This is for Glory!"

Behind him, Muldoon said, "I don't understand; I thought Two Arrows was leavin' the lass behind for you."

David whirled on him. "Muldoon, are you sure it's Glory?"

The Irishman rubbed his hands together and grimaced in pain. "Aye, I swear by all that's holy."

David swore under his breath as he strode into the stable, ignoring the confusion as the other troopers saddled up and Muldoon gave orders. David led Second Chance out, began to saddle him, good to see his favorite horse. "Good boy! Good boy!"

To the sergeant, he said, "So Two Arrows has dragged Glory along as a hostage again to protect their retreat. Damn him for his cruelty!"

"I—I don't think that's the case, Davie." The older man fell suddenly silent, and David wondered what the sergeant was thinking.

"Saddle up Gray Mist, too," David ordered. "We'll need blankets and medical supplies, canteens. Get the cook to fill one with hot broth."

"Sure, lad." Muldoon saddled up the fat buckskin and pulled his heavy buffalo fur coat closer around his ears.

Abruptly, David remembered. "I'll be right back!" He ran to his quarters where his luggage stood unopened on the floor. He grabbed up the box, ripped it open, took out the fine sable coat with its fox-trimmed hood. It was meant to be Glory's Christmas gift; now its warmth might save her life. David pressed its soft richness against his face, praying she was still alive. His concern for her was equaled only by his fury at the drunken scout. There was no doubt in David's mind that Two Arrows had taken Glory from the barracks as a final, defiant gesture against the officer he neither liked nor respected.

Throwing the fine coat over his arm, David ran back out to the stable, where Muldoon had the three horses saddled and equipped as ordered. The troop was mounting up now.

David threw Glory's fur coat across the cantle of his saddle and mounted Second Chance, took Gray Mist's reins from the sergeant. Then he turned in his saddle, looking back at the troopers. "Men, Captain Wessells has offered a promotion and reward for whoever brings in the ringleaders." He paused. "I assume he meant dead or alive. That big one, Two Arrows, may have a hostage, so take care. Lead out, Sergeant!"

The troop left the stable area at a smart canter, the horses spirited in the cold weather, blowing and snorting. They crossed the snow of the parade ground, following the echoing sounds of gunfire past the old barracks. There was infantry out there following the tracks through the snowy woods. Now and then, they heard shouts or echoing gunfire. David reached to touch Glory's fine coat for reassurance, not even wanting to think that those screams might be hers.

God, it was cold. David had a sudden vision of warm yellow sunshine and lazy guitar music, fiery chili peppers and tortillas. Texas. Perhaps now he could finally face the tormenting past, get on with his life.

David glanced back to see Muldoon pulling his fur coat closer around his red ears and rubbing his aching hands together. "Rheumatiz gettin' so bad, sir, I don't know if I can pull a trigger."

"You've got to find a warmer clime," David said with affection, trying to keep his mind off Glory's fate.

"Army only sends me to frozen hells like this," Muldoon muttered, "and I know nothin' but horses."

The shots were louder and echoing up ahead as they pushed into the woods. The snowdrifts grew heavy enough that they had to slow the horses to a walk. David looked back at Gray Mist, reassuring himself that the food, blankets, canteens, and medical supplies were there. If she were hurt, all these supplies might make the difference between life and death for his beloved. As for Two Arrows—David gritted his teeth and reached for the reassurance of his rifle. He would cut him down like a rabid dog without a thought of mercy.

The Irishman rode next to him.

"Damn it, Muldoon, if you knew she was with the Indians, why didn't you take her out of that barracks?"

"Well, sir," Muldoon lowered his voice as they rode, "if I'd identified her, I was afraid before you could get here, the soldiers might try to make free and easy with her, figuring if some Indian buck already had—"

"Don't even think that!" David commanded, gnashing his teeth in fury. "Even if—if that's what happened, it doesn't count; leastways, not to me. I'm going to kill that arrogant, drunken bastard, and then I'm going to marry Glory and take her away from all these terrible memories."

"Yes, sir."

Up ahead in the snow lay a small body covered with blood. David's heart lurched in fear, and then he realized it wasn't Glory after all. It was a young Indian boy, sprawled as if he'd been running when he was shot down. The heat of his thin body had melted the snow beneath him.

"Holy Mother of God," Muldoon whispered, "we're killin' children."

David blinked, staring down at the pitiful form. The boy couldn't have been much younger than his brother, Joe. He swallowed hard and urged his stallion forward. Up ahead lay another body, a young woman. David rode over and looked down. Glory? No. In his mind, he saw Susan dead on the prairie. White men could kill women and children, too, he realized, just as Indians had done. "It shouldn't have come to this," he whispered. "What drove these people to such desperation?"

He must not show pity; these were enemies, courageous and daring as they might be. David had vowed to track down one of them and execute him as coldly as if he were the colonel shooting a colt with bad legs. Absentmindedly, he reached to pat Second Chance's neck.

David looked around. They must be at least a mile from the fort, coming up behind the infantry scattered through the woods and across the prairie. Gunfire echoed ahead. People were dying out here in the cold night, some of them only wounded and freezing to death. He didn't hate Indians enough to do that to women, children, and old people.

"Sergeant Muldoon, order the men to fan out and search;

back up the infantry, gather up any wounded Indians and take them to the fort infirmary. Then you come with me."

"Yes, sir." The old Irishman turned the fat buckskin and rode back to shout orders while David pulled his hat down farther on his pale hair and waited, his breath hanging like icy fog in the bright moonlight.

Oh, Glory, I'm so worried for you. He looked around, wondering where she might be. The countryside would have been beautiful in spring perhaps, but now it was stark and windswept and so very cold. David shivered in spite of his heavy fur coat, thinking about the Indians who were out there without coats or boots or horses. For the most part, it was going to be like tracking down helpless rabbits as they floundered through the drifts, struggling vainly to escape the well-armed cavalry coming relentlessly behind them.

Muldoon rejoined him. "The men are spreading out, as you ordered."

David nodded, looking around him. "What's up ahead, Muldoon?"

"A creek and some bluffs, sir."

"Let's go."

They rode through the snow, their horses at a walk because of the drifts until, in the distance, they could see the looming shadows of the bluffs.

"If the Cheyenne could reach the top, they might be able to make a stand," David thought aloud. "But I doubt they have much in the way of weapons or ammunition."

"I imagine the poor devils aren't worried about makin' a stand, Davie boy. They're just tryin' to get away."

"I know one that's not going to get away," David said through clenched teeth, urging his horse through the snow again. "I'm going to kill him!"

Up ahead, David saw a little knot of soldiers gathered around. Oh God. He could only pray they hadn't found Glory's body. After all they'd been through, she just couldn't be dead, not when he'd finally arrived to rescue her. He reined in and dismounted. "What's the story, men?"

They saluted. A young, red-faced corporal, pointed to the ground. An old Springfield single-shot rifle lay in snow that was scarlet with blood where someone or something had fallen. David leaned over. The outline of a woman's very small footprint showed clearly. He picked up the weapon. "Is this the best they've got?"

"Most of them only have clubs or knives, sir. If they've got guns, they don't seem to have any cartridges. One of them dropped this." The man held out a small daguerreotype. In the bright moonlight, David recognized that proud, lovely face immediately. Glory. His heart seemed to twist in his chest. Oh, Glory. "What—what happened here?"

The corporal said, "We was close on their heels, sir, and this big buck was running way ahead of us; we never would have got him; but there was a woman laggin' behind."

David looked down at the blood-smeared ice. He wasn't sure he wanted to know.

The corporal, encouraged by his silence said, "The woman tripped and fell. We thought we shore 'nuff would get her; but then she screamed out. That big Injun was almost to safety, but when she screamed, he turned and came back for her, swinging this empty rifle at us; biggest man I ever saw!"

There was a murmur of agreement from the others.

David took a deep breath. Two Arrows, they had just described Two Arrows. "And then what?"

"We was layin' down a deadly fire," another said, "but that Injun came right through it. He must have knowed he'd get hit, but he kept comin' until he got to her. He dropped this weapon and this here picture when he was hit. Pretty, ain't she?"

David looked at it again. For a moment, he could not speak, only nod. "The—the most beautiful woman I ever saw," he said.

"The big Injun was hit more'n once, I reckon," the corporal volunteered, "but still, with her screamin' and reachin' for him, he kept comin'!"

"No." David shook his head. "You must be mistaken; she's his hostage. She was trying to get away; screaming for help from you soldiers—"

"Beg your pardon, sir," said another trooper, "but I don't think so. She was reaching for him like a drowning person reaches for a life preserver, and he kept coming, even after he was hit. You should have seen the look on his face as he scooped her up."

"Never saw anything like it," the corporal said with awe. "Him bad hurt and coming back for her, right through a line of gunfire. He must love that squaw something fierce."

David didn't attempt to correct the soldiers this time; they didn't know about the white hostage and how Glory must have been attempting to escape. Of course Two Arrows wanted to hang on to his hostage. Poor thing, she must be terrified. David's anger waxed even hotter. "So did you lose them?"

The corporal pointed at the bluffs. "They went up there, sir; didn't think they'd make it with him hurt so bad, but she seemed to be encouraging him, urging him up the trail."

Muldoon didn't say anything.

"Corporal," David snapped, "I don't think you men know exactly what you saw. Why didn't you go after them?"

The young man gestured toward the top. "I think there might be a few up there with guns; not certain how they got them, but we don't know how much ammunition. We was waitin' for reinforcements while we tried to decide what to do. That's a pretty steep climb with someone shootin' at you."

The others nodded agreement.

Muldoon blew on his hands and stuffed them in his pockets. "Did you blokes see an old woman and a little girl?"

"Seen lots of them," one said. "Some dead, some just hurt; dirty shame."

A murmur of agreement from the soldiers. Their expressions betrayed that they were not happy about being out in the cold darkness shooting women and children.

Muldoon described the pair he meant and a private said he might have seen them climbing that trail earlier.

David took no part in the discussion, his mind busy assessing the bluff. It was suicide to attempt that trail if armed men waited at the top. Worse than that, he didn't want a stray bullet injuring Glory. He only hoped Two Arrows didn't die of his wounds before David could find him. He didn't want to be done out of the pleasure of killing him.

"Corporal," David said, "scatter out and look around; there may be some Indians hiding in these ravines."

The younger man saluted. "Yes, sir; if you don't mind, we'd like to try to pick up some more of these wounded and get them back to the infirmary."

David saluted. "Permission granted. Come, Muldoon, let's see what we can do about trailing Two Arrows."

Muldoon urged his buckskin forward, but he looked none too happy. "Davie lad, suppose she was reachin' for him?"

"Have you taken up liquor along with your gambling habit?" David was incredulous. "Glory's a hostage, trying to escape and—"

"Captain, I didn't tell you how I knew she was with the Cheyenne."

"I figured she managed to slip you some desperate note or—"

"He told me," Muldoon said. "Two Arrows told me and asked me to contact you, get you to come after her."

"Muldoon, you've been on the sauce. Why would that savage do that?"

"He loves her, Davie; he wanted her to be safe; he wanted you to take her away from here."

"No"—David shook his head—"he was trying to get me to this fort where he might have a chance to kill me. He's holding Glory as a hostage against her will."

Muldoon sighed and shrugged.

David turned his attention to the terrain as they rode closer. "There must be a path up the back side of these bluffs that the others don't know about. Muldoon, you know about this bluff from the Indians, don't you?"

"Davie, why don't you let the poor devils go? There can't be many of them left alive up there—"

"Because I've got a man to kill and a woman to rescue. I can't believe my ears, Sergeant. I think you're actually trying to thwart me." He glared at the older man, his temper rising. "Muldoon, if you know a way up the back of these bluffs, I order you to take me there."

"Yes, sir." Muldoon sighed and rode past him, his shoulders slumped in resignation.

So Muldoon does know, David thought, and fell in behind him as Muldoon swung in a wide circle. How he had dreamed of this moment! David reached for his rifle, checked to make sure it was fully loaded, balanced it in the crook of his arm as he rode. He wanted to be ready for any danger. His poor Glory! Even now, she might be begging her kidnapper for mercy—no, Glory was proud, David remembered, she wouldn't beg anyone for anything; not even her own life. His arms ached to hold her, take her to safety.

The path began to wind up the rear of the bluffs. Good, David thought with satisfaction, staring at Muldoon's back, they'd be coming up behind any unsuspecting Indians. That gave him a better chance to get Two Arrows before the savage could harm her. He had waited a long time for this moment!

She was resigned to dying as long as they died together. She lay holding Two Arrows, attempting to keep him warm. He seemed to be drifting in and out of consciousness as she stared out at the snowy terrain and awaited the inevitable.

A movement caught her eye and she tensed. Three horses appeared suddenly, coming up the back trail. In the moonlight, she recognized David and Muldoon and the horses. Almost she shouted out in relief, then noted the grim expression of David's square, calm face, and the way he carried his rifle at the ready.

He hadn't come to help; he had come to kill. The wind carried his faint words to her as he dismounted.

"Look around for footprints, Muldoon, they must be up here somewhere."

"Yes, sir." Muldoon dismounted, began to search farther away, finally disappeared over the rise.

Glory held her breath, pressing herself against Two Arrows, who lay still as if he might be unconscious. Perhaps David would find nothing and leave.

Instead, he tied the two horses to a bush only a few yards away and looked around.

Misty. Thank God the wind was blowing toward Glory; if her beloved horse smelled her, the filly might nicker a welcome and alert David to her whereabouts. Glory stared at the two horses wistfully, noting the canteens, the blankets, and the saddlebags, no doubt full of food. Everything she and her love needed to escape and make it to safety was out here—and between her and all that was a grim man with a loaded rifle, looking for tracks. The silver bars on his shoulders gleamed in the moonlight. Captain Krueger. So he, like Muldoon, had finally gotten another chance. She was glad for him.

Glory hesitated, watching him as he squatted, studying the terrain, looking for tracks in the snow. Maybe she could make a deal with him; maybe if she went with David, he would let her lover go.

At that moment as she tried to decide what to do, David leaned over and picked up a dead leaf and smiled in triumph. In the moonlight, she could see the bright blood on the leaf. "He's hit!" David said, and smiled in triumph as he clicked the safety off his rifle.

Her heart fell at the hard look of vengeance on his face; David would give no mercy.

She tried to keep from breathing, fearing David might hear her. He walked a few steps closer, leaned over and picked up something, held it up. Her little beaded bracelet. Even from here, she saw the expression on his face soften.

David stared at the little object in his hand. For a moment, he was seated at the piano again while Glory leaned on it, her lovely face profiled in the dim light. She was wearing that blue calico dress and this very bracelet, and she smiled sweetly. *In the gloaming, oh, my darling. . . .*

David's vision blurred, and he blinked rapidly to clear it, reached inside his coat to put the bracelet in his shirt pocket. They were up here, all right; he imagined Glory held captive and terrified. David would kill that disrespectful son of a bitch for everything he'd done to her.

He looked around the bluff, his rifle at the ready. Good, Muldoon had disappeared over the rise, searching around. David didn't want any witnesses nearby in case he stumbled onto the wounded scout. He intended to execute Two Arrows with no more guilt than he'd expend on a big rattlesnake. Like rattlesnakes and just as dangerous, the Cheyenne could be holed up here in these rocks; except that rattlesnakes would hibernate in all this cold, and Cheyenne were always deadly.

He hefted his rifle again, eager to have this long rivalry between him and the disrespectful scout over and done with. The promotion and reward would be nice; his father would be proud; but none of that mattered. This was personal.

Ahead lay a rock outcrop. Yes, that would be a good place for a wounded predator to hole up. David moved to one side of the outcrop so the moonlight would light up the shadows. At that moment, David saw them. The pair were lying under a rocky ledge, Glory's eyes staring back at him, wide with fear. Except for those beautiful dark eyes, he might not have recognized her, dressed as she was in buckskin and braided hair.

Then Two Arrows moved ever so slightly, and David realized just how hurt the man was. The big Indian was all but helpless; no weapon, he might not even be conscious. There weren't a dozen yards between David and his quarry.

I'll save you, Glory, don't worry, my love. Very slowly, David brought the rifle to his shoulder, smiling a little. He had the Cheyenne's forehead in his gun sights now.

In that split second before David could squeeze the trigger, Glory threw herself across the half-conscious man, shielding him with her body, putting herself between danger and the Cheyenne. She looked up at David in the moonlight, and her lips moved silently. *Please,* her lips and her eyes begged. *Oh, please don't kill him!*

Glory begging? No, she was too proud, and this man was her kidnapper, yet she lay so that David couldn't shoot without hitting her.

David blinked, saw the tears running down her beautiful face, *please,* she begged silently, *oh please, I love him.*

Abruptly, David knew. She wasn't a hostage. Back there when she fell and could have been rescued by the soldiers, she had instead reached for Two Arrows, who loved her enough to run through deadly gunfire to reach her side. David had thought no man could ever love Glory as much as he did. He'd been wrong. Tears came to David's eyes and blinded him. She was lost to him forever, lost.

Two Arrows opened his eyes slowly, too wounded to even move, looking without fear into the cocked rifle; yet injured as he was, he tried to pull the girl into the protection of his embrace.

David had waited a long time for this, dreamed of this moment. He stared down the rifle sight, looking into the other man's eyes. "This is for Glory," he whispered. Then, very slowly, David lowered the rifle to his side.

Glory began to sob silently, relief on her beautiful, blood-smeared face, still shielding the wounded scout with her own body. Her love for that man was there in her eyes for all the world to see.

David stared at her, seeing that love reflected in her face, a love that was not for him; imagining the Cheyenne running through deadly gunfire to return for her and Glory reaching for him. Two Arrows was the man she loved.

David had never felt such inner pain. For only a moment, David considered, then he made his decision. He pulled off the buffalo coat, hung it across the chestnut's saddle. He threw his arms around his stallion's neck; knowing the sacrifice he would make. "Good-bye, Chance, boy, take care of them; they're depending on you."

Then he turned to walk away, leaving the two horses behind. It was cold without a coat. David shivered and kept sloughing through the snow, his rifle in the crook of his arm. He turned once and looked back. The pair were wearing the fur coats now, mounted on the horses. The expensive fur hood framed her features, and she had never looked as beautiful to David as she did at that moment, sitting that gray filly in the moonlight.

Her lips moved silently. *Thank you,* she said.

He nodded to show he understood. *I love you,* he whispered, and the cold wind took his words away and lost them on the wind. *Have a wonderful life.*

Two Arrows sat the chestnut stallion, staring at David almost in disbelief. Then very slowly, he raised a bloody, trembling hand, snapped David a salute.

David paused only a moment, then he returned that salute. They looked at each other a long moment; two men who had reached an understanding of mutual respect. "Take care of her," he whispered, and the other man nodded.

David was suddenly so blinded with tears, he could not see. He turned again and strode away. If he looked back, he might weaken and not be able to let her go. Muldoon was out here someplace. He heard a step crunch through the snow, and the sergeant came out of some trees. He was without his fur coat and afoot, carrying his rifle in one hand, a small object in the other.

"Muldoon?"

The other paused, smiling, looking at what he held. "Did you know, lad, that when you give an Indian a gift, they insist on givin' you something in return?"

David took a good look at what Muldoon carried; it was a little china doll.

"That wasn't much of a trade for a smart gambler like you," David said.

"Aye, and look who's talkin'." Muldoon suddenly noticed. "No coat and missing the two finest horses in the West, now, just what—?"

"I got the respect of a better man than I am." He smiled at the memory, and abruptly felt good about what he'd done. "And this." He reached into his shirt for the small bracelet and held it up. "Let's go, Muldoon; it's colder than hell up here without coats."

The Irishman clapped him on the back and they started walking toward the back trail together. "Ah lad, they'll bust us down again, you know that; maybe even drum us out of the corps, comin' back without any of our supplies, without our horses. Why, we ain't even fired our rifles!"

David shrugged and put the bracelet back in his pocket. "I never was cut out to be a soldier, and winter's too cold in Nebraska for an old guy with rheumatism. Have you ever thought about Texas? We could catch and break mustangs, build us a herd."

Muldoon's broad face broke into a grin. "Now that sounds just fine! Let's go, lad!"

Glory watched the two top the rise, disappear over the other side. She sighed with relief, reached for the canteen, discovered it was full of hot broth, held it to Two Arrows's lips as he swayed on the chestnut stallion's back. "Here, drink this, my love; we've got everything we need to make it now. We've been given another chance."

He looked stronger as he sipped the broth, the food and David's coat bringing warmth back into his big body. He was a tough dog soldier; he would live.

The wolf howled somewhere far away, as if it were running hard across the prairie, moving away from the fort, headed toward the Cheyenne's own country. The echo rang almost like a clarion call in the starry darkness, signifying that *Heammawihio,* the Great One Above was still in charge and looking out for his own.

She smiled. "It is a good omen. Now I will tell you; I am expecting your son; we will call him Wolf Song."

For a moment, his jaw trembled, and he seemed overcome with emotion. "Why—?"

"I didn't want to worry you," she whispered. *"Ne-mehotatse,* my dearest, I love you."

"Ne-mehotatse, my Proud One," he answered. "We have a long life ahead of us together."

"Together!" she agreed. "Forever together!"

Then they turned and rode away into the snowy night, following the wolf toward freedom.

To My Readers

Yes, the basic story you have just read is actual history. Approximately three hundred Cheyenne, less than a hundred of them poorly armed warriors, traveled fifteen hundred miles, fought four major skirmishes, and outwitted ten thousand soldiers, who were equally determined to stop these ragged, hungry Indians from returning to their beloved homeland. While accounts differ, it appears the Cheyenne dead in that flight were about ten warriors to about forty whites. The attempted escape from Camp (Fort) Robinson, on the other hand, was a slaughter.

Glory Halstead, Two Arrows, Lieutenant Krueger, and Corporal Muldoon are fictional. If the character of Two Arrows seems familiar, you have met him before as a minor character in my earlier books: *Cheyenne Captive, Cheyenne Splendor,* and riding as an army scout against the Nez Perce tribe in *Song of the Warrior.*

So what happened to the northern Cheyenne after that bloody, desperate flight from the barracks at Fort Robinson? Most were either killed or recaptured over the next several weeks, and the majority of the captured were wounded or badly frostbitten. The army trailed a handful of the survivors to the Hat Creek bluffs forty-five miles west of Fort Robinson, where a final battle ensued. When that was over, only eight or ten were missing and never accounted for. The army assumed these had either frozen to death or were wounded and had crawled away to die. Perhaps, instead, that handful of missing Cheyenne escaped to follow the wolf to freedom; at least, I want to think so.

Finally, the government, because of popular sentiment and mounting criticism, decided against sending the brave little group of captured survivors back to Indian Territory.

Five of the warriors were sent to Kansas to stand trial for the killings of whites there, but were finally released for lack of evidence. Perhaps it would have been embarrassing to try the Indians when so many Cheyenne children and old people had just been slaughtered by whites. Today, in the cemetery of the little town of Oberlin, Kansas, near the Nebraska border, there is a monument to the eighteen whites killed in that area during the Dull Knife raid. You'll also find the nearby Decatur County Museum interesting. For more complete details on the Sappa Creek raid, I suggest a booklet the museum sells, authored by a local resident, George Nellans. The title is: *Massacre of Indians and Cheyenne Indian Raid.*

Dull Knife survived that infamous night in the escape from Fort Robinson. Both he and Little Wolf had been part of the 1866 so-called Fetterman Massacre, where a reckless captain led his troops into ambush and total annihilation by a combined force of Cheyenne and Lakota. Dull Knife died in 1883 in Montana and is buried in the Indian cemetery just north of Highway 212 on the east side of Lame Deer, Montana.

Little Wolf, who had also fought at the Little Bighorn battle, took his group to winter among the Lakota in Montana, and thus spared them from the bloody incident at Fort Robinson. It is perhaps ironic, that later, Little Wolf and many of the Cheyenne warriors who had been part of the exodus from Fort Reno ended up scouting for the white soldiers against their allies, the Lakota. Years later, while drunk, Little Wolf finally killed Thin Elk, gave up his position as chief, and went into exile. Almost forgotten, blind, and helpless, Little Wolf lived until 1904 and is buried next to his friend, Dull Knife.

At least twenty-five of the Cheyenne dead from the exodus were turned over to various museums for study by order of the army surgeon general. In October of 1993, the remains of these twenty-five were retrieved from display cases and dusty storage cabinets and returned to the northern tribe, who reburied them with traditional ceremonies to honor Cheyenne war dead at Busby, Montana. After 114 years, these brave ones went home at last.

Like Colonel George Armstrong Custer, Colonel William H. Lewis died in battle against the Cheyenne. In case you are curious, only one general was killed during all the Indian wars of the West, Brigadier General E.R.S. Canby, during the trouble with the Modoc tribe in 1873.

Major "Tip" Thornburgh, whom the New York papers had chided about being lost, would be killed in action in the autumn of 1879 during the Ute uprising in northwest Colorado. I've already told you that story in my February, 1997 Zebra romance, *Warrior's Prize.*

Fort Reno still exists as an agricultural station. Many of us would like to see the neglected historical site turned into a park or museum, but ownership of the fort is in dispute between the government and the Cheyenne tribe, and until that is resolved, the old fort continues to deteriorate. If you're curious, the site is near the town of El Reno, overlooking the famous Route 66 highway. Fort Reno boasts the best example of a Victorian-period cavalry barn still in existence, and the historic cemetery is worth a look.

If you're interested in the U.S. Cavalry, its two most famous horses are both in Kansas. Comanche, the famous bay gelding that was supposedly the only survivor of Custer's last stand, has been stuffed and is on display in a glass case at the University of Kansas in Lawrence. The last mount on government rolls, Chief, also a bay gelding, died in 1968 at the age of thirty-six, and was buried with full military honors. There's a magnificent, monument on his grave at Fort Riley, Kansas. The U.S. Cavalry Museum is also located at this fort. You may be surprised to hear that the last U.S. mounted cavalry charge took place during World War II in the Philippines against the Japanese on January 16, 1942.

As for forts, Fort Robinson, Nebraska, is now a state park. During World War II, Fort Robinson was used to train war dogs and as a center for German prisoners. I have walked its grounds with my fellow members of the Order of the Indian Wars. The barracks that housed the Cheyenne is long since gone, but there's a good museum operated by the state historical society and a monument to the Lakota chief, Crazy Horse, who was murdered at Fort Robinson in 1877.

If you want to read more about the Cheyenne exodus, the best work on the subject is *Cheyenne Autumn* by one of my favorite authors, Mari Sandoz, reprinted in 1992 by University of Nebraska Press. A John Ford movie was made from this book in 1964, starring Richard Widmark and James Stewart. You can probably find it at your local video store. By the way, as you watch it, you might be interested to know it was not filmed in Oklahoma, Kansas, or Nebraska, where the actual events took place, but in Monument Valley, Arizona, using Navahos instead of Cheyenne.

Other books I would recommend are: *Bury My Heart at Wounded Knee* by Dee Brown, *The Fighting Cheyennes,* by George B. Grinnell, published by University of Oklahoma Press, and *Death on the Prairie,* by Paul I. Wellman, University of Nebraska Press.

Cheyenne Song is my sixteenth Western/Indian romance for Zebra Books. Those of you who have been reading my novels for a while know all my books connect in a long continuing saga called the Panorama of the Old West. For those who want to write me to receive an autographed bookmark explaining how my stories all connect, plus news of upcoming books, please send a stamped, self-addressed #10 envelope to: Georgina Gentry, P.O. Box 162, Edmond, Oklahoma 73083-0162. Residents of foreign countries, please enclose postal vouchers I can exchange for U.S. stamps, as our postal authorities will not allow me to use your foreign stamps.

So what story will I tell next? There are two famous bank robberies in the history of the old West; I'm going to tell you about one of them. It's probably the strangest tale I've ever written; part time travel, part paranormal, about a handsome, half-breed gunfighter named Johnny Logan. Johnny served time in the Nevada State Prison with Nevada Randolph, the hero from my earlier book, *Nevada Dawn.* After that, Johnny did time in Arizona Territory's infamous Yuma Prison. Yes, this is one tough hombre!

Johnny has been riding with the Dalton gang and gets in such a desperate fix that he makes a deal with the devil. Johnny thinks he's gotten the best of the bargain—until a blond divorcée named Angelica Newland enters his life and makes him regret his crooked past and his deal. Is he willing to trade it all for her love?

And is this girl from the twentieth century brave enough to travel back in time and risk getting trapped there in order to help him break that damning contract?

Come along and relive the romance and excitement of the old West with this half-breed gunfighter and his lady in the most unusual story I've ever written. In the following pages, you will find an excerpt from this romance, titled *Eternal Outlaw*.

Hahoo naa Ne-mehotatse,

Georgina Gentry

Eternal Outlaw

Kansas. Late afternoon, October 5, 1892

Johnny Logan was bleeding to death, and he knew it. It was all he could do to stay on his paint stallion as it slowed to a walk. Only a couple of miles behind him in the frontier town lay a botched bank robbery, citizens and fellow outlaws dead or dying in the streets. Soon Johnny would be dead, too . . . unless the posse got there first.

He put his hand to his bloody, gunshot arm and winced, as the horse stopped. God, he hurt so! Crimson blood dripped dark and wet onto the stallion's white-and-black coat, then onto the saddle and into the prairie dust.

Johnny struggled to stay conscious, hanging on to the saddle horn, his head whirling. Where was he? He looked around at the desolate prairie. He saw a broken chair, some empty boxes, garbage, shattered dishes, and other refuse. Johnny threw back his head and laughed.

"A garbage dump! This is Coffeyville's ash heap! How ironic! How funny!" He began to laugh as he reeled in the saddle, the stallion looking back at him as if questioning his sanity. "Don't you get it, Crazy Quilt, old boy? I'm human trash; fittin' ain't it, that I should die here?"

The horse snorted and stamped its hooves as if awaiting orders to move on.

Johnny glanced at the sun soon to set on the western horizon. "You're right, boy," he mumbled, "gotta get outa here; law's lookin' for me. Reckon all the others are already dead."

Johnny tried to urge his horse forward, but he no longer had the strength. Instead, he felt himself falling. He hit the ground hard and lay there a long moment, willing himself back into consciousness despite the pain. He lay in the midst of the rubble, his blood-smeared horse now munching stray blades of grass growing up through the trash.

If he could just stand up and get back on the horse. Johnny struggled, but he was growing weaker by the moment. He couldn't even get up, much less mount and ride across the border into Indian Territory, where he might find refuge among the Kiowa. It would be dark soon, and Johnny was afraid of the dark; silly weakness for a tough, half-breed gunfighter. *No matter,* he thought; he wasn't going to be alive to see the sun set.

"What a rotten end to a rotten life," he muttered, and tried to staunch the flow of blood from his arm, but he didn't even have a bandanna to tie around it. "The fastest gun in the West dies amid a pile of trash."

Well, he was human garbage himself; the unwanted bastard of a mixed-blood Kiowa Indian girl and a frontier soldier. He didn't even have a real name; Logan's was the name of the saloon where, as a starving urchin, he'd been fed in exchange for sweeping up and emptying spittoons.

Johnny licked his cracked lips in desperation and screamed at the sky, "I don't want to die! I want to live! I'd do anything to live!"

Abruptly, a rider seemed to appear out of nowhere, loping toward him. It must be the sheriff or a bounty hunter. If it were a posse, they'd string him up right here. Johnny managed to turn his head and look around, chuckled softly. "No tree," he whispered. "Can't lynch me; no tree."

The stranger reined his shadow gray horse to a halt, leaned on his saddle horn, looking down at Johnny. "You've left a blood trail. I'm surprised no one but me has noticed it yet."

Johnny stared up at him. The handsome stranger's voice was deep as a tomb, and it seemed to echo through the stillness. His eyes glowed dark and hard as obsidian, and he fingered his small mustache. He was dressed all in black with the finest boots, Western hat, and a long frock coat.

Something about him sent a chill up Johnny's back. "Don't—don't I know you?"

The lean stranger nodded and lit a slender cheroot as he stared down at Johnny in the twilight. "We've known each other a long time. I didn't figure you recognized me when we played cards earlier today in the Lady Luck saloon. You cheat as badly as you rob banks. No wonder you're a loser; you don't have any real talent for evil."

"Hot, so hot. Help me." Johnny gasped, ran his tongue over his dry lips again. "You've got a canteen, give me just a sip of water."

The other grinned and shrugged as he dismounted. "You'll think hot and thirsty when you get where you're going."

"Going? I can't even ride. I—I don't want to die," Johnny begged, holding out a bloody hand in appeal. "Please, get me to a doctor—"

The gambler yawned and squatted next to Johnny, looked at the setting sun. "Stop whining, Logan, you've always been brave, no matter what."

"I—I've never been this hurt before."

"It's almost over; you'll be dead when the sun sets."

Johnny stared up into the soulless dark eyes and then at the ghost gray horse. An eerie, troubling memory came to him of an old preacher on a street corner in a lawless trail town shouting scripture at the sinners passing by.

. . . and I looked up and beheld a pale horse and his name that sat upon him was Death and hell followed with him.

Johnny fumbled for his Colt. "Whoever the hell you are, help me, damn you, or I'll—"

"You'll what?" the gambler blew cigar smoke into the air. "Your pistol is empty."

"How—how do you know—?"

The other only smiled.

Of course his Colt was empty. The bank robbery had been an inferno of gunfire. Johnny knew who this rider was now. Ironic. He had not planned to die like this. Handsome, tough gunfighters went out in a blaze of bullets in some wild saloon with half the town and all the pretty, adoring whores watching. "You—you've come for me?"

The other nodded and tossed away his cigar. "Of course, there is an option. . . ."

Johnny looked at his life running out, mixing with the dust beneath him. "Anything," he gasped, "I'd do anything—"

"Fine." The stranger pulled a paper from his black frock coat, knelt next to Johnny. "Here's a contract; good for one hundred years with option to renew."

Johnny began to laugh through his pain. "A joke; it's a joke; I'm dreamin' all this."

"Just sign it," the gambler snapped. "I'm running out of patience, and you're running out of daylight."

Johnny looked toward the dying sun. "What's the catch?"

"No catch." The other unrolled the ancient-looking parchment and laid it next to Johnny's hand. "People make bargains with me all the time."

Johnny felt so very weary and in pain. "Nobody ever did nothin' for me, and I don't do nothin' for no one."

"Sweet guy; about like my other clientele."

This couldn't be happening. Something about a contract. "I—I don't have a pen."

"Just dip your finger in your blood and sign."

"What?"

"Either sign it or let your miserable short life end here amidst the garbage; I'm late already, and I've got thousands of eager customers waiting." The forbidding stranger turned toward his horse.

"Wait! Come back; I'll sign." Johnny didn't care anymore what was on the paper; all he knew was that he wanted to live.

He dipped his forefinger in the warm scarlet stream dripping down his arm and slowly and painfully scrawled his name across the paper.

"Smart hombre." The other grinned. "All your dreams of long life and riches are about to come true."

"Nobody gives nothin' for free," Johnny gasped incredulously. "What do you get out of this?"

The other looked at him, and the triumphant expression in the soulless eyes sent a sense of dread through Johnny's very heart. "Why, don't you know? I get you!"